A GIFT FOR A PRINCESS

He was in his mid-forties, a deep tan over his strong, cleanshaven face underscoring the health and vigor he seemed to emit like the scent of cologne. His dark brown, almost black, hair was worn long. It curled behind his ears, and his temples were streaked with hints of gray, caught by the soft lighting of the room. But his eyes were what captured Aurora's own for they were so like hers—emerald green, intense, yet sparkling with wit and promise.

She knew immediately that this was the man with whom the countess had been talking, but Maritza was nowhere in sight.

"Hello," he said, his deep baritone revealing the trace of a Midwestern drawl.

"Hello," she responded.

"Maritza sent me over to keep you company."

"That was nice of her, and of you."

He nodded an unspoken thank you and extended an arm, his closed hand turned upward.

"Hold out your hands," he said.

Aurora placed her cupped palms together, puzzled but curious. From his fist fell a trickle of walnuts. She looked up into his twinkling eyes with amused surprise.

"I wish they were diamonds," he said.

And Aurora knew that someday they would be. . . .

Places

ROBIN ST. THOMAS

ZEBRA BOOKS
KENSINGTON PUBLISHING CORP.

Cover photo © 1987 Anthony Loew

ZEBRA BOOKS

are published by

Kensington Publishing Corp.
475 Park Avenue South
New York, NY 10016

First printing: February 1987

Printed in the United States of America

For Bern and Martha, Kathleen . . . and Lou

Thanks, Jasper

Prologue

For one week Aurora Styles had been the most famous woman in the world. A legend had been created around her.

On the front pages and covers of every major newspaper and periodical, her name pushed aside reports of war, politics, famine, and flood. Her journey to this exalted position had taken a decade. That was of little consequence now; those years were merely a prologue to the events of the last seven days. A hungry public and a voracious press clamored for more news— any news—of her whereabouts.

Had she not been forced into hiding, she mused, perhaps her notoriety would not have been so readily attained. She had longed for—hungered after— recognition. Once before, she had achieved it and had held it fleetingly, only to see it slip quickly away.

And now . . . Fame had come in a way she never could have anticipated or desired. Nor could she have envisioned the cost, the unreimbursable price of her recognition. Certain actions had set off a series of events that could never be undone. She alone possessed the key to their resolution.

Two men were searching for her; that much she

knew. They intended to force her onto a plane bound for New York, or to prevent her from boarding a plane, should she decide to return to that same city. She had no way of knowing which, not without also knowing who had hired them. She had narrowly escaped these men twice before: in London and then in Paris, the worst time of all.

Who were they? Detectives, surely, hired by the lawyers. But whose lawyers?

The Steuben-glass flute caught the fading light and made a rainbow prism across her jeweled hand as she raised the champagne to her lips. It had gone flat, while she had been contemplating the sun as it dipped behind the snowcapped mountains guarding Lake Lucerne, hoping that here, finally, she was free of her pursuers. She had flown to Lucerne from Paris only four days ago.

At twenty-nine, Aurora Styles' womanly beauty had begun to emerge. Her lustrous hair, the color of burnished umber, fell loosely to her shoulders, one errant lock persistently straying over her right brow to partially shield a high forehead accented by a perfect widow's peak.

She tossed her head, flipping her hair back into place in a characteristic gesture that seemed to reflect her attitude toward her present circumstances and in general. This gesture was familiar to those who knew her well.

But who did know Aurora Styles well? She had been a different woman to so many people that at times she hardly recognized which of her various incarnations could be considered real. Perhaps none; probably all. Only one person had almost discovered her true essence; only one man had seen past the mystique, been unimpressed by it. He had shed his own light, allowing her the freedom, had she taken it, to illuminate the person within her.

She had seen him last in London, before her current predicament had begun, or, rather, during its inception, although neither of them could have known it at the time.

Where was he now?

Aurora gazed out the window, past the deceptive serenity of the vast lake. Why hadn't she tried to reach him? Hadn't he said she could count him as a friend? She'd sensed he'd really meant it. Perhaps that was the source of her reluctance. At any rate, she felt she had no right to seek his help. No, she thought, but perhaps someday, if I survive this dilemma . . .

Fool, she reprimanded herself. You can trust no one. Your salvation is in your own hands.

She glanced down at those hands. On her left she wore the four-carat diamond. On her right, the emerald, now as famous and photographed as she.

"A gift to match your eyes," Otto had said.

Were these, then, all that was left to her? On one hand, a souvenir of the marriage she had coveted; on the other, a reminder of the loveless affair that had ended with her ex-lover on trial for murder. The rings would bring a handsome sum, were she to sell them. She'd thought about it often enough lately. But the diamond represented the most important relationship of her life. Regardless of the scandal, it remained a symbol of Harper's devotion and love. And, although she needed money now more than ever before, she had sworn to herself that she would return the emerald to its donor in person; only then could she sever her ties to him forever and bury the past that had turned her into a fugitive. Only then could she be free of guilt.

Thank God for her friends! From across the world

they had come to her assistance: from Hollywood, Paris, London, and New York.

New York, she reflected. Could I return there? And what would happen to me if I did?

She had been known as Rory during her Hollywood years, and that was what most of her friends called her. Having exhausted what little funds she had, she now lived at the mercy of the wealthy and the well-connected. This was a strange situation for one who had ranked among the royalty of the film capital and of Beverly Hills. She had been, for a time, the darling of the international crowd or the Jet Set or whatever they were calling themselves these days.

And what does that matter now? she mused with a smile.

Always generous with her own money when she'd had it, Aurora was quickly learning that there was no guarantee of treatment in kind when the proverbial chips were down. Not that anyone really knew in what dire straits she was. People in the inner circle never wanted to be privy to such confidences, nor would she have volunteered the information. Oh, they were free with the use of their houses; they all seemed to have houses scattered about the globe and left unoccupied eighty percent of the time, these idle rich, parsimonious with ready cash, yet always willing and eager to open their doors to guests of their class—temporary custodians. And Aurora, having no other available choice, hastily accepted the invitations.

At first, in search of breathing space. Lately, as a means of escape.

Before Paris it had been bad enough. She'd been in London when the first news of the indictment and trial had reached her, and, with it, the suggestion that her testimony might be required. She hadn't been sub-poenaed yet, merely watched. They'd come all the way to London, it appeared, to *watch* her.

Eventually, she came to know them by sight, so often were they seated in the lobby of her hotel, in the restaurants where she dined. She'd even noticed them at the theater. It had seemed only a coincidence at first.

But soon there was no pretense. They stared openly, following close behind and making no attempt to hide the fact that she was under surveillance.

Both tall. One, the redhead, always in a black suit; the other, a painfully thin blond, forever dressed in gray.

During her second week in London, Aurora confronted them outside Harrods. They were behind her as she left the store and she turned to look them squarely in the eyes.

"Why are you doing this?" she asked.

The redhead answered, "Someone wants to know where you are. All the time."

"*Who?*" she demanded. "Which side are you working for?"

But they only smiled and retreated to the corner of the building, waiting for her to move on.

She lost them for an hour or so, only to have them turn up again.

She fled to France, but the pair were there within a few hours, dogging her tracks. It was on her third day in Paris that the threat of their presence became a real danger.

Alone in the borrowed flat, Aurora had received a telephone call from Tadzio Breslau in New York. Countess Maritza, who had arranged for her to occupy the sumptuous apartment on the Avenue Georges Mandel, had learned the latest news. She and Tadzio were following the trial proceedings, and at regular intervals were keeping Aurora abreast of developments.

"Rory!"

"Oui! Tadzio?"

"Yes, darling! We must be brief and you must act quickly. Get on the next plane to Switzerland—they've stepped up the search. They may even know you're in Paris!"

Aurora knew Tadzio well; this was no joke, no idle warning.

She packed immediately.

On the plane to Lucerne she read a newspaper. Tadzio's alert had been more up-to-date than the current information in print; obviously, her pursuers had access to the same data; that explained the harrowing incident she had just survived.

Aurora had not expected to see her face monopolizing the entire front page. After the recap of the case, the article stated:

Although a search for Otto Danzig's former mistress, Aurora Styles, has been conducted by the defense and the prosecution for the past two weeks, Judge Meyers today declared that the wait is over. The beautiful film actress of the late 1970s will be subpoenaed. If Styles does not appear within one month, her testimony will be discounted. In March, the defense moved to have her signed affidavit thrown out as inadmissible, since they would be unable to cross-examine the witness. The prosecution has fought this move for some time, but it appears that Judge Meyers will brook no more delays.

The motive for murder rests on Styles' testimony. In her earlier affidavit, the actress affirmed that her affair with Danzig was over before the death of his heiress-socialite wife, Elizabeth "Buffy" Houston-Danzig. However,

Styles claims that Danzig swore he'd win her back. This, the prosecution alleges, was sufficient motive for Danzig, whose wife was found murdered last year. Whereas the defense maintains that Mrs. Danzig was the victim of an intruder. Several burglaries had been reported in the North Shore area at the time of the murder.

Aurora, rather than folding up the newspaper, disappeared behind it for most of the flight.

By the time she arrived in Lucerne, her hair was tucked tightly beneath a turban she'd retrieved from her beauty case, and dark glasses camouflaged her green eyes. Aurora hoped these ploys would help her to avoid detection until she arrived safely at Tadzio's chalet.

Four days had passed and so far she'd seen no sign of the sinister shadows she had acquired in London. Perhaps she had finally given them the slip, or perhaps they had called off the search. A slim chance. Nothing to count on. The press, radio, and television were still flashing her name and descriptions or photos of her. The media were obsessed with the mystery of where she was hiding.

The sun had nearly set when Aurora removed her sunglasses and stood. She'd been seated for a long time on the sun deck of the small chalet, and now she stretched, bringing herself up to her full five feet eight inches. Five-ten in heels, but she wore them less often lately. They hampered speed and agility. The ability to move quickly and freely was essential now.

It was mid-April, a cool day turned chilly by approaching night. Aurora tugged at the ends of her mink jabot, then tucked her teal blue silk shirt into the

13

chocolate suede slacks. The Piaget on her wrist read six o'clock. She picked up the half-empty champagne glass, but decided against finishing its contents.

Glancing restlessly at the vanishing horizon, she hesitated and then passed through the French windows, pushing aside the white curtains that billowed in the wind now rising from across the lake.

The room was white, as was everything within it, and both walls and furniture had taken on the pink glow of twilight. Her kidskin riding boots sank into the plush carpet as she crossed to the mirrored bar.

"Sabine," she called, not bothering to use the petit-point pullcord to ring for the housekeeper, the only servant kept on while the chalet's owner was away.

At length, Aurora heard the padding of the woman's feet along the tiled entrance hall. A momentary flash of guilt passed over her. Sabine had insisted upon catering to her young guest, who had forgotten that age was slowing the older woman down. The housekeeper was in the employ of Tadzio Breslau, Aurora's savior-prince. A prince by birth . . . a prince without a country, she mused, reflecting on their similarities. She had almost been a princess. And she, too, was now without a home. The chalet was, for both of them, a haven, but at that, only an address.

She reminded herself to speak to Tadzio about Sabine. Installing intercoms room to room would make it far less wearing on the poor woman who appeared now in the archway, presenting her image in the mirror before which Aurora stood.

Sabine was some years past sixty and looked it. Her faded graying hair was pulled back severely into a tight bun at the nape of her neck, and she wore black by choice. Her garb gave her the appearance of an aged widow, although Aurora wasn't sure if Sabine had ever married, and the black was a stark contrast to the

14

pristine white of the room surrounding her. Cotton stockings hid her varicose veins, but she had a stooped posture, as if poised for a blow.

"Madame?" she asked breathlessly in a slight French accent.

"I'm sorry, Sabine. I shouldn't have bothered you. I could have done it myself."

"What is it? Tell me. It is what I am paid for."

"Well . . . it's just that the bar is out of ice. Would you mind, Sabine?"

"Eh bien!" the older woman said, shrugging her shoulders.

Aurora handed her the silver bucket.

"Merci." The woman waddled off again down the long corridor between the salon and the kitchen.

Sabine was aware of Aurora's predicament, yet she continued to treat her with the utmost respect, as though her guest were a grand lady. Aurora was grateful for that. She hardly needed the housekeeper to remind her of her fall from grace. Some grand lady, Aurora mused. She wondered how much Sabine knew about the "grand lady's" actual beginnings.

From the front of the house came the sound of a speeding vehicle. The motor's hum grew louder and louder until the screech of brakes pierced the quiet evening and a car door slammed. Seconds later, the brass chimes were ringing madly and fists pounded at the door.

Aurora crossed the room with haste, furtively parting the curtains to peer out the window at the unexpected guest. Immediately, she recognized the Bentley; it was Anton Kalmar. She had made her film debut with Anton. But more than that, he was a treasured friend.

15

His career as a film director had come to a grinding halt due to his taste for cocaine, a habit he was said to have overcome. Aurora wondered if that was true. His behavior, while amusing and always loyal, was frequently erratic, often bizarre. Still, during his glory days he had invested wisely, and those investments now afforded him a comfortable, if obscure, life of luxury and exile in his adopted Switzerland.

Sabine rushed into the room with the filled ice bucket. "Shall I answer it, madame?" she asked, on her guard for Aurora's welfare.

"Yes, yes, please. It's Anton," she answered, taking the silver container. Anton's drink was a Manhattan, which would suit Aurora as well as anything, she supposed. There was no time to chill the pitcher.

She was pleased at the prospect of seeing him, but visits with no word beforehand irritated her, now more than ever. Each unfamiliar noise, each stranger, every ring of the telephone had her nerves jangling. Aurora never knew from minute to minute whether she would have to move on. There was a barely discernible tremor in her hand as she poured the vermouth.

Anton's voice boomed from the hallway, Aurora's name echoing throughout the house.

He had pushed past Sabine and now entered the coziness and warmth of the salon.

Aurora raised her head, looking into his eyes through the mirror's reflection. Something was wrong. Usually when Anton came calling he was careful to present himself as casually elegant. But the tweeds, suedes, and corduroys were absent. His steel-gray hair was disheveled, and he wore only a heavy wool sweater, opened to reveal a yellow T-shirt, blue jeans, and sandals. He was middle-aged, but lines of worry and concern now marred his face, adding to his years.

"What is it?" Aurora asked, the pitcher still poised in

16

her shaking hand.

"I have news."

Sabine stood silently, waiting to be dismissed. At last she asked, "Will there be two for dinner, madame?"

"You'll stay?" Aurora asked him.

"No!" he roared. "There will be no dinner. Not even for one. There is no time, Aurora! Sabine, pack madame's bags immediately!"

Sabine's eyes darted to her mistress, who nodded. Aurora trusted Anton, and she had become philosophical about moving on in haste. The phrase *so be it* now came easily to her.

"Do as he says, Sabine, please."

The housekeeper retreated once more into the hallway as Anton crossed the room and grabbed the pitcher from Aurora's hands. "I'll do this. I could use one. And you're going to need it."

Aurora sat on the sofa. The sound of glass against glass came to her, the sharp tinkle of crystal ringing in her ears as Anton stirred, poured, then placed the drinks and pitcher on a tray, setting them on the glass coffee table.

She sipped. He waited for her to swallow and to sip again. She was aware of too much ice.

"They are here, Aurora. In Lucerne. Now."

She felt her heart sink as tears began to well in her eyes, but she shook her head, tossing the mahogany mane about her shoulders. She must not lose courage now, when it was so essential. Think, she ordered herself. You must think!

"How do you know, Anton?" she asked.

"The men . . . one is red-haired, the other blond?"

She nodded and he continued. "It's the same two. There is a young girl whom I see occasionally. She works for customs at the airport. I told her something of the situation, described the men to her. She

17

promised to keep an eye out for them." He drew a deep breath. "Well, she rang me up. There can be no doubt—the two you described to me. That's why I came here immediately. You are as good as found, Rory. You must leave at once."

The stakes *were* high; Otto's freedom—or conviction—hung in the balance. There was no way to learn which side they worked for; London and Paris had proved that.

Why couldn't they be satisfied with her affidavit? Why couldn't they leave her alone? But she knew the answer: The prosecution suspected that she had withheld evidence. She alone knew whether her former lover was guilty—or innocent—of murder. But was her knowledge proof beyond a reasonable doubt? Could she testify for, or against, a man, any man, without tangible evidence?

She glanced down again at the enormous green gem on her finger. A woman was dead. That woman's husband had given Aurora this ring. Would her testimony ensure that justice would be carried out?

And what of the two men who pursued her now? Judge Meyers had set the limit at a month. Could she last a month?

"How long?" asked Aurora. "How long before they find me?"

Anton took her hand and gently squeezed it. "My dearest Rory, why do you think I told Sabine to pack your things?"

"But can we be so sure they'll find me here?"

"Do not be so naïve. Your friendship with Tadzio is . . . well . . . a publicized one, is it not? It is only logical that they will come here."

He was right again. Tadzio had frequently been her escort. Rumors had flared, died, and flared again regarding their relationship, their "affair."

It was ridiculous, of course.

Nonetheless, they would track her to Tadzio's chalet. And even if they didn't, Aurora couldn't afford to take the chance.

"Thank you, Anton," she said finally. "Of course I must go."

But where? Where could she go?

She felt the pressure on her hand once more and looked up into his eyes.

Rome, she thought. Perhaps, after all, there was Rome. . . .

"Darling," he said softly, "please . . . there is very little time. . . ."

Aurora leaned her magnificent head against the sofa and heaved a deep sigh.

"What is it, Rory?"

"Tired," she answered in a whisper. "I'm so awfully tired, Anton. Will this never be over?"

"It will, it will. And it is to that time you must look. To a time when you will be relaxed, secure again, with all this behind you. It will come, you shall see."

"I want to believe you!" she cried, throwing herself into his waiting arms, tears illuminating her smooth pale skin.

Anton held her for a moment, allowing her to calm herself, feeling her racing heart slow to an even, steady pace. Then he did something he had not done in years. Taking her face in both his hands, his fingers delicately lifting her chin, he kissed her, long and tenderly. Her warm lips opened slightly to his, and her arms folded around his neck as she gave herself to the embrace.

When their lips parted, she opened her eyes. Anton was looking deeply into them, smiling.

"You are one of the strongest women I have ever known. I wish I had one-tenth of your courage." He wiped a tear from her cheek with his index finger and tasted it. "Now," he went on, "go and change your clothes. Save yourself. I will put your bags in my car."

They rose and started for the hall.

"Rory, wait!"

She turned. In his hands were a set of keys. "Take these extra keys to my car . . . in case, later, there's no time."

As Aurora took the keys, her fingers and Anton's entwined briefly as if in anticipation of farewell. Then they left the room and hurried up the stairs.

Sabine had worked quickly. The last of Aurora's three Vuitton bags were just being closed as Aurora swept into the room, followed by Anton. With haste he collected the luggage, and struggling under its weight, a garment bag over his shoulder, he made his way down the stairs.

"Ah, Sabine, you are an angel!" Aurora exclaimed, seeing that the housekeeper had left unpacked a pair of black corduroy jeans and a black silk crepe blouse. Beside them on the bed lay her sable coat. "I thought you should wear it, madame," the woman said, fingering the opulent fur. "It is still cold at night."

"Thank you," said Aurora, kicking off her boots and tearing herself free of her clothing. The dark mink jabot at her neck came away, and Aurora held it out to Sabine.

"Take this," she said. "I can't repay you for your kindness in any other way, so you must take this."

"No, madame. For you it has been a pleasure."

"This is no time for arguing. Please. I want you to have it."

Sabine's hands reached out and fondled the jabot. *"Merci, alors,"* she said quietly.

Within minutes Aurora was dressed again. She pulled a brush through her mass of dark hair, then reached for her black leather driving gloves. Sabine helped her into the fur coat, and Aurora took one more moment to survey her image in the full-length armoire mirror. She appeared to be totally encased in black, her hair reflecting none of its titian highlights in the shadowy dark of the room. The whiteness of her face and neck created a cameo against the ebony frame of her hair and fur.

Grabbing her black leather shoulder bag, Aurora was about to call for Anton when she heard a speeding auto, followed by screaming brakes.

"Oh, madame!" cried Sabine in a small voice, her hands at her mouth.

Aurora ran to the window and carefully parted the lace curtains. She spotted a tan Fiat parked outside in back of the Bentley. In Paris they had driven a Citröen.

From downstairs they heard the door open and Anton's voice speaking rather too loudly in Italian, feigning only a minimal acquaintance with his fluent French. Bless him, Aurora thought, he's buying me time!

At the window once again, Aurora and Sabine peered out. There was a small roof just beneath the ledge. From there it was only eight feet or so to the ground. If she could make it that far and get around front to the Bentley, she'd have a chance.

She tugged at the window, but it refused to open. Then she saw the lock. Twisting at it, she tugged again. Still the window did not budge.

"Sabine!" she whispered. "Help me!"

The housekeeper took the right side and together they pulled and heaved frantically, Sabine nearly hysterical as she choked back sobs. At last the window flew open.

Aurora climbed through and out onto the white tiled roof. Quickly she grasped Sabine's hand, kissed it, then said, "Good-bye—and thank you!"

21

There wasn't a steep slope, although Aurora wished the heels of her boots were not quite so smooth as she tentatively made her way across to the edge, trodding as softly as she could in fear that her footsteps might be heard within the house.

She listened.

So far, so good.

A gust of wind from the lake sent her hair and coat flying wildly about her in the new night, the moon spotlighting the tall, dark figure poised and looking down. Eight feet seemed a lot farther from where Aurora stood than it had earlier that day from below. She glanced over her shoulder; Sabine still leaned against the window frame. The older woman blessed herself, crossed the fingers of both hands in front of her, and nodded, tears glistening on her cheeks.

Aurora smiled weakly, turned back to the edge, and looked down once more.

Then she tossed her shoulder bag to the soft grass below, took a deep breath, and jumped.

The ground came up to meet her and suddenly there was the shock of impact. Evening dew had come to rest upon the earth, and the coolness against her cheek felt, for a moment, revitalizing. Aurora lay there, listening. She could still hear Anton's voice speaking loudly, but now the other male voices, two of them, were raised.

She pulled herself to a standing position. Having gone over on her left ankle during the jump, she took a few halting steps to test it. It was all right.

She darted across the lawn, making for the front of the house. Slowing her steps when she reached the driveway, she carefully avoided creating noise as her boots moved cautiously atop the crunching gravel.

The door on the driver's side of the Bentley was unlocked. Slowly, painstakingly, Aurora opened it and slid behind the wheel, not slamming the door but letting it lean, half-closed. She slid a gloved hand into the pocket of her sable coat.

The keys!

Where were the keys! To come so far. . . .

Could she have left them upstairs? Had she been so carelessly stupid?

Wait! Her hand searched the other pocket. Yes! There they were!

Aurora inserted the key into the ignition. She sighed, turned the key, gunned the motor, and took off.

The car wheels sent a shower of pebbles up from behind. They landed in loud cracks against the tan Fiat. The door of the Bentley flew out as she maneuvered a fast turn around the drive and it nearly snapped off as the Bentley approached the edge of the stone gate. Aurora's hand reached out, trying to grab at the handle while avoiding an oncoming tree that loomed before her.

At last her fingers clutched the leather handle. Pulling it shut with a thrust of her entire body, she veered right with her free hand. A scraping against the far side of the vehicle was followed by a cascade of small branches and leaves across the windshield. But she was free.

Her eyes were not confined to the road as she drove furiously into the night. They kept checking the rearview mirror. She saw the front door of the chalet open, and then two men stood on the threshold, pointing after her. The redhead struck Anton in the face, and her friend went down. Sabine ran out onto the porch and knelt over Anton as the two men raced to the Fiat. They were soon on the road and in pursuit of Aurora, less than a mile behind the Bentley.

Two days later, two nuns sat in the second-class

23

compartment of the *rapido*. They were leaving Milan to attend a retreat. Their order was an old one and did not subscribe to the new, lighter cottons and shorter hemlines that had become acceptable for their sisters. They shifted their legs, arranging their woolen habits as they tried to make themselves more comfortable on the warm imitation-leather seats. They were swathed from head to toe in wool. White wool.

One of the nuns was old; the other a novice, having just taken her vows. She had wanted all her life to devote herself to God and was grateful to be on this journey to retreat. She still needed to erase certain thoughts from her young and vulnerable mind, thoughts that bothered her now as she looked across at the woman seated opposite and guiltily realized she was envious.

She was envious of the woman's long golden blond hair and the fur of the woman's coat—what was it made of, this beige- and white-flecked jacket? And she envied the woman's eyes, visibly emerald green even behind the smoke-tinted sunglasses. And the suntan . . . and . . .

The young novice glanced furtively at her elder, who had taken no notice of their compartment companion but sat engrossed in her newspaper, waiting for the train to depart.

How, wondered the young nun, could anyone just sit there and gobble up the news and glamour of the world when right in their very compartment was a beautiful, mysterious, sophisticated woman. All that they had renounced . . .

"Putana," muttered the old nun under her breath. She pointed to the photograph on the front page. The younger nun remained silent.

Across from them, Aurora raised one eyebrow from beneath the Dior frames, suppressing a smile at the old

24

nun's remark. Well, there were many people who, upon seeing her picture in the paper, would make the same, mistaken comment.

She'd been aware of the younger nun's stare. At first it had alarmed her, but after studying the child's face, Aurora decided to follow her instinct, which told her that her secret was safe.

She wondered if the wig was too much, but it was all she'd been able to find on a moment's notice. The skullcap underneath that hid her own dark hair was too tight, and she disliked the darker shade of makeup she'd chosen for her "tan," but the disguise seemed to be effective. She'd packed the sable coat in the garment bag that now lay folded on the rack above. The redhead and the blond hadn't seen her lynx jacket. She hadn't worn it in London or Paris.

Both sides would have assumed it unlikely for Aurora to travel second class. And it was cheaper; unfortunately this was an aspect she had to consider.

She was fairly convinced that her pursuers were not on the train. She felt she'd lost them on the road, just before the Swiss-Italian border.

That had given her a start. Approaching it, she'd panicked at the sudden realization that the border guards might have been alerted. She hadn't yet had time to buy the wig or change cars or clothes, and even if she had, her passport was authentic—and the only one in her possession. But, surprisingly, perhaps due to a flirtatious exchange in her more than passable Italian, she'd been waved through without problem.

The modest inn where she'd stayed had neither radio nor television, and the most recent newspaper was over a week old. She had been able to spend one night and enjoy one meal in total obscurity.

The chase from the chalet had been movielike but far more harrowing in real life. Fortunately it had not been of long duration. Aurora was well acquainted with the labyrinthian roads that surrounded the chalet so it had been easy for her to lead them far away, then lose them down a dirt lane. After hearing them whiz past, she'd waited nearly half an hour before venturing forth, turning back in the direction from which she'd come and heading circuitously toward the main highway that led to the Italian side.

Once in Milan, she had parked the Bentley in the garage of a friend, afraid to leave it on the street where it might be recognized; a Bentley attracted attention even if it was not transporting a fugitive. With her luggage in tow, Aurora had taken a taxi to the *Stazione Centrale,* checked two of the bags in a locker, purchased her second-class ticket, and boarded the train.

The bright Italian sun was warm in the overheated compartment.

"Fa caldo," she said in an attempt at polite conversation, sympathizing with the nuns. *"Posso?"* She indicated the window.

"Sì, sì," answered the older nun.

Aurora rose and tried to release the window locks. She smiled as she recalled Sabine's help with another window; that one had led to her freedom.

The lock gave, and air rushed into the compartment, filling Aurora's nostrils with diesel engine exhaust. But that was soon replaced by the clean perfume of the northern countryside. Small villages began to appear, dotting the landscape along the rolling green-carpeted hills, then vanishing as quickly as they filled the window frame; animals, farms, peasants all flashing by with increasing speed.

Like my life, Aurora reflected, slipping off the lynx jacket and laying it beside her on the vacant seat. Flying past me as if I had no control over it.

She glanced across and caught the young nun staring at her again. The girl immediately averted her eyes to the window and her cheeks went bright scarlet.

A babe, Aurora thought. A child with no inclination of what might be out there waiting for her if she chose to reach for it.

She stared at the crimson blush of the child lost inside the voluminous white wool habit.

Yes, she mused. A babe. A child. As I was.

Once.

Part I

Chapter One

It was a myth, perpetrated by those who didn't know, couldn't know. Everywhere, adoptive parents told children that they were "special" because they hadn't just "happened"; they had been "chosen."

Aurora knew it was a lie; she'd understood that early, from the time she'd begun school. Nothing could cut as deeply as the taunting of classmates: "You're adopted! Your parents didn't want you!" Whatever pain her peers suffered, as an adopted girl, she bore a heavier burden. In their insular worlds brothers and sisters and *real* parents couldn't possibly imagine what it was like.

And yet she hadn't been abandoned, unwanted. Her mother had died in childbirth and her father in a plane crash. Aunt Frances had explained it all as soon as she'd been old enough to comprehend. It had saddened her to think of parents she would never know, but that was preferable to the jeers of neighborhood brats. Her situation had nothing to do with "not being wanted."

Aurora—or Rora, as she had nicknamed herself before learning to pronounce the extra syllable—had always known that Frances Gifford wasn't a blood relative. Indeed, the story of her involvement with

Aurora had been exciting to a five-year-old child.

Elmira, Aurora's mother, whose photographs bore an uncanny resemblance to the child now in Frances' care, had exchanged a vow with her best friend: If either of them should marry and bear a child, the other would serve as godmother. Frances had never married, but when Elmira wed, Aurora, even before her birth, had been assured of a "second" mother.

Frances Gifford was plain. She might have made more of her looks, but she despised artifice of any kind. She was bookish, more out of a passion for learning than for escape, and as Rora grew more beautiful, even in her youthful inexperience she could sense a gradual withdrawal on the part of her adopted "aunt." Nothing was ever said, yet an ever-increasing barrier arose between them.

Rora had seen photographs of her mother and Frances, arm in arm, at school outings, then at graduation, and later in front of the Ben Franklin Five and Dime where both got their first "paid positions." Always a twosome, inseparable, closer-than-sisters best friends.

And then Henry O'Brien had come on the scene. Tall and handsome, as striking for his dark green eyes as Elmira was for her burnished mahogany hair that reflected reddish gold in the sun. The photographs became pictures of a threesome, their smiling, laughing faces as close as the twosome's had been. Rora had devoured the albums in Frances' desk, searching for pictures that included a fourth, a little child with a name that meant sunrise. But there were none. Not a single snapshot of Henry or Elmira with their daughter. Rora's only assurance that her classmates had lied in their jealous outbursts was the proof she herself presented: deep emerald eyes that seemed to turn hazel in the light and waves of dark auburn hair that fell upon her shoulders when she undid the elastic that held her tresses in tight, austere braids.

As she filled out and began to mature, Rora resembled her father more. "You have Henry's stride," Aunt Frances told her. "Elmira took small, dainty steps. But Henry . . . you are certainly your father's daughter."

That helped when Joanie Harmon down the street teased her. "Your parents aren't really dead. My mother told me. You weren't supposed to happen! You're ill-e-git-imate! You're a bastard!"

Rora hadn't understood the full meaning of Joanie's words at first; yet some inner instinct, an unknown but very visceral reaction, had made them sting. She'd rushed home to confirm her fears by looking in the dictionary. The definition of the word had burned deeply into her mind, but she hadn't dared to mention it to Aunt Frances. The shame would have shocked her mother's closest friend.

Then, when Rora turned thirteen, her godmother grew ill, a gradual decline that ended, months later, in an overcrowded hospital ward, in agony and pain. Rora, feeling doubly cheated, having first lost parents she hadn't known and then her only remaining "family," withdrew into a shy, quiet teenager. Her physical development contributed to her retreat; she was tall, slim, and not quite sure of what to do with her long arms and legs.

She was sent by the state to live with a foster family. The Linns had children of their own and three others, like Rora, who boarded with them in the large, sprawling old house on the outskirts of town. Although Joseph Linn received money for each foster child's care, Rora had hoped this situation would provide a real family for her. However, the rivalries in the house-hold were as fierce as those she had encountered in school. Her two foster "brothers," Johnny and Ralph, regarded her in anything but a brotherly fashion, and her foster sister, Clara, resented Rora's presence. Until Rora had arrived, she'd had most of the Linns' attention.

Rora was never sure how many children really belonged to the Linn family; there was a baby, Abby, entrusted to Rora much of the time; a boy, Cal, around her own age; a girl, Jen, who was out of school and who dropped by occasionally but rarely stayed the night; and there was Artie, the eldest, in Rora's eyes an "older man" because he was at least nineteen or twenty. The way he looked at her made her uncomfortable, but she said nothing to Betsey or Joe Linn; after all, she was an extra mouth to feed, even if Betsey and Joe were getting money with which to fill her plate.

Rora, alone and introverted, discovered the joy of books; for the first time she understood her aunt Frances' love of reading. She spent hours at the local library sampling the classics, then opting for fantasy and romance. She became as avid a reader as Frances had been, albeit for different reasons. For Rora books were an escape and a means of survival until she was old enough to go into the world alone. She laughed, ironically: She *was* alone. Totally alone. She had been alone for years. To be grown up she'd thought would ensure that she'd never have to be alone again. But she'd known she had to wait until she was old enough so that nobody—neither Betsey nor Joe Linn nor her teachers or the state—could control her life. And she dreamed of falling in love. Her heroes had wonderful names: Heathcliff, Rhett, Vronsky; they changed with regularity and the use of her library card. Her weekly allowance, meager as it was, paid for a double feaure at the Main, and she fell in love with new heroes: Newman, Redford, Connery, Moore.

Her sixteenth birthday had begun like any other day. She rose at six-thirty and was second in line for the bathroom. She showered, dressed, and went downstairs. It was her job to feed Abby, ten years her junior and recently enrolled in school.

Rora loved the little girl and lavished upon her all the affection and attention she herself had missed as a baby. She found Abby sitting on the floor in the dining room, under the table, playing with her dolls, talking to them, admonishing them, a veritable mother-in-miniature. Rora was taken aback. The child was imitating not Betsey, her mother, but Aurora!

"Now this is very good for you," she was saying, "so open your mouth." And she pantomimed spooning some invisible vegetable into the doll's painted smile.

"There," she said. "Isn't that 'licious? If you eat your dinner and say your prayers, you'll grow up to be just like Aunt Rory."

Rora laughed. The prayers part had not come from her; she hadn't prayed since the night Aunt Frances had died; she had asked God not to let Frances die and He hadn't listened. She hadn't asked Him for anything since.

Abby looked up at the sound of Rory's laughter. "Wha's so funny, Rory?" she asked, her eyes wide with wonder.

Rora knelt on the floor beside the child. "Nothing. I'm just happy." But the word had a strange ring, and as she uttered it, she knew it wasn't true.

"Why are you happy?" asked Abby.

Rora smiled to herself. God, kids are so literal minded, she mused. Aloud she said, "I'm happy because today is my birthday, Abby. I'm sixteen."

The child reflected for a moment. "Tha's old, isn't it?"

"Very." Rory's hand absently stroked the top of the

little girl's hair.

"Rory," said Abby, "when I grow up and I'm old, I want to be just like you almost."

"Almost? Thanks a lot. Why only 'almost'?"

"Because I don't want to be an orphan."

Tears welled up inside the birthday celebrant, tears she quickly submerged; doing so had become a habit. She rose and forced a smile. "Well, it's time for breakfast, Abby."

"Okay," said the child brightly, unaware that her words had caused any pain.

Oakdale High School had a custom that had, over the years, become a tradition. On each female student's birthday, a poster was affixed to her locker, together with a corsage, and a lettered message: HAPPY BIRTHDAY. A large area was left blank for fellow students to sign as they passed the locker en route to classes. Rora's freshman and sophomore years had seen a modest collection of signatures and the usual "roses are red, violets are blue" rhymes, silly and impersonal. She thought the custom childish and dismissed the fact that her poster was never covered with as many signatures as other girls' by telling herself that her locker was at the end of the long hall; fewer students passed her poster than those in more prominent locations. But it didn't matter. She'd repeated that to herself several times on her fourteenth birthday and on her fifteenth as well.

Today, however, she was confronted by a surprise. The poster had been signed by so many students that the white cardboard beneath could barely be seen. And instead of the usual carnation corsage, pinned to the top of the poster was a beautiful white orchid! It was surrounded by sugar cubes, also part of the tradition, signifying that this birthday girl had turned sixteen.

Rora examined the signatures. Many belonged to students she barely knew, seniors for the most part. She didn't understand her sudden popularity until she spied one of the scrawled messages. The name was that of the senior class president, Bud Randall. It read: "To the most beautiful girl in the school—now you're old enough to f——" The blank was not filled in, although the first letter of the word left no doubt as to the other three.

Rora's face reddened. She read the rest of the messages. There were several puerile remarks and a few innocuous wishes, but the entire football team had, it seemed, elected to give Rora girl-most-likely-to status. She didn't know whether to feel complimented or deeply insulted. She had become accustomed to un-popularity; to be robbed of it after it had taken on a certain familiarity was something for which she wasn't prepared. After all, she reminded herself, she'd only been sixteen since midnight.

Rora was further surprised that afternoon when Bud approached her on the school steps.

"Hey, want to go to a movie tonight to celebrate your birthday?" he asked.

Guardedly, Rora answered, "Thanks, Bud, I don't think so."

"Look," he urged, "I know you've got a secret lover at the library, but give me a break, will you?"

She blushed; she didn't think he'd ever noticed where she spent her free time.

"C'mon, Rora. I've seen you at the movies. You shouldn't go to the movies alone . . . people might talk."

"About what?" She suddenly felt naked, embar-rassed at having her private life so visible to someone she'd thought didn't know she existed.

"Rora," said Bud, "I'm not giving you a line. I'd really like to take you out. It's just that . . . you usually seem so . . . well . . . so wrapped up in your own thoughts. Some of the kids think you're a snob, but I think you've just got your mind on a lot of stuff."

"I do," she said coolly. She wasn't a snob—couldn't the kids see that? She was just protecting herself, that was all.

"C'mon. I've been taking a lot of ribbing all day on your account." But he was smiling.

"Ribbing?" she repeated. "Why?"

He took his time before answering. "Well . . . who d'ya think put the orchid on your poster anyway?"

"Are you serious?" Her voice rose in surprise.

He nodded. "It was the only way to get your attention, without hanging out at the library myself."

In gratitude she allowed herself to be persuaded into a movie date. Besides, she thought, that would be better than having the whole family ignore her birthday. It wasn't a question of forgetting; they knew the date. They just had too much to do and didn't bother to remember.

It wasn't a drive-in; she was grateful for that. She'd never been to one, but she'd heard stories and she knew what went on. Girls suddenly had to drop out of school and just as suddenly get married. Or worse, they had babies without being married. Aunt Frances had said the only bigger sin was to give the baby away, the way the grammar-school kids had claimed her own parents had done. Not for Rora. Never for Rora. She didn't know which was more unpardonable: bringing an unwanted child into the world and subjecting it to an unloved existence or having an abortion. She didn't

38

want to ever find herself in the position of having to make that choice, so she was determined to be very smart. And smart meant no drive-ins with Bud Randall or anyone else.

She laughed as she brushed her long wavy hair. Her ruminations had made her feel like an old spinster. Well, sometimes she thought like one, even at the tender age of sixteen. It was true that morals were changing; she read about the hippies and the flower children in the magazines. And her miniskirts were as short as any of the other girls'. But she was always careful about the way she sat and moved so people couldn't see what they weren't supposed to see. And even though she hated wearing a bra, she did so if her blouse was the slightest bit see-through. She didn't wear the new "transparent" styles, nor did she discuss sex with the girls at school; she wasn't that friendly with any of them. But she read and saw films, and she was intelligent. She was not a flirt or a tease; she saw examples of such behavior at school and thought it despicable. Still, she wasn't a prude. In fact she feared being the opposite—too preoccupied with sex. It frightened her. It was something about which she knew absolutely nothing, yet it filled her thoughts and, at night, her dreams. In a way, she was glad she didn't have a best friend in whom to confide; she would have been too shocked at her own dream carryings-on to divulge them.

Rora finished dressing. She wore the standard issue of the day: prewashed faded jeans, a navy blue crewneck sweater from the local army-navy store, and penny loafers. The doorbell rang just as she blotted her lipstick.

Artie knocked at her bedroom door and entered before Rora had time to answer. "Well, jail bait," he said, "you're looking good."

"Thanks." She didn't remind him that it was her birthday.

"You going out with that football jock downstairs?" he asked.

"Oh, we're going to the movies." She tried to say it nonchalantly as though she had been on many movie dates, but Artie knew better. He'd seen her sitting at home week after week buried in her books and magazines.

"Well, behave yourself," he said. "Fifteen is pretty young to keep out of trouble."

"Sixteen," she corrected before she could catch herself.

He nodded as his eyes roamed from her amber barrette to the tarnished pennies in her shoes. "All the more reason," he said slowly, turning to go. "Have a good time—but not too good a time."

She'd heard a line like that in a movie. The hero had spoken it to the heroine. "And why not 'too good'?" she asked in the same tone of voice the actress had used.

"'Cause I want you to save it for me," Artie said with a leer as Rora's face went bright red. He was down the hall before she could reply.

She descended the stairs to find Bud in jeans and a sweater, too, but instead of loafers, he wore sneakers. He is cute, Rora thought, and with his freshly washed blond hair falling over his forehead, he was a sort of seventeen-year-old Dennis the Menace. Cute, yes. But he looked so *young;* at school he seemed like all the other boys, but out of context, well . . . Rora had read in several psychology magazines that girls matured sooner than boys, but she suddenly felt years older than her chronological age.

Bud had brought his car, appropriately named "The Heap." It rattled loudly, making Rora even more glad

40

they weren't going to a drive-in.

Rora had already seen the movie the previous Saturday, but she decided to be tactful. It was a James Bond film. She wasn't a Bond fan, but Sean Connery was one of her heroes and at least it wasn't a war story or a "message" film. She and Bud settled into seats in the back, and although the sound system did not boast the latest in amplification equipment, Shirley Bassey's throaty voice enveloped them, transporting Rora into the make-believe world of intrigue and romance.

Nonetheless, she was very aware of her surroundings and of Bud's arm as it slid around the back of her seat and "fell" onto her shoulder. She didn't mind that, actually; the air-conditioning was running at full throttle and there was a chill in the theater. However, when Bud's hand began to roam around her neck and then down the front of her sweater, she stiffened and, as casually as she was able, pushed his hand to the right, back toward her shoulder.

But Bud had two hands, and his left managed to appear suddenly at her temple. His right then turned her face to him, and before Rora had time to think, Bud had kissed her. It was a soft, gentle kiss that made her heart pound, but she shook her head and pulled away.

"Let's watch the movie," she said.

The movie didn't help; James Bond was wrestling with a beautiful woman on a huge bed, the music crescendoing, and the dialogue was as suggestive as the scene onscreen.

Bud tried again, but this time his hand was on Rora's thigh. As agent 007 explored his leading lady's anatomy amidst a flurry of silks and satins, Rora was struggling with Bud's hand, a battle of denim against denim. How could she tell Bud, without hurting his feelings, that the scene in the movie was far more thrilling than the scene at the back of the theater?

41

Spilled popcorn did nothing to add romance to her situation.

Bud gave up and sighed. "The guys were right," he said under his breath. "You're a cold fish. An ice princess."

Now she was angry. "I'm only cold to *boys,*" she said. "It's different with *men.*"

"Sure," muttered Bud. "Always blame it on the other person. Some girls are just . . . frigid. It's okay, Rora. I'm not taking it personally. It's *your* problem. Happy birthday."

They didn't speak a word to each other during the rest of the movie. On the way to "The Heap" after the show, Rora made an attempt at conversation, but Bud's only response was an occasional grunt. So she withdrew and stared out the dirty passenger window until Bud pulled up in front of the Linn house. It was early, but most of the lights were out. The smaller children were probably in bed and the older ones were out on dates—dates that weren't ending at nine-thirty as was Rora's date with Bud.

She didn't speak when she opened the car door; Bud had made no move to open it for her. He didn't even say good night, so she went up the walk and into the house without looking back. She knew he was gone only because his car's ancient muffler dragged along the street.

She entered the hall and locked the door. There was a glow from the living room—not an actual light, as from a lamp, but a grayish glare. She realized that the last person up must have forgotten to turn off the TV set. A western, circa 1945, was on. Two handsome actors were fighting over the leading lady. Rora watched for a moment as the heroine, a "B" starlet with ridiculous gestures, whispered to her lover not to fight the villain. Rora walked toward the set; no sense in leaving it on; she'd seen it before and knew the outcome.

Her eyes had accustomed themselves to the darkness in the room, but she hadn't looked about. She was startled to hear a low voice whisper, "Happy birthday, Rora. You're home early."

She reeled about at the sound of Artie's voice. Then she saw him. He was stretched out on the sofa, an empty bottle of Scotch on the table beside him. A half-empty glass stood next to the bottle, and a cigarette had burned itself out in the ashtray.

"You must have fallen asleep," said Rora, attempting to cover her surprise.

"Not really. I was waiting for you." She didn't like the tone of his words.

"Let me turn on a light," she said.

But he had bolted upright and grabbed her hand. "No. It's nicer like this."

She tried to pull her hand from his grasp, but he wasn't about to let go.

"How come you're back so soon?" he asked. "Buddy boy get fresh?"

In the dark, she blushed.

"You're too grown up to bother with little boys from school," said Artie. "You've always been too grown up, Rora, ever since you came to live with us."

"Uh . . . where's everybody? Betsey? Joe?"

"They're at bingo night. Won't be home for hours. And all the kids are in bed. Nobody to bother us or interrupt—"

"Interrupt what?" she asked. But she knew. She knew the moment he pulled her down onto the sofa beside him.

"Rora, honey, you're special. You're too good for those babies at your school. You need someone mature to take care of you." His hand brushed a tendril of hair

43

alongside her cheek. Bud had done the same thing at the movie, but Bud's hand was clumsy; Artie's touch was . . . different.

"Artie, I—"

"Shh. Don't talk. Just let me love you. I do, you know. For a long time now, Rora. But I didn't want to rush you. I wanted to be sure you were ready, that you trusted me."

Her heart was pounding so loudly she feared Artie could hear it in the silence of the room.

"You do trust me, don't you?" he asked. He leaned forward as he spoke and his lips brushed hers, first lightly, then with more insistence, more pressure. Rora was becoming dizzy. She was afraid—not of Artie, but of herself. This was Artie, practically family—almost her brother! It was wrong!

Bud's words rang through her mind. How could I be frigid with these feelings going on inside me? she thought. She began to ache between her legs as Artie's hands went beneath her sweater and caressed her breasts. She heard herself moan as his head disappeared under the sweater. When she felt his tongue on her nipples, teasing them and causing them to harden, she wanted to say *no*—to shout *stop*—but she was overwhelmed by sensations she had only read about or dreamed about. She was helpless to fight him, and she wanted so to be loved, to be wanted.

When Artie's hands fumbled with the zipper on her jeans, Rora shocked herself by placing her own hand on his, guiding his fingers until the fastener was freed so Artie could slide her pants down. "Artie—" She tried, but his mouth covered hers and silenced her. His hands slid inside her panties and his stroking fingers elicited several responses at once. She knew she should stop him, yet was unable to resist; the pleasure of his touch shocked her senses, but she wanted more.

The sound of a key turning in the front door lock caused Rora and Artie to sit up and dart to opposite ends of the sofa. Rora's face burned with fear and shame. She was grateful for the darkness; it hid her color as well as her guilt.

"Who's in there with all the lights off?" asked Betsey, unsuspecting. "Mustn't take your eyesight for granted. After all, you only get one pair of eyes."

"I guess we fell asleep," Artie lied. Rora didn't speak; she didn't trust her voice.

"Well, don't forget to turn off the TV before you go to bed," reminded Joe.

"Okay," Artie replied.

"Good night then." Betsey headed upstairs, Joe following.

"'Night," Rora managed as her breathing returned to normal.

As soon as Joe and Betsey were gone, Artie reached for Rora's arm. "C'mon back over here," he coaxed. But the mood was broken. Rora wasn't sure whether she felt relief or disappointment. Conflicting emotions warred within her, and all she wanted was escape.

She tiptoed into the room she shared with little Abby and quietly made her way toward the closet. Opening the door a crack so as not to wake the child, she turned on the light and began to undress. She could see the shadow of a pair of shoes as they paused outside the bedroom door—the hall light was still lit—then their owner passed by. From the sounds of the creaking floorboards Rora knew exactly who that was. She quickly changed into her nightshirt and turned out the light. She wanted to wash her face and brush her teeth, but she suddenly feared confronting Artie in the hall. She tiptoed slowly to the bed and crawled under the covers.

"Did you have a happy birthday?" asked a tiny voice.

45

"I thought you were asleep," said Rora.

"No. I wanted to wait up for you. Did you?"

"Did I what?"

"Have a happy birthday. I crossed my fingers that you would, Rory. I wish you were my real sister."

In the dark, Rora smiled. "Me too," she answered. "And yes, Abby, now you've given me a happy birthday."

If the child did not understand, she said nothing to that effect. She mumbled "G'night" and immediately fell asleep.

Rora stared vacantly at the ceiling. Her eyes, slowly accustoming themselves to the darkness, saw patterns made by the shadows; formless, they played with her imagination until they had transformed themselves into eerie creatures, headless bodies, elongated insects—the nightmare images that had once frightened a lonely child. Now they caused Rora to laugh, a silent, self-deprecating laugh; she was sixteen and had no time for imaginary ghouls or nonexistent fears. The real world offered far too many flesh-and-blood demons, and her greatest fear was that she herself was possessed by one of them. She managed to stifle her laughter so as not to interrupt the innocent sleep of the child in the bed beside her, aware that Abby represented the only love in her otherwise empty sixteen-year-old life. Yet Rora sensed that was about to change.

Chapter Two

Aurora's personality underwent a drastic transformation during her last year at Oakdale High. She had already withdrawn from extracurricular activities; sports held no interest for her, and the senior drama club was staging *Harvey* for the umpteenth time; she had loved the James Stewart movie but wasn't the least bit tempted by the "talent" presenting the revival. She applied for a sales position at Lloyd M. Roth, the downtown department store, and instead was hired as a part-time model. Her work was not involved in high fashion or haute couture, but in teen clothing for the junior figure. Still, it paid better than the minimum-wage clerk positions available, and it afforded Aurora the luxury of pretending to be Jean Shrimpton or Twiggy. She spent much more time in front of the mirror in her bedroom, little Abby mimicking her pose as a bored sophisticate, right hip slung almost out of joint, one eyebrow slightly arched, observing the overall effect first front, then sideways.

At school this only added to her reputation of aloofness; now the "look" accompanied her wherever she went.

Some of the change in Aurora, however, was due to

Nature. Her figure was developing from that of a promising young girl to that of a striking young woman; tall and slim, but with curved hips and just enough bosom. At times she was bewildered by the stares of men on the street, men far older than she. Her practiced air of sophistication, together with an inner sense of style, caused her to appear more knowing than she was. From a constant study of movie stars, both onscreen and in interviews, she developed a repertoire of clever, suggestive answers to the questions being put to her with growing frequency. In the beginning she was shocked by the comments of the middle-aged men accompanying their teenaged daughters to the fashion shows held at Roth's on Saturday afternoons. Didn't they see that Rora was only a year or two older than their own girls? Would they speak in such a manner to their daughters?

After several months of weekend modeling, Rora learned to hide her blush when confronted with a proposition. Fortunately, the head buyer, her immediate boss, was a homosexual; she wondered about his roommate, one of the handsomest men she had ever seen. Both men treated her like a kid sister and advised her on makeup and hairstyle. The future Aurora O'Brien slowly, and stunningly, began to emerge.

Betsey Linn was made aware of the transformation by household tension. Joe Linn, although a decent, loving husband and father—and foster father, too—couldn't keep his eyes off her. That did not go unnoticed by anyone, including Artie.

Rora had taken great care since the night of her sixteenth birthday to avoid being alone in the house with Artie. She'd even managed to keep one or two rooms between them. If he sat down to watch TV, she went upstairs to her room. If he found her in the kitchen, she found a chore to do outside. She sensed that he was waiting for the slightest encouragement, and she exerted every effort to withhold it. Yet this situation troubled her sleep and filled her mind with sexual fantasies, leaving her breathless and frustrated, fearful that wherever he was, even down the hall in his own room, he could read the innermost wonderings and wanderings of what she considered her wanton mind.

She found a copy of *Peyton Place* in, of all places, Betsey's knitting box. With a pen-sized flashlight, and only when Abby was fast asleep, she devoured every page, spending the most time on "certain" passages. Pent-up feelings, unexpressed emotion, added to her disquiet. During her waking hours, she appeared calm and poised, a model of charm. But at night, with no one to observe her, she was a sad, lonely, little girl of seventeen. When she lay awake listening to the six-year-old sleeping beside her, she envied the child, feeling far younger than her charge.

This dichotomous behavior led people to think of Rora as moody and neurotic, and she herself would not have argued that point. She felt as though she were two separate individuals housed within the same body. For a month or two she wondered if perhaps she were schizophrenic or manic depressive. She bought psychology books with her allowance and earnings, too embarrassed to be seen borrowing publications on such subjects from the local library where everyone knew her.

When she had read enough to realize that she wasn't crazy, simply lonely, she enrolled in a community theater group in an attempt to meet people who were beyond the "teenybopper" stage. But most of the members were older married couples and her appearance proved disruptive. The men stared at her while their wives openly ignored her. Rora couldn't understand their behavior at first. She had dressed "down" for the occasion, wearing her oldest jeans and her baggiest sweaters.

So she escaped once again into the world of movies and romance. The Main opened early on Saturdays and was the only movie house in town that did not cater to children on weekends; no cartoons here, but regular features at discount prices before two o'clock in the afternoon. This fit perfectly into Rora's Saturday schedule. She wasn't due at Roth's until one-thirty. She began leaving the house early and taking in a movie at eleven in the morning. No seniors like Bud Randall were necking at the back of the theater at that hour; he and the rest of his cronies were probably at football practice or sleeping late in anticipation of a "heavy date" that evening.

Rora maintained this Saturday morning schedule for several months, relishing the intimacy of the empty theater. There was something cozy and reassuring about the smells of leftover popcorn and chocolate candy; their familiarity seemed to promise safety. But the same question always occurred to her: safety from what? The only reply was the monotonous, impersonal drone of the air conditioner.

Rora consciously chose "easy" films; comedies, musicals, intricate spy plots that were always too convoluted to understand and therefore pure escapism. She didn't want to challenge herself on any issues she was unprepared to confront; she sought only solace and comfort on Saturday morning, never films to set her curious head to spinning further.

She fell in love with *Breakfast at Tiffany's* although she knew from the novella that the movie was a fairy tale. But she was a fan of Audrey Hepburn and of Capote, and that film and *The World of Henry Orient* she replayed in her dreams as rehearsals for the freedom she would one day find in New York.

One Saturday, she saw a New York film that depressed her, a film about the Manhattan singles scene in which lovers didn't even bother to learn each other's names. That wasn't what she wanted; that kind of freedom wasn't freedom at all. But what did she want? Her regular reading and Saturday-morning movie fare would not provide the answers. She began seeking out books and films that might tell her more about the world, teach her more about herself and her own, unique, as-yet-uncomprehended place in it.

Rora, along with most of the seniors with above-average grades, scored well on her SATs. Yet college was out of the question unless she could win a full scholarship, which she did not. However, her major disappointment in this area derived from the news that Barnard and Hunter had turned her down. Not that she had entertained hopes of entering either, nor had she relished the notion of an all-girl school. But these were New York schools; that made all the difference.

So it was that Rora wrote away to several less traditional institutions; namely, the Actors' Studio and the National Academy of Acting. The latter was in the heart of Greenwich Village, a plus before she even saw the catalogue.

She didn't know how to approach Betsey and Joe on the subject, although a sixth sense hinted that Betsey might not be brokenhearted to see her ward depart. A foster child was one thing; a grown woman—a beautiful one—in the house was another matter. Both women knew this without speaking about it.

But as Rora nourished thoughts about New York and acting school and a life outside of Oakdale, circumstances, or fate, whichever one chose to call it, intervened and her decisions, one by one, came about as the result of a movie.

It was unusual for the Main to be showing a foreign film; Oakdale was not a sophisticated town and the movies of Ingmar Bergman and Vittorio de Sica and Federico Fellini were as foreign to the town's citizenry as were the names of these filmmakers. So it was definitely odd that on the Saturday preceding Rora's graduation from Oakdale High the Main selected a limited run of Fellini's *La Dolce Vita*.

The theater was almost empty, so Rora decided to pretend that she was at a private screening in Hollywood. This morning there was no smell of popcorn or cigarette smoke, no grumbling from the ancient Coca-Cola machine; the theater was still asleep as the curtain opened and a solitary audience of one was transported to Fellini's Rome.

The story unfolded and reached out to Rora on one level; the actors touched her on another. From the moment Marcello Mastroianni's image filled the screen, Rora was in love, though her competition consisted of some of the most beautiful women in Italy. She envied them, hated them, adored them. When Anouk Aimee whispered to Marcello, Rora mouthed her own whisper, as intimate as any in her limited sexual vocabulary. She shared a voyeur's secret as she watched Marcello and the women in his life. She sympathized with his mistress, Emma, but at the same time resented her for wanting Marcello all to herself. Emotions and sensations, as unfamiliar to her as the language of the actors on-screen, converged upon her; in awareness, if not in experience, Aurora O'Brien was coming of age.

She understood that Maddalena was a word she had recently discovered in one of her "dirty" books, Betsey's description of current popular fiction. *Nymphomaniac.* She had looked it up for two reasons: for its definition, and to learn whether or not it described her. Because in her attempt to read and explore the human psyche, she feared above all that she might fit into that category. The thought had seldom left her mind since her sixteenth birthday and the sofa episode with Artie.

One article she had read discussed masturbation. She had tried it. Once. And the article was right on one count: She had felt no guilt afterward. But the author had erred on another point. Aurora had not experienced "sexual fulfillment" or orgasm; she wasn't even certain how it would feel if she *did* experience it. In short, the article didn't say how to recognize it—just how to achieve it. But she hadn't, she was sure. She felt more titillated and aroused when reading a sexy passage in a novel or sitting in the darkened theater, as now, watching a very suggestive scene with a man to whom she would gladly succumb if she had the opportunity. Her legs quivered as she watched Nadia Grey do her strip, and as Marcello pursued the wading Sylvia into the Trevi fountain. No, she thought. I'm not a *nymphomaniac*. And I'm not *frigid* either. I'm just waiting for the right man. Marcello . . . or someone like him.

She left the Main feeling years older than when she'd paid her admission and entered. This part of her life, graduating from Oakdale High, working at Roth's on Saturdays, coming and going, seeing the same shops, the same people, the same everything—all of it was temporary. It would pass. That made it bearable.

She wasn't pleased to learn, upon her arrival at the store, that she was expected to model bathing suits that afternoon.

"I really feel a bit . . . undressed . . . in them," she told Margo Gold, the manager.

"Really, Rora, you wear a bathing suit at the beach, don't you?"

53

"Yes, but everyone does there. I don't feel so . . . exposed."

Margo eyed her model. "Honey, if I had it to display, I certainly wouldn't hide it!" She handed Rora three different suits, two halter-top, one-piece styles and one bikini. "Take your pick, but that's your wardrobe today."

Rora selected the black suit. It had a starkly simple line that reached her neck in front and was cut very low in back. Maybe she wouldn't have to turn around on the runway. She laughed at herself, knowing that she'd be expected to model the suit from every angle.

Well, she reminded herself as she changed out of her jeans and T-shirt, this, too, is temporary. As soon as I save enough money, I'll go to New York. I can put up with this for now. . . .

But she hadn't expected to see Artie among those attending. The fashion shows at Roth's were informal displays, lasting only twenty minutes or so. They were held at the center of the Young Elite shop on the third floor. The men's section was on the ground floor. As far as Rora knew, Artie had never visited the floor where she worked.

He was seated on one of the striped loveseats when she came out of the dressing room. He winked, which made her doubly uncomfortable. But she managed to do her turn as she had been taught—the model's walk and the model's slouch were already second nature to her—and in a few minutes it was over. The fashion show would be repeated in an hour, but for now, she had forty minutes to herself.

He was leaning against the dressing-room entrance when Rora came out in her jeans and T-shirt. "Hi," he said casually. "Got time for a Coke?"

"What are you doing here?" she asked, avoiding his question.

"Watching you," he said in that unnerving way of his. "I do that a lot."

"Well, I hope you're getting something out of spying on me."

He smiled. "I haven't yet, but I'm not giving up." He took her arm. "C'mon, let's get out of here for a while." He steered her toward the escalator.

"Where do you think you're taking me?" she asked.

"Wherever you want to go, Rora," he answered. Why, she thought, do all of his remarks seem to have double meanings? Or do I just have a one-track mind?

"Did you like the movie?"

That took her aback. He *had* been spying on her! "How did you know where I was? God, don't I do anything that you don't know about?"

He shook his head. "Not much. Rora, you really don't get it, do you? Don't you remember your birthday?"

How could she forget? "What about it?" she asked abruptly as the escalator deposited them on the ground floor.

"You know what would have happened if Betsey and Joe hadn't come home just then, don't you?" Actually he was not asking a question; he was stating a fact.

She blushed. A third-floor clerk provided a momentary distraction, but still her color remained.

"You really do something for a bathing suit," he said when the clerk had passed.

"Artie, I wish you'd leave me alone."

"No you don't. You're saying it because you think you should, but it isn't what you feel. Remember, I know that."

Rora was becoming irritated, but because of a duality of feelings. His words were not the romantic, poetic ones she wanted to hear; yet they tantalized her. That she didn't want. Or if she did, as Artic claimed, she didn't like wanting it. Why did he affect her this way?

They had reached the street. "Rora, sooner or later you're going to give in. It's only a matter of time, and you know it as well as I do. You want to lie there and let me show you what it's like." He took a long, audible breath and then added, "I'd be a very good teacher, someone you could trust. I'd never hurt you. I just want to love you."

Rora couldn't speak. Her knees suddenly turned to Jell-O and she was aware that Artie knew it. She had to reach out for his arm to steady herself. The rough texture of his blue cotton work shirt only drew attention to the warm spring afternoon, to aftershave mingling with Artie's own, particular body scent, to the soft breeze blowing in her hair. Everything seemed suddenly to create a heady, dizzying intoxication. Again, Rora was repulsed as well as seduced by conflicting sensations.

"I . . . I have to get back upstairs soon," she stammered.

"I'll pick you up at five-thirty," he said.

"No—" She tried to protest.

"Yes. It's Saturday night. You're graduating next week. Commencement—that means *beginning*. I'll see you at five-thirty."

She was helpless to resist. A little voice reminded her that despite his dark curly hair, Artie wasn't Marcello Mastroianni, but that same voice also whispered that she wasn't Anouk Aimee, either.

When she returned to the third floor, Margo Gold hurried to her. "Who *was* that guy, Rora?"

At first Rora didn't understand. "What guy?"

"That gorgeous guy you went on your break with. Honey, he's too old for you." She grinned. "He's more my age."

56

Rora laughed. "That's Artie. My older brother." She didn't add the word *foster;* if it had elicited jeers five years earlier, now it only served as a bid for attention, and that was not the kind of attention Rora sought from anyone.

"He's your *brother?*" Margo echoed. "The way he looks at you? Christ, Rora, I've read about 'close family relationships,' but you just don't strike me as the type." Margo was teasing, of course; how could she know what was being contemplated by Rora's "brother" for five-thirty that evening?

He was waiting at the employee entrance to Roth's when Rora came out of the store. When she hadn't seen him on the third floor, she had thought he'd changed his mind, and again had experienced that odd conflict of relief and disappointment. But he was leaning against the passenger door of his Ford, and nodded, beckoning her to the car.

She hesitated for only a moment, then walked slowly toward him, her legs slightly unsteady.

"I'm glad you didn't run away," he said as they settled into the car. "I figured you might sneak out the front entrance."

She laughed nervously. "And I thought you'd changed your mind."

"Nope. Some things never change." He cast a glance at her, but any reaction was hidden behind sunglasses. "C'mon over," he said. "It's silly to sit on top of the passenger door. You could fall out if we hit a bump."

"Isn't it locked?" Rora asked, attempting to sound casual.

Artie leaned across and pushed the button down, brushing his arm against her breasts as he did so. "It is now," he said.

57

Rora felt the color rise in her cheeks. "It's warm in here," she said.

"It'll get a lot warmer. Trust me."

"I wish you hadn't said that!" she exclaimed.

He just grinned, that slightly off-center grin she remembered from the night he'd kissed her. She also remembered that his lips had tasted salty and his breath had smelled of Scotch.

"Where are we going?" she asked as they passed through the last of Oakdale's downtown section and headed toward the highway.

"Well, you looked so great in that bathing suit, I thought we'd go to the beach," he answered, his eyes on the road.

"I didn't bring the bathing suit," she said defensively. "Besides, it isn't hot enough for swimming—the water must be like ice."

Again he grinned. "I wasn't thinking about swimming."

The Jell-O feeling gripped her once more. She stared out of the passenger window as the countryside went by.

Before long they reached a deserted area off the main road. It was not far from the beach, although it could not be termed a part of it. Set off in a bower of lush trees, it seemed a perfect hideaway, and its seclusion stirred images in Rora's inexperienced senses.

"Just remember, Rora," said Artie, "I know you. I mean *really*. And that's nothing to be afraid of. Rather it's something to be grateful for."

She didn't answer. He didn't frighten her. She didn't know why, but she felt safe with Artie and this was certainly new to her.

"C'mon," he said, leading her from the car. He took a sleeping bag from the back seat. "You know, I really think girls should always have their first experience with an older man, someone they know will be good to them. So be glad you're not my real sister 'cause I don't believe in that kind of stuff."

Still she hadn't said a word. He walked toward her and traced his left index finger down the front of her T-shirt, lingering at a nipple. "I remember you like that. Right?"

Her breathing was growing shallow, her voice weak. "Artie—"

"Shh. Let's take that off. It gets in the way." In one movement he removed her T-shirt and she stood before him, her breasts exposed to Artie and the soft breeze, her nipples taut and erect.

"Oh, God, you're beautiful!" he exclaimed, taking one of her breasts in his cupped hand and fondling it. "Tell me how you like this," he said, bending his head to lick the tip of the nipple back and forth.

Rora groaned with pleasure.

"I thought so," he said. "Now the other one." He repeated the teasing and then rose to his full height, taking Rora into his arms while they still stood, his hands moving up and down her smooth back as he kissed her. His tongue parted her lips and explored her mouth, and soon she responded with her own kisses and caresses. Her body reacted independently of her mind's instructions as Artie held her closer. Then his hands unzipped the fly of her jeans and teased her before he pulled her pants down to her ankles. He knelt as she stepped out of the denim.

Artie unbuckled his own jeans and let them fall to the ground. Then he removed his Jockey shorts and stood before her in naked, sun-bronzed, muscled glory. Rora's head began to swim as Artie knelt and parted her legs with his face. "Put your hands on my shoulders if your legs go weak," he said, and his tongue slipped beneath her mound of pubic hair. When he reached her clitoris she began to shake, but he didn't stop. His tongue increased its pulsating rhythm.

Rora did as he had instructed and gripped his shoulders, digging her fingers into his flesh as she grew more and more excited. The wetness and the heat inside took over, and she moaned as multiple spasms of pleasure overcame her.

"Lie down," Artie commanded, and for the first time Rora caught sight of his erect penis. Fear flashed through her. "Artie! Don't make me pregnant!"

"Shh! Don't ruin the mood!" He reached over to where his jeans lay and withdrew a condom from the pocket. "I used to be a Boy Scout."

She was relieved, but her body had tensed; he was going to enter her; she was going to let him. There was no backing out now. But once it was *done,* there was no going back either.

Would she really see the world differently afterward? Through wiser eyes? She almost laughed at herself as Artie lay down upon the bedroll alongside her.

"Lie back," he instructed, "and just let me do everything. You'll like it. You like it already. It'll just be like what we've been doing but better. And don't be afraid. The books are all wrong—it isn't going to hurt."

"You're sure?"

He answered by teasing her and bringing her around. "How could anything that makes you feel that good hurt, huh?"

She didn't respond. She came. Again and again, lying there and letting him tease, arouse, play with her until he said, "Now!" with an urgency she hadn't heard before.

He slipped the condom on his waiting erection and rolled Rora flat on her back. "Now!" he repeated, and her legs opened and wrapped themselves around him as though she had performed the ritual countless times.

Their two bodies established a magical harmony, riding tandem with one another as he thrust himself deeper and deeper into the mystery of her, obliterating all sounds and sights around them.

Rora wanted their bodies to merge and become one. They were rocking faster and faster now, and he alternated his long, penetrating thrusts with quick, short insertions that made her gasp, fearful that he would leave her body. But they only served to heighten her sensations, to bring her closer and closer—and then they came, together, crying out in unison and joy. Rora's tears were of gratitude and release.

Her universe had changed. Aurora O'Brien remained the same person she had been an hour earlier—with one exception: the doubting was over. She *knew*. And she had no regrets; she was ecstatic. She was no longer a child. She was a *woman*.

Aurora graduated from Oakdale High the following week and modeled at Roth's on Saturday. Nothing had outwardly changed except that Artie was waiting for her outside the employee entrance each Saturday at five-thirty and they drove to their own secluded spot where they made love until it was dark. Then they shared a pizza or ate hamburgers and went back to the house to watch television. Nobody at home seemed to notice that foster brother and sister were spending more and more time together, as nobody had noticed the year in which Aurora had avoided him. In short, nobody noticed her comings and goings any more than they had before. Only little Abby, had she been old enough, might have been aware that whenever Aunt Rory was present Artie was not far away.

At first, Rora found it difficult to be around her foster brother in the company of Betsey or Joe, particularly Joe, for he seemed to enjoy watching her, being in the same room with her. But gradually she realized that she was projecting her own thoughts onto them; Betsey was occupied with keeping a busy house clean and in order; Joe was behaving no differently. The major change was in Rora. For more than a year her body had stiffened in Artie's presence, withdrawing as a way of denying her attraction to him. Now there was a fluidity to her movements, a subtly languid relaxation. If he brushed against her as he passed in a hallway, his touch provoked a remembered response and she longed for Saturday and their appointed hour. Her dreams were no longer filled with fantasies of secret trysts with movie stars—even Marcello had faded from them—but were evocations of hours in Artie's arms. If Rora had once feared being frigid, Artie had erased her qualms forever.

She was aware that summer could not last, that when September came she and Artie would part. She also knew that this would be her choice, not his. A future in Oakdale with her current lover was not enough. She wanted more of life, of herself. Artie had shown her possibility, passion, love. She would always be grateful for that. But he had also shown her that life offered more than she had allowed herself to imagine. And she wanted to taste it, to hold it, to possess it. At times she was shocked by the needs unleashed by her sexual knowledge. Perhaps Freud was right, she speculated, and we are, indeed, governed from infancy by the libido. And what if that is so? She wasn't base enough to use it, and unlike many heroines she'd met in films and books, she wasn't willing to sell it. But it was an advantage to be aware of it. The better one knew oneself, the better one fared in the world.

As August approached she saddened. Artie sensed it, although perhaps he couldn't give name to it.

"Something's on your mind, isn't it?" he asked after they had made love.

She didn't answer, but instead traced his dark eyebrow with one of her long, slim fingers.

"Wondering how to tell me?" he asked.

She turned to look into his eyes. They were dark eyes, but not deep or mysterious. Artie was not complicated; she had once thought him to be, but it was simply that he had wanted her. Once she was his, the intense brooding she had seen in him was gone. He didn't seem to ask more from life. She didn't know whether to envy him his simplicity or pity him for it.

"I'll be going to New York in September," she said at last. "To study," she added, as if to justify her action and to assure him that she wasn't rejecting him, just Oakdale.

"I figured you would," he said without emotion.

"I didn't want to hurt you." She was still looking at him.

"You're not. I always sensed you wouldn't be satisfied following in Betsey and Joe's footsteps. You've got too much going for you to settle for that."

"Going for me?" she repeated. What did she have going for her except a desire to see more of the world? To do something?

His fingers separated the tangles in her long, mahogany waves. "You think I don't understand?" he asked. "Look, Rora, I read you better than you read yourself." He reached over to take a cigarette from the pack in his shirt pocket. "Maybe you figure what we have is something special." He lit the cigarette and took a long drag. "Or maybe you realize that it's just what it is."

"What do you mean?" She didn't understand; maybe he was right and perhaps he did "read" her better than she did herself.

"I mean that our Saturday-after-work fun and games affair—because that's what it is, after all—is great. But that's what we're talking about, not love. We dig each other. Period. That's terrific, but it isn't anything more. And in a way that's lucky. Because if you thought it was love, or if I thought so, we could really screw ourselves by deciding we were destined to be together for the rest of our lives. And we'd do like millions of people do when they find they're compatible in the sack—we'd get married and have a couple of kids and settle down with a house and a mortgage. See, you're turning your nose up already. Then, after awhile, we'd grow bored with each other and get a divorce or, because of the kids, we'd stay together and find something on the side. We'd lie to each other and to ourselves, and eventually we'd come to hate each other because it'd be easier than admitting we'd really fucked it all up." He took another drag and then said, "You see? We're really the lucky ones. We see each other for exactly what we are. A guy and a girl who really know where it's at. You dig me, I dig you, so we fuck each other's brains out and come out of it friends instead of enemies. You go to New York with ideas about what you want, and I stay here because I don't have my sights set as high as you. And five or ten years from now we can still get together, whether it's for a coffee or a roll in the hay, whereas if we got married, ten years up the pike we wouldn't be talking to each other and I'd probably be banging my head against a wall trying to meet alimony payments and child support." He paused to take a swig from the thermos they had filled with Scotch. "So I repeat, we're the lucky ones."

Rora had listened quietly, his words disturbing her if only because of their matter-of-factness. But she couldn't argue with him. Artie did read her all too well.

Probably the reason she had allowed him to seduce her—she hadn't known it at the time—was that she had trusted him, trusted him not to fall in love with her or to create illusions as most of the boys at school would have done. She laughed aloud then. Bud Randall, clumsy Bud Randall of her aborted movie date, had announced his engagement at the graduation luncheon. His bride-to-be was no doubt a girl he had gotten pregnant! Thank God Artie was pragmatic. He had initiated her into the joy, the wonder of sex. He had unlocked a new world to her without any promises, without any lies. She would always be grateful for that.

Why, then, was she feeling so empty, and suddenly so sad?

Chapter Three

Aurora yawned as she reached over to turn off the alarm clock. She attempted to open both eyelids at once, a task made difficult by the caked mascara she had neglected to remove the night before; her eyelashes were all but glued together.

Eleven o'clock. It was impossible to tell the time of day in her cramped, minuscule hotel room at the women's residence on east Fifty-seventh Street. That apartment *had* to be available!

But her appointment to see it was set for noon, and so, after allowing herself the luxury of a five-minute stretch, Rora jumped out of bed, collected soap and towel, and, sticking her tongue out at the image presented in the medicine-cabinet mirror, headed down the hall to the showers.

Icy needles of water welcomed her into the day; then she quickly dried herself. This was not a shower in which to linger.

A subsequent look in the mirror assured her of an improvement, but not totally convinced, she added dark glasses to her apartment-hunting ensemble, a modest-length miniskirt and a beige turtleneck T-shirt.

After descending from the bus on lower Fifth Avenue, she made her way to Greenwich Village and arrived at the Cornelia Street address at five minutes before twelve. The exterior of the building didn't hold much promise; a crumbling Victorian façade with cracked steps and peeling paint. She entered the once-elegant vestibule and rang the super's bell.

A chubby, ruddy-faced woman of fifty or so responded after the fourth ring, shuffling to the door in worn felt slippers.

"Yeah? Whaddya want?" she asked, squinting to adjust her bloodshot eyes to the noonday sun.

"I came to see the apartment," said Rora. "I have a twelve o'clock appointment."

The round face scowled. "Yeah? Well nobody told me about it."

Aurora consulted the slip of paper the real-estate agent had given her. "Here it is. Mrs. Marini sent me."

The super glanced at the paper and shrugged. "Okay." Then she examined Rora. "You some kind of actress or model? Or a stewardess? I don't want none o' them in my building."

Rora hesitated for only a second. "I'm a school-teacher," she said.

"Yeah? Kinda young, aren't you?"

"I skipped in school. It's my first year."

The super didn't seem interested in Rora's academic accomplishments. "Well, c'mon, then. I'll show you the room. Ain't much, though. I keep it clean, but that's about it."

She led Rora down a dark, smelly corridor to the rear of the ground floor, and as they entered a small room, the rotund woman switched on a stark overhead bulb. The floor was covered with large black-and-white linoleum squares. They were cracked. The walls, a dismal, peeling, greenish gray, were drab and unin-

68

viting. At one side of the room was a marble fireplace—inoperable, the super was quick to point out—and on the wall opposite was a set of louvered doors behind which Rora found a compact sink, a refrigerator, and a two-burner stove.

The only furniture in the room consisted of a formica table with two unmatched chairs and, under the room's single window, a folding cot. Rora peered out the window at what once had been a garden but was now overgrown with weeds and dead shrubbery. Aloud she said, "Well, I guess it's quiet." The street outside the women's residence was being torn up and the riveting began at eight o'clock each morning.

"And it's clean," the super put in. "I keep it very clean. Exterminator comes in once a month and you won't see too many cockroaches."

Rora glanced around. "I don't see a bathroom."

"For this rent she wants a private bathroom?" The super spoke to the air as if Rora were invisible.

"Excuse me," said Rora, "but is this an apartment or a rooming house? I had expected my own bathroom." She'd waited outside the bathroom at the Linns' house enough times to appreciate the luxury of her own bath.

"Look, honey," said the woman, warming only slightly, "you only gotta share with the guy in the front apartment and he's hardly ever here. Travels. You get your own key and it's closer to your room than his." Then she added, "*I* ain't never had a private john, and I don't miss it none."

Rora sighed. "Well, let me look at it." The woman led her down the hall. It was indeed clean, private, and close enough to the apartment to almost qualify as her own. Furthermore it had a new showerhead.

"What about the deposit?"

"Ain't none, except the commission to Mrs. Marini. It's month-to-month. No lease. You pay in advance, cash preferred. You decide to move, you gimme thirty days' notice. I do the same if the owner sells. Correct the 'if' to 'when.' Which is why there ain't no lease. They'll knock this down by next summer, you'll see. Put up a big high-rise and triple the rent. Whole Village is changing. So take it or leave it—it's Saturday, and it's my day off."

Rora reached into her purse. Anything was preferable to her closet accommodations uptown. And this was only a few blocks from the National Academy of Acting, whose entrance audition she had passed on Monday. Less than a week in New York and she was already on her way!

By the end of the week the tiny room had been transformed. With the help of the super's nephew Jimmy, the walls had been repainted in a cheery antique white, and colorful throw pillows in bright oranges, pinks, and purples had been tossed onto the charcoal gray cot. The super had contributed a carton of assorted dime-store plates and kitchen utensils left by a previous tenant. By the time Rora's classes began later in the month, she would be settled into the Village as a bonafide New Yorker. She had found herself a part-time job at an answering service only two blocks from Actors Equity, so she would have money in the bank to boot.

The super, Josie, told her about Loehmann's in the Bronx, where Rora could find inexpensive clothes for her "teaching" position.

The subway ride to Jerome Avenue was an experience in itself. Rora had never ridden an elevated train before. Her stomach felt queasy each time she looked down through the window. A herd of loud, boisterous children, dripping ice cream cones and cracking bubble gum, invaded the car. Workmen, smelling of sweat and guzzling beer from cans wrapped in brown paper bags, crowded one end, and a drunk slept, sprawled out lengthwise and taking up three or four seats. None of the other passengers seemed to notice, although the smells and the lurching of the train caused Rora's stomach to swirl. She couldn't possibly imagine this trip as a normal, everyday commute.

The mass of humanity exited with Rora at the Jerome Avenue stop. She hoped they weren't all headed for the same discount destination.

Josie had advised her to grab anything she liked that fit her size eight figure. "They're a bunch of barracudas," the super had said. "Don't be afraid to shove—it's part of the act!"

Rora had steeled herself for the onslaught, but the racks of designer dresses in the smaller sizes were relatively uncrowded; most of the activity was centered on the aisles catering to double-digit figures.

She tried on several summer cottons in the communal dressing room, modeling each for herself as she had done for Saturday shoppers at Roth's, although Loehmann's was a far cry from Oakdale's leading department store. She chose two in crinkly Indian cotton so she wouldn't have need of an iron. Admiring a pale blue chiffon Givenchy and a taupe wool crepe Halston, she was tempted. However, her budget did not yet match her taste; designer labels would come later.

She made only one other clothing purchase. Employing restraint to curb her weakness for buttersoft kidskin shoes, she treated herself to a pair of black pigskin stacked-leather heeled shoes; they'd be perfect for making the rounds or, as she soon learned, pounding the pavement.

The pace of life in New York, particularly in the

Village, was accelerated in comparison with Oakdale, but Rora was energized by it, even in the hot summer sun and a sticky, humid apartment. Her new life had begun!

Rora worked the six-to-midnight shift at the answering service. At first the prospect frightened her; she was alone in the one-room office with the tiny outer lobby on the eleventh floor of the building. Bustling with activity during the day, it took on the aspect of a haunted house at six each evening when the rest of the Broadway–Times Square area was coming alive. But Rora was careful to lock the lobby door with the dead bolt and Sylvia, the daytime operator, assured her that the place was impenetrable; the night guard on the ground floor saw to that.

"Charley's your relief man and he's very prompt. Sort of a loner, but a decent guy. He's into heavy reading and therapy. He'll probably try to psycho-analyze you, but don't let that scare you off. He can be a very loyal friend."

Charley, it turned out, had been a Broadway gypsy until he broke his ankle in a very awkward fall during a tour of *West Side Story*. It hadn't healed correctly, and his dancing career had ended. This Rora learned from Sylvia: Charley was more than quiet; he was downright taciturn.

Rora's classes at the Academy were due to begin in two weeks, so rather than take the afternoon shift and then have to reaccustom herself to the change in schedule, she opted from the start for the later turn. Once the school reopened she would be able to take the Sixth Avenue subway from the Village to midtown in less than fifteen minutes. And she would have her weekends free as soon as Saturday classes were over.

After the first few days on the phones, Rora found that she could recognize the voices of the majority of subscribers. Most were performers and possessed, by nature or by cultivation, distinctive speech patterns. One very sultry, slightly British-accented woman named Lorene phoned every evening at seven. At first Rora assumed this woman was on her way to the theater, but as time passed she realized that Lorene was a call girl; all her messages were from men with first names only, and each was confirming a different appointment. Rora was amused, rather than shocked, when she learned that Lorene's address was an exclusive and expensive one on Sixty-third Street between Madison and Park avenues.

Sylvia had instructed Rora to remain businesslike with all the subscribers, to be polite but to keep a certain distance. That was easy to do with Chauncy Whitmore, a snobbish third-rate Shakespearean actor, and with Jerry Townes, the service's resident juvenile with a twenty-five-year-old adolescent yodel. But it was impossible to be anything but friendly with Stanley Roach, a borscht-belt comic who never called Rora by her name or even by her nickname. It was always "Hiya, doll, Stanley here!"

Stanley was very precise, checking for messages at six-thirty nightly, without fail. Rora could tell it was he before she answered the phone; all she had to do was glance at the clock on the wall. She also knew, from his messages, that Stanley was a good man; they all expressed gratitude or warm wishes. Even the calls from his agent gave that impression. "The hospital says thanks," or "You really cheered the kids." And at least twice during Rora's first week on the phones he received a message expressing appreciation for a loan.

At the end of Rora's second week, only three days before her classes were scheduled to begin at the

Academy, she picked up the phone at six-thirty on the dot and said, "Hi, Stanley."

"My God!" he exclaimed. "How'd you know it was me?"

"ESP," she teased, reaching for his messages. She read them off one at a time and came to the last one. "It's from Manny." She knew by now that Manny was his agent. "He wants you to meet him at Rosoff's at seven o'clock. And he says not to eat beforehand because he's buying dinner."

"But doll, I just ordered a takeout from the Stage Deli—wait a minute! You like chopped liver on Russian rye?"

Rora's mouth watered, although she had never tasted either. She had been living on doughnuts and coffee from the Humpty Dumpty Café on the corner of Cornelia and West Fourth.

Stanley said, "Listen, I'm two blocks away. I'll be right over!" And he hung up.

The main entrance to the building was open until nine o'clock, but Rora wondered what she should do. Stanley sounded safe enough; however, Sylvia had cautioned her about familiarity with the subscribers. Now he was on his way up, and there was nothing she could do to stop him.

Within minutes Stanley was knocking on the frosted glass in the outer lobby. Rora put all the phones on HOLD and ran to get her dinner. She opened the door and tried to refrain from giggling as she greeted the five-foot-tall perfect double for Pinky Lee. He grinned until his eyes disappeared, and as he extended the brown paper bag to Rora, cole slaw began to drip onto the black-and-white tiled floor. Rora was so hungry and the pickle was so aromatic, she almost swooned. But she recovered her manners and grabbed an oversized ash tray to serve as an improvised platter.

74

"You're an actress," said Stanley.

"How'd you know?" she asked.

"ESP," he answered, still grinning. The phones suddenly came to life and Rora hurried back to the huge round oak table to cope with impatient callers. As she swirled the alphabetized listings, she congratulated or placated, whichever served the occasion, and Stanley waved from the doorway.

"Gotta run, doll—lock the door as soon as you have a chance. Be seein' ya!"

The chopped liver was only the beginning. The following evening Stanley arrived with pastrami, still warm. Then came corned beef, knishes, tongue. Rora gained a pound and Stanley beamed with pride. "There! A little more and you won't look like a waif!"

But Rora didn't mind looking like a waif. It was chic to look like a waif. Twiggy did, and Jean Shrimpton was losing her place as the number-one cover girl to more boyish models. And wearing her long dark hair in a ponytail, her T-shirts baggy, and her jeans too loose to be provocative gave her a kind of anonymity when traveling the subway late at night.

When classes began at the Academy, Rora's wardrobe fit right in with those of the other young hopefuls. She was glad to be attending school in the Village; uptown, she would have felt shabbily clothed. It seemed that actors who couldn't afford to attend the more expensive schools and who didn't have the professional credits to gain admittance to classes at Actors' Studio wound up at the National Academy, where the classes were small and informal, more like actual rehearsals.

In regard to training, the school left much to be desired. Its students were not the cream of the season's crop, nor were its instructors, who chose to call themselves directors, possibly because most of them

75

had tried—and failed—to direct, or act, or both.

Rora liked Hannah, a robust woman in her fifties who taught voice and diction technique. Hannah had been a music-hall performer in England before coming to America. She had a wonderful voice which resounded down the hallways without ever becoming raucous. Rora was delighted when she was told she had no regional speech patterns that needed "fixing." Hannah made a few suggestions to enable her to make her voice carry; the most helpful was an admonition to lean toward "Standard Stage." It was closer to British than to general American speech and made Rora feel . . . continental. She employed her excellent ear and such speech soon became second nature. Only Stanley noticed the change.

"You're startin' to talk funny," he commented one night over stuffed derma. "I mean actressy. Foreign. Y'know?"

She certainly did know.

Rora did not particularly like her scene study director. It was said to be an honor to attend his classes, partly because he'd written a book on acting technique, but mostly because he claimed to have studied with Stanislavski. Rora found that difficult to believe. She had read *An Actor Prepares,* and found little connection between it and this lecherous old man whose hands were constantly upon her. She didn't succumb to his flattery as the other young girls did, and after three classes, Rora knew that Hubert complimented any girl who had what he termed "promise"—except the promise to which he referred had little in common with theater or acting. His reputation with women was as well known as his book.

His wife also "directed" at the school. Rora did not know of Madame Skrepova's lesbian tendencies or activities, but she did notice that the woman eyed her when they passed each other in the hall. However, Rora had all she could do to fend off Hubert, and since she was not in any of Madame's classes, she didn't give her a second thought.

The Academy contained the usual assortment of very intense neurotics, flighty effete young men, and older "angry" actors inspired by Brando and Dean. There were several interesting students; one was a funny freckle-faced boy of Rora's age. His name was Billy and he had run away from a farm to become an actor. With his hillbilly accent and his Huck Finn appearance, Rora wondered how he had passed the entrance examination. But when she reflected further, she was amazed that she had been accepted. Her audition had been a five-minute reading of a scene from *King Lear,* and the little she had studied thus far was enough to convince her that her reading had not been very good. Artie had said her looks would gain her acceptance anywhere, but that provided little consolation. Now she was compelled to admit that he was probably right. She determined to work harder at her craft.

She admired an actress in her scene class, a girl of about twenty-two whose name was Miranda. Blond, ethereal, angelic in appearance, she had a natural ability; her body didn't cross a stage, it glided. Her voice resembled that of Julie Harris. And the emotion! Even when portraying a tree in improvisation class, Miranda *became* that tree! Her best roles were Tennessee Williams' characters, tortured souls with whom Miranda, at her tender age, seemed able to identify. Rora wondered if that was due to an incredible imagination or to a wanton, sordid past.

They shared a table at Humpty Dumpty's on more than one occasion, but Miranda never discussed her personal life. She appeared more interested in hearing other people's stories. Perhaps she was collecting information to use in her repertoire, her storehouse of sensory recall and experience.

Miranda chose to befriend Rora, and because of this, Rora found herself telling the actress her deepest secrets. She had never had such a close friend. Artie knew one side of her, but it was only the sexual side, not her thoughts and feelings unrelated to sex. Rora even told Miranda about Artie, as a show of trust and in the hope that Miranda would share herself, or at least a part of her that would shed light on her wonderful acting ability.

But Miranda merely clasped Rora's hands in hers and exclaimed, "Oh, Rora! How marvelous! Your own foster brother! And nobody in the family knew a thing about it! Oh, I envy you!"

Rora found that an odd reaction, but it only added to her fascination with Miranda. "What about you, Miranda? We've only talked about me," she said.

"Well"—Miranda lowered her voice to a whisper— "I have a secret, too, but you mustn't tell a soul! I'd have to leave the Academy if they knew."

"Knew what?" Rora leaned closer for privacy.

"I'm going to have a baby!"

Rora gasped, in spite of her attempt at nonchalance. "You're *what?*"

Miranda smiled, her mouth a replica of Leonardo's *Mona Lisa*. Rora recognized the smile. It wasn't enigmatic, after all. It was a pregnant smile.

She observed the mother-to-be. Not a trace of a stomach. Miranda was even thinner than Rora, mannequinlike, with cheekbones to match. Rora wanted to ask when, but the word that issued forth was *who*.

Miranda's eyes glistened. "I don't know yet. I have to find him first."

Rora used whatever acting technique she'd acquired in two weeks to withhold visible signs of shock. The girls paid their check and went out onto the street.

"Want to come over for some Minute Rice and Cheddar cheese?" asked Rora. "Billy's coming over and I can add garlic powder and turn it into a feast."

Miranda laughed. Even her laughter sounded theatrical, musical, yet on the edge of hysteria. "Some other time. I'm meeting Raoul tonight."

"Raoul?" echoed Rora. "Sounds exotic."

Miranda's face assumed a tragic air. "Oh, God, how I adore him! But he can't decide whether he's straight or not. And I don't know how long I can take his not knowing, Rora! I've already told him he'll have to choose between Jeffrey and me!" She waved a farewell-performance-style good-bye and was across Sixth Avenue before Rora could say another word.

Rora prepared the Minute Rice without the garlic and she and Billy enjoyed two helpings apiece.

A seamstress occupied the ground floor apartment in the adjacent building. Maria was short and plump, and in addition to doing sewing, she took in stray cats and stray neighbors. She seemed to possess an eye for anyone in need, and Stanley's "waif" did not escape her notice. She introduced Rora to the Roman standby, pasta *aglio olio,* and to the world of Italian haute couture or, as she called it, *alta moda.* In exchange for standing atop Maria's round kitchen table for an occasional hour or two, being pinned and hemmed and intoxicated by the smells of Maria's herbs and spices as they simmered on her neighbor's ancient stove, Rora was included as part of Maria's *famiglia:* Vito, the dry cleaner from west Fourth Street; Pete, who owned the secondhand bookstore on Bleecker; Sergei, a pixie with a gray beard who had actually danced with the Bolshoi. In addition, if Rora passed by in the company of Miranda or Billy, Maria's arms beckoned. *"Venga, venga!"* she would exclaim. "I make you a cappuccino!" It was never an invitation; it was a command.

Maria disappeared once every two months when the Italian liner *Raffaello* arrived in the port of New York. Her longtime lover worked as a steward aboard the ship and during Aldo's visits not a stitch was sewn. Park Avenue matrons and Village residents alike were unable to retrieve their garments until the *Raffaello* had pulled anchor and headed for Genoa or Naples. Maria was always quieter, more subdued, after Aldo's departure, which made Rora think of Artie. She seldom thought of him these days, but she was aware that even with her new friends, far more than she had ever known in Oakdale, there was a kind of closeness missing. And it was more than just sexual. She couldn't have explained it if she had tried.

Maria occasionally earned extra money by permitting film crews to photograph her apartment; it had appeared in countless movies and television shows. Rora was fascinated when she saw huge trucks parked along Cornelia Street, long cables running from them to Maria's front windows. Once in a while the apartment was used for more than "background," and an actual scene was shot inside. Rora watched as each crew member performed his job. Dozens of personnel were involved for hours, and the result was a mere ten or fifteen seconds onscreen.

"The next time they shoot here," Maria suggested, "you must make yourself more visible. You never know, with your looks that might do more for your career than a hundred years at that academy of yours."

"Oh, Maria, I'd love to, but I'd be in the way."

The wise woman laughed. "You show up early and let me dress you and do your makeup, and I promise you will not be in the way."

It was too tempting an offer to refuse. Rora skipped her diction class several weeks later when a Hollywood crew arrived to shoot exteriors.

First Maria announced, "You will wear this." She reached into the closet and pulled out a hand-crocheted slip of a dress, a wispy, gossamer maze of burgundy cobwebs magically held together by invisible threads.

"Oh, it's beautiful, Maria! But I couldn't wear it!"

"Nonsense! The owner is a client who will be in Europe until October. Put it on. A crochet knit will show off your figure just enough."

Rora obeyed, aware that the intricate design was striking yet simplicity itself. "It looks like one of a kind," she said as she stepped in front of the mirror.

"It is. One should never gain weight when one wears originals. To alter them, especially to let them out, ruins the line."

"But it isn't ruined," said Rora, turning to see the side view.

"This is because I sew cleverly. But also because you are wearing it. Its owner should wear it with such style."

Maria didn't do much with Rora's hair. "It is magnificent as it is," she said. "But we must do more with your eyes and mouth." She went to work with makeup brushes, as seriously as an artist at his canvas.

The effect, however subtle, changed Rora from a pretty acting student into a professional-looking model/actress. Rora felt the change only externally, but by the time the film crew had set up their gear, she was comfortable enough in her new surroundings and wardrobe to greet the assistant director in tandem with Maria.

"Ciao, Eddie!" Maria shouted through the window. "Come have a cappuccino. I got someone I want you to meet."

Eddie Calvert was the first assistant on the New York unit. He had sandy brown hair and deep blue eyes. And his manner, unlike that of most straight men Rora had met in New York, was not threatening or compromising. He exuded a warm, natural friendliness. Rora took to him immediately.

Eddie shook hands and said to Maria, "Where did you find her?"

"She lives in the next building, and she's *different,*" answered Maria protectively. "You got some work for her maybe?"

Eddie turned to Rora. "You're beautiful enough to be in the business. Are you?"

From anyone else it would have sounded like a line, a come-on. But Eddie asked it without guile, without a double entendre, so Rora answered directly. "I'm studying to be an actress, and I've done a little modeling."

"Ever been in a movie?"

Under the makeup Rora blushed. "No. Maria's just trying to be nice."

Maria cast her a look and made an Italian gesture that Rora recognized as a signal to shut up. But there was no point in lying. If Eddie put her in front of a camera, she would have to be told in which direction to look.

"Then you're not a member of the union."

Rora knew he meant Screen Actors Guild. "No. I guess that lets me out."

"Well, if you want to be an extra, we can get you a Taft-Hartley waiver, but the next one you do, you'll have to join SAG."

Was he offering her work?

82

"Does it pay money?" she asked.

Eddie grinned. "What do you do to pay for your classes?"

She told him about her job at the answering service.

"And what does that pay? Minimum wage or lower?"

She admitted that she was at the bottom of the pay scale.

"Well," he said, "I don't mean to put down your job, but extra work probably pays per hour what you're earning for a whole day." He paused, thinking, and then said, "I have an idea. Got any eight-by-tens?"

Rora shook her head. "Not yet," she admitted. She knew the first item on a model or actress' list of acquisitions was a good set of photographs. She just hadn't been able to afford pictures; once her rent was paid, even with Maria feeding her at least four times a week, there was nothing left over. And on her Academy tuition, low as it was, she still had several payments to go.

"Look," said Eddie, "I can use you in one of the shots we're doing in front of La Groceria. But we're only doing the one scene today because it involves the actors going from here"—he indicated Maria's living room—"to the restaurant. They have a couple of seconds of dialogue and that's it. Thing is, if you do an extra today, you're dead for the rest of our New York stuff because you'll be right up front in camera range. But . . ." Another pause while he turned it over in his mind and then he said, "We'll be needing a stand-in for Audrey Hepburn. Your coloring's right. How tall are you?"

"Just under five-eight."

"Hmm," Eddie said. "What about heels?"

Rora began to understand. "As tall as you need me."

"Okay. Tell you what. Let's go outside and talk to Mel. He's the SAG rep. I don't want to do anything that isn't by the books." He turned to Maria. "Is that dress hers or yours?"

Maria laughed and threw up her hands. *"Jesù,"* she said, "Eddie, you know me too well!"

He turned back to Rora. "Those yours?" He nodded toward the jeans and sweater over the kitchen chair.

She was grinning now. "Shall I change?"

"I think it might be a good idea. The job won't reimburse you enough to replace that if you lean against anything on the set, and if Mel okays it, we still have to clear it with casting *and* get you the waiver. Then you've got to join SAG and that'll wipe out your answering-service nest egg." He looked down at her pigskin shoes. "Got any higher heels than those? Audrey is really tall."

Rora said, "I have a pair of spindly heels." She laughed. "My friend Billy calls them my hooker shoes, but they're probably high enough."

"Let's get 'em, then," said Eddie, checking his watch. "Maria, the coffee's great and you may have done more for your friend than just make sure she's eating regularly." He bent over and kissed Maria's cheek. Then, taking Rora's arm, he led her to the door.

He had collected the jeans and sweater, but Rora was still wearing the borrowed dress. Eddie said, "C'mon, let's get you changed. Then I'll take you over to meet Mel."

For a moment Rora hesitated. She didn't want to take Eddie up to her apartment while she undressed. He could wait outside on Cornelia Street while she changed at Maria's, yet something about him told her she could trust him. Perhaps he even wanted to test her trust. Or perhaps movie people were accustomed to such casual behavior. She wasn't stupid or naïve; she exited Maria's apartment and he followed her. Josie was sweeping the steps of her building, and she gave

84

them both a disapproving look.

"Uh-oh," said Eddie as Rora took out her keys. "Is den mother upset?"

"She shouldn't be," Rora declared. "I'm not in the habit of inviting men into my apartment." Billy had been her sole visitor.

"I'm honored," he said lightly.

She opened the door and they went inside. There was a pleasant early autumn breeze circulating in the room, but it seemed suddenly to have grown smaller, more claustrophobic.

"Ah," mused Eddie, "suffering for your art?"

"Well, it's home," she answered. "Have a seat. I'll change and be back in a minute."

While Eddie looked around, Rora disappeared into the closet and pulled off the dress in the dark. She dropped her jeans and had to fumble around for a moment before retrieving them.

"Hey," called Eddie, "don't fall in!"

"I'll be right out," she said. She zipped her jeans and adjusted her sweater. *Voilà!*

He appraised the new Rora and smiled. "The dress is gorgeous, but frankly I like what you do for a pair of jeans."

Her face warmed with color, causing Eddie to remark, "My God, I didn't think there was a girl left in this city who could still be embarrassed and not try to hide it."

"I *am* trying to hide it," she said. "I'm just not having any success at it."

"Well, I like it. C'mon, let's go talk to Mel. He's probably scorfing up more food across the street—he loves shooting at restaurants."

They passed Josie on the way out of the building. Eddie pantomimed tipping an imaginary hat; then he whispered to Rora, "She's probably clocked us and can't figure out if we've set a new speed record."

Rora's face reddened more than before.

"Please forgive that," said Eddie. "I just wanted to see you blush again."

Mel Collins explained the SAG rules and waiver procedure. Then the casting director had to meet Rora. She didn't like him at first sight: wrinkled, stocky, shiny trousers, a pot belly, cigar-stained teeth. She didn't care for the way he looked at her either. She wondered what his reaction might have been if she'd shown up alone for an interview instead of on the arm of the first A.D. She was grateful to be with Eddie.

"She yours?" asked Harry Slater.

"Does her getting the job depend on the answer, Harry?" Eddie shot back.

Harry snorted. "Only thing that depends on—her height," he said, studying her legs and then fixing his gaze on an area that had nothing to do with height. "Turn around," he said to Rora. Even those words had the ring of sexual innuendo.

But she did a model's 360-degree turn and when she faced him again, she had assumed the impenetrable mask she'd learned to assume at Roth's department store when approached by classmates' fathers.

To Eddie, Harry said, "Well, if she wears those heels every day, she's got the job. I can't find any girls the right height and coloring. Did you clear it with the union?"

"All set," said Eddie. "We'll be ready to go in about half an hour. See you—and leave some room for later," he added, indicating the casting director's protruding belly.

"God, are all casting people like that?" asked Rora when they had reached the corner.

"Nope. Some are much worse. Harry's been in the business for years. He's less crooked than most, and I guess his staying power does give him some kind of credibility."

Eddie led her to the coffee wagon behind the star's trailer. "You have to remember that you find the creeps at the bottom. For extra work, everyone is willing to pimp. When you get to the big roles with other people's cash riding on them, the business becomes a little more respectable." He poured them each a cup of the fragrant brew, then took a sip of the steaming coffee. "The movie business can eat you alive. But it can also take you where you want to go. As long as you keep your head—and don't let yourself be taken in by the bums." He indicated the spot where Harry had "interviewed" Rora. "His type is easy to spot. It's the pimps who wear five-hundred-dollar suits and travel in limos and talk like gentlemen—they're the ones to watch out for. Because underneath it all, they're still pimping. They just give it a nicer name."

Rora listened intently. Maybe Maria was right and she could have a more valuable learning experience outside the rehearsal environment of the Academy. Her training was just beginning.

Chapter Four

Taking leave of the answering service was not difficult. When Rora told Morty, its owner, about her stand-in assignment, she was fired. Sylvia thought it was a wonderful opportunity, and Charley, the night relief, thought she was crazy. Glancing around the small office as she collected her belongings—several books she'd kept there for slow evenings, a personalized coffee mug (a present from Stanley), pens and pencils—she said aloud, "I'll miss the pastrami, but I'll never miss the ringing phones." She left a message for Stanley, kissed Sylvia and Charley good-bye, and left the eleventh floor.

Being excused from classes at the Academy was more complicated. Hubert took the request as a personal affront. "The theater requires discipline," he reminded Rora. "Films? Television? What do they offer besides money?"

Rora chose not to mention that she was in need of money to pay her tuition and that she had seen Hubert on television before she'd been old enough to appreciate his acting talent.

"You must not expect shortcuts if you wish to become a great actress," Hubert declared, fondling her hand in a more than paternal way.

Rora, in spite of herself, answered, "But Hubert, you don't really think I'll ever become a great actress, do you?" Somehow she was disappointed by that realization; nonetheless, she felt light-years removed from Miranda's natural ability and denying it would not change the situation.

Hubert squeezed her hand. "My dear, you have a wonderful potential"—his Russian accent was thicker with certain words, *potential* being one of them—"but you are still a child! What do you know of life?" The vowels were getting longer. "You must first experience so much—"

"That's why I want to take advantage of this opportunity," Rora interjected while removing her hand from his grasp. "And also," she added, "so I can continue at the Academy."

Hubert rose. "Well, then, we must not stand in your way. You will be welcome when this . . . *filming* . . . of yours is finished."

She bumped into Miranda on her way out of Hubert's office.

"I just heard!" her friend cried tragically. "Oh, I'm thrilled for you! Oh, it's fabulous!" She hugged Rora, who wondered if Miranda ever just spoke like other normal, everyday "civilians." But Miranda's scene from *Streetcar Named Desire* had been so incredibly moving—Madame Skrepova had called it "acting from the womb"—that Rora was not about to pass judgment on her friend's offstage personality. Acting of that ilk was to be treasured; Miranda would someday be one of the great stars of the American stage, of that Rora had no doubt.

Now, Rora decided, each of them had to survive the present; Miranda with her hostessing job at the famed La Grille, and Rora as stand-in for a beautiful film star.

It was all part of what Hubert called "life experience."

As Eddie Calvert's protégé, Rora enjoyed special privileges. The production secretary was friendly to her, the crew considered her one of them and shared their jokes with her, and Eddie served as her guide, showing her the ropes. She learned how to laugh at her own faux pas, such as when one of the gaffers shouted from high up on a scaffold, "Gimme a hand—quick!"

Rora was standing where she'd been instructed to stand, in the center of the shot. There were no other actresses on the set that morning, no extras, and the gaffer repeated his request, louder this time. Rora looked down at her hands—people had often commented on their slim, graceful beauty, asking if she were a pianist or violinist—and she raised a hand high in the air, calling to the gaffer, "Here. Is this high enough?"

From all around, laughter erupted—leg-slapping guffaws—and Rora blushed deeply.

The gaffer, when he'd calmed, shouted, "Honey, that's gorgeous, but it's not exactly what I had in mind!" He had to stifle another convulsive attack.

Rora would never forget that when a gaffer called for a hand, he was requesting a particular kind of light. She managed to laugh at herself, which endeared her to the crew, but she didn't relish her performance.

Eddie promised to clue her in on any other possible "gaffes" before they happened.

"To do that," he said, "I'll have to take you to dinner. How about it?" he asked casually shortly before the day's wrap.

"Fine. But I'll have to change shoes. These heels are getting to me."

A shorter Rora emerged from the trailer moments

later, tired from the long day, but happy. It was a Saturday—double pay—and they had gone into overtime. Her check would be substantial. She handed her voucher to Harry Slater, still not liking the way he looked her over, and left to join Eddie at the Transfer truck where he was bidding the crew good night. They weren't planning to shoot again until Monday; they were still on schedule, and a Sunday shoot would mean another double-pay day.

"Well, where to?" asked Rora.

"It's your choice, lady; I'm just visiting your town."

She had received a message at the answering service that morning from Stanley. It had said something about missing their Stage Deli dates on the eleventh floor. "Have you ever been to Rosoff's?" she asked.

"In the west Forties, you mean? What tourist hasn't?"

Rora hadn't expected to see Stanley at the restaurant, but he was standing at the bar with several of his friends, all male, all similar in height, dress, and age. He waved as Rora and Eddie entered. "Hiya, doll! Come and meet the boys!"

They were introduced to Morey, Josh, Hymie, and Bobby, who was the smallest of them all and only reached Rora's shoulder. "You wanna join us or you two romancing and wanna be alone?"

Rora was embarrassed by the question, but Eddie didn't seem to mind. He looked at her, his eyes asking her preference.

Rora smiled "yes" and Stanley signaled the maître d' for a large table in the back "so we can talk," he said.

But they didn't "talk." Amidst steaming platters of brisket and potato pancakes, Rora and Eddie could barely hear or think, for shtick zoomed back and forth across the table with gravity-defying speed. There was much laughter, much food, and Rora and Eddie, rather than compete with the professionals, surrendered and just enjoyed the "show."

Over the rice pudding, Bobby announced, "Listen, folks, Myra is fixing dessert and coffee, and we are all moving uptown to my place. Gotta new print of one o' the tramp's films."

Stanley leaned over and said to Rora, "You two like Chaplin?"

Eddie did; Rora had never seen any of his work.

They managed to cram themselves, illegally, into a Checker cab. The men were very attentive as the taxi bounced over potholes, the cabbie hitting most of those along the route. Rora was seated in a coiled position on Eddie's lap, her long legs cramped, her feet under the jumpseat on which Stanley provided a living definition of how the seat had acquired its name. Eddie didn't speak during the trip to the west Eighties; he laughed at the jokes and kept his hands on Rora's waist to prevent her from falling. She hoped the intimacy of the ride would not be misinterpreted; she was simply trying to keep from banging her head against the cab's roof.

They tumbled out at the corner of Eighty-fifth and West End Avenue. Their next trip, in a pint-sized elevator, amused Rora. This is why Bobby's friends are all five feet tall, she thought. Bobby did a rat-a-tat-tat on the door, then winked at Rora.

"Our signal," he explained as another Munchkin opened the door. Myra looked up at Rora and observed, "Who's the Amazon? And her friend?"

Thus welcomed, Rora, feeling like Gulliver among the Lilliputians, offered to help their hostess with the coffee.

The men, including Eddie, sat in the living room as Bobby set up the movie projector. Their cigar smoke

93

filtered into the kitchen, and Rora coughed.

"Hope you like cheesecake," said Myra. Rora's eyes bulged at the sight of the homemade masterpiece topped with the biggest strawberries she had ever seen. "You eat enough of this stuff," said Myra, "and you'll fill out." She shook her head. "Skinny. Every girl today has to be skinny."

Rora and Myra carried the cake and coffee into the living room as Bobby proclaimed, "We're ready to start, so sit down." To Rora he said, "You sit in back, honey, with your boyfriend. If you sit up front, none of the boys will be able to see!" Everyone laughed as Rora seated herself beside Eddie on the loveseat.

"Quiet! A little respect, please!" The buzzing voices and gags ceased immediately as Chaplin's tramp appeared onscreen. Rora was transported into a wonderful, magical world, a silent world in which a sad, funny little man in baggy trousers and oversized shoes, reduced grown men, however short in stature, to uncontrollable laughter, then within a split second, turned that laughter to tears. Rora howled until her ribs ached, yet the film's end found her and the others wiping away tears. Myra leaned over in the dark and whispered, "First time, huh, kid?"

Rora nodded. Eddie's arm brushed against hers and when Bobby turned the lights back on, she could see that he, too, had been moved by the little tramp.

Only Stanley spoke. "Wish I had that," he whispered in a hushed, wistful voice, almost to himself.

It was late, past three, when the party broke up. Myra kissed Rora's cheek and said, "So come visit now you know where we are." To Eddie she said, "But feed her, willya?"

Eddie and Rora climbed wearily into a taxi and

headed downtown. Rora was exhausted, but relaxed; the evening had been fun.

"Where are you staying?" she asked as they sped past Times Square, past Macy's at Thirty-fourth, unimpeded by traffic at the late hour.

"With you?" Eddie said softly. He had voiced it as a question, without any words between the lines.

And Rora responded in the same vein. "Yes," she said, "with me."

She turned the key in the lock and Eddie followed her into the small room. The streetlights on Cornelia were at the front of the building, so Rora's apartment was pitch-black. She and Eddie stood still for a moment until they got their bearings.

When his hand touched her face, it was not a seductive move, but a friendly one. His touch brought a feeling of warmth to Rora, quite unlike the passion she had known with Artie.

"Shall I turn on the light?" she asked.

"Not just yet," he answered, coming closer to her.

She felt good in Eddie's arms. He was strong, he was relaxed, and she liked him. More importantly, she trusted him. She had trusted him from the moment they'd met in Maria's apartment. They'd known each other only a few weeks, but she felt as though she'd known him since childhood. He was, in Maria's words, a really nice guy.

As Eddie unbuttoned Rora's blouse, she found herself saying, "I don't invite every man I meet up to my apartment."

He kissed her at each temple. "I didn't think you did. You told me that the first time, remember?"

"But I meant it, Eddie." She was kissing him back.

"I know. I knew then." He removed her blouse and

95

reached out to unzip her jeans.

Rora was puzzled. With Artie she had felt awkward, unsure, at odds with herself. With Eddie, it was she who led him to the cot. Had she changed so drastically in such a short time? Or was it because she was with Eddie? And did it really matter?

But neither Eddie nor Rora expected what followed. When he joined her on the cot, its legs gave way underneath them and the bed collapsed, sending them both to the floor. They broke into convulsive laughter in the darkness.

"You okay?" he asked.

"Yes," she giggled. "And you?"

"No bones broken. C'mon over here. Let me make sure you're all right."

She pretended he was checking her for bruises; he did the same. "God," he said between laughs, "I haven't had this much fun since I played doctor and nurse with my cousin—and that must have been thirty years ago!"

She stiffened momentarily.

"Are you shocked?" he asked. "She was a second cousin."

Could Rora tell him she had done more than play doctor and Artie had been much closer than a second cousin? She decided against it, and her body responded to his touch.

Eddie began tracing a pattern, an invisible map of the contours of Rora's body. Neither of them spoke for a time; they both seemed to be concentrating on his fingers and the feelings they evoked. The darkness of the room added to the silence; neither of them wanted to break it.

Eddie had removed his jeans, although he still wore his safari shirt. Rora reached over and slid her hand between the two middle buttons. He helped her by slipping it off, but he took each move slowly. She was growing moist inside and wanted him; she felt desire rising, her breath becoming higher yet deeper. She was surprised by her sudden response; minutes earlier she had felt only friendly toward him. Now she wanted him inside her, wanted to feel his thrust, to touch and taste him. The thought of him penetrating her heightened her desire, and thought fed on desire, desire on thought.

But Eddie was in no hurry. He could sense her body's tensing and releasing, but still he only stroked her, imitating the steady brushwork of a painter exploring his subject before making the final touches to a canvas.

It was Rora who finally spoke. "Eddie—please!"

"Shh!" he whispered. "We've got all night." He kissed the tip of her nose. "I'm busy," he explained softly.

"You're what?"

He laughed quietly. "I'm marveling at the female form. Truly one of God's masterworks. You're beautiful, Rora, even in the dark. I was busy thinking about that."

"Why busy?" She didn't want to break the mood, but she was curious.

"I was thinking that I don't deserve you."

"That's not really up to you," she said, drawing him closer.

He heaved a sigh and then turned her face to his. "I don't want to hurt you, Rora."

"You won't," she said.

Their kisses grew more urgent. His hands, no longer teasing gently, pressed her against him, hard. He sucked her breasts and she gasped from pleasure. "Eddie!" she cried.

"Rora, here!" He pulled her on top of him until she was sitting astride. "Oh, honey!"

Her body arched as he quickly entered her. Without

breaking their increasing rhythm, she bent down over him, careful to keep him inside her. Her mouth covered his, her long hair falling over them both, a cloak of perfumed softness swaying back and forth. It grew damp as their lovemaking became more intense.

She withdrew her mouth and his lips sought her breasts again. And all the while she rode him, faster, faster, like a galloping steed. She grasped his shoulders as the plunges came stronger and stronger from below. She saw shooting sparks, and her head bolted wildly from side to side like that of a bucking mare.

Eddie's pace accelerated, deepened, and Rora felt as though her insides were about to burst.

"Oh, honey!" cried Eddie. "Rora, honey, you're beautiful!"

She was too breathless to speak. Gasps of pleasure poured from the depths of her throat; orgasm upon orgasm spasmed through her, a frenzy of sensation. She was certain she would die there on the floor with Eddie still inside her. She wanted him to stay inside her all night—forever! Never had she known such bliss, or that it was possible.

Did poets find words to describe this joy? She knew only that she felt alive—wonderfully, ecstatically, blissfully alive! Oh, God, she thought, this *has* to be Paradise!

She and Eddie slept in each other's arms on the tiled linoleum floor, the Salvation Army blanket tossed over them.

Desire awakened Rora in the morning. She glanced at her sleeping lover, not wanting to disturb his rest, yet wanting him, wanting more of what they had already shared. Perhaps that was the difference between Eddie and Artie, she thought. With Artie it hadn't been *sharing.* Oh, she had enjoyed it; nonetheless, it had been Artie making love *to* her. Teaching her. Leading her. Instead, she and Eddie had shared something and that made her feel warm, close to him, free. And she wanted it to happen all over. Again and again.

Fear assailed her briefly; Eddie hadn't used any protection. But her period was due within the week, and from what she had read, this should not be her fertile time of month. Good, she thought as she gently lifted the blanket. This was Sunday. They didn't have to be on the set until seven o'clock the following morning. She was glad, because she had decided, after all, to disturb his sleep.

They spent the entire day in Rora's apartment. They made love, slept, ate, and then made love again. Rora didn't care if he had to carry her to the set the next day. Toward evening they crept down the hall and showered together.

"This has been the most wonderful day of my life," said Rora as they finished the last of the doughnuts.

Eddie reached across the formica table and gently squeezed her hand. "Be careful," he said. "I could easily fall in love with you."

"What's wrong with that?" she asked.

He was quiet, reflective, but only for a moment. "Not a thing," he said. "Now, we have to see about getting you some decent pictures. When this gig wraps, you'll be without a job, and my so-called connections don't go beyond the lower echelon in this town—yet."

"Will you be going back to California when we wrap?" Rora asked.

"Have to. I've spent the last five years laying the groundwork. I don't want to carry a megaphone and direct 'background' traffic for the rest of my life." He carried the paper towel to the sink and emptied out the crumbs. "But first things first. Your pictures." He was checking a mental list. "Got a telephone directory?"

She nodded. "Under the cot. We fell on it in the dark."

"Oh," he said, smiling, "that's what broke our fall." He retrieved the large book and began scanning the second half. His finger stopped at the bottom of one of the pages.

"Christ, he's still at the same address! That's lucky." Eddie dialed a number and while it was ringing he explained, "We went to NYU together a hundred years ago. I think he's heavily into fashion stuff, but maybe, just for old times'—" He interrupted himself to greet the voice at the other end.

"Tony! It's Eddie Calvert. How the hell are you?" He covered the mouthpiece and said to Rora, "I think he's come out—way out—but he's a terrific photographer." Then he returned to the phone and told Tony the reason for his call.

Rora sat nervously on her chair, worried about what this would cost. She was paying off her SAG membership initiation fee and covering her dues on a weekly basis, but pictures . . . by a top New York fashion photographer. What was Eddie thinking of?

Whatever Eddie was thinking of, it worked. He hung up and reached over to kiss Rora, a triumphant smile on his face.

"Tony has offered to do test shots of you."

"Test shots? What does that mean? Eddie, I can't afford—"

"Test shots are on the house, honey. That's how Tony got his start. They all do it in the beginning, just to get their work seen. Of course, Tony may have forgotten how to work gratis—he gets a couple of thousand a day now—but we won't worry about that."

Rora's eyes widened at the mention of Tony's fee. "Do film photographers—I mean directors—make that much too?"

"Not until you're running the show. But on the way there, the union is pretty strong. We do okay." He looked at his watch. "Speaking of which, it's dinnertime. We've been eating junk food all day. Why don't you let me take you somewhere romantic and cozy and we'll have a quiet little dinner?"

"You mean 'just like in the movies'?"

He nodded. "But please, no potato pancakes tonight. And no Munchkins. Just the two of us. Okay?"

"Okay," she said. "I'll even dress for the occasion."

It was all they could do to keep their hands off each other as Rora slipped into one of her Indian cotton dresses. It really wasn't cotton weather, but she hadn't been able to afford warmer clothing; that would have to wait until the bills were paid.

The following evening after the day's wrap, Eddie escorted Rora to a town house in the east Thirties. The décor was entirely a two-color scheme: shell pink and slate gray. Even the flowers were pink, the vases gray porcelain. The single third color was the green of plants and flower stems. Rora half-expected Tony Rogers to appear in a pink shirt and gray pants; however, only his beard was gray. He was dressed in shiny black overalls, a kind of polished cotton jumpsuit.

"Eddie!" he greeted his former classmate. The two men seemed a generation apart, Tony's gray hair and beard aging him, Eddie's deep blue eyes maintaining his youthful appearance. And he keeps himself trim, Rora thought, blushing as she called to mind his firm muscles. Tony, however, was thinner than Audrey Hepburn, and he looked like a mannequin: The jumpsuit hung from his frame; he didn't *wear* it.

Tony bowed theatrically when Rora was introduced

to him. "Edward, my dear, you always *did* have taste."
To Rora he said, "You're lovely. Are you already in the
business or has my friend seduced you into it?"

Her face grew warmer as Eddie said, "A little of
both, Tony. So do your stuff. She has lousy pictures."

Rora thought, But I haven't *any* pictures. However,
she didn't argue. If Eddie was flattering Tony, that was
okay. She'd let him handle things.

Tony led her into a dressing room with wall-to-wall
mirrors and trays filled with makeup. He examined her
face, turning her by the chin and checking every angle.
Then he ran his hands through her hair. "Gorgeous,"
he said to the air.

"Come with me," he instructed, and together they
went into a closet that was larger than Rora's
apartment. It was filled with clothing, three tiers of
garments, and there was a tall ladder along one wall,
the sliding kind that Rora had seen only at libraries.

"Eddie!" he called. "Question-and-answer time."

Eddie joined them in the wardrobe closet.

"Okay. Now, are we going for high fashion"—he
shook his head at his own words after glancing at
Rora's low heels—"or TV or *theatuh*, dahling?" This
last was spoken in his best Tallulah Bankhead style.

Eddie shrugged and Tony answered for him. "Too
short for high fashion and too pretty to waste her bod
on catalogues. I'd say go for commercials—and some
dressier stuff for films and the boards, provided she can
act." To Rora he said, "Dahling, can you? Act, I mean.
And I *don't* mean the mumble-and-scratch garbage. I
mean the real McCoy."

Rora was still recovering from his "show." She'd
never encountered a Tony Rogers before.

"Well, *can* you?" he repeated.

"I think I can, although I'm not exactly Bette Davis
or Geraldine Page."

"Well, my dear, we wouldn't want *two* of either of them, would we?" He turned to Eddie. "My God, an actress who isn't pure ego. Eddie, either she's *very* new or you're a genius at finding diamonds in the rough."

Rora was growing uncomfortable. Repartee and banter were not part of her repertoire yet, and she felt as though she were a fish swimming in a bottomless glass bowl.

"All right, then, we'll go for natural and ingenuous," Tony decided. "Come over here. We'll just pat your nose with a touch of powder so we don't reflect all over the room, but we won't even do lipstick." To Eddie he said, "It's all the eyes and mouth, anyway. No matter what you do to the rest of the face. The eyes have to look 'come hither,' and the mouth should offer to . . ." He didn't finish the sentence but ran his tongue over his lips. "Lip gloss will take care of that. Nice and wet." He winked at Rora. "It's a business, dear. Something tells me you're shocked. Well, don't be. Just smile your winningest, sexiest smile and the camera will do the job. The rest is, as they say, in the eyes—and imagination—of the beholder."

He turned to glance at Eddie, who had seated himself in a director's chair and seemed amused by Tony's lecture.

"So my friend, how are things out West? Tell the young lady. It's no different there, only more out in the open. Here we pretend that talent is a premium. In Hollywood, it's up front. A meat market. That's why *I* love New York." He was setting up lights and moving equipment during his speech, and Rora felt she was in limbo. Eddie was leafing through eight-by-tens, and although the three of them were assembled for Rora's benefit, she perceived herself as the outsider, the one not in the know.

The photo session lasted only an hour. Tony's choice

to "go natural" did not require many changes of wardrobe or complicated poses. With the little fan blowing her hair, it became tangled, but in Tony's words, "that turns the casting guys on. They see all that hair flying over *them*. Let's get them excited, dear. That's what it's about!"

As a result, the clothes consisted of oversized sweaters and tight jeans for fresh-girl-next-door commercials and filmy, gauzy chiffon—almost, but not quite see-through—for perfume or cosmetic ads. For the last set, Tony handed Rora an ecru gown of gossamer transparency and said, "Take off your underthings and let's really do it right."

"Tony," she protested, "I'd rather not."

The photographer turned to Eddie. "You didn't tell me she was a Puritan, my dear. They *never* work!"

Eddie's eyes twinkled. "A Puritan she's not. Just modest, hmm?" He winked at Rora.

"It's just . . . well, *that's* not what I'm selling—"

"Sweetie," interjected Tony kindly, "*that* is exactly what they're *buying*. Now I'm not suggesting you pose nude, and I suggest you turn down any offers for bra and girdle work. If you do underwear, you're dead for anything classy. But this"—he ran his fingers over the ecru gown again—"this is the color of skin without anything underneath. Suggestive, you bet. Lewd? *Never!*"

Rora looked from Tony to Eddie. Her lover nodded. "I'm afraid he's right, Rora. Besides . . . I'd love to see you model that for me."

It was settled. Rora changed into the gown and Tony shot a roll of film with the fan wind blowing the layers of almost-but-not-quite-transparent chiffon to almost-but-not-quite areas of intimate exposure.

When Rora had changed back into her street clothes, Tony kissed her on the cheek and said, "If you ever decide to do any stuff in the buff, remember, you owe me. It'd be such fun!"

Rora blushed and Tony said to Eddie, "You'll have to assure her that I'm safe." To Rora he added, "Eddie's not. But *moi? I* wouldn't touch you, my dear."

They descended the stairs and inhaled the crisp evening air. "What did Tony mean? About his being safe but you not?"

Eddie stroked her cheek. "That he likes men, not women, and I am not so inclined." He bit the tip of her ear. "In fact, I'd like to take your pictures too, but they wouldn't be for circulation. And I don't think I'm that double-jointed."

"Double-jointed?" She didn't understand.

"To do and photograph at the same time," he said in a low, intimate voice. "I'd love you to see the way you look when we're making love."

Rora's heart began to pound as Eddie squeezed her hand.

"But that's personal," he added. "I'm not eager to share you with anyone."

"Don't worry about that," she said as they hailed a taxi and climbed inside.

Chapter Five

The New York location shooting wrapped. Rora had saved a small amount of money after paying off the union and the Academy, but this last night had its share of sadness. She and Eddie went out for drinks with several of the gaffers and the best boy, who, as Eddie explained, was the head electrician's first assistant.

"Then why isn't he called that?" she asked. "Best boy sounds really strange. What would they do if the best boy were a woman? Call her best girl?"

"Slim chance of that happening, Rora. It's a man's job."

She didn't like the ring of that. "You mean it might not be 'safe'? 'A woman's place is in the home,' et cetera?"

He leaned forward and kissed her lightly; they were in a crowded bar and the atmosphere was not given to intimacy.

"No, lover. Your job is to be gorgeous and do the things you do so well, not to worry your beautiful head about best boys or anything else. If you looked like Eleanor Roosevelt, you'd have to do something noble with your life. But you . . . you don't have to do a thing."

"Eddie," she said, "somehow I'm getting the icky feeling that you think a woman is supposed to be window dressing, just an ornament. You didn't strike me that way when I met you."

"Don't get your bowels in an uproar, honey. There's no need to argue, for Christ's sake. Here. Have another beer."

But she didn't want another beer. When Eddie was with his cronies, he assumed a different personality. She had ignored that until now, but he would be leaving for California in a day or two and she couldn't just forget it. She was crazy about him, which made it imperative that they understand each other if their relationship was to have a future.

She reflected while he drank. Perhaps she was feeling edgy because he was leaving. Three wonderful weeks were ending and she couldn't change that. Maybe he was right. Maybe she ought to have another beer, not take any of it seriously, just relax and have a good time. But his attitude had irritated her, and she was tired of tuning out unpleasantries as though they never happened. She had done that in Oakdale. It was one of the reasons she had left and come to New York. To become herself, whoever that person turned out to be.

They made love when he took her home. At first she'd thought she might refuse him—or at least be cool because they hadn't resolved their altercation—but her body responded to him the moment he touched her and she was unable to resist. In bed she was very much the woman he wanted her to be, but aware that she didn't know when she would see him or be held by him again, she found herself voicing the question.

"When will you be back in New York?"

He was lying on his back beside her on the floor. "When I'm on another picture, I guess." He traced her eyebrows with his index finger. "Why the scowl? We'll see each other again. Either I'll be here or . . . who knows? Maybe Tony's photographs will land you work in L.A. You'd like it out there."

"From what Tony says it doesn't sound so terrific."

"He doesn't drive a car. Likes to be chauffeured everywhere. But you'd fit in anywhere."

"Like a chameleon, you mean? Adaptable? Accommodating?"

He sat up, sensing her tone. "Wait a minute. I meant it as a compliment. You fit in because you're not a phony. That's what I meant."

"Oh. I thought I fit because I don't make waves. I just go along, you know, part of the background."

"You? Background? Never, honey. Page one, all the way."

"I see. Eleanor Roosevelt would be on the back page, but not me."

"Rora, you're in a feisty mood and I'm not going to argue. Let's not spoil the past three weeks. C'mon, now. I've all but fallen in love with you."

"All but . . ."

He heaved a sigh. "Okay. I *am* in love with you. Is that what you want to hear?"

"Only if you mean it." Why am I doing this? she asked herself.

"I mean it. I'm crazy about you. You want me to get on my knees? You want to get married and come to Hollywood with me?"

"*What?*" Now she, too, sat up. "Eddie? Are you serious?"

"Sure. Why not?"

There was a constriction in her chest. "I thought you were married," she lied, stalling for time.

"I have been. Twice. But I'm not now. What gave you that idea?"

"Well . . . the first night you stayed over you said

109

you didn't want to hurt me. Isn't that what married men usually tell the girls they seduce?"

He laughed. "Wait a sec. *You* almost seduced me, remember? And when I said that . . . frankly, you seemed so young and . . . inexperienced. I was afraid you might be a virgin."

"But I wasn't."

"No, thank God. I don't need that on my conscience." He turned her face toward his. "Okay, you've had enough time to think up an answer. Yes or no? With me, Mrs. Eddie Calvert. Without me, Miss Aurora O'Brien."

She had to rely on instinct because reason refused to assist her. After a long pause, she said quietly, "Eddie, I . . . I think I love you . . . but I'm not ready . . . it's too soon."

He simply nodded and reached over to the table for his beer. "Too soon for what? I thought we were great together."

"We are. But I want to have a career. I want to do so much—"

"You're not that ambitious or that conniving, Rora. The business could turn you into someone even your mother wouldn't recognize."

"She couldn't recognize me anyway," Rora answered with a trace of bitterness. "And if the business is so rotten, how come it hasn't corrupted you?"

"I'm a man, lover. It's different."

"Goddammit!" she exclaimed. "Why the hell does everybody keep saying that?"

"Because," he said, trying to pull her to him, "that happens to be the way it is."

"Why?"

He reflected on her question. "I guess maybe . . . because it's the women who have the babies."

Tears welled up in Rora's eyes. "If we're careful not

110

to bring unwanted children into the world, I don't see why we can't do anything men can. But nobody wants to give us a chance—including you!"

Eddie swallowed the last of his beer. "Look, Rora, don't get me wrong. When I get a contract to direct a picture, I'll be the first one to say, 'Hey, Rora baby, come out to the Coast and be in a movie.' I'm just saying that it isn't that easy unless you play the game by the rules."

"By whose rules?" She was almost pouting.

"Whoever's running the show. I told you to be aware of that. If you're setting your sights on the stars, you'd better keep those emerald eyes wide open at all times." He leaned over and kissed her; this time she kissed him back. "And if you decide it isn't worth it, give me a call. I'll wait for you."

She smiled through her tears. "You'd never be second choice. I care too much about you."

He brushed her cheek with the side of his hand, drawing his fingers through her dark hair. "Well," he said, "maybe one day that'll be enough."

Tony's photographs were excellent; Rora had copies made and sent them out to every advertising and casting agency listed in the Ross Report. She had nothing to put on a resumé, so on the back of each picture she wrote, under her name and answering service number, the title of the film she had just done. Although she had been a stand-in, the letters *SAG* indicated that she was a bonafide member of the profession. The enigmatic message, Additional Credits Upon Request, was added at Tony's suggestion. "Besides," he'd said, "when they take one look at the face on that glossy, they won't give a damn if you've ever done a thing!"

111

That relieved her, although it did nothing to reassure her. New York was crawling with beautiful girls, actresses and models, and too many were willing, as Eddie had put it, to "play the game." She tried not to concern herself with such thoughts. If she dwelt on them, she wouldn't have a chance.

Classes continued at the Academy, and Miranda helped Rora find a job in the checkroom at the restaurant where she worked as a hostess. The salary was not much higher than what the answering service had paid, but Rora did get free meals and there were tips to be made in the checkroom.

It wasn't part of the training session, but it was widely known throughout the plush establishment that anyone working the checkroom "lifted" tips. Doing so was a matter of survival.

Rora thought the practice justified when she heard what the waiters were earning in tips, tips the IRS never heard about. Captains withheld tables until their palms were sufficiently "greased," and busboys, who did the bulk of the heavy work, were generally stiffed by the waiters. More than once Rora saw a large tip being pocketed by a waiter who told his busboy that the party had left nothing. It was a house rule that the busboys receive ten percent of the waiters' tips, but they were young and inexperienced, usually just learning English and in fear of losing their jobs, so they said nothing.

Rora was told by the manager that all tips were to go into the slot at the center of the checkroom counter. "Do you mean we can't accept tips?" she asked naïvely.

"You're being *fed,* aren't you?" asked Mrs. Smythe.

Jane, Rora's partner in the checkroom, whispered, "I'll clue you in later. We'll make a fortune."

Rora resisted for the first several weeks. Dinner guests handed her quarters and she obediently dropped

112

them into the slot. But gradually, when she realized that guests didn't know the tips were going to the house, she decided the rule was unfair. Particularly when she was handed a dollar bill, or occasionally a five or ten, which she thought to be error on the part of a drunken patron. Nobody in his right mind would tip a checkroom attendant five or ten dollars for parking his hat!

But when one guest said to her, "No, gorgeous, that's no mistake—I want you to have it," she quickly learned that the restaurant was squeezing every extra cent it could from its customers. There were no signs posted that read NO TIPPING PERMITTED or YOUR TIPS DO NOT GO TO EMPLOYEES, so Rora began to see Jane's point. Furthermore, she reasoned, if they don't want us to take the tips, they ought to pay us more than two dollars and twenty-five cents an hour. The food wasn't that good, and steaks were off limits to employees.

Jane had it down to a science. She explained the procedure to Rora. "It's one for the house and one for you. Don't get greedy and don't take paper money—the manager sends 'checkers' in from time to time, just to test us. Just quarters. You'll do fine." She eyed Rora's long, dark hair and slim figure. "Oh, yeah, you'll make out just fine."

She, too, wore the simple little black dress, the polyester-passing-for-silk that the restaurant assigned to all the girls who worked the checkroom. Stylish, sophisticated, and wrinkle-free, it was also pocket-free, to discourage the concealment of clandestine quarters, but Jane's ample bosom jingled merrily with coins.

Rora didn't wear a bra, so the only place she could put her unofficial earnings was inside her shoes, the spindly high steel heels she'd worn on the film. She took very careful steps when she went on her break, and quickly transferred her collection to her purse in her locker as soon as she reached the ladies' room. She told no one, not even Miranda, about the tips. Jane had warned her that the enormous restaurant was "crawling with spies."

These additional earnings enabled Rora to purchase a few pieces of clothing. At Bloomingdale's, she invested in a black cashmere sweater; at I. Miller, a pair of antique leather boots—with walking heels—and a matching leather portfolio for making the rounds. This last was preferable to the standard bumpy-grained leather carried by most actors in the city. At Saks she found a black suede skirt and the perfect jewelry accents: a simple hammered-gold choker and a pair of earrings, for which she immediately had her ears pierced. The necklace wasn't solid gold, but because it so closely matched the color and design of the earrings, which were fourteen karat, only an expert would be able to tell the difference. Rora decided that until she could afford to buy an entire wardrobe—and that would *not* be possible on checkroom quarters alone—simplicity was the key word. And quality. With that in mind, she checked the better designer coats at both Saks and Bloomingdale's, and then bought the very coat she wanted, *sans* label, at Loehmann's in the Bronx.

But when Tony Rogers telephoned to invite her to a Christmas party at his town house, neither the checkroom nor Loehmann's could provide the wardrobe.

"Don't worry," Maria reassured her over cappuccino, "we'll find something for you. Many of my clients forget to pick up their dresses until the last minute. What color you want? It's gotta be something to set off your white skin. For Christmas, the kind of party you're going to, they'll all dress like Christmas trees—

114

you know, red satin, green silk. And jewels. Diamonds down to here"—she indicated her navel and Rora began to laugh—"and their hair piled up three feet high." She got up from the oak table and went to the armoire.

"So we gotta do something dramatic. Like—" Maria almost disappeared behind a flurry of chiffon and velvet and Rora couldn't hear a word she said until she reemerged, several layers of dresses and gowns covering her shoulders.

"Okay," she said. "Try these on."

"But they're all black. I wear black every night at La Grille. It's Christmas, Maria."

"Listen to me, Rora. Try this on." She handed Rora a long, filmy black gown, weightless, and bearing no resemblance, except in color, to Rora's five-times-a-week ensemble.

Rora changed into the dress. "It's lovely, Maria, but I think it's too short, don't you?"

The woman nodded. "Let me see if there's enough silk to let down the hem." She checked the underside and shook her head. "Okay, then, try this one."

It, too, was black, a sheer wool crepe that was starkly simple. It came up to Rora's neck—a bateau neckline, one of her favorites—then plunged to her waist in a deep V at the back. It was fitted without being too tight, and its long sleeves reached Rora's wrists. It looked as though Monsieur Givenchy had designed it specially for her.

"Maria! Oh, I love it! But you're sure its owner won't need it before the party?"

"No. She left for Paris only two days ago and will not return until New Year's Eve."

Rora laughed. "Good. Then I don't run the risk of meeting her at Tony's party. I'd die if that happened."

115

Maria surveyed her model. "No, I think you would not. You would smile and say that you had seen it in a magazine or at a fashion show and you liked it so much that you had a copy made for yourself. That flattery would make her your friend."

As Rora envisioned the dress set off by her new gold jewelry, Maria brought forth a black beaded handbag and a black velvet cape. All Rora would have to do was buy a pair of evening shoes, and for that, La Grille's quarters would be sufficient.

"Remember to wear your hair loose," said Maria as Rora left with her booty. "They will all overdo. You must wear yours around your shoulders, and use very little makeup. That is how Tony photographed you, and that is why he has invited you to his party. You will be an asset."

"Oh, yes. Window dressing. I'd almost forgotten my role." But, she reflected, being window dressing at a chic East Side brownstone in a Paris original had its compensations. . . .

Tony had invited Rora to bring along a friend "as long as she's gorgeous. Unless," he had added with a laugh, "you have something for me!"

She ended up asking Miranda to go. Her response came as no surprise. "Oh, Rora! How divine of you to think of me! You are truly a wonderful friend!"

Actually Rora had planned to invite Jane. Although her partner in checkroom crime might not fit Tony's conception of "gorgeous," she could be attractive, and since her "savings" no doubt exceeded Rora's, she could afford to dress for the occasion. Besides, Rora wanted to know her reclusive partner better, if only to have a friend in whom to confide. Maria was too many years her senior, and Miranda was too neurotic.

However, upon punching her time card, Rora noticed that Jane was late. She was not at her post, nor was she in the employees' lounge. La Grille opened for dinner at five o'clock each evening; Rora usually arrived around a quarter to five, but Jane was always there ahead of her. At five-twenty, she knocked on Mrs. Smythe's office door.

"Yes, Aurora?" said the manager. "Something wrong?"

"I was wondering . . . about Jane. She's late. Has she called in or changed her night off?"

Mrs. Smythe folded her hands in front of her. "Come in for a moment. This seems as good a time as any to remind you."

Rora took the stiff-backed chair closest to the door.

"Well," said the woman with an imperious flaring of her nostrils, "our Jane has been fired. She's a thief. We're doing her a favor by not reporting the matter to the authorities."

"She's *what?*" exclaimed Rora, the word still registering.

"A *thief,* a common criminal! We've had our eyes on her for some time but we just couldn't catch her in the act." She paused, staring meaningfully at Rora. "Until last night. She didn't know that our checkers know how to locate missing coins, as well as paper currency."

"Your checkers?" Rora had never dreamed that the woman would acknowledge that the staff was under surveillance.

Mrs. Smythe continued. "Your friend Jane was with us for two years. So she knew enough to take only coins. But she didn't know that quarters could be marked. In red. Like this!"

She produced a piece of evidence from her desk

117

drawer. On the serrated edge there was a small streak of red; shiny, possibly nail enamel.

Rora examined it and handed it back to the manager. "I don't think I understand. If she was taking them, how can you detect it unless you follow her everywhere she spends money?"

Mrs. Smythe grinned her Cheshire cat smile. "My dear, if the marked coins are missing from the strongbox underneath the slot, then we know they've been taken. Now do you see?"

Rora's adrenaline was rising. "But how do you know it was Jane? It might have been the spy"—there, she'd said it—"who went through the box."

"That, my dear, is Mr. Fitzhugh, and since he is the owner of La Grille, there seems little point in his doing that, wouldn't you say? Besides, Aurora, we caught her in the act, fired her on the spot. We must set an example, after all."

Her final sentence took Rora aback. "You should feel relieved. We weren't certain whether it was Jane . . . or you."

Rora's hands began to shake, imperceptibly, but she placed them flat against her hips. "Why should I be relieved when *I* know what I am or am not doing?" she asked, careful to phrase her words so as not to lie outright.

"Because I think you've been in the city long enough to understand survival, Rora. Better Jane than you, yes?" The question was uttered with a tone of dismissal.

Rora left Mrs. Smythe's office without voicing an answer.

"I do feel guilty about it," she confided to Miranda as they walked from La Grille to Nick's Bar, their nightly rendezvous after work. "I ought to call her, but I didn't even think to get her last name, and when I punched out, her card was already gone. If I ask in the office, they'll be suspicious."

"Don't feel guilty," said her friend. "I mean, it isn't a life-and-death matter. It's only a checkroom job."

Rora was surprised that Miranda, who always overreacted, seemed distracted, disinterested. Perhaps it wasn't dramatic enough; Jane hadn't been caught stealing diamonds, only quarters.

On most nights Rora ordered an Irish coffee, but tonight she opted for a Bloody Mary. Miranda always ordered a vodka martini. She said that drink had "sentimental attachment and significance."

Nick's was crowded for one-thirty in the morning, but they found a quiet booth at the back. Nick knew them well enough by now to say "The usual?" when they came in.

Rora had never tried his Bloody Marys, and the vodka made its impact felt immediately.

Miranda sipped her first martini without talking. That too was a departure from her normal behavior, talky and keyed up from eight hours of smiling at guests.

"You said not to worry about Jane," said Rora.

"Oh, I wasn't thinking about her."

"Raoul, then?"

Miranda's eyes grew wide. "Oh God, Rora, that was over ages ago! He and Jeffrey left for Greece . . . together."

"Then what is it? You seem preoccupied tonight."

"I saw Farley on my way to the restaurant this afternoon."

Miranda loved to use the first names of stage and film stars she'd never met. Rora exclaimed,

119

"Farley Granger?"

Miranda shook her head, tears forming in her eyes. "No, no, no. *My* Farley." She drew in her breath. "Oh God, Rora, I'll kill myself if he marries her, I swear! I'll just die!"

Rora was tired and the drink was strong. But she was alert enough to ask the one or two lead-in questions that she knew her friend wanted as cues.

Apparently, Farley was the first candidate Miranda had selected as a prospective father for her child. She'd seen him in a B movie when she was in her teens, and had followed his career all the way from the Bronx to Broadway. He had been divorced by his wife when she'd caught him in bed with his leading lady—it had been in all the papers, Miranda assured Rora—and the teenage fan had then determined to be his next love.

She had decided to become an actress in the hope of playing opposite him, and had moved into his neighborhood after finding him listed in the phone book. Feverishly she reached the climax of her tale, drawing Rora into it by her excitement. "He used to drink here all the time! At Nick's! And here *we* are!"

Rora considered this. "You mean that's why we come here every night?"

Miranda was nodding "yes" and almost jumping up from her seat. "Oh, and don't you see, Rora? It's fate! He hasn't come here once that we've been here, but I saw him on the street! Out of the blue! Doesn't that mean something?"

"It might mean that he lives in the neighborhood."

"But he *doesn't,* that's just it!"

Rora finished the last of her drink and made a child's slurping noise through the straw. "Miranda, did you ever read *The Best of Everything?* There's a character in the book that's obsessed, too. Please don't get carried away."

And then, as though a moment of ecstasy had passed and a world of normalcy had returned, Miranda said quite matter-of-factly, "I saw the movie. Don't worry. *I* wouldn't do anything foolish—unless he remarries and it isn't me."

"Have you ever met him?" asked Rora.

"Met him! Rora, he was my first *lover!* Don't you understand? I met him here—at Nick's!"

"How long ago?" Rora expected her friend to say a year or less. A rational reason for not having recovered from the affair as yet.

"When I was eighteen. I'm older than you think, you know. I look young and that's good for my career, but I'm actually twenty-four." She glanced furtively around the bar. "But don't tell anyone. My agent says it could stand in my way."

Rora signaled to Nick for another Bloody Mary. Although she wasn't in the habit of having more than one drink after work, she felt this would be a long night.

"Miranda, forgive my asking, but do you mean to say your affair was six years ago?"

The blond actress nodded.

"How long did it last?"

Miranda's eyes were glazed again. "Just that night." She raised her glass in a toast and cried, "To love!"

Rora leaned closer. "Miranda—"

"Oh, Rora," she interrupted. "Try to imagine what it was like! A night of bliss and then, afterward, he never said another word. I saw him here the next night and he didn't even know who I was!"

"Was he drunk? I mean, you met him in here, so maybe—"

"That didn't matter. I was drunk, too, but *I* didn't

121

forget! I thought I would die—"

"What did you do?"

She was toying with the matches and now began to light them and blow them out, one after another. The bar was half-empty and no one seemed to notice except for Rora.

"I went home with one of his friends," Miranda said. "I thought it would make him jealous."

"Did it?" Artie's words about love and sex flashed through her mind; they seemed to be part of a previous lifetime.

"He didn't notice! Like today! He saw me, Rora, but he *didn't* see me! I've got to do something to make him remember!"

Nick came by and stopped at their table. "Another round, girls? It'll be last call before long."

Rora surprised herself. "Yes," she said. "Another for each of us." Then she turned back to Miranda, who didn't speak until Nick was out of earshot.

"He's been dating his ex-wife. I read it in the paper. If they remarry, I'll take pills again—only this time I'll take enough." And to emphasize the point, she drained the contents of her glass. "But that would wreck my plans," she added. "About the baby."

"The baby?" Rora repeated.

"You remember. I'm going to have a baby."

"I thought you hadn't found a father yet."

"But I want Farley to be the father. Anyone else is only second choice."

Rora was beginning to feel dizzy; she didn't know whether it was Miranda's story or the third Bloody Mary, but whichever, it was time for her to be getting home.

She took out her wallet and Miranda said, "Please, let me pay."

Rora responded with a firm no. "This is on me," she

said. "And . . . Jane."

Miranda didn't even remember Jane by the time they rose from the booth. "Who knows," she confided to Rora as they climbed into a taxi, "maybe at that party we're going to I can find a suitable father!"

The taxi's brakes obliterated Rora's response.

Chapter Six

Tony Rogers' party was a cocktail-and-canapés extravaganza. The host stood at the entrance to his sunken living room flanked on one side by a beautiful young man, blond and bronzed from either lamp or sun—it was difficult to distinguish which—and a woman in her forties with a close-fitting hat that revealed a single blond curl, called a guiche. All three—Tony, the striking male model, and the older woman—were wearing black tuxedos with satin lapels. The woman sported a diamond brooch and held a black and gold cigarette holder in which a Gauloise had gone out.

Rora and Miranda smiled their best Academy-actress smiles as Tony bent to kiss each of their hands.

"Ah, welcome, my lovelies. I'm so glad you could join us!" he said. "I would like you to meet my dearest friends, Tadzio Breslau and Countess Maritza." The countess nodded while Tadzio clicked his heels, and Rora stifled a girlish urge to giggle. She wondered if Fellini had directed the production.

Invisible hands removed Rora's velvet cape and Miranda's heavy wrap; then both girls were invited to enter the salon. It was early, but already guests were sardine-packed at the bar, at the center of which was an enormous swan carved of ice. Inside its wings were pink roses, somehow frozen in time; the middle was a scooped-out punch bowl filled with champagne—also pink. Uniformed bartenders and waiters, dressed much like the three hosts—wove their way through the throng, trays held high above their heads.

Rora and Miranda accepted flutes of champagne and nibbled at the hors d'oeuvres, tasting the shrimp, salmon, and caviar. A stage director Rora recognized from a magazine interview appeared with his male lover; his wife was nowhere in sight. A soprano, en route to drunkenness, leaned against the gray piano and warbled unintelligibly and off pitch to the accompaniment of two guests, neither of whom could play the instrument.

"I wonder who pops out of the cake at midnight," Rora mused aloud to Miranda.

"Oh," her friend replied in all seriousness, "that won't happen tonight—that's a New Year's Eve event."

Rora noticed that Miranda's eyes continued to scout the large room, and she realized that the actress was no doubt seeking her Farley. She secretly prayed he would not show up, for her friend's sake.

Before long many people were crammed around the food and drink. Miranda had gone to "powder her nose," and Rora stood at the side of the room feeling much like an abandoned child surveying a circus merry-go-round. She invented wicked little titles for the face-lifted matrons and the opera queens—Billy's descriptive term for flagrant homosexuals. Rora noted that among the assemblage of jeweled, sequined models and actresses there were a number of famous or near-famous Broadway and film faces. She was glad she had taken Maria's advice; she was a striking contrast to their glitter. A ballerina from the Balan-

126

chine company waltzed by—not dancing, doing a waltz walk—draped from head to foot in gray ostrich feathers. A film star whose name escaped Rora tossed her mane of golden curls at the dancer. She wore a scant costume. Her midriff was bared and the sheer fabric that did not conceal her body was bikinied in jet and bugle beads. Rora marveled at the needlework, the illusion that the beads were attached to skin instead of fabric.

Several men wore more makeup than the women present, but Rora turned as an elderly woman with violet hair teetered by. She was exquisitely gowned in a matching violet which clashed with Tony's color scheme. As she maintained her precarious balance on stiletto-heeled violet satin pumps, she amused herself by pinching men's bottoms. As each man registered surprise, this spritely predator disappeared into the crowd. As more guests arrived, the noise level became deafening and conversation was rendered impossible. Guests gestured, grimaced, pantomimed, their gyrations of face and body grotesque. Although somewhat fascinated by the scene, Rora wondered if she could locate Miranda and then slip away without being noticed. She laughed aloud at the thought: how could anyone miss her? Nobody knew she was there!

But then she wasn't alone. A voice asked, "Are you amused by the charade?"

She turned to face Tadzio Breslau, and her face grew as pink as Tony's walls.

"It's all right," he assured her. "If you knew the truth you would find Tony laughing as well. That's why he has this annual 'do.'"

"It's quite a . . . performance, isn't it?" Aurora said uneasily.

"That's as appropriate a description as I've heard," he said. "How did he find you? You don't strike me as one of his models."

Rora stiffened. "He . . . he shot my portfolio." She wasn't so vain as to think she was as stunning as the jet setters at Tony's party, but she had thought she looked attractive. Tadzio's comment had come as a disappointment.

"I didn't say it as an insult. You have a . . . freshness—if that doesn't add to my gaucherie—that his girls lack. You don't strike me as jaded. Is that word more to your liking?"

"Are you making fun of me? I really don't understand what you mean." Where is Miranda? Rora wondered. She wished her friend would return so that the two of them could escape.

"Not at all. Look around you—Tony said your name is Aurora, yes? You're surrounded by 'the beautiful people' and they are desperately trying to give the impression they're having a good time."

"Aren't they your friends?" she asked.

"My dear, in these circles one doesn't really have 'friends.' One has acquaintances. One acquires them. Collects them."

"To use your word, that seems rather *jaded,* doesn't it?"

"It does, I agree. And I admit that I am jaded. That's why I wanted to chat with you. New blood, so to speak."

"Another 'acquisition'?" she asked more coolly than she had intended.

"Let's be friends. You strike me as . . . well, let's say—"

"Fresher," she interrupted.

"Sorry. I repeat, I meant it as a compliment."

"Why?"

"Why what?" he asked, taking two glasses of champagne from the tray of a passing waiter and handing one to Rora.

"Why is it a compliment not to be one of Tony's models? Isn't he a well-known photographer?"

"Oh, yes," said Tadzio, but he said it with an inflection Rora could only detect; she could not decipher it. "He's very well known. But more in some circles than in others." He took a sip of champagne. "But tell me. If he did your photos, you must be a model or an actress. With those eyes, I hope it's the latter." His own blue eyes flashed as he added, "And that, dear Aurora, is a compliment." He smiled, and his handsome face warmed, causing the corners of Rora's mouth to turn up, too.

"I'm sorry. I haven't had much experience with drawing-room comedy scripts. I'll learn, but I guess my amateur status is less invisible than I'd hoped."

"Ah, but you have humor. You'll survive. A woman with humor is rare. Beauty and intelligence and humor . . . now that's an unbeatable combination. Are you intelligent?" He addressed the question to her eyes, and they flashed as Rora began to enjoy the verbal fencing match.

"I was under the impression that an intelligent person—male or female—knows when to remain silent."

"Fifth amendment?" he teased.

"Something like that," she replied. They both laughed as Miranda joined them.

"Oh, I've had the most marvelous conversation with Donny Everett! He wants me to read for his play!"

Rora turned to her friend. "I'm afraid I don't know who—"

"He's *only* directing the revival of *Miss Julie* on Broadway this spring, Rora. And he wants me to audition for the understudy! Can you believe it?"

Rora said simply, "Yes, I can, and I think it's

wonderful." Then to Tadzio, she explained, "Miranda is a really great actress."

"And she's very fortunate to have you in her corner," Tadzio answered. Lifting his glass, he made a toast. "To friendship. A rare commodity in today's world."

The girls clinked their glasses with his as Rora added, "And to Miranda's becoming the understudy."

Tadzio smiled enigmatically. "Oh, yes. To that, too."

Tony insisted on introducing Rora to several of his guests then—he referred to it as "meaningful mingling" —and Rora's jaw began to ache from smiling. She met stage and film directors and producers, several agents, and others whose names and occupations she forgot almost as quickly as she heard them. It seemed that nobody present had a mere name; some guests also had titles and the others had labels. Labels followed names; Arthur, the producer; Ralph, the designer; Karen, the agent. Titles preceded them: Princess Serena, Baron von Kroft, and as Tony had said, *"of course,* Countess Maritza."

Countess Maritza seemed the most interesting of all the nobility. She did not dismiss her title when anyone used it, but she did not take its pronouncement seriously. She wore her background graciously, and while she did possess a regal carriage, plebians had no need to feel uncomfortable in her presence.

She and Rora took to one another immediately, although Rora couldn't understand why. She found the countess fascinating—her clothes, her manner, her glamour, her nobility—she was surprised that the countess even spoke to her, however.

She was further surprised when Tadzio returned to her side with a suggestion. "Look, it's late and canapés won't hold us until dawn. The countess and I are going to the Brasserie for omelets. Will you and your friend join us?"

Rora did a quick mental rundown of the cash in her purse before she realized that she and Miranda were being invited to go.

"If Miranda says yes, I'd love to." Her eyes sought her friend.

"And if she's managed to disappear with Donny or Denny or whoever he is, will you still come with us?"

She considered the offer. It seemed that Tadzio had anticipated Miranda's behavior. The crowd had thinned out, yet her friend was nowhere in sight.

"Just let me make sure. If Miranda's gone, well . . . yes, I'd love to join you."

Miranda had left with the director; Tony had seen them duck out only half an hour before. "She's in excellent hands," he assured Rora with a wink. "And she'll probably land the job."

Eddie's words flashed through Rora's mind. She wondered if he was wrong, if New York and California were more alike than people thought, if the whole business was nothing but a meat market. And if it was, what was she doing in it?

Brushing this disturbing question from her mind, Rora wrapped the borrowed black velvet cape around her shoulders and allowed Tadzio and Countess Maritza to escort her to the waiting car.

It was a small limousine by Hollywood standards, but it was the first luxury conveyance Rora had seen from within; she sank into the velvet seat, drinking in the plush carpeting and mahogany paneling, the small television set and the bar with *T. B.* engraved on its tray and glassware. Summoning whatever acting technique she had thus far acquired at the Academy, she smiled politely as though accustomed to chauffeur-driven Rolls Royces. When Tadzio inquired, "Are you comfortable, Aurora?" she replied, "Oh yes, thank you. Perfectly comfortable." It wasn't a lie, and the words were pronounced with the Standard Stage diction that would have made the Academy's "director" Hannah proud.

The Brasserie was as crowded as Tony's town house, and its clientele was dressed much like his guests. Aurora recognized film and television stars. Liza Minnelli waved, and although her eyes briefly met Aurora's, she knew the wave and smile were for someone else. While the countess led the way to her regular table—"I always sit there to observe the show," she said—names were dropped all around them. It was "Liz said this" or "Roddy told me" or "Well, I said to Barbra." Aurora heard one shrill voice cry, "Oh, but Farley is such a dear, I'd forgive him anything." She wondered if the woman was referring to Granger or to Miranda's Farley.

The clatter of dishes and the tinkling of glasses served as a backdrop, as did the food and drink. The crowd wasn't there to eat, but to see and, more importantly, to be seen. Tony's party, as outrageous as it had seemed only a short time ago, was subdued, understated, and dull by comparison.

The countess and Tadzio were treated like visiting royalty. Several people referred to Tadzio as Prince.

"How did you come to be called that?" asked Aurora as champagne was poured for her. It was her first at the Brasserie this morning, but actually the fifth or sixth glass she'd had.

The countess explained over the din. "But, my dear, Tadzio *is* a prince, didn't he tell you?"

Aurora's eyes widened, but she feigned only casual interest. "Really? I thought perhaps he was a prince of a person."

Tadzio's eyes flickered as a grin curved the corners of his mouth upward. "I think titles are a bore," he said, winking. "You see, Maritza," he said to the countess, "Aurora is totally unimpressed. That's why I invited her along."

Aurora leaned forward and said quietly for him alone, "I'm acting. Frankly, I've never met a prince before."

"And he's simply Prince Charming!" announced an effete male model who had bent to hear her words.

Aurora stifled a blush as Tadzio introduced her. "This is Jimmy. Tony photographs him from time to time. Pay no attention to him."

"And who is the pretty thing?" asked Jimmy in his high-pitched tenor.

"Aurora." The countess answered for her. "But I think we shall christen her Rory, yes?"

Aurora shrugged her shoulders.

"Everybody goes by the countess' nicknames," said Jimmy. "Rory is an improvement on some she's invented, believe me!" He swept down and kissed Aurora's hand, after which he planted a kiss on Tadzio's cheek and floated off into the crowd.

They ate and drank and laughed and sang until the sun began to rise. "What time do they close?" asked "Rory," suddenly weary and more than slightly dizzy from all the champagne.

"Never!" sang Tadzio. He nodded and a waiter appeared. "I think we'll be going now, George," he said. Taking a wad of bills from his pocket, he peeled off quite a few. Aurora was too bleary-eyed to notice their denominations, but her thoughts flashed to the checkroom at La Grille; the waiter had been handed at least several weeks' worth of Aurora's combined wages and "gratuities." That awareness only made reality

133

more blurred for her.

They blew kisses—Aurora, too—to the few remaining patrons whose voices had dropped several octaves and whose faces had ceased to glow in the hours between three and sunrise.

Sunrise, she mused as they came out onto the street. That's my name in Italian. Tadzio had told her earlier. "We'll take you to Rome one day," he'd murmured over one of the toasts. It was drink talk, Aurora reflected, but it did bring a smile to her lips.

Chapter Seven

The sun was bright for a cold December morning.
Aurora shielded her eyes, but that did nothing to
steady her walk. The trio swayed against one another
until they reached the corner of Park Avenue.

"Shall I get you a taxi?" asked Tadzio. "I told Max to
go home when he dropped us off."

Countess Maritza, who seemed in worse shape than
the prince or Aurora, mumbled, "She should always
ride in a Rolls. Never in a taxi." Tadzio caught her arm
before she fell against a wire trash receptacle.

"Well, I . . ." Aurora hesitated, not knowing if the
few dollars in her borrowed evening purse would be
sufficient to take her to Cornelia Street.

"Darling," said the countess, "where do you live? Are
you in the neighborhood?"

"No," she answered. "In the Village."

"Oh, God!" She turned to Tadzio. "The poor dear
simply can't go to the Village dressed like that. It's
broad daylight!" She took a pair of dark glasses from
the pocket of her Russian sable coat as if to emphasize
the point. "We'll take her home with us!"

Tadzio's face brightened at the prospect.

"Oh no," protested Aurora. "I can't impose. You've

both already—"

"Shh! Not so much noise or I'll be sick," cautioned the countess. "Come now, Rory. We're only a few blocks' walk and you'll feel wonderful after a few hours' sleep." To Tadzio she added, "And I may die without it."

She slipped her arm through Aurora's, and Tadzio smiled as he flanked her on the other side. Then the three walked slowly, Aurora almost staggering, until they reached Fifty-seventh Street.

"Ah, home!" said the countess with a relieved sigh.

Aurora looked up at "home." Did Tadzio or the countess actually live at the Ritz? But they steered her halfway down the block to another entrance that seemed to be separated from the famed hotel.

They passed the doorman, who tipped his hat and appeared not the least surprised by their dress although it was six-thirty in the morning. Tadzio pulled gently on Aurora's arm and said, "This way, madame."

He didn't stop at the bank of elevators but headed toward a single one at the corner of the rear lobby. "Going up?" he asked as the ornate brass doors opened.

The three stepped inside and fell almost simultaneously onto the Wedgwood blue, velvet-covered bench. The interior of the cage was paneled with antique mirrors set off by subdued lighting, for which Aurora was deeply grateful. A pounding had already announced the arrival of a headache. When the elevator doors opened onto the foyer of the vast penthouse, Aurora was too exhausted to be impressed. She was aware of having her velvet cape and black shoes removed, and somehow she walked across the plush Wedgwood blue carpeting—even with a hangover, she appreciated the way her toes sank into it—and into an enormous bedroom.

Tadzio bowed. "Yours. We'll see about aspirin and

136

coffee later."

"But where—" Aurora cut off her own question. In such an elegant penthouse, obviously there were a dozen bedrooms. Too much champagne had not totally numbed her mind. If she asked about Tadzio's sleeping arrangements she might invite problems for it seemed that the countess and Tadzio were a recognized twosome, and although Maritza was a good fifteen years older than he, Aurora was less shocked than she might have been at an earlier time—and an earlier hour. Rules were different when the scenario was *La Dolce Vita*. She fell across the bed, visions of Marcello Mastroianni floating through her head. She hadn't thought about him since Oakdale, a world ago. But then, she had never before stayed out all night, and had never, ever drunk so much champagne.

Nor had Aurora ever felt so miserable before. She awoke around two that afternoon, her hair a disheveled mess, her makeup all but gone. Only traces of lipstick reminded her that she had looked attractive the night before. She wondered when she had removed her dress, then wondered if someone else had taken it off for her. Panicked by that thought, her eyes fell upon the dress, neatly arranged on a satin hanger hooked over the door of the armoire. On second thought, she was grateful. To hell with modesty; if she had slept in the borrowed Givenchy, Maria would have killed her!

She was wearing a striped, man-tailored silk nightshirt, and she definitely did not remember having seen it before. But her present preoccupation did not revolve around whether she had been compromised; it was of a far more practical nature. She was thinking of immediate necessities: aspirins and black coffee.

She rummaged through the armoire, which was

137

ornamented with intricate inlay, until she found a man's silk dressing gown. When she wrapped it around her, the length and fit were almost perfect. Barefoot, she tiptoed into the living room, which she had failed to notice upon arrival that morning. It had a sunken pool at one end, and two walls were ceiling-to-floor windows that overlooked the city. A quiet Manhattan from twenty stories up, cars and people reduced to miniature size as Aurora peered down at the afternoon bustle on Park Avenue.

"Feeling better?" Tadzio asked from behind her.

"My head is still swimming, I'm afraid."

"Here," he said, offering her two tablets, "for whatever ails you." When she hesitated, he added, "They're only Bayer. I'm not slipping you a Mickey Finn or LSD or whatever." His eyes twinkled as they had the night before. "You really model that robe quite well."

She felt her cheeks warming. "Tadzio, I . . . I'm a bit embarrassed to ask . . ."

"But you'd like to know who undressed you because you passed out cold. Yes?"

She was unable to control the blush, which now went beet red.

"I did," he admitted, bowing slightly. "It was safer that way."

Before she could speak, he added, "By the way, you're really lovely to behold. Don't let that embarrass you, I beg you. I would do nothing to harm you."

He wasn't the first person to say those words, and she had only met him the night before. Were all of Tony Rogers' friends so liberal and immodest, or was this just what was to be "expected" in show business? And was Tadzio part of that business? Had it purchased this sumptuous palace, or did a princely kingdom accompany Tadzio's title?

The snap of his fingers brought her back to the present.

"I'm sorry, my mind was wandering," she said.

"No apology necessary." He poured a glass of water from the pitcher on a tray on the mahogany desk. "Swallow the aspirins. If you still don't trust me, read the trademark. It's on the tablets."

She was looking at him seriously, and he began to laugh.

"You *are* different," he said. "Tony was right."

Aurora swallowed the pills and then asked, "What did Tony tell you about me? He hardly knows me at all."

Tadzio reached out to take her hand and led her to the blue-and-ivory satin loveseat. "Don't be afraid of me," he said reassuringly. He brushed aside the lock of her hair that had fallen across her brow. "You're lovely. So lovely."

This time she managed to suppress the blush as she said, "Thank you. I—"

"You must accustom yourself to compliments, Rory." Then he smiled. "Do you mind the name? I prefer Aurora, but Maritza does usually impose her taste."

She was warming to him. His smile was too engaging to resist, and his face was one of the most handsome she had ever seen. "I don't mind Rory," she said. "It's more relaxed, I suppose, than Aurora."

"Okay, then Rory it shall be. The countess will be pleased."

Aurora shifted her legs, uncomfortable with his closeness, for his mistress might enter the room and misunderstand.

"What shall we do this evening?" he asked.

"This evening?"

"Yes. You didn't think you could disappear at

139

midnight—or noon—like Cinderella, did you?"

She laughed. "Ah, then I'm being held captive?"

His hand touched hers. "How I'd like that! Would it be against your will?"

"Tadzio—"

"Rory, my dear, sweet, and, I fear, naïve Rory. You have, as I have said, nothing to fear from me. And you must take none of us too literally. We exist to enjoy—and to provide entertainment for the masses."

"You're in theater, then? Or films?"

"Not for commercial release," he said with a grin.

Her eyes widened and this time she made no attempt to hide her reaction. If he and the countess were involved in pornography—if such films had paid for this luxurious penthouse—Aurora, Rory, Miss O'Brien wanted no part of it!

She rose. "Tadzio, just what is it that you and the countess do? And has it anything to do with Tony Rogers?"

He stood and placed his tanned hands on her shoulders. "Rory, you must understand several things because I don't want our friendship to begin on the wrong footing, as they say. I don't *do* anything for this"—he indicated the opulence around them—"I am, with no apology, independently wealthy. I go where I wish and do as I please. And," he added, flicking the collar of her nightshirt—his nightshirt—a lightness in his voice, "I do not take advantage of lovely young ladies who happen to pass out in my bed."

"In your bed—"

"Correction. *On* my bed. The countess passed out on hers and you passed out on mine."

She lowered her eyelashes. "Where did you sleep?"

"In the den. I have other bedrooms, but I prefer the den. Now, is there anything else you'd like to know?"

"Yes. If it isn't too presumptuous, is the countess . . .

is she . . ."

"My lover?" He burst into spontaneous laughter. "Oh, Rory, I *do* think you're marvelous!" He stepped forward and spoke softly. "She is not my lover. She lives with me when she is in New York, just as she lives with Ugo Balestrino when she visits Rome and Harper Styles when she travels to Hollywood."

"And her home?"

"I have no home." The sultry voice came from the doorway. "I am at the mercy of my friends." The countess crossed to the bar and rummaged through several bottles. Into a tumbler she poured three different liquids, stirred them with a silver swivel stick, and then downed the contents of the glass in one long gulp. "The only way to treat a hangover, my dear," she said to Aurora, and she added, "May you never find yourself at the mercy of friends—except, of course, for Tadzio here. He's special." She came from behind the bar and greeted him with a peck on the cheek. Surveying Aurora, she said, "Hmm, some women can wear anything. Even that suits you."

Aurora laughed while Tadzio said, "It should. It's from Sulka—and you've forgotten, but *you* bought it for me."

She shook her head. "My, one can suffer lapses of taste, can't one?" She seated herself on a striped satin chair. "Well, where are we off to this evening?"

"We were discussing that when you came in, Maritza," said Tadzio.

"Really? Somehow I thought you were discussing something else. But no matter," she said, lighting a Gauloise. "The opera? The ballet? What's on?"

"Well," said Aurora quickly, "I have to . . . to work." She said the word apologetically.

"You have to *what?*" asked the countess.

"*Work,*" said Tadzio. "Some people do, you know."

141

He turned to Aurora. "Rory darling, are you in a play? Tell us and I'll get tickets."

"No. I . . . uh . . ." Well, she thought, here goes the fairytale. As soon as I tell them, it's good-bye, Rory. She took a deep breath and said, "I work in a restaurant. In the checkroom."

The countess squinted, but Aurora couldn't tell whether it was from the afternoon sun, the hideous concoction she'd just consumed, or the answer to their question. Suddenly the time dawned on her. "My God, I'm late! I'll be fired!" But what would she wear to La Grille? The overdue Givenchy? Tadzio Breslau's dressing gown? Somehow she doubted that Mrs. Smythe would be impressed by either outfit.

The countess stubbed out her cigarette after taking a puff. "Rory darling, we have all worked at one time or another." With a quick glance at Tadzio, she added, "Well, most of us. If you simply must go to your job, *eh bien*. But we can meet you afterward. Yes! Tadzio, we'll pick her up at the restaurant."

Aurora had never heard the word *job* pronounced in quite that manner before. She looked down at Tadzio's dressing gown. He anticipated her dilemma. "What are you going to wear to this job of yours?"

"I . . ."

"What size dress do you wear?" asked the countess, giving Aurora a once-over while she tried to maintain her balance.

"Usually an eight unless—"

"Well, the size is close to mine, but I'm afraid my dresses would be up to your navel. You *are* tall, aren't you?"

The clock over the marble mantelpiece read four-twenty. Discussing height and fashion would not get Aurora to La Grille by five o'clock. This had been an exciting interlude, but it was time to return to the real world where she worked in a checkroom and lived in a pint-sized studio with a bathroom down the hall.

But suddenly Tadzio said, "Maritza, do you have a belt? Something in a neutral leather or suede?"

"I'll look. But why?"

Aurora picked up on the idea. "Are you sure you don't mind?"

"Why should I? You'll do more for it than I ever did."

The countess disappeared and then returned, carrying a taupe kidskin tie-belt, which she handed to Tadzio. "I still don't understand what—"

Tadzio took the belt and handed it to Aurora, who removed the paisley silk dressing gown and tied the belt around Tadzio's nightshirt, transforming it into a stunning silk minidress. The fit and length were perfect, as if tailored to Aurora's proportions.

The countess nodded in approval. "Stunning, Rory. Just stunning! It couldn't be better, could it?"

Aurora smiled and thought to herself, If only it had pockets.

The evening at La Grille dragged by. Aurora had no one to confide in; Miranda had taken the night off. At times the party at Tony's and the night she'd spent at Tadzio's penthouse seemed to have been a dream, but on her two coffee breaks, when she deposited quarters into the makeup case in her locker, Tadzio's "glass slipper" nightshirt-minidress hung from its hook as a reminder—verification—that she had not lived the previous twenty-four hours only in her imagination. The remnant of her hangover headache underlined that fact.

However, the most vivid confirmation appeared in the form of her two new companions who entered La Grille at one-thirty A.M. completely swathed in furs.

The countess sported knee-length chinchilla; Tadzio, a three-quarter jacket of black-dyed mink. His matinee-idol face and Maritza's meticulous makeup and coiffure caused every head in the restaurant to turn. La Grille, while a moderately expensive eating establishment, was not in Tadzio's or the countess' circuit. Mink and chinchilla were occasionally worn by guests, but never with such flair.

When the maître d' summoned Aurora to his desk, Mrs. Smythe's eyes bulged with curiosity and envy. Smiling to herself, Aurora mused that the manager would think twice before suspecting *her* of stealing mere quarters; Tadzio and the countess obviously did not consort with petty thieves!

The restaurant had served its last customer of the evening and Aurora had returned the last hat to its owner when Tadzio entered the checkroom. "Come, Rory," he said, "that Scotch could ruin my liver. I asked for Chivas, but the bartender obviously thinks no one can taste the difference." He grimaced and she laughed.

"How did the countess like the wine list?" Aurora was no authority on wine, but she'd heard guests complain about the limited and prosaic selections at La Grille.

The countess joined them then. "My dear, it's easy to see how you maintain a size eight figure. You are on your feet so many hours."

The three of them left as soon as Aurora had changed, and they found Max outside with the Rolls. He stepped out and opened the rear door for Aurora and her hosts.

"Where to?" asked Tadzio. "The Brasserie all right with you?"

Aurora smiled. "It's fine. But tonight I'm sleeping in my own bed."

Tadzio and the countess laughed merrily as Max

headed across town to Park Avenue. Aurora saw that someone had thoughtfully laid her borrowed Givenchy over the passenger seat beside the driver. She would return the dress to Maria in the morning, and the striped silk nightshirt to Tadzio as soon as she could climb back into her own blue jeans and sweater. And my loafers, she added to herself, rubbing her ankles. She'd been wearing her "hooker shoes" for two days in a row. A jet setters' legs must get terribly tired, she thought as the Rolls sped them to another late night of name-dropping and playacting and fabulous omelets.

Miranda was rehearsing the role of Miss Julie when the star left the cast, and Aurora could barely understand her when she called.

"Donny's going to let me take over!" she cried. "He's not getting someone else! Rora, do you *know* what this could mean!"

Aurora shared Miranda's enthusiasm. She felt her friend deserved every chance, and indeed this could be the break for which she'd been waiting.

"The only flaw in the entire picture is Donny," said Miranda, calming.

"Flaw? What do you mean? I thought you and he—"

"Oh, Rora, wake up. I'm not in *love* with him! Oh, I didn't know that when I went to bed with him—I'd never have become involved as a means to further my career, I hope you believe that!"

Aurora hoped she believed it. "Then why—"

"Well, it was fine at the beginning. But now . . ."

"But now what?"

"He thinks he's in love with *me!* What can I do?"

"What's wrong with that?" Aurora stopped herself before asking more. Donny's love couldn't hurt Miranda's career, but she was shocked because that thought had crossed her mind.

"He wants to *marry* me! I told him we'd both be miserable, but he really thinks it would work."

"Could it?"

"No, silly. First of all, I don't *love* him. *You* know that. He asked if there's someone else, but—"

"Is there?" asked Aurora, knowing the answer.

"Rora, I've *told* you . . . *you* know. . . ."

"Oh, yes. Farley." Inadvertently she shook her head.

"Besides," Miranda added in a confidential voice, "Donny doesn't want children. He doesn't like them."

There was a pause in the conversation. Finally Aurora asked, "Then what do you plan to do?"

"Well, I'll stay with him till after the show opens. It'll help the publicity for both of us, you know, the blurbs in the columns." As Miranda outlined the benefits of continuing the relationship, Aurora's mind wandered. Finally there was a dramatic pause, and then Miranda said, "Besides, it's a way to make Farley see me. He can't fail to notice, this time!"

Aurora sensed the manic breathlessness in her friend's voice. "Miranda, don't you think that your Farley fantasy has gone—"

"*Fantasy!*" cried Miranda. "Rora, you're my closest friend—how can you call that fantasy? I'm going to pretend you never said it."

The way you pretend everything else, Aurora wanted to say. But she said nothing. She was beginning to wonder if her friend's onstage life seemed so authentic because she believed in it as fervently as she believed in her offstage fantasies. Was Miranda a truly gifted actress or, as Aurora suddenly began to suspect, was her friend merely living an imaginary life both onstage and off? In short, Aurora asked herself, is Miranda not sane?

Into the telephone, however, she merely said, "Look,

146

I think it's wonderful about the play, and I hope everything will work out the way you want it to." She wasn't even certain as to the meaning of her own words.

But Miranda seemed placated. "Rora, thank you! You're truly a friend. You're the only person I know who isn't green with envy about the play. People have been saying some nasty things about Donny and me, as if I'd actually *use* him! He's been so sweet and understanding . . . it's just that I'm not in love with him. And jealous actors can be so petty and cruel!"

"Well," said Aurora, "as long as you know where you stand." She spoke the words more for herself, her thoughts suddenly darting to California and Eddie; she doubted anything she said would register on Miranda. Her friend might possess a great acting ability, but as to knowing where she stood, she probably knew even less about that than Aurora. At the moment Aurora sensed a metamorphosis was occurring inside her, as well as in her external surroundings. Glancing about her tiny studio made her aware of that. Maria was lending her another designer dress for Christmas Day, which she had been invited to spend with Tadzio and Countess Maritza, but it would be someone else's Christmas at someone else's apartment, not so different from the Christmases in her past. Always someone else's. Only the trappings were changing. . . .

Chapter Eight

The holidays came and went. Aurora was grateful when they were finally over; she had exhausted Maria's supply of gowns and was compelled to wear one dress for the second time only a day before its owner returned to Cornelia Street to claim it.

The parties had been fun for a while; certainly they allowed no time for loneliness. That was a first. Christmas' and the New Year's celebrations had always left Aurora with an aching emptiness, a nostalgia for a past she had never really known, but this year the holidays had been a social whirl. A trio had been formed, but a trio quite unlike the previous threesome that had preceded her birth. No photographs in front of a five and dime for Aurora O'Brien. She and Tadzio—Prince Tadzio Breslau, as the captions always read—were accompanied or chaperoned, depending upon the publication, by Countess Maritza at the 21 Club or the Stork Club or The Four Seasons. The enigmatic *terzetto,* they were labeled in the current *Oggi;* in Paris *Match* their pictures were printed above the question: *Menage à Trois?* Aurora, with Tadzio's help, was acquiring language skills, not by attending classes or listening to records but by leafing through the latest Italian and French periodicals.

"But Tadzio," she asked, "why do they include me? I'm not royalty or anyone famous."

And he answered, squeezing her hand, "By association, my love. And it cannot hurt your career."

Of course, it wasn't helping either. It was only making a minor celebrity of the young actress studying at the Academy and thereby arousing a stir of interest at local clubs and "in" places. She learned not to blush when old acquaintances of her two friends inquired as to the nature of their "relationship." She polished her verbal skills and at times even found herself enjoying the conversational games.

The restlessness in Aurora's nature surfaced from time to time, however, though Tadzio was attentive, affectionate, great fun, and more beautiful than any man had a right to be. It was true, perhaps, that he drank too much, as it was true that the countess smoked too much. Occasionally, Aurora picked up a copy of *Gente* or *L'Europa* and saw herself seated at the theater between Tadzio and Maritza, the eyes of all three beaming at the camera. But if interviewed, Aurora would not have been able to define their relationship, and that had begun to trouble her.

She and Tadzio were seldom alone, and on the rare occasions when the countess slept the day away or spent the afternoon at Elizabeth Arden, Tadzio made no overtures beyond friendly kissing or caressing. On the nights when he had an opportunity to do more, Tadzio was usually too drunk to care. On one night in particular, after seeing the countess to her door, the "newsworthy couple" repaired to the den for brandy. It was quite late, past three, and a chill permeated the room.

"I'll pour," said Tadzio. "It'll warm us both." He opened an ornate wooden chest and withdrew a fur blanket. Tossing it to Aurora, he said, "Wrap yourself in this while I stoke the fire."

She slipped her shoes off and curled up on the leather sofa, enveloping herself in the luxurious fox throw. Tadzio, meanwhile, had brought the dying embers in the fireplace to life; their light flickered against the amber liquid as he filled two snifters.

He kicked off his shoes and removed his jacket before joining Aurora on the sofa. Then he loosened his tie and unbuttoned the top of his shirt.

Silence added to the intimacy of the moment and the room. Both Aurora and Tadzio swirled the brandy, sipped, and gazed at the fire, each lost in thought. She was experiencing the melancholy that had become a late-night companion since her entry into the inner circle. She wondered if Tadzio drank because he felt it too, but hesitated to ask. Instead she took another sip, unaware that he had shifted his gaze and had been staring intently at her.

"You're even lovelier in this light," he said, with only the slightest slur to his words.

"Is that because we're in the dark?" she asked brightly.

He laughed, but not the way he did at parties. "Rory . . ." he said.

She turned to look at him. His Grecian features were accentuated in silhouette, and she wished she were a sculptress so she could immortalize his beauty.

"A penny for those thoughts," he said, still watching her.

Smiling, she took another sip of the brandy.

"A refill?" he asked, reaching for the decanter.

"Mmm," she replied. A warm glow accompanied each swallow and banished her sadness.

Tadzio drained his own snifter, poured another, drank that, and said, "Finish your drink and come with me."

He hadn't spoken with any unusual or seductive inflection; nonetheless, Aurora's knees buckled. Perhaps, she mused, it's the brandy. I've never drunk so much brandy.

He led her down the hallway, past the countess' door to the master bedroom, the room in which Aurora slept on the first night of their friendship. Her steps faltered, partly from indecision, more from the brandy she'd consumed.

"Here," said Tadzio quietly, a husk suddenly overtaking his voice.

They were standing at the foot of his bed. Tadzio, four inches taller than Aurora, who was wiggling her bare toes in the carpeting, bent down to kiss her. She lifted her face to his and closed her eyes, swaying in his arms as a familiar sensation coursed through her. Should she? Shouldn't she? Her mind refused to answer as her body made its own response.

What was she doing? This wasn't Eddie. Or Artie. This was a prince, a worldly, wealthy, Park Avenue prince. This was crazy, foolish, and in the morning she would be just another addition to his list of conquests. Girls from her world were a dime a dozen, his for the asking. She was just harder to get than those who said yes on the first occasion. With her it took a few weeks of wining and dining.

But reason deserted her when his hands began to trace the outline of her breasts through her dress. Then his lips parted hers, and his expert kisses sent shooting sparks through her. Aurora murmured only once, "Tadzio, no . . ."

"Yes, darling," he whispered into her ear. "So beautiful . . . you are so beautiful. . . ."

Her heart was pounding wildly, her head swimming from brandy and desire. Together they fell back upon the bed, where Tadzio caressed her gently, warmly, but never impatiently as he untied the bow that held her dress around her. He helped her slide from its confinement and then tossed it into the darkness, the fingers of his other hand lightly brushing back and forth across her breasts as he did so.

"So beautiful," he continued to murmur, and Aurora grew more and more aroused with his every touch. Her hands were clasped around his neck, playing with his curling hair, until he moved from beneath her fingers. His mouth traveled from her lips to her neck, placing tiny kisses on her clavicle; then lower on her nipples; then down to her navel where he stopped, his crown of curls teasing her breasts, now taut and firm with excitement.

Aurora had never been so slowly aroused. She lay still, her arms over her head, waiting, the waiting stirring even deeper responses within her.

"Tadzio," she whispered, with her own urgency now. But he didn't answer.

She brought one of her arms from under the back of her head as she repeated his name. "Tadzio."

And that was the moment when she realized that Tadzio, the prince of Park Avenue, had passed out and was sound asleep.

She was alone in his bed the following morning when she awoke. The draperies had been pulled back, and Parsons, the very silent butler-valet-factotum, had brought her a tray upon which rested a buttered croissant, marmalade and jam, a small pot of steaming espresso, and a mauve rose in a silver vase to the left of the butter plate. Indeed, that gentleman's gentleman was standing in the doorway, his attention focused discreetly on the far wall, well beyond the bed.

153

Aurora was unaccustomed to servants but she quickly realized that if she did not dismiss him, Parsons would stand there all morning. She had expected him to say, "Is that all, miss?" as she'd seen butlers do in countless films, but he remained motionless, not a trace of surprise on his face.

At last Aurora smiled at him and said, "Thank you, Parsons."

He bowed politely and turned to go. It is that easy, she mused.

"Parsons, did—" She stopped, not knowing whether to refer to Tadzio as Mr. Breslau or the prince or His Highness. One required coaching for such amenities when one had not been born to the station.

"Yes, miss?" he asked when she didn't finish the sentence.

Aurora couldn't decide how to inquire about Tadzio. "Is the countess awake yet?" she inquired.

"I believe she is breakfasting, miss," he replied.

"Thank you, Parsons," she said, with a studied combination of polite interest and indifference. The butler bowed and made his exit.

Aurora laughed aloud when he was gone. He probably saw right through me, she thought. His etiquette is better than mine! She was relieved to find herself amused rather than alarmed.

She showered and dressed and casually entered the den, where she found the countess leafing through the *Times*.

"Well, Rory, what's on your agenda?" asked Maritza, not the least surprised to find Aurora there.

"I have a class this afternoon at three—"

"Splendid! You'll let me take you to lunch, then. I have an appointment later myself, so Max can drop you at your school"—she said school the way she said job—"and we can meet Tadzio afterward." She didn't glance at Aurora when she mentioned his name. "He'll be back in time for dinner. I think we have tickets to the symphony this evening. Do you like Mahler? Tadzio simply adores him."

Aurora's classical music course at Oakdale High had not been wasted, after all. "I like some Mahler. I do find much of it . . . brooding, though."

"That's true. But Tadzio gets into a Mahler mood from time to time. It's best to let him vent it. It always passes and after that, Mozart takes over, which is always a welcome improvement."

Aurora picked up the theater section of the paper, and small talk ceased as the two women scanned the *Times* in the glow of the late winter sun. Its golden haze washed over the leather furnishings, erasing any remnant of sensuality from the scene of only eight hours before. Perhaps it had never happened except in Aurora's lonely imagination.

"How wonderful!" she exclaimed, holding up a page. "An interview with Miranda!"

"I've read it," answered the countess. "Your friend is a bit strange, Rory."

Aurora perused the entire two-column piece, a frown of concern wrinkling her brow. She sighed and said, "I'm afraid you're right. She identifies with every tragic heroine she plays."

"Hm. Good thing she's not about to play *Medea*. I mean, many of us may occasionally *feel* like Miss Julie and have some masochistic desire to be brought down from our pedestals, but God knows why *anybody* would admit it in print!" She shook her head, but her meticulously coiffed blond waves remained as immobile as the expression on her face. Her hours spent away from Elizabeth Arden, Aurora mused, seem only extensions of her hours spent inside the salon—always the pursuit of perfection.

155

"I'll reserve at the Russian Tea Room, if that meets with your approval," said the countess. "A quiet lunch. We have to talk."

Aurora wondered what they had to talk about.

They were led to the countess' usual table, a cozy booth far enough to the rear of the restaurant so its occupant could observe everyone who entered, but far enough from the door to avoid anyone she did not choose to see. She was known to everyone, patrons and staff alike, and heads bowed in obeisance as she and Aurora settled in.

"I must admit, Rory," said Maritza, "that there is an ulterior motive in my asking you to lunch."

"Is there?" Aurora had wondered about the sudden invitation but hadn't thought to question it.

The countess was studying the menu, though Aurora was convinced that her hostess had memorized it long ago, perhaps for occasions such as this.

"Tadzio told me about last night."

Aurora felt her color rise and was helpless to stop it.

"I think it's important that you understand certain . . . factors, Rory."

"We were both drunk last night."

"I know. If Tadzio would drink less, then perhaps explanations of . . . unusual behavior . . . would be unnecessary."

"I'm not sure I know what you mean, Maritza."

"I was afraid of that," she said. Taking a deep breath, the countess stalled for time by rummaging through her enormous totebag for a Gauloise. "Tadzio adores you. I've never seen him quite so taken with a woman as he is with you." She found the cigarette and now searched for its ebony holder.

Aurora decided to remain silent until the countess

voiced whatever it was that had prompted her to suggest this lunch.

Maritza's eyes flashed as she said, "Tadzio needs . . . credibility, Rory. And you must believe that he cares a great deal about you. He didn't just pick you out of the crowd and say, 'Oh, now here's a sweet young thing who can give me an alibi.' He would never have done that."

Aurora's color had begun to subside, but now her adrenaline rose. "Just a minute, Maritza. First of all, that's exactly what he did—pick me out of the crowd. Secondly, what kind of credibility or alibi are you talking about?"

"Rory," said Maritza, her voice that of a patient schoolteacher addressing a very slow pupil, "you weren't expecting Tadzio to seduce you last night, were you? Because he won't. He's mad about you, but—"

"But I'm nobody, is that it?" Aurora was having difficulty in containing her temper.

"Not at all. Rory, darling, don't you understand? Oh, dear. I can see that you don't. Rory . . . Tadzio is *gay*. . . ." The countess' words faded away as she saw their impact on Aurora. She reached across the table in a maternal gesture, but Aurora shrank away.

"Then *why*, Maritza? Why all the pretense? All the attention and the photographs in the papers and magazines? Why the charade?" Anger was giving way to consternation.

The countess stubbed out her unsmoked cigarette and addressed Aurora in a flat, emotionless voice. "Rory, you should feel flattered by what I am about to tell you." Then she softened somewhat. "Tadzio comes from one of the wealthiest families in Europe. Their title no longer means much"—she laughed as if at a private joke—"so few titles mean anything today. But

157

in his family's circle, certain ... persuasions ... are simply not acceptable. They are practiced, of course, quietly, discreetly. It's a game. Everyone knows it's a game. But there are rules to be observed."

Aurora's curiosity had been piqued. "And just how do I fit in? As his 'alibi'? His credibility?"

The countess smiled, and for the first time Aurora saw tiny, almost imperceptible lines where the woman's face had undergone some kind of cosmetic transformation or rejuvenation. She wondered how old the woman was, and why this should cross her mind during such a conversation. Was everything in life a charade? Tadzio's "front"? The countess' face? Her own existence? And why, in place of anger or disappointment, was she suddenly feeling cheated, sullied, used?

"Tadzio was right," Maritza was saying. "You are intelligent, Rory. Your naïveté is due simply to your inexperience. That's good."

"Why is that good?"

"Because it means you can learn. There is always hope for one who can learn—and I say this having myself been in your place."

"How could you have been in my place?" asked Aurora. "You come from the nobility, don't you?"

"Ah yes, the nobility. My dear Rory, there are rules to be observed and lessons to be learned in every class. But let's return to your question—how you fit in, as you say."

A waiter appeared then, and the countess ordered for both Aurora and herself, dismissing him before continuing.

"I'll come to the point so that we can enjoy our lunch. We'd like to invite you to join our ... family."

"I'm afraid my naïveté is resurfacing, Maritza. What are you talking about?"

The countess took a quick swallow of her vodka, her

eyes flashing with excitement. "The game . . . is nothing more than what you've already done. Except that you can move out of that Village hovel and leave that horrendous job of yours. You will move in with us."

"You mean be *kept?* Is that what you're saying?" But Aurora recognized that the countess was right; except for her address, she was already being kept.

"And what do I do in return? Nobody offers something for nothing, even I know that."

"You just continue to be seen with Tadzio. Allow the world to believe what they already believe."

"You mean that he and I are lovers?" Her eyes opened wide at the memory of the previous night. "He suggested that?"

The countess nodded, motioning Aurora to silence as their waiter delivered two portions of blini. When he had departed, Maritza spooned a generous helping of caviar onto her pancake and concentrated her attention on her meal, while Aurora watched her and followed the same procedure.

"You could do worse," the countess said. "You are fortunate that you possess a . . . regal bearing, if that phrase doesn't embarrass you, Rory. It shines through all the attempts at sophistication and all the borrowed clothes—"

"How do you know about that?" Aurora demanded.

"Rory, please listen. I myself have known great wealth and great poverty. I know what it means to live by one's wits. I do it even now." She paused for another mouthful of blini. "If you see the waiter, I need more sour cream," she said.

Aurora handed her the dish of cream from her plate. "Take mine," she said, and the countess accepted.

"As I was saying, Rory, I *know.* Take the labels, for example. And forgive my bluntness, but a little checkroom attendant can't possibly earn enough to

159

dress in Givenchy and Halston and Norell night after night. Last week you began to repeat. Don't be offended," she added upon seeing Aurora's reaction. "I *notice* these things. I make it my business to notice."

"You seem to know a lot more about me than I know about either of you, titles notwithstanding," said Aurora, not too kindly.

"I'll tell you my story over coffee if it won't bore you," said the countess. "Tadzio's is shorter. He was born into wealth and will die in wealth—even without an heir. In fact, one of the reasons he'll never marry 'for appearances'—believe me, Rory, that's a common occurrence—is that without a wife, he can share his money with whomever he chooses. And he can be a friend, without having anyone dictate to whom he is a friend." Reaching for another cigarette, she said, "And I must add that to have Tadzio for a friend is to be rich indeed. You will learn that, Rory, in our company." She lit the Gauloise now and launched into her own personal history.

"I was an infant, newborn, when the Revolution came." She studied Aurora for a reaction, but none was forthcoming.

Her guest, meanwhile, made a quick mental check. If this woman had departed Russia in 1917, why she *had* to be in her mid-fifties! Could regular visits to the Arden salon and cosmetic surgery have made the countess appear a decade younger? And if that were so, could Tadzio have undergone a similar transformation? Aurora shuddered and wondered if she had stumbled upon two living Dorian Grays.

". . . so they killed poor Papa," Maritza was saying, "but Mama, so I was told, carried me in her arms all the way to Paris. We lived with friends. There were no more relatives—the entire family had been assassinated, just like the czar." Her eyes misted, although

160

Aurora was certain she was not the first to be privy to this tale that could have served Tolstoy.

"We had friends while we had money," the countess went on. "But one by one, Mama had to sell the diamonds. She had been clever, you see. To get those stones out of Russia—and to get us out—we had to dress as peasants. Mama covered the jewels with cloth. Cheap, simple cloth. They became black buttons on a black sweater that belonged to her maid. Nobody thought to question us, and we—she—walked right across the border."

Aurora listened attentively, fascinated. Even if the countess had really been old enough to walk with her mother, it was an amazing story, impossible to invent. For an inexplicable reason, Aurora suddenly yearned to know more about her own mother and father.

But the countess hadn't finished. "We lived well enough until the last of the diamonds was sold. Then we soon found out what it meant to fend for ourselves, to *work* for our bread. Oh, only when we *had* to work, you understand. I wasn't brought up to work and do not find it at all pleasurable. As I imagine you do not?"

They were now sipping brandy, which was making Aurora even more reflective. "Whether I do or not, I haven't been fortunate enough to choose."

"Ah, but you can leave that in your past, Rory."

Why did she feel as though she were Eve, being tempted by the serpent? "What past?" she said aloud.

"Whatever you come from, wherever you've been. Although you are too young to look upon it with anything but distaste."

Aurora laughed wryly. "Maritza, maybe you think you see a 'regal bearing' or some phony nobility, but believe me, my past is very dull. What you see, I'm afraid, is what you get."

"Rory, don't say that in such a derogatory manner,"

cautioned the countess. "You must never apologize for your past. Whatever it is, it has brought you to this point. That means you've survived it, which is certainly more than some can say. You're a survivor, Rory, as I am. And those of us without Tadzio's advantages—whether we possessed them at birth or not is unimportant—we must simply shrug our situation off, say *eh bien,* and continue with our lives. And if you think about it, you'll see that you and I, in practicing the art of survival, are far stronger than those who have been handed the world on a plate. Tadzio is the exception—he has wealth, but he is also strong. And beneath his playboy image is the most loyal friend I have ever known. That is more than unique in the circles in which we travel."

Maritza's voice had assumed a gentler, more natural inflection. Aurora didn't know whether it was to avoid unwanted ears or if the countess, the epitome of sophistication, had truly been touched by her own words.

Max collected them and the Rolls headed east across Fifty-seventh Street. The countess waited, her eyes fixed on Aurora, who gazed out the window in silent contemplation. They passed the Automat, a grim reminder of the choice being offered. So near to the Oriental splendor in which they had just lunched on caviar and blini, so far if she refused. Aurora could spend years at La Grille, hoarding her quarters, before receiving such an opportunity again.

She wasn't being asked to sell her body; the scene played out last night, now that she knew the truth, would not be replayed. Her dubious reputation might come under scrutiny, but what harm could there be in silencing gossip mongers? And really, what reputation did she have? None. She was to be included *only* because people thought her to be Tadzio Breslau's "girl." How different would that be from the speculative labels captioning their photographs now? The only change would lie in her acceptance, her awareness of the situation. She would be part of the game, not the outsider she had always been. She would belong.

"Well?" asked the countess once more.

Aurora answered the question with one of her own. "What do I have to do?"

Tadzio never mentioned the unsuccessful seduction or Maritza's conversation with Aurora. The guest room had been readied by the time Aurora and Max had picked up her clothes and deposited the keys with the super on Cornelia Street, and Tadzio greeted the new member of the "family" with open arms and a bottle of Dom Perignon.

"We must celebrate," he said, popping the cork and filling three flutes to overflowing.

"To the three of us," he exclaimed.

"To the three of us," echoed Aurora and the countess.

The following day before Aurora's theater history class, Tadzio, Maritza, and Aurora went shopping. Aurora, after an initial hesitation, accepted a limited number of what she felt were necessary clothes, although she firmly refused jewelry of any kind. "I prefer my own, thank you."

Tadzio relented only when the countess observed that Aurora's decision would simply serve to distinguish her as modest, quelling any rumors that might arise regarding her intentions. On her part, Aurora was

163

amused by the backward reasoning of the inner circle; it seemed not unlike that in Alice's topsy-turvy Wonderland. But as long as she could survive in it, Maritza was right, it was preferable to checking hats and borrowing dresses and showering in a bathroom down the hall. As she crawled between the silk sheets in her new bed at Tadzio's penthouse, she was reminded of little Abby's question on her sixteenth birthday.

"Are you happy?" the child had asked.

"Everything is relative," Aurora said to the empty air, "and I'm just along for the ride."

Chapter Nine

Aurora hadn't seen Miranda for three days. Her friend was busy rehearsing for *Miss Julie,* and everyone at the Academy spoke of little else.

At the end of the week, Aurora spotted a notice on the student bulletin board outside Hubert's office. It gave the date, time, and place of the rehearsal to which Miranda had invited the school. Aurora was scribbling the information on a piece of paper when Miranda came rushing into the building.

"Oh, Rora! I've been looking for you everywhere! You've moved! The super told me, but she didn't say where to!"

Aurora pulled her friend into a corner before telling her the news, not wishing to make a public announcement of her new address.

"God, Rora, how incredible!" Miranda sighed romantically. "Imagine, Tadzio Breslau and my friend! He's *so* gorgeous!"

Aurora didn't feel it wise to share Tadzio's secret with someone who fantasized as much as Miranda did.

"You've got to bring him to the rehearsal, Rora!"

"Well, that depends on your director—"

"Oh, Donny knows you two are dating—it was his idea to invite you. He also said to bring that weird countess along."

"Actually, she's not so bad, once you get to know her."

"Well, no matter. It's going to be so exciting, Rora! I can hardly wait! Olga has offered to take notes, so in addition to Donny, I'll get feedback from the horse's mouth. Did you know she played Miss Julie in Moscow?" She paused to think. "Maybe it was Leningrad. But anyway, isn't it absolutely thrilling?" Tears welled in Miranda's eyes.

Aurora nodded but not with manic enthusiasm.

"Rora! What's wrong? I thought you'd be so happy for me—you're the only true friend I really have."

"I am happy for you. It's just that . . . I read your newspaper interview, Miranda."

"Did you? Do you think *he* did?"

Aurora did not need to be told who *he* was. "Miranda, you really ought to be concentrating only on the play. It's a big responsibility, and—"

"Well, I tried to be subtle. I'd hate to hurt Donny after all he's done for me. I just wanted to phrase it so that if Farley *did* read it, he'd understand the message. Do you think he did?"

"Read it or get the message?" Aurora asked flatly.

"*Read* it, silly! Of course he'd understand it—nobody else would, but Farley would *have* to!" She was breathless from excitement.

"If I were you, Miranda, I'd forget Farley. Period."

"God, Rora," said her friend, "sometimes I wonder about you!"

Tadzio and Maritza accompanied Aurora to the rehearsal at the Shubert. The threesome sat apart from

166

the rest of the invited audience, in the balcony. The student body of the National Academy of Acting almost filled the orchestra section, and halfway back, to the left of the stage manager, sat Madame Skrepova holding a clipboard on which was a large yellow pad. Hubert paced the aisle, ignoring his wife, while she flirted openly with an actress she appeared to know.

The lights dimmed and Tadzio whispered, "This had better be good. I turned down something really special tonight." Aurora's senses went on alert, although his remark had been made to the countess.

The curtain opened and the play began. There were constant stops and starts, since it was a working rehearsal and not a run-through. However, Miranda Vale maintained an intensity of concentration throughout, and at the final curtain, Tadzio turned to Aurora and said, "You were right, Rory. She's a wonderful actress."

Maritza was silent, but she was slowly nodding her head. Her eyes were still upon the stage, although the curtain had closed and was now reopening, revealing the cast assembled onstage in a semicircle with the director.

"This role will make her a star," said Aurora aloud, happy for her friend but feeling strangely used. Not jealous, definitely not that, but sad. Perhaps because Miranda was about to find her place, and Aurora had just begun her search.

Below them, a man arose from one of the seats to the left of the acting students. He was tall and muscular, not overweight, but large. His hair was thinning and gray, and although his features were individually attractive, in combination they gave him the appearance of a heavy rather than a leading man. He had the kind of face and physique that Aurora would never have noticed had it not been for Miranda's onstage reaction.

"Oh, my God!" cried the actress who had just electrified them as Miss Julie. She jumped from her folding chair, almost tripping over the stage manager, and tore down the steps and into the house.

Aurora leaned over the balcony railing to better see below. He had already gone up the aisle as Miranda flew after him calling, "Farley! Farley!"

Aurora mumbled a breathless "Excuse me" to Tadzio and rushed past him to the balcony exit. She reached the bottom step as Miranda, out of breath, tears streaming down her face, came back into the theater. Farley had been there, and Farley had gone.

"Oh, Miranda," said Aurora, at a loss for words.

"He was here! Oh, why did he disappear again?" Miranda's voice broke, and she threw herself into Aurora's arms as a small crowd, Tadzio and Maritza among them, appeared in the lobby.

"Is she all right?" asked the stage manager.

Despite her friend's convulsive sobbing against her shoulder, Aurora nodded. "She'll be all right. She'll be all right." She tried to use the soothing voice she had employed with Abby when the child had awakened during a nightmare.

The group dispersed, those from the audience leaving the theater, those involved in the production going back inside for their notes.

"Who was that man, anyway?" asked Tadzio when the three had reached the street.

"A long story," Aurora replied.

"Darling, I hope you realize that your friend is playing with something less than a full deck," Maritza observed. "No matter how good she is in the play." Then, with her usual practicality, she added, "I hope it's a limited run, for all the angels' sakes."

"I hope so too," said Aurora, although her wish had

168

nothing to do with backers' investments.

Aurora was unable to attend any subsequent rehearsals of *Miss Julie*. The Academy, in its annual scenes' evening for Broadway agents, producers, and casting personnel, had announced its role assignments. Aurora was simultaneously learning three different roles from three very different plays: in one scene she would play Eliza Doolittle—"from the *play*," Madame Skrepova had stressed, "and *not* from the *musical* version!" In the second, she would portray Stella in a scene from *A Streetcar Named Desire,* and although she would have preferred to have Miranda playing opposite her as Blanche, the actress chosen was not a poor choice.

The third and final scene had been selected, as were the rest, by Madame, who would also direct. It was from *The Children's Hour,* and although Aurora liked the Hellman play, she felt she had little in common with either of the protagonists. Her portrayal of Martha Dobie reflected her uneasiness with the role, and Madame's constant criticism was a hindrance, not a help.

Hannah, her voice and diction coach, worked with her on projection and dialects, and Aurora's natural ear quickly picked up Stella's Southern accent. She found Eliza's cockney speech slightly more tricky, however, and mastered it only after three sessions with Hannah.

These two characterizations presented few problems. She sympathized with Stella and Eliza. She searched and found something of their emotional life in her own. Both Stella and Eliza needed love, and each of these women knew herself, possessed an inner strength, an inner life. Portraying Martha Dobie was difficult for her though. As a result, Olga Skrepova was pressuring her.

Aurora studied and rehearsed and reread the scene over and over without finding a handle, without discovering its hook. Tired and frustrated as she was, she began to take Madame's unrelenting badgering personally. Tadzio even remarked on it on one of the dozen evenings Aurora worked instead of accompanying Maritza and him. "Don't you think she's riding you a bit much?" he said. "Why not play hooky tonight and come to the theater with us? You'll probably learn more!"

But Aurora shrugged her shoulders and refused. "She's trying to find the key, I guess. Maybe she thinks she can get a performance from me. I'm not so sure anymore." Her eyelids were heavy from poring over the script.

"Darling, I thought acting was supposed to be *fun*. I mean, otherwise, why do it?"

She smiled wanly, then returned to her room to dress for rehearsal.

But when she arrived at the Academy that evening, the other actress in the scene was absent. "I dismissed Margaret for tonight," Madame Skrepova explained as Aurora entered the small room, its gray enameled walls and sparse furnishings, a folding card table and chairs, highlighted by the starkness of the unshielded overhead light.

"I want to work with you alone on the character. I'm sure that together we can find it," said the director, her Russian accent thicker than usual.

"Madame, I've gone over it and over it. Maybe I just can't do it."

"Olga," the teacher said. "Call me Olga. We will dispense with formality. Perhaps that is distracting you." She was seated on one of the two folding chairs.

170

"Aurora, do you find it difficult to relate to authoritarian rule?"

Aurora stared at her blankly. "What has that to do with *The Children's Hour?*"

The woman smiled, a studied smile. "Ah, even that response is defensive. Did you get on well with your parents?"

"They're dead. I was raised in a foster home."

"I'm sorry." But her tone showed no remorse. "Tell me, then, what about your childhood? Did you have friends? Were you part of a group? Or were you lonely and shy?"

Memories stirred, but Aurora did not like this woman enough to share her confidences. "I'm afraid this might sound defensive again, Madame"—she quickly corrected herself—"I mean Olga, but I don't really see the connection—"

"That may be the problem, Aurora. Have you thought about the character, the background, the feelings experienced by the young teacher in the play? What in your past can you bring to light and use that is appropriate to her? Things you share? Factors that make you . . . similar?"

Frustrated, Aurora sighed. "That's just it; I don't *see* any similarities. I mean, sure, she's been sad and I've been sad. And she and I both share a love for children. But the rest—"

"What about the rest?" Olga interrupted.

"What?"

"Aurora! Think! You are resisting some facet of the role, and as long as you do, you will be unable to play Martha!" The director's voice had risen and her cheeks were flushed.

"I can't relate to—"

"To what, in God's name? To *what!*"

The small room was heavy with unexpressed

emotion. It was a barrier between the two women, as impenetrable as if it had been built of brick and mortar.

Aurora sank into the other chair, shaking her head. It was Olga who broke the silence.

"Child, have you ever been in love?"

Slowly Aurora looked up.

"I mean deeply, truly in love." The director rose from her chair and leaned against the table more in a pose than as a means of support; if she had leaned more weight against it both she and the table would have toppled. Olga Skrepova was not about to cede center stage.

The unkindly glare of the uncovered overhead bulb shone down upon the older woman's head. For the first time Aurora was aware of the snow-white roots of the woman's jet-black hair; the ugly shadows cast upon the director's face gave her jet-black eyes a sinister aspect.

"I'm waiting for an answer, Aurora." Olga impatiently, but imperiously, tapped her foot.

"I've . . . I think I've been in love."

"You haven't!" snapped Olga. "If you had, you would know! That is the problem, Aurora! You are not relating to the woman in the scene because she knows what it is to be in love—to be hopelessly, agonizingly in love. You know nothing of love!" Her black eyes narrowed, and Aurora's heartbeat quickened.

"What do you mean, you *think* you have been in love! You are talking like a ninny, like a stupid teenage virgin!" When she spat out the last word, Aurora almost grinned.

"You find this amusing, Aurora? You think you're smart perhaps because you've been in bed with a few men—*boys*—and because you let them paw you and climb on top of you, you *think* you've been in *love?*" Now Olga's face and neck, even her scalp beneath the white roots, had turned red.

172

Aurora breathed deeply and then rose.

"Where do you think you're going?" demanded the director.

"Home. To work on this scene alone."

"You're here to rehearse with me," said Olga. She pointed her finger to the chair. "Sit down."

Aurora remained standing.

"Sit down!" The older woman bellowed.

"I don't think so, Madame," said Aurora, moving toward the door.

Olga jumped in her path and before Aurora could move, the director embraced her clumsily, simultaneously trying to caress and detain her.

Aurora pushed her away, shoving her against the wall. Angry now, she tried to maintain control in her voice as she said very evenly, "If you think that in order to play a woman who loves another woman, Madame, I must submit to your"—she hesitated, unable to find an appropriate word—"advances, you are wrong! Maybe you're right. Maybe I haven't ever been in love! Maybe I don't know what love is!" She was furious now. "But I'll tell you one thing, Madame, I know what love *isn't*—and I have no intention of letting you anywhere near me!"

She didn't wait for the director's reaction but ran down the corridor to the exit. Madame Skrepova's response echoed down the hall as she opened the huge metal door of the school.

"You're out of the scenes—you're through at this school! And if I have anything to say about it, you'll *never* work in this town! Never!"

Aurora reached the street and hurried across to Max and the waiting limousine. As she climbed inside, she saw Olga, framed in the doorway, her arms flailing. Her wild gyrations looked comical and pathetic to Aurora. As the car swept away, she only hoped that

173

Madame Skrepova had no real influence in the theater.

"Rory, darling, you ought to feel relieved," said Maritza, pouring sherry as Aurora recounted the evening's episode. "I'm sorry you were all alone when you got here, but Tadzio and I had no idea you'd be back before midnight."

"It's all right," she said, accepting the drink. "I've had time to think."

"About what?"

"Oh, about a lot of things. One of them concerns something you've both often said to me."

"We said something wise? Helpful?" Tadzio said playfully.

She laughed softly. "I suppose you did. About acting schools being a waste of time. They are, you know."

"Oh, good," Maritza said, joining Tadzio in the teasing. "It's so much fun to be right about something —at least once in a while." The countess, Aurora noted, was en route to being drunk.

"I'm serious. A private coach is different. But these classes—frankly, they're exercises in egomania. An actress like Miranda doesn't need the school, and the rest of us at our varying degrees of talent need to learn technique. We don't need to get up and play roles we'd never get in the commercial theater."

Tadzio was sitting on a barstool, studying her. "Then why haven't you quit before now?"

Aurora shrugged her shoulders. "I don't know. It made me feel as if I were part of something—of the theater, I guess. It's a family, of sorts."

"We're enough family for anyone," said Maritza, sitting beside Aurora on the sofa. "And we'll take care of you." An idea seemed to strike her then. "Tadzio! Who do we know in the theater?"

"Who?" he echoed. "Why everyone!"

"No, darling. I mean people who could help Rory." She considered her suggestion. "Or at least people who can make sure that this Olga woman can't hurt her."

"Well," he replied. "Most of my close friends are on the other coast. They're movie people."

"Hmm." The countess drained her glass of sherry and then poured more into it. "Anyone else? Helps me to think better."

Tadzio shook his head and tried to intercept Maritza's glass. "You've drunk a lot tonight, darling."

Sleepily, she rose from the sofa, but she managed to down the sherry before Tadzio could make it from the barstool to the sofa.

"There," she said with a slight slur. *"Now* I've had enough." Turning toward the door, she said over her shoulder, "Don't worry, Rory. We won't let anyone hurt you. We're your family."

For a reason Aurora could not fathom, the countess' remark unsettled her and filled her with sadness.

Chapter Ten

Tadzio arranged for center aisle seats for the opening performance of *Miss Julie,* and Maritza and Aurora went shopping together at Henri Bendel for accessories after selecting their gowns at Bergdorf Goodman. Aurora chose one in her favorite color, deep burgundy. It was a clinging, floating wisp of silk. The countess, as always, chose black. "I'm not in mourning," she observed. "It's just so *basic.*"

Tadzio insisted that Aurora parade her ensemble for him, so she employed her model's slouch in the den, turning a full 360-degree circle for him. "Well?" she asked, one eyebrow arched.

"Spectacular!" he said. "You'll make Madame Olga suffer like hell!"

The crowd of opening night regulars showed up in full regalia; it appeared that the lobby and Shubert Alley had simply exchanged guest lists with 21. The same names, the same name-droppers. If it were not for Miranda, Aurora reflected, they could have saved themselves the bother and stayed home.

Hubert Skrepova and Madame Olga were there.

177

Apparently the director of the Academy had not been told about the scene between Aurora and his wife, for when he passed her in the lobby, he kissed his former pupil's hand. Then he looked at Tadzio, nodded aloofly, and moved on. Madame Olga said "Good evening," to the air and brushed past before she could be answered or ignored.

As Aurora had expected, Miranda's performance enthralled the capacity audience, her opening-night adrenaline charging her tragic portrayal of Julie and stimulating the whole company. Indeed, electricity emanated throughout the house. When the curtain fell people rose to their feet and cried "Bravo!" Aurora, Tadzio, and the countess did likewise.

The single jarring note in an otherwise magical evening was an exchange overheard by Aurora as she exited the ladies' room. As she made her way toward Tadzio and Maritza, a male voice greeted an acquaintance in the anonymity of the crowd. Had he not addressed his colleague by name, Aurora would have paid no attention. But the name uttered jolted her.

"Farley!" boomed a Shakespearean actor whose face Aurora had seen on television countless times.

Expecting to see Farley Granger, whose work she had so enjoyed in the film *Strangers on a Train,* Aurora turned.

But it wasn't Hitchcock's Farley. It was the man she'd seen at the rehearsal, the man who had caused Miranda to collapse in tears. Still, Aurora would not have been upset but for her eavesdropping.

"Farley, you old bastard! What in God's name are you doing here?"

"The same as you, I'd imagine. Strindberg is one of my favorite playwrights."

"Grim, but brilliant," said the first man. "And I must say Donny's brought it off wonderfully. A keen eye for

178

casting, wouldn't you say?"

"Damn keen," said Farley. "She's fabulous."

"Wonder where he found her," said the friend. "Program says Miranda Vale. Ever seen her before?"

Farley shrugged his shoulders. "Can't say that I have," he said. "Although I certainly wouldn't mind . . ."

Both men laughed knowingly, and the first speaker said, "Damn that Donny, he really knows how to do it!"

They laughed again as Aurora stumbled toward the lobby.

She sent a note backstage to Miranda, hoping her friend would understand a sudden "indisposition." Then she explained to Tadzio and the countess that she couldn't stand being polite and making light conversation at Sardi's while they awaited the reviews.

"It *is* part of the show," Maritza reminded her.

"I really don't think I can take that part of it tonight."

She suggested that they go on to Sardi's without her, but Tadzio wouldn't hear of it, so the three made their way through the glittering crowd and past the rows of sleek black limousines until they located theirs. It was exactly like the others lining West Forty-fourth Street, but only they had a chauffeur like Max, whose white handlebar mustache and wavy white hair stood out from the more somber drivers in their dark caps. Max, whose demeanor was correct and quiet, observed the customs of his position with one exception: he absolutely refused to wear a cap. Aurora liked his insistence on this individual note, and she liked his employer for permitting such a defiance of convention.

On the opening night of *Miss Julie,* convention was

tossed to the winds on more accounts than Max's cap. When Tadzio asked where she'd like to go, Aurora said, "I'm really not in a mood for celebration. Sometimes this all seems too much. I just can't—"

"Well, darling, tell us. We'll do whatever pleases you."

Aurora sighed. "I think I'd like a hamburger and french fries at Howard Johnson's," she announced. "And I'd like Max to join us."

"God," muttered Maritza as she stared out the smoked-glass window. "I hope she's not bringing the play we've just see *home.*"

Parsons delivered Miranda's reviews on Aurora's breakfast tray. Excitedly, she tore through the news-paper until she found the theater page. "Oh, my goodness!" she exclaimed, jumping from the bed and running from her room.

She knocked on the countess' door but there was no answer, so she put her ear to the carved wooden paneling and listened. The soft, consistent buzz of snoring came from within. Glancing at the tall grandfather clock in the hall, Aurora saw that it was only ten A.M., a time Maritza referred to as "the middle of the night."

Slowly she crept down the hall to Tadzio's door and rapped on it. She knew by now that the prince was a heavy sleeper, so when she got no response, she knocked a second time with more force. Still no response. She turned the knob; the door opened.

His room was empty, and the bed was turned down. It had not been slept in. Speculation on where Tadzio could have gone provoked an uneasiness in Aurora, but she tried to ignore it. She returned to her room to eat her cooled croissant and to drink her tepid coffee.

As she did so, she reread Miranda's reviews and spent the major portion of the morning rejoicing in her friend's triumph. Even Parsons was nowhere to be seen, so Aurora rejoiced alone.

She pondered over whether to tell Miranda of Farley's presence. Then she wondered if perhaps he had gone backstage. Her misgivings might have been for nothing. For all she knew Miranda and Farley could be sharing the joy of her success. Wasn't anything possible?

She sighed. Watch it, Aurora, she cautioned herself as she dressed. You don't want to let your own imagination run away with you.

Maritza was still asleep and Tadzio had not yet returned when Aurora left for her first appointment of the day. She would telephone Maritza later with her congratulations, but right now she had to concentrate on her own career, and the appointment Tadzio had arranged for her was too important to receive anything less than her full attention.

Byron Endicott handled a modest list of actors and actresses. He had begun as an actor and, as Tadzio had explained, had found he preferred the security of being on the controlling side of the desk.

"But agents aren't guaranteed a secure income, are they?" Aurora had asked.

Tadzio had laughed. "No, my love. Byron doesn't need the money. He just enjoys being in the driver's seat."

He hadn't told her what Byron Endicott confided to each young actor or actress seeking representation. Although the agent used it as a means of discouraging all but the most determined, his disclosure did shed more light on his present occupation.

"I simply wasn't a very good actor," he said to Aurora. "And even if one is very, very good, the

181

competition is so tough that only a fraction of those entering into it actually get anywhere."

"I know," said Aurora, "but one of my closest friends has just made it." She shared her excitement about Miranda, finally able to discuss it with someone; even Max had been off somewhere so Aurora had walked to Endicott's office on West Fifty-seventh Street.

The agent was nodding. "She's a fine actress," he said. "If she makes the right choices and is given proper direction, she could go far. But I'd hardly call last night 'making it.'" He was looking straight at Aurora, seeking a reaction.

Smiling, she said, "What would you call it?" He wasn't going to use this tactic to discourage her.

"I'd call it an auspicious beginning, if I may quote the *Times*. Or a 'promising debut,' if I may borrow from— pardon the expression—CBS news. I don't usually trust television critics," he added quickly. "They tend to flatter unless the performance is dreadful."

"Well, I'd say Miranda's on her way," Aurora responded.

He said nothing but continued to study her.

"Mr. Endicott," she said finally, "why are you staring at me?"

"Byron. Does it make you uncomfortable?"

She was surprised that her face retained its usual color with no hint of a blush. "No. I'm just wondering if you stare at every actress who comes into your office. And if so, why."

The corners of his mouth turned upward in a grin. "To see what kind of a response they'll give me. Yes, Miss O'Brien, I do tend to stare throughout the first interview."

"In that case, your first interviews must be a waste of time—for you as well as prospective clients."

His grin widened and became a smile. "Miss O'Brien,

you are . . . different from most of the actresses who come into my office. I don't know if you're talented, but you are definitely different."

"How is that?" she asked, beginning to relax.

"Most actresses, particularly those of limited experience, tend to gush or try too hard to please. You don't seem concerned about whether I add you to my list or not. Or did Tadzio Breslau coach you on how to be interviewed?"

Not angered, Aurora replied, "He didn't have to coach me. As an agent, it's my understanding that if you add me to your list—if *I* choose to be added to your list—then you'll be, in effect, working for me." She spoke softly, graciously, with warmth in her voice. "Isn't that what being an agent is?"

"Miss O'Brien," said Byron Endicott, "I repeat, I don't know if you can act, but I do like your style." He rose, for the first time, having remained seated when Aurora had entered his office, and came around to the front of the desk. Still seated, Aurora realized at once that should she stand beside him, he would come up only to her shoulder. She saw no point in embarrassing a man who might become her agent, even if he had just tried to embarrass her.

He leaned against the desk and lit a cigarette. When he offered her one, she shook her head, waiting for him to return to business.

"I don't know Tadzio Breslau well," said Endicott. "This is more of a favor for Donny, who's an old buddy of mine, but please understand that if I do act in your behalf, it'll be because I think I can do something for you and not because of an obligation or friendship. The interview is a favor. Anything else is strictly business."

"Can you?"

"Can I what?" he asked, still leaning against the desk.

"Can you do something for me? In short, can we

benefit each other?"

"I haven't seen you onstage. What have you done?"

"A stand-in on a film," she said honestly. A resumé was one thing. There could be no pretense between agent and client.

"You're damn good-looking," he said.

"Thank you."

"What else have you done?"

"Not much. That's why I need an agent."

"Hm. Smart, too."

"Thank you again."

"Well . . . what shall we do about you?"

"Would you like me to read? I have a few monologues, or if you have a script—"

"Naw. You don't have enough credits to get Broadway auditions yet, and there's no money off Broadway. I can get you commercials, and for those, I don't need you to audition." Then he paused. "You realize we're talking to each other like agent and client, don't you?"

A slow smile crept onto Aurora's lips. "We are, aren't we?"

"You know, Miss O'Brien, it's not what you see in the movies—or even with your friend Vale. Usually somebody becomes an overnight sensation—*after* twenty years in the business." He was watching for a reaction again.

He didn't have long to wait. "Well"—Aurora rose to her full height—"if it takes that long, we'd better get started."

She wondered, when she reached the ground floor of the building, if Byron Endicott had been as surprised by their interview and its outcome as she was. Rushing to a phone booth, Aurora called the penthouse.

Only Parsons was at home.

"They'll be back to change for dinner," the butler

said. "Is there any message, miss?"

"Yes, Parsons. Please tell Mr. Breslau"—she chose to dispense with the title, protocol be damned—"that I've been out shopping . . . for an agent. And I think I've found a perfect fit."

Byron Endicott began arranging auditions for her almost immediately. They were all for television commercials, usually for the more expensive perfume and cosmetic products. She was told by one casting director that she simply didn't have a "housewife's face."

At the first advertising agency she was given several pages of copy to study. She glanced around the reception area at the other young women, eight of them, all actresses or models, all beautiful and expertly made up, all studying their scripts.

Aurora took a seat and followed suit, trying to analyze the copy, to pick out the words to be stressed, considering various inflections. Forty-five minutes went by. One after another, an actress was ushered in, an actress was ushered out. A stunning assembly line.

Finally, Aurora's name was called. She followed the receptionist's instructions as she worked her way through a maze of orange and white walls, and came at last to the door marked Room C. She knocked.

"C'mon in," a woman called out.

She entered a room in which four men and two women sat at a conference table. One woman held a Polaroid camera while the other said, "Miss O'Brien?"

Aurora smiled and heard one of the men whisper, "Lovely smile."

"Here, dear," said the woman who had spoken. "Give me the copy and please stand over there, next to the mark."

185

Aurora did as instructed, wondering how much of the script she would remember.

"Okay, now give us the same smile we just saw a second ago," said the woman with the Polaroid.

"But don't you want me to read?" she asked.

"No, we really haven't time. We're going to take your picture, though, and see how you match with Lex."

"I beg your pardon?"

"No, no, another foot to the right, honey. Right where the mark is, okay? Otherwise we'll get half your face in shadow."

Aurora wondered if she had stumbled into the wrong room.

"Excuse me, but I thought I was supposed to be auditioning for—"

"You are, honey—that's what the picture's for. C'mon, let's have that smile."

Aurora smiled. Byron was right on one count, she mused; credits didn't matter. But he was mistaken on another; the smile on her lips as she posed for the Polaroid camera had required more than a little *acting*.

She landed an extra on her tenth or eleventh audition; she was beginning to lose count. Byron had submitted her for a wine commercial; her "audition" had consisted of clinking a champagne flute with a handsome actor. Another actress was chosen for the principal, but the agency called to say they had been impressed by her poise—Tadzio commented that her experience with champagne flutes was due to him— and would she be willing to do an extra? It was better than doing nothing, she decided, and no sense in letting her SAG card accumulate dust.

So Aurora filmed her first commercial, as one of two dozen "poised" actresses laughing and enjoying a party—background for the two principals on-camera. It was longer than any party Aurora had ever attended; she arrived at the penthouse fourteen hours after she left it. She was several hundred dollars richer, thanks to overtime and meal penalties, but neither her legs nor her smile muscles had ever ached so much.

Miranda and Aurora were having coffee at the Howard Johnson's on Forty-sixth and Broadway when three small people passed their booth. Before Aurora glanced up, she heard, "Look, Stan. It's your Amazon!" It was Myra, standing between Bobby and Stan.

The diminutive comic shook his head as greetings were exchanged. "Hey, doll!" said Stanley. "I didn't reco'nize ya! How's it going?"

"Okay," she answered, embarrassed that she hadn't tried to contact him since the night of the Chaplin film.

"How's that boyfriend of yours?" asked Myra. "He feedin' you enough?" She was examining Aurora's still-slim frame and shaking her head, while she made little tsktsk sounds under her breath.

Aurora answered uneasily, "I . . . uh . . . Eddie went back to California."

"Well," said Bobby, "why don'tcha come up and see us? Must get pretty lonely, huh?"

She nodded. "Thanks."

"Listen, doll," said Stanley, "we gotta go. But gimme a call, willya? Your boyfriend won't get jealous if we take care o' you while he's away, will he?"

Aurora smiled a sad smile. "No, he won't get jealous."

They said good-bye and disappeared through the revolving doors into the taller crowd of tourists, passersby, actors, and bums. To Aurora they were as unreal as a mirage.

Miranda had been dividing her attention between her friend and the fried clams on her plate.

"You don't miss Eddie, do you?" she asked finally.

"Not really," answered Aurora. "Strangely enough, I don't. I haven't even thought about Eddie lately."

"Since you moved uptown?" her friend said.

"I haven't had time." She considered her answer. "No, that's not it. I . . . it's funny, but I miss his company. Eddie's a friend." A sudden memory made her blush. "Well, I mean I was able to talk to him."

"I thought you fell out of love with him," said Miranda.

"I thought so too. If I was ever in love with him to begin with," said Aurora reflectively. "It's just that . . . there hasn't been anyone to take his place. I guess that's it."

Displaying a pragmatic side for once, her friend said quietly, "Rory, you can admit it to me—you're just horny."

"Possibly." But first she had to admit it to herself. She hoped that Eddie had meant more to her than that, although she wasn't sure whether that was for his benefit or her own.

After Miranda went off to her matinee, Aurora walked uptown to Byron's office. He had gotten her a Day Player contract, an under-five as it was called because the part had five or fewer lines. Still, as her agent reminded her, it was a credit in a Hollywood film, a big-budget extravaganza with locations in several countries. The New York segment only involved three days' shooting, but it was a credit and Aurora was very much in need of credits.

The conversation at Howard Johnson's was on her

mind as she entered Byron's office.

"Do you know how I could contact a friend of mine in L.A.?" she asked him.

"Try the Los Angeles phone book." He was seated behind his desk. "Or is his number unlisted, assuming it's a he?"

"You know, Byron, I never even thought of that."

"That," he said, reaching under his desk, "is what agents are for." He brought forth a telephone directory similar in size to the Manhattan book but with Los Angeles printed on the cover, then plopped it on his green blotter and asked, "What's the name?"

"Calvert. Eddie Calvert."

Byron leafed through the *C*s, slowing as his eyes passed the appropriate page, and said, "Sorry, hon. No Calvert. But you could try the Guild or Equity—"

"He's not an actor. He's an assistant director."

"Well, then he's a member of the directors' union."

Aurora rose. "I hadn't thought of that either. You're a good agent."

"As good as they come," he said. "That's why you hired me, isn't it?" He winked as he handed her a copy of the contract she had just signed.

"You bet," she answered, winking back.

"Wait a sec," he said as he scribbled a number on one of his business cards.

"What's that?" she asked as he held it out to her.

"Directors' Guild. Happy hunting."

She blew him a kiss and went out the door. She'd have to call after her next audition; she had to be at Madison and Fifty-third in ten minutes.

This time she was actually given an opportunity to read the audition copy on videotape, although the casting director told her immediately that she was years too young for the type they were seeking.

This surprised Aurora; Byron was the kind of agent

189

who didn't push his clients where they weren't wanted. He submitted them only when they fit the age range and physical type requested. "Otherwise they won't call me, and if they don't, how do I get work for you?" he'd pointed out at the start.

But she was told that between calls to agencies that morning and the auditions in the afternoon, the advertiser whose money was financing the commercial had decided that he wanted a mature beauty in her forties, someone who would lend more credibility to the product. Aurora sighed as she read the lines. Another afternoon wasted, albeit on videotape. It did not compensate to be told they could probably use her at a later date for another job because she was such a good type and had given a good reading. Wasted time was still wasted time. Lately a restlessness had come over her because it seemed that her waking hours could be better spent than running from go-see to go-see, from one cattle-call audition to another. She wondered why nobody ever publicized the humiliating aspects of the performing arts, the hours of waiting to read and then, alone on a stark stage with only glaring worklights for mood, reading a scene, or a page, or four lines when time permitted no more. And, as she had suspected even before Byron told her, most roles were already cast anyway, everything but the bits and walk-on parts, those invisible jobs for which the competition was as steep as for leading roles—perhaps even steeper. Aurora had read the casting notices for *Miss Julie* for a month following Tony Rogers' party and Miranda's meeting with the play's director. The entire theatrical community quickly learned which parts were available in any given show, yet it was always the same. The union demanded open interviews and open auditions, and every unemployed actor in Manhattan showed up filled with blind optimism, somehow believing that all the rumors were nothing more than gossip and that *this* one part was really *open*. One by one, day after day, the hopefuls lined up outside the theaters. They practiced at the nearby rehearsal studios and guzzled quantities of coffee at lunch counters in the theater district, between auditions. And every once in a while a story was circulated about an actor who was the last to audition, nonunion, no agent or any Broadway credits to his name, and bingo! The waiting had paid off. Someone had seen him, singled him out from the rest, and he was being given his chance!

Then there was the actress who was signed as understudy to the star, and when the star suddenly took ill, the understudy got the role. They *weren't* replacing her with another star as was generally the case. Another break! Another reason not to give up hope!

This spring much of the optimism was due to Miranda Vale. The scuttlebutt implied that she and Donny Everett were lovers. But wasn't that *after* she'd been cast? everyone asked in hushed whispers. Everyone who didn't know Miranda or Donny Everett. Nobody else had to ask.

Rumors in the columns hinted at movie deals and TV series; and an ideal professional marriage might be in the air, suggested more than one gossip columnist.

But Aurora knew the truth because Miranda had told her, over cappuccino at The Peacock on a rare return visit to the Village.

"We're through, Rora, and I'm afraid he may replace me in the show!" Miranda said through a mist of tears, although Aurora couldn't tell whether they fell from sadness at the breakup with Donny or the possibility of unemployment.

"How did it happen?"

"He kept after me and after me about getting

married. He even accused me of sleeping around, and I haven't done that since the night I met him! Finally"—she gasped between sobs—"he asked if there was someone else."

"And what did you say?" But Aurora already knew.

"Rora," said her friend, "I'd never lie to him. I couldn't bear to lie." She lowered her eyes and then looked up, straight across the table into Aurora's stare. "I told him."

"About Farley."

"Yes."

Aurora considered the information. "How did Donny react?"

"That's the worst part—he didn't! He just stood there without saying a word, never taking his eyes from mine. And then . . ."

"Then what?"

Miranda heaved another deep sigh. "He said, so quietly I could barely hear him, 'You're out of your mind.' In this weird tone of voice, as if he'd never seen me before in his life. He kept shaking his head and repeating those same words. I thought eventually he'd lose it and hit me. I could feel the intensity, it was . . . tangible! But he didn't. He didn't raise his voice or say anything else."

"What did he do?" asked Aurora.

"He took his keys and walked to the door . . . and"—the tears were welling up again—"and said he . . . he wanted me gone by the time he got back."

Now Aurora breathed a sigh. "How long ago was that?"

"A few hours ago . . . Oh, Rora, what'll I do?" She burst into fresh tears.

"About Donny or the show?" she asked slowly.

"About *Farley!* How can I make him understand how miserable he's making me!"

Aurora resisted the temptation to voice her thoughts aloud. They would have been wasted on Miranda, who plainly was beyond accepting responsibility for her own actions. It seemed strange that only months ago Aurora had wanted to be more like her friend; now she wanted to help Miranda and she felt only pity for her. Had they each changed so greatly or was Aurora beginning to see more clearly? Neither possibility comforted her.

"Aurora," repeated Miranda, "what am I going to do?"

Aurora finished the last of the french fries on her plate, her mind far from the clatter of dishes or Miranda's dilemma. "I don't know," she said.

In the role in which she had her four and a half lines Aurora played a fashion designer in a chic Madison Avenue boutique. It was just up the street from the Getty building, lodged in between an art gallery and an antique shop. Her lines were disconnected: one phrase in the first scene, two in another, and her final one and a half lines were spoken as she exited the store on Madison Avenue, a portfolio of designs under her arm. As she explained to Tadzio and Maritza, any attractive young woman with reasonable intelligence could have played the role. She was happy to be on a movie set, but less than thrilled about the demands made upon her acting ability.

Nonetheless, she hit her marks and didn't squint or blink when the lights were turned on, and—she laughed to herself at this—she kept her graceful hands to herself when one of the grips called out for a hand.

During the lunch break, Mel Collins, the SAG representative she'd met through Eddie Calvert before getting her first job, came over. They were seated in a coffee shop around the corner from the location.

"How's it going?" he asked, moving his chair closer to hers.

"Okay," she said. "Nice to see you again."

"What do you hear from Eddie? He back from Rome yet?"

Aurora was surprised. She hadn't had time to get his number from the Directors' Guild and hadn't thought that he might be out of the country.

"What's he doing in Rome?" she asked casually.

"Something for De Laurentiis, if I remember." Leaning in closer, he said, "Can I ask you a personal question?"

She assumed it would concern Eddie. "Sure. What?"

"Is all the stuff in the magazines true? About you and that prince? I mean, it's none of my business, but I figured you and Eddie—"

"Are very good friends. And as for my prince, don't believe everything you read, Mel."

"Just another friend?" He grinned, but not suggestively.

Aurora was uneasy nonetheless, and she decided it was best to drop the subject. "Yes," she said with finality, "just another friend."

But the brief conversation did make her wonder whether Eddie had seen her pictures in the gossip magazines. The Italian weeklies, along with one or two supermarket newspapers, seemed to print the most provocative captions. Surely Eddie had been in the business long enough to pay no attention to them. And why should it matter anyway? He had wanted to wrap Aurora up in his own particular package and she had refused. Why should anything he might think have any effect upon her?

But she was troubled over more than Eddie Calvert. In fact, he was the least of her concerns. Tadzio was drinking himself into a stupor nightly and often disappearing until the following day. She was less naïve than when they had first met and now assumed two things: that he was with male lovers on his frequent nights out and that she mustn't interfere. She could appear on his arm at social functions, but she couldn't be responsible for him or his reputation.

And that brought to mind another worry. She couldn't be responsible for Miranda's sanity either. Her friend was in desperate need of professional help, of that there was little doubt. Donny Everett had not fired her, which, Aurora surmised, must only be adding to Miranda's torment. Over the telephone, she had said that she was all right, but Aurora felt that Miranda was losing her grip, and she knew she was unable to prevent it. When Miranda confided that Madame Olga had befriended her, Aurora decided she could only wash her hands of the entire matter.

She and the countess did attend a matinee of *Miss Julie* at which Maritza confessed a morbid curiosity about how Miranda's life had affected Miranda's art.

It hadn't. Her performance as the tragic heroine had deepened and grown since opening night. It seemed as though a different entity was embodied in her as soon as the curtain rose. It was impossible to explain.

"Have you ever seen *A Double Life?*" the countess asked.

But Miranda offstage was not the sharp, finely tuned instrument she was as a theatrical personage. She was becoming vague, forgetful, distracted. Twice Aurora made appointments for lunch and twice Miranda did not show up. She neglected to answer telephone calls and her appearance, offstage, became sloppy. Her silken blond hair was often dull and uncombed; her clothes were haphazardly chosen and wrinkled. Tadzio commented that he had passed her on Eighth Avenue and called her name, but she had walked right past him as if in a daze.

Finally one Wednesday afternoon at two-thirty, Aurora received a telephone call. She stiffened at the sound of Olga Skrepova's voice. "I am calling about Miranda Vale."

Aurora's heart skipped a beat. "What happened?"

"We thought you might know since you are her friend." She was calling from the Shubert; Miranda had not shown up for the matinee. Half-hour had been at one-thirty; at one forty-five they had phoned her apartment, then Donny Everett's hotel. No Miranda. They had checked everywhere, and called everyone connected with the show; but no one had seen her since the night before.

"I haven't heard from her in several days," said Aurora. "If I do, I'll contact you at once." She hung up the phone, an icy dread coursing through her.

Tadzio had mentioned meeting Tony Rogers for lunch; the countess was at Elizabeth Arden. Aurora paced back and forth in the den trying to imagine where Miranda could have gone. She couldn't understand her friend's sudden lapse in theatrical discipline; *Miss Julie,* especially of late, had become a substitute for everything missing in her life. Not to show up . . . Something had to have happened to her. The theater had called the police and the nearby hospitals before contacting Aurora, but no one answering Miranda's description had been seen.

Erasing one frightening image after another from her mind, Aurora grabbed her purse and went out; wearing out the carpeting would do nothing but turn her into a nervous wreck. She sensed something but didn't know what—didn't want to know what.

Distraction. She needed distraction. She left the building and, turning left on Fifty-seventh Street, walked to Lexington. She paused while deciding whether she was up to Bloomingdale's and, realizing that she wasn't, crossed Fifty-seventh where the women's residence still stood, the awful place where she had slept upon her arrival in New York. She laughed in spite of herself, remembering her morning ritual; the prickly-needled shower, the doughnut and coffee across the street at the Mayflower, then back to her room with the newspaper to hunt for apartment vacancies. . . .

Inadvertently her eyes took in the familiar newsstand on the corner. Her heart began to pound rapidly, and her pulse raced so loudly that dizziness overtook her. To diminish these reactions, she inhaled deeply several times, intent upon recovering her composure. Then she focused her eyes upon the headline and the accompanying full-page photograph: "Film Star Weds Ex; Blessed Event Due." And below, with his arm around an attractive woman who bore a striking resemblance to Miranda Vale, was Farley.

The woman in his arms was not Miranda but a very pregnant blond bride, her happy smile beaming out at the camera. The caption beneath the photo read: "I'll never let him go again."

Aurora stood, immobilized, for several minutes, and finally the woman running the newsstand asked, "Are you okay, lady?"

Aurora nodded. She was all right—but Miranda wasn't. She knew that for a fact. She needed to find her friend. But how?

She hailed a passing taxi and climbed inside. As it traveled across Fifty-seventh Street toward the West Side, places to look raced through her mind only to be dismissed as quickly as they came to her. When the cab reached Broadway, the cabbie said, "Lady, where you wanna go already?"

"Drive down Broadway. I'm looking for someone."

He glanced at her through the rearview mirror, shrugged his shoulders, and said, "It's your money."

When they reached Forty-second Street, she hadn't yet decided on a definite course of action. The cabbie turned again. She didn't know why she felt compelled to stay inside the taxi, but she decided to follow her instinct; if nothing else, doing so might help her to determine her next move.

She instructed him to go across Forty-second and turn up Eighth Avenue. Still she didn't know why. When they stopped for a traffic light, she found herself asking, "Do you have a copy of today's paper?"

The driver handed her a rumpled copy of a tabloid. Her hands shook as she again saw the happy couple staring at her from the page. "Take me to the Village," she said suddenly, as bewildered by her words as was the cabbie.

"Lady, I thought you said Eighth Ave—"

"I did. I changed my mind. Please hurry."

"Where to in the Village?" he asked.

"I . . . don't know yet. . . ."

The downtown traffic was light for a Wednesday. Aurora wondered if the matinee had been canceled or if Miranda's understudy had gone on in her place. She'd neglected to ask Olga.

As the cab headed down Seventh Avenue past Sheridan Square Aurora peered out the window. On the right was an off Broadway theater and small eating places, on the left were restaurants. Aurora directed the driver to circle the area. She wasn't worried about the cabbie's impression of her; she had to find Miranda!

The cab turned into a small side street lined with coffee houses and boutiques. Aurora had often come here with Miranda after classes at the Academy. She noted the revival movie house, but the cab was almost three doors beyond it before the words on the marquee registered on Aurora's brain.

"Stop!" she cried.

The driver slammed on the brakes and she jumped out of the cab.

"Hey, lady—"

"Wait here!" She pulled several bills from her purse, paid the cashier, and ran inside.

She stood at the rear of the theater, her eyes fixed on the wide-screen image of Farley—Miranda's Farley.

There was no usher; none was needed. As Aurora's eyes accustomed themselves to the dark, she saw that the theater was almost empty. An old man sat alone, munching on popcorn, and two women occupied seats halfway down in the center. But no Miranda.

Then, suddenly, she knew. She turned as if guided by an invisible force, passed the Ladies' Room sign and headed to the stairway. Smoking in the Balcony Only, the sign said.

Slowly she mounted the stairs, a heaviness descending on her.

She waited until the screen lighting was bright enough for her to check the entire balcony.

Only one person was there. In the last row at the very top.

"Miranda!" Aurora whispered as she made her way up the steep incline, tripping in her haste.

"Miranda!" She reached the top row, breathless, hyperventilating, fear gripping her chest and squeezing it like a vise.

She tiptoed to the seat beside her friend. "Miranda!" she spoke into the void as she took her friend's hand.

The hand was limp. Miranda didn't answer.

Chapter Eleven

Tadzio handled everything. But the events that followed the discovery of Miranda registered on Aurora's brain like a film speeded up and later replayed in slow motion. And the sequence of the scenes was reminiscent of the shooting schedule of a film; ends before beginnings, middles suspended in a meaningless time frame.

Now as Aurora lay between the sheets of her elegant bed in the safety of Tadzio's penthouse, disjointed images flashed through her brain—jarring images. Ambulance sirens. The police. St. Vincent's emergency room. Tadzio and Max with the Rolls. A bewildered cabbie. Television cameras. News reporters. And the doctor, his soothing voice calming her whimpers of "Miranda . . . Miranda . . ."

The sedative accomplished its purpose immediately, and Aurora slept through twelve hours of TV news, network and local, of anchormen repeating the same, senseless, numbing words, over and over until they acted upon viewers in the same way the doctor's needle had acted upon Aurora. Across the city, friends, colleagues, agents, and directors were invited to assess the reasons for Miranda Vale's suicide. "The rising star," said one publicity agent. "Everything to live for. It would have been a great PR stunt if she'd called someone before it was too late." Of course, the public relations man had missed the point. So, while the city of New York was told that a brilliant young actress on the brink of stardom had killed herself due to fear of success or her recent breakup with Donny Everett, Aurora O'Brien mourned in sedated slumber the wasted love and the wasted life of her best friend.

In her dreams Farley—Miranda's Farley—danced. Balletic leaps propelled him, a vertiginous blur, high into the air, then into a movie balcony where a lonely girl sat alone, an empty bottle in her purse, a sad-sweet smile across her lips. Farley's arms went out to her and then withdrew. He turned to another girl, this one with her arms extended. And they danced together over the balcony, onto the stage, into the screen. And the movie faded from view.

On and on Aurora slept, Tadzio and Maritza, in turn, keeping vigil. It was not a peaceful sleep. Aurora's mind saw clock hands forever set at two, matinee curtain time. The movie marquee. And throughout the evening and long into the night she envisioned a stage manager calling "Places!" She turned restlessly every so often and murmured, *"Why?"*

But the only reply was "Shh," uttered by Tadzio or the countess.

Tadzio and Maritza did their very best to see to her comfort and to provide distraction. Either money or Tadzio's title—Aurora never knew which—kept reporters from the door, and Parsons followed instructions to the letter; any telephone inquiries received a very British, very polite "no comment." The penthouse on Park Avenue had temporarily become a fortress.

However, it could not protect Aurora from her innermost thoughts, nor could it shield her from depression. For days she remained shut indoors, a recluse, declining dinner and theater invitations, and shunning auditions and shopping sprees. So Tadzio had her meals catered by the finest restaurants, and he secured whimsical films to be viewed in the den.

Both he and the countess were bewildered when a delightful Chaplin comedy caused Aurora to burst into uncontrollable tears. But gradually Aurora came to realize that her tears were not for Miranda alone. They were for Frances Gifford and for little Abby in Oakdale, and for the parents she had never known. They were tears she had heretofore denied herself, tears she had to shed alone because, appearances to the contrary, she was alone. As alone as she had been as a homeless child. That emptiness again, and a longing as deep as before.

When she became aware that she mourned her own past, Aurora ceased to mourn Miranda.

She came out of her depression with renewed energy, a sudden sense of purpose. It was she who telephoned Byron and told him that things weren't moving fast enough. She went to as many auditions as he could arrange, she partied every night with Tadzio and Maritza. It seemed as though Aurora didn't want to waste a single minute of the day or night; the wasted life of her friend had triggered this behavior.

Aurora's photographs began to reappear in magazines and columns, always with Tadzio's arm linked through hers, beaming smiles on their faces. When the *paparazzi* adopted her as their darling, she found herself enjoying the publicity and Byron made every attempt to capitalize on it.

Several commercials materialized, and this time Aurora was the right age and type for them. When she landed a small role on a soap opera, the part was expanded to offer more "visibility." Still, as she confided to Tadzio and Maritza, they would miss her if they blinked, but she was learning to find her way about a set, becoming aware of which camera was focusing on her even before she was told. And while a secret part of her refused to take her success too seriously—perhaps as self-protection; even Aurora wasn't sure—she did begin more and more to relax on a set and onstage. Her work wasn't a real home, but it was as good a substitute as any—and she could pay her own way. That enabled her to spend more time with Tadzio and to feel no guilt or obligation. She didn't care what the gossip columnists said about her as long as she knew the truth.

Of course, the truth is sometimes difficult to bear. It was true that she was becoming ambitious. It was true that she sought success. It was true that, despite occasional twinges when she thought of Eddie in faraway Rome or little Abby, who, most likely, was not so little anymore, or Maria on Cornelia Street, she was concentrating solely upon her career and what was commonly referred to in the business as "making it." She wasn't willing to take certain routes: She wouldn't pose nude or sleep around or pay kickbacks of any kind. No. She was developing an unerring ability to charm, both on screen and off. Her banter often exceeded her experience—several times directors misread her responses as encouragement—but she was a quick study and soon learned to employ a delicate balance. Her intelligence was serving her well; as the countess had predicted, she was living by her wits.

Tadzio and Maritza, meanwhile, informed Aurora that soon they would have to move.

"But I thought this penthouse was yours," she said to the prince.

"It is, darling," he said with a laugh. "But I grow bored if I spend too long in one place. And besides, the countess and I miss our friends on the Coast."

Aurora was surprised. Actors she knew who had worked in California hated the place and spoke of it only in the pejorative sense.

"I'll miss you both," she said.

"There's no reason you should, Rory," said the countess, pouring another drink. "You'll come with us, of course."

"What?" Aurora looked from Maritza to Tadzio. "I can't! Things are just starting to open up for me on this coast—nobody knows me out West!"

"But we know people there, darling," said Tadzio. "I don't mean to be a bastard about it, but don't think that the little parts you're getting on TV or the perfume commercials are going to make your name a household word. Even with leading roles, it's still the small screen."

"He's right," the countess chimed in. "We can introduce you to people who can make a difference. We've talked it over and decided. It's the best move for all of us. And especially for your future, Rory."

"I beg your pardon?" she said. *"You've* decided what's best for *my* future?"

"Your future, our future! The three musketeers!" Tadzio had drunk several glasses of champagne already and was about to start another.

"Don't argue, Rory," Maritza intoned, as she spread herself across the long sofa and gazed toward the ceiling of the sunken living room. Realizing she was crushing the folds of her linen dress, she rearranged herself before continuing. "You'll love Beverly Hills." She eyed Aurora and added, "And Beverly Hills will *adore* you."

"I'll have to think it over," said Aurora, sipping her own champagne. "It's very nice of both of you, but it is, after all, *my* decision as to how I handle my career."

"*Your* decision," agreed Tadzio, imitating her voice. "Absolutely."

"And it's your career," added the countess. She lit a Gauloise and then, as if reminding herself that she was trying to curtail the habit, stubbed it out and sat, or reclined, champagne glass in one hand, the empty ebony cigarette holder in the other. As she spoke, her hand waved the holder back and forth as if it were a magic wand.

But Aurora wasn't amused. "Look, both of you, I'm very grateful for everything you've done for me. But I do want to have some say in what I do with my life."

"Absolutely," said Tadzio in the same, slightly slurred voice as before.

"And I'm just not sure I want to leave New York."

"Absolutely."

"Especially for the West Coast—and please, *don't* say absolutely again!"

"Ab—" Tadzio bowed so low that he fell into the deep corner of the sofa at Maritza's feet.

"I mean," continued Aurora, "it's wonderful of you two to be so concerned, and I appreciate it more than you know . . . but—"

"But it's your career and your life," finished the countess, staring at her.

"Yes."

"You're right, Rory darling. Of course. It's your decision. We were foolish to try to speak for you, weren't we Tado?" She had taken to shortening his name as of late.

He looked at her, his face a mixture of curiosity and the effects of too much alcohol.

In turn, they both looked at Aurora, who was standing at one of the ceiling-to-floor windows that overlooked the long stretch of Park Avenue going north. They were right and she knew it. The residual checks for advertising Arpège and L'Oréal were more than welcome in her bank account, and the experience she had gained on the afternoon soaps was invaluable; but it was a drop in the professional bucket. Movies were the only way. She could stay in New York for fifty years, go from walk-on to bit part to good roles on Broadway, yet only a handful of people would know. She didn't need Miranda, alive or dead, to remind her that she was not Geraldine Page or Julie Harris. Right now she had youth on her side, beauty. And she was smart enough to handle the business end of it. What was it the countess had said that afternoon they'd exchanged confidences? Something about a regal bearing. Style. She was discovering that style could be developed, enhanced, but the basics had to be there from the start. One either had it or one didn't, but, Aurora acknowledged to herself, it was one attribute she possessed. That was the single factor that set her apart. On Broadway it might be overlooked for rarer abilities, but in California, she could probably make it work in her favor.

Turning from the window and downing her champagne, she smiled the smile she displayed on the lipstick commercial every night during the eleven o'clock news.

"I've decided," she said to Tadzio and the countess.

It was the countess who had chosen to fly at night. "It's so much more *ethereal* from above, don't you think?" She was making a pronouncement, not asking a question. No more had been said about it, although it was Tadzio's Lear jet, and the prince preferred flying in broad daylight. He wasn't fond of air travel and deemed it safer by day.

However, the countess had made known her preference, and that was that. Aurora realized that the trip had probably been Maritza's idea, which was why Tadzio was letting her make all the arrangements.

In the long run, it hadn't mattered to Tadzio because of the way in which he traveled, the hour notwithstanding.

As Aurora observed his slim, elegant form, casually attired in pink silk shirt and gray gabardine slacks, she wondered if Tony Rogers had selected the ensemble. He was reclining across the leather sofa in a drugged sleep, his cashmere coat pulled hastily over him. The dosage was calculated to wear off so he'd awaken just prior to landing at LAX in Los Angeles, thus saving him anxiety while flying or the embarrassment of arriving unconscious in a city that never slept.

The countess rose and crossed to the bar, nearly tripping over Tadzio's gray suede loafers in the process. Aurora noted the grace with which the woman moved, an ability the two women shared. With a practiced hand, the countess began to mix a pitcher of martinis, putting in a bit too much gin for only two glasses. The pilot wouldn't be drinking, and Tadzio was out cold.

It was still difficult for Aurora to believe that they were aboard a plane. A private plane. But for the constant roar of the engines, they might have been in someone's study or living room.

According to Maritza, one of Tadzio's hobbies was decorating and redecorating the interior of the jet. When asked why, Tadzio, as quoted in one printed interview, had thrown up his hands in a helpless gesture and cried, "But what can I say? I've seen *Auntie Mame*—the *first* one—too many times!"

He changed the décor at whim, whenever he grew

bored with it, which Maritza confided was usually three or four times a year. The most recent transformation, number two for the current calendar, was responsible for their present cabin surroundings, which were reminiscent of an old English manor-house library or game room. The walls were paneled in dark mahogany and three of them were lined with set-in bookshelves crammed with books. Not ordinary books, Aurora saw immediately. Treasures. Leather-bound, gold-tooled editions of all the classics. None of which had been read; the bindings were untouched. Aurora thought fleetingly of her childhood, of the hours she'd spent at the local library, devouring the same titles that now surrounded her.

The fourth wall, the one on the opposite side of the cabin, was decorated with a collection of severed heads; magnificent animals' heads, but severed, nonetheless. Deer, tiger, mountain goat. Aurora wondered how much courage it required to shoot a mountain goat. She glanced at the prone figure of the prince, oblivious to them all. Tadzio hadn't felled any of these poor beasts; surely they had been provided by an interior decorator. But whoever was responsible had been off his mark. The total effect was at once ridiculous, impressive, and disgusting. Aurora made a promise to herself never to wear the fur of an endangered species. She looked up at the tiger's eyes. I promise, she said almost silently. Mink, yes. Sable, of course. But never one of you.

She was further repulsed by the realization that in another few months this interior would be replaced. And by what? she wondered. An Indian harem, a Japanese geisha house, a Chinese pagoda, or an Art Deco bedroom? And still the walls would be confining. . . .

She turned to peek out the window over her left

shoulder. The jet had ceased its ascent into the dark sky and had leveled off into its flight pattern. Below, Manhattan was just slipping away beneath the black velvet cover of night. Is this the right move? Aurora thought, experiencing a moment of panic.

It had to be. It was time to leave New York. To arrive. To *begin* to really arrive. Success was beckoning, and she would grasp it firmly with both hands and claim it for her very own.

The swirling sensation, she reasoned, must be the result of a too-strong martini on an empty stomach. It couldn't have anything to do with the flight.

It had, at one time, been the home of a famous movie star. Her name had faded more quickly than her image on film, but neither had attained immortality. Acid was gradually eating away at her scenes as celluloid disintegrated in a can on a shelf in a Hollywood warehouse.

But she had been famous and rich for a while, and her home had been a testament to that success.

Tadzio had borrowed the house from its present owner, a friend of Maritza's. These people, Aurora thought, have houses everywhere! She stood between her two friends, staring up at the sprawling, sun-drenched stucco façade of the Spanish-style hacienda.

The car had stopped at the foot of the sloping drive to deposit the passengers. Tadzio had insisted that they walk up to the house and send the limousine ahead for the unloading of their luggage—that alone would require at least fifteen minutes.

Aurora could see the shiny vehicle behind the palms that lined the narrow road, then ended in a circle before the heavy, dark, carved wooden doors. She recalled Tadzio's description of a large fountain at the center of the circle, and of a statue depicting the nude form of the house's previous owner. It had since been removed. "It was tacky," Tadzio had commented. "She was all chipped away."

They crossed the broad expanse of lawn, the cool blue Spanish tiles of the roof no longer visible as they drew near. The chauffeur and another man were just lifting the last of the matched suitcases from the trunk of the Rolls. Aurora noticed Tadzio's raised eyebrow and quick glance at Maritza, who seemed greatly amused. Tadzio stood dead in his tracks, awestruck by the figure before them.

The sunlight caressed the gleaming golden hair that lay like corn silk over the tanned skin of his raised arms, the muscles clearly defined beneath the pure white T-shirt that encased his well-formed chest. Growing over his strong jaw was a day's growth of darker stubble. In a way, he resembled a healthier Tadzio in the full bloom of manly youth. No longer a boy, he was fully aware of his effect upon them all, the prince in particular. Aurora guessed that this first impression had been calculated to stun, to entice; and the bright sun did serve to highlight his cool strength. His thighs were bound in bleached denim cut-off shorts that strained to contain what was scarcely left to the imagination.

"Who is that?" Aurora whispered to Maritza.

"Tadzio asked Anton Kalmar to hire some . . . help," she replied softly.

"You must be Vance!" Tadzio called to the "help."

Vance looked up suddenly as if he had been unaware of their presence and had awakened from a trance. He flashed a dazzling grin and stood perfectly still, one suitcase balanced on his shoulder, the other in his hand; he was a living California icon. "Hmm," mused Tadzio. "Albee's American Dream . . ."

211

He moved swiftly across the driveway as Vance answered, "Yes, sir. Mr. Kalmar said you'd be needing an extra hand around the place."

"Mr. Kalmar read my mind," said Tadzio with a smile.

Aurora felt an uncomfortable stirring inside her. Rarely had she seen Tadzio so animated, so outwardly happy. Why, then, should she be feeling anger? Could he be so easily deceived by such an obvious display of obsequious friendliness?

"Take those bags in, please," Tadzio continued. "Then join us for a drink . . . and a swim."

Vance nodded and muttered a "thank you" as he turned toward the front door. Pausing long enough to catch the countess' eye, he deliberately let his gaze travel down the length of her body. Aurora, observing the entire scene, sensed an unfamiliar, crawling feeling on her skin. Instinctively, she feared that Vance would turn that gaze upon her. The same look, the identical smile offered to Tadzio, was now flashed at Maritza, who raised her head in response, regarding the "golden boy" through half-closed eyes that stared back at him down the length of her regal nose.

The exchange was not lost on Tadzio, who turned his head sharply toward the countess as Vance strode into the house, the sound of his bare feet slapping on the tiles of the entrance foyer.

Aurora decided that she disliked Vance. Why, she couldn't say. Perhaps she felt insulted for Maritza. The look Vance had given her clearly indicated that he did not discriminate between her and Tadzio. He was instigating competitiveness, attempting to manipulate them, which Aurora found repugnant.

Tadzio and the countess remained for a moment with their eyes fixed upon each other. Then Maritza moved to him, kissed him quickly on the lips and held

212

his face between her hands. She looked deeply into his eyes and smiled. He responded with a beaming grin and then laughed. Whatever had passed between them belonged exclusively to them and, Aurora knew, did not include her. But she found herself strangely moved by their silent communication. Together the three walked up the steps and entered the house.

Aurora had been overwhelmed by Tadzio's penthouse in New York, but even that luxury paled in comparison with this sumptuous hacienda. Its white stucco walls and terra cotta floor tiles exuded coolness and warmth at the same time, and its furniture, though massive, was never overbearing. Earth colors provided the accents in the form of vases, cushions, paintings, and sculpture. Whether the furnishings were the result of the owner's impeccable taste or the skill of a Beverly Hills interior decorator, they were impressive. Aurora made every attempt to appear accustomed to such luxury, and in a way, the past months at Tadzio's had been a preparation for it.

While Tadzio changed for his swim ("Everyone into the pool! You too, Vance!" he'd said), Maritza showed Aurora through the dining room with its sleek, long table; the circular library where there was a floor-to-ceiling stone fireplace, and the six bedrooms and six baths. Each of the baths had sunken marble tubs, the faucet spigots gleaming with polished brass handles, and the kitchen sparkled with copper pots and kettles. In addition to the pool the hacienda was equipped with a hot tub and a sauna.

"A cook will be engaged tomorrow," she told Aurora, "and the housekeeper comes in twice a week. And of course . . . there's Vance."

"What does he do?"

The countess regarded Aurora for a moment, then put an arm around her and hugged her. "He'll clean the

213

pool, I suppose," she answered, smiling.

"Maritza," said Aurora, "I was wondering . . . well
. . . have you met Vance before? Do you know him?"

"Yes and no," replied the countess, still smiling.

"What do you mean?"

"Well, I've never met him before, no. But . . . yes, I
know him."

By the time Aurora had changed into a claret-
colored crochet-knit bikini, the others were already at
the pool. Vance, soaking wet and wearing the briefest
of bathing trunks, sipped a beer beside an enraptured
Tadzio, whose Margarita, abandoned on the glass-
topped table, was turning to slush.

Aurora was again struck by the magnificent appearance of the countess. In a black, one-piece halter-
topped swimsuit, she reclined beneath the shade of a
canvas canopy, her body and face belying the
chronology of her years.

When Aurora turned to Tadzio, her eyes met
Vance's. She colored, quickly averting her glance, and
he took another swig of his beer, then set it down, and
dove into the pool. Tadzio laughed in delight as Aurora
seated herself on the chaise beside his.

"Ah," he declared, "I'd forgotten how I do sometimes enjoy California."

"And just think, darling," said Maritza, grinning,
"this is only the first day."

He leaned in closer to the countess and said quietly,
"He has an eye for you too. Tempted?"

"Oh, please," she said, "he's in *your* employ, not
mine."

Although it was a shared joke, Aurora recognized in
Tadzio's sigh an unmistakable relief. The situation
made her uneasy.

214

"Don't take too much sun, Rory," Maritza ordered. "It's aging. Besides, you'll be far more striking tonight with your ivory skin. *Everyone* out here has a tan."

"Tonight?" said Aurora.

"Anton called," Tadzio explained. "There's a party this evening, supposedly in my honor, at his place."

"Who is Anton?" Aurora reached for her Margarita as she spoke.

"A very big—and very *good*—director, Rory," Maritza answered.

"A director who succumbs easily to the charms of a beautiful woman," Tadzio added.

"True," the countess agreed. "You might do yourself some good tonight, darling."

She proceeded to outline the plans she and Tadzio had made for Aurora, their calculated blueprint for the construction of her career.

That evoked further uneasiness in Aurora, because these were big plans. This first week would include a series of introductions in the offices and homes of directors and producers. The following week, she would see agents and casting people; she would make immediate contacts that even Byron Endicott could not have arranged. These visits and meetings would acknowledge her awareness of the powers' importance, while at the same time they would bring her name and face to their attention. She would, as in New York, be seen everywhere on the arm of Prince Tadzio Breslau or in the company of the countess Maritza. Screen tests and roles would follow.

"By the way," Maritza said, interrupting herself as she puffed on the ebony cigarette holder and the perpetually lit Gauloise, "you *can* act, can't you darling? Not that it matters all that much, but it would be a definite plus."

Aurora was almost insulted by the question until she

215

realized that Maritza had no way of judging her talent, a talent Aurora doubted much of the time. "Yes," she said quietly, "I can act."

"Fine. You'll do just fine, darling." The countess leaned over and patted Aurora's hand in the now-familiar gesture. Aurora noticed that Vance was lifting himself from the pool, and drawing their attention away from a discussion of her career.

"Like Neptune from the sea," Tadzio observed aloud.

The countess smiled slowly, then turned to Aurora. "Welcome, darling, to Beverly Hills."

Chapter Twelve

"Simple! I said— What *is* this?"

The countess lifted the necklace of diamonds and rubies, and let its weight fall with a thud against Aurora's sternum.

"Tadzio told me to wear it."

"The earrings and bracelet are enough. Tadzio can wear the necklace if he is so fond of it!"

Maritza moved behind her and undid the clasp at the back of Aurora's neck; then she studied both of their reflections in the mirror. Leaning in closely to examine her handiwork, she inspected her charge from the mass of titian waves falling loosely to her shoulders, down to the deep forest green silk sandals that matched the green of her Trevilla gown, a shimmer of silk chiffon that clung to Aurora's body in soft, flowing lines. She had wanted to wear her hair piled high on her head in Audrey Hepburn fashion, but the countess had vetoed that idea. "What if Audrey is there tonight? No, no. You'll wear your hair down." And, Aurora noted as she observed herself in the mirror, Maritza had been right again; her dark hair with its red highlights provided a dramatic frame for her alabaster shoulders. The effect would have been ruined by the addition of a necklace, no matter how brilliant or precious the jewels.

When Maritza was finally satisfied, the two women proceeded to the waiting limousine. They were four now, no longer three. The "hired hand" on this occasion wore evening clothes as elegant and as expensively tailored as Tadzio's; Aurora understood that he'd performed this kind of "work" before.

Upon entering the Tudor mansion of director Anton Kalmar, Tadzio took Aurora's arm while Vance escorted Maritza into the foyer.

The house was already filled with the great and the near great. Aurora had been briefed in the car as to the scale of Anton Kalmar's party. It was on the "A" list. Maritza explained the unwritten rule: A-list people did not attend B-list or C-list parties. Nor were B- or C-list guests invited to "A" parties. Apparently the ups and downs of a career could be gauged by who was seen at which party. Anton Kalmar, Tadzio added, was still A-list, "despite his problems." Aurora wanted to inquire about the qualifying remark, but they had reached the house. It would have to wait until later.

After twenty minutes, she realized that this was similar to soirees they had attended in New York. For all the talk of A-, B-, or C-list parties, it was not unlike a Tony Rogers bash transported to another coast. The single noticeable difference was the quality of the conversation; fragments of exchanges she overheard revealed a single subject: movies. No one spoke of anything else. After a while, the gathering seemed to Aurora to be one enormous, formal business meeting masquerading as a party. Famous minds, dazzling intelligence were reduced to indulging in innocuous exchanges as a means of entering the latest schemes into the cocktail banter, a "new script you really ought to look at," or a client who would "be perfect for that

218

adventure flick you've optioned."

Since Aurora was a stranger, people approached her on one of two levels: the sexual, which she was gradually learning to handle; or the guarded, which fascinated and repelled her. In these last approaches, many questions were asked, superficial ones, in order to seek answers to the questions that could not be voiced: How important are you? Are you someone I should know? Can you do anything for me? When the answer turned out to be no, her questioners quickly excused themselves and moved on.

But the most disturbing discovery was that everyone emitted the same uneasiness—an almost palpable insecurity—despite the fact that each person present was at the very peak of his or her profession! These A-list people, the most successful in Hollywood, were all frightened, worried about their next moves.

Aurora found herself alone near the bar, a glass of champagne in her left hand, poised self-consciously. Maritza was deep in conversation with an aging glamour queen who had herself once been a princess. Aurora searched among the sea of guests for Tadzio, spotting him finally at the French doors leading out to the terrace. He was talking with Vance. *Why* did she feel that angry reaction at seeing them together? Was it necessary for Vance to stand that close, so very close, to Tadzio?

"Miss O'Brien?" said a male voice.

She turned to face her host, Anton Kalmar, who was brandishing a fresh bottle of champagne. They'd been introduced upon arriving, but Tadzio had immediately whisked her off to meet another group of people whose names she'd already forgotten.

"Mr. Kalmar. Hello."

"Hello," he replied. "I'm sorry we didn't have a

chance to talk earlier."

"You were busy greeting your guests. It's a lovely party."

"It's only as lovely as its guests. Your presence helps."

"Thank you," Aurora said with a modest laugh.

Kalmar smiled. His dark hair was tinged with gray, and he would have been handsome but for the sickly pallor evident despite his perfect tan.

"Tadzio has been telling me wonderful things about you." He lifted the champagne bottle, offering to refill her glass, and Aurora nodded.

"Tadzio is biased, I'm afraid. But thank you anyway."

"So you want to act?" His slight German accent was only revealed in the word *want,* the *w* pronounced as a *v.*

"I *do* act. Tadzio thinks I could do well out here."

"And you? What do you think?"

"I only arrived here today, Mr. Kalmar. I think I'm too green to venture a guess at that."

"'New and shiny'?"

"I'm sorry, but—"

"Ava Gardner to Clark Gable about Grace Kelly. *Mogambo.* John Ford for MGM, 1953."

"Oh," she said.

Kalmar smiled again. "You have no idea what I'm talking about, have you?"

"I've . . . well, I have seen the movie . . . on TV."

"You don't know that *I'm* the man you were brought to this party to meet, to be nice to. Do you?"

A conversation that had begun pleasantly enough had become ambiguous, and Aurora felt as if she were losing her footing. Trying to keep the color from rising in her face, she replied, "It's your party. I'm just another guest, Mr. Kalmar."

"Anton. Please."

"All right. Anton, I'm as 'nice' to you as I am to anyone I've met for the first time and know nothing about."

"Ah," he said with a sigh, filling his own glass from the bottle, "new and shiny . . . *and* smart."

"Thank you for noticing."

"Are you afraid I am going to seduce you?"

She met his stare with her own and said, "No. I'm just hoping you won't try."

He bowed slightly. "Touché." Then, coming up to his full height again, he asked, "Are you busy tomorrow afternoon?"

"I'll have to ask Tadzio."

"For permission?"

"Not for permission. I am his guest and he may have made plans for tomorrow afternoon. It would be rude to make him cancel them."

"Whatever they may be, they can wait. Tadzio will agree, that I assure you. Can you come to the studio at . . . say three o'clock?"

"Well, I suppose so . . . although—"

"I shall clear it with your prince. I am directing a new film, and we begin shooting in about two weeks. You are gorgeous—and right for the role. I would like you to read for me."

"Seriously?" Her voice rose.

"Seriously." Her question seemed to amuse him.

"Well . . ." This time Aurora was unable to control the warmth in her cheeks. "Yes. . . . Thank you . . . Anton."

"Don't be too grateful too soon. If you read well, there will be a screen test, but getting the role depends on the producer approving that test. There are a dozen other girls already at the test stage, and it is only a small role. Important, but small."

Aurora took another sip of her champagne, then smoothed a crease in her gown. "Actually, I'm relieved. I mean, if I do get it, I'd rather my first time out was not a leading role."

"Seriously?" He said it in the same tone she had used a moment before.

"Yes. Why?"

"Never mind." A grin had formed, crinkling the deep lines around his eyes. "One more question. Will you dine with me next Tuesday evening?"

"Is the seduction part of this about to appear?"

"I would be a liar if I said I did not have my hopes. Short of that, I would very much enjoy your company at dinner."

"In that case, I'd be flattered."

"I'll clear that with Tadzio too. See you tomorrow," he said. Then he moved off through the crush of guests, stopping to chat with Warren Beatty before he was lost in the crowd.

Aurora caught her own reflection in the mirrored wall to her left, and was surprised to see a silly, slightly dizzy smile on her lips. Her satisfaction with herself amused her and she giggled softly, wondering how much the champagne contributed to her new, good mood. She was pleased at the way she had handled her "interview" with Anton Kalmar and she liked him, whether or not she landed the role.

Feeling braver and more self-confident, she began to inch her way through the partygoers. The rustle of silk and the caress of chiffon mingled with the glitter of beads, sequins, and jewels. Physical perfection surrounded her on all sides as strains of music filtered in from the terrace where a band played. Through the French doors she could see couples dancing at the poolside.

The French doors. But no Tadzio. And no Vance.

She was momentarily relieved to find that they had separated, although that feeling was quickly replaced by doubt: what if they were still together, somewhere in private? Yet that possibility seemed less disturbing to her than it had before.

All the people in the room seemed to be talking, laughing, dancing with *someone*. Aurora was suddenly aware that only she was alone. A familiar, friendly face would be welcome now. A man in the entranceway resembled Eddie. Could he be here?

She wondered if that was beyond the realm of possibility. Did assistant directors get invited to these kinds of party? Was he A-list? She was fairly certain the answer to that question was no; still, she looked around the room, just in case. . . .

"Rory, darling."

Aurora turned to face Maritza. The ebony cigarette holder was empty, held as a prop between her index and middle fingers while two other fingers pinched a champagne flute, and her bejeweled pinky curled outward. The countess had obviously drunk more than her share. Aurora sensed a contentment in her, but didn't know if that was due to a champagne glow. Maritza's beautiful face and smooth skin shone with well-being.

"I didn't know where you'd gone," said Aurora. "You look happy."

"You see? I have my moments. You must come with me—instantly!"

She took Aurora's arm and dragged her a short distance, to a low chair near the fireplace. "There is someone you must meet, someone who must meet you. Sit here and do not move."

And she was gone.

Aurora watched her move away. Elbowing through and around various groups, she came to a halt before a

223

very tall man who stood at the center of the room. His back was to Aurora, but she could see the countess stare up at him and gesture toward the fireplace behind him.

"Champagne?" asked a red-jacketed waiter as he bent toward her, proffering his tray of sparkling, brimful glasses.

"Oh . . . why not?" Aurora accepted with a laugh and he handed her a glass and continued on his way.

When she turned to face the room once more, the figure of a man blocked her view. He stood quite near, the crush of the crowd having forced him almost to her chair.

Aurora's eyes traveled over his elegant black, silk-vested tuxedo and the shining V of his white silk shirtfront. This last was dotted with small sapphire studs, which winked at her. Her gaze then turned up to his face.

He was in his mid-forties, and deeply tanned. Health and vigor emanated from him as if they were colognes. His dark brown, almost black hair was worn long and curled behind his ears, and his temples were streaked with hints of oncoming gray, caught by the soft lighting of the room. But his eyes were what captured Aurora's own—for they were so like hers: emerald green, intense, yet sparkling with wit and promise.

She knew immediately that this was the man with whom the countess had been talking, but Maritza was nowhere in sight.

"Hello," he said, his deep baritone revealing the trace of a Midwestern drawl.

"Hello," she responded.

"Maritza sent me over to keep you company."

"That was nice of her. And of you."

He nodded an unspoken thank you, then extended his arm, the closed palm of his hand turned upward.

224

"Hold out your hands," he said.

Aurora placed her cupped palms together, puzzled but curious. From his fist fell a trickle of walnuts. She looked up into his twinkling eyes with amused surprise.

"I wish they were diamonds," he said.

Aurora knew a line when she heard it. She didn't care. It was a very good line.

He'd given his driver the night off, so he was driving the Porsche himself. She liked watching him drive. He maneuvered the exquisite machine with such assurance that the speed at which they were traveling did not alarm her. He took the curves with relaxed grace.

A full yellow moon hung low in the brilliant blue starlit sky, and the road before them seemed open and unobstructed, as they sped down its wide length, bathed in golden lunar light.

As they rounded a turn at the top of a hill, he took her hand in his and held it gently. "There," he said, nodding toward the shore.

Ahead of them lay the ocean, dark and silent but for the roar of waves that slapped the beach and then rushed away, leaving behind a glittering carpet of drenched, cool sand. A short distance from the shore, a shimmering glow twinkled in the quiet waters, the lights of a yacht beckoning, a welcome refuge from the land.

"The ship—" Aurora began.

"Boat. Or yacht, if you prefer," he corrected with a grin.

"It's yours?" Aurora tried not to sound impressed.

He nodded once more, and they began the quick descent down the incline toward a small dock.

"But I thought . . . I mean, when you said _home_, I assumed—"

"I didn't think you'd mind. After all, you've forced me to move here." Even in the dark, his eyes twinkled mischievously.

"I've forced you?"

"Yes. You have put me out of my own home."

"Excuse me, Harper," Aurora said, utterly confused. "I really don't understand."

He stopped the car at the foot of the dock, alongside which speedboats and a dinghy bobbed lazily in the soft swells of the harbor. Turning his face to hers, Harper leaned close, his green eyes penetrating hers.

"That house you and your trio are visiting. It's mine. I lend it to Maritza whenever she's in town."

"But why should you have to move out? It's enormous—there's certainly more than enough room for everyone."

"But this gives me my much-needed privacy, Aurora. And an excuse to bring you out here where we can be alone."

Her heart began to pound as his hand came to rest in the waves at the back of her neck. Then he opened the door of the car and led her to the dinghy.

He rowed swiftly and when they were alongside the yacht he swung himself aboard, then reached down and grasped her hand firmly. When he pulled, Aurora lifted herself up out of the dinghy and onto the ladder hanging over the side. After she was aboard Harper led her carefully and slowly to the rear deck, where she slid out of her silk sandals.

The only crew aboard was a man of about thirty, who had obviously been awakened by their arrival.

"Anything I can do, Mr. Styles?" he asked sleepily.

"I don't think so, Jack," answered Harper. "We can fend for ourselves. Thanks—and good night."

Jack grinned and headed below to his quarters.

"Where's he going?" asked Aurora.

"Crew sleeps through there," he said, nodding in the general direction Jack had taken. "I'll show you around tomorrow. For now . . . come with me."

The yacht was spacious but not ostentatious. Harper explained that he'd owned a larger vessel, an ocean-going yacht, but this better served his needs. "She's a seventy-seven foot Hatteras," he said. "I'm entertaining less these days, and the upkeep and crew required on the bigger one were becoming too time-consuming. It's more equipped for a quick getaway," he added as a joke.

Even this smaller boat offered more than ample space, however. The main deck, of rubbed teak, led to the main salon some twenty feet wide—"full beam," Harper explained. It had an enclosed bridge, mahogany walls, and polished brass appointments, sunken beige velvet sofa, and dark brown suede chairs. In the corner stood an antique jukebox, casting its neon glow of primary colors—reds, yellows, and blues—across the room. Harper turned on only one lamp, a ship's lantern, which gave off a candlelike pink light that was strangely harmonious with the glaring jukebox hues.

"It's exquisite, Harper!" Aurora exclaimed.

"I'm glad you like it. Come, I'll show you the master stateroom. It's just down those stairs. We'll leave the rest of the tour for later."

"Tomorrow, you said."

"Yes." He was across from her, beside the bar, but his eyes studied her, transfixing her as they did so.

She broke their gaze to move to the jukebox, her fingers lightly scanning the selection buttons of the vintage Wurlitzer.

"Does it work?" she asked.

"Oh, yes. And it's stocked with my favorites. A bit

227

eclectic, perhaps, but it's for my own amusement."

He joined her and led her back to the bar. "It was champagne, wasn't it?" he asked.

She nodded, accepting the crystal goblet from him. "But I've drunk quite a lot already tonight."

"A little more won't hurt. It'll help."

Now he was beside her, his green eyes again penetrating her very thoughts, Aurora felt. Her knees weakened and, as he reached up to caress the soft down of her cheek, she sighed, a long, shivering sigh. Harper pressed his body against hers, forcing Aurora against the smooth side of the jukebox, his mouth barely touching hers, teasing, promising; the warmth of his breath on her face, the sweet tingle beginning between her legs. Still he did not kiss her. Instead, he lifted one silk strap from her shoulder, the hot breezes created by his breathing caressing her smooth skin. His lips only brushed her as his mouth moved, lingered, and moved again down her shoulder.

Aurora's hands rested in his soft hair, her body arching to meet his, and a wave of pleasure surged up from inside her as she felt him harden between her legs, through the layers—too many layers—of clothing. Her hands dug into his hair now, pulling, forcing his head up to meet hers. Their eyes held for an instant before his mouth went hungrily to hers, their lips ravenously seeking, their tongues insatiably searching.

Aurora was amazed that this was happening. Never had she felt such a sudden, overwhelming need to have a man—*this* man—make love to her! It was right. It had to be! This she knew even before her body took control and erased any last doubts she might have entertained.

Harper began to lead her below toward the master stateroom, but as they moved to the stairs, they stopped and kissed again. His hands traced the outline of her hips, then held her firmly as his own gentle, thrusting movements sent the stronger, fiery flashes achingly through her groin. Her hand slid from his shoulder, down the front of his shirt, and slipped between their merging bodies, palm down over the length of his erect penis, now bulging beneath his velvet trousers. Harper's head bent then, his tongue circling the rising swell of her left breast. She wriggled free of the silk chiffon that still covered her nipple and his mouth replaced the silk, sucking deeply as the cap grew hard between his teeth, which gently nibbled at the crimson peak. Then he continued to journey down her body, his expert hands unfastening the zipper at her back and letting the green silk chiffon fall to the floor. Aurora heard herself cry out as Harper, now on his knees before her, inserted his tongue between the lace folds of her panties and into the moist sable mound beneath them as he burrowed his face deeply between her quivering legs.

Then his hands were at her hips, her knees, her ankles, and she was naked. She fell to her own knees to meet his mouth, the tongue that had plunged inside her, and he tore at his clothing, his bare chest coming against her breasts as they lay back together on the rug. Harper's index finger entered Aurora, and his thumb found her swollen clitoris and played with it before he moved inside, deeper and deeper. Aurora moaned at each new sensation, every new touch. She struggled with his belt, trousers, and shorts until he was free of them. Then she broke their kiss and bent to gaze upon his large, thickly veined penis, rolling back the last of the foreskin. Gently, she rolled her thumb across the eyehole at its tip, gleaming wet in the glow of the lantern light. She spread the sticky lubricant oozing from within over and across that orb. Harper's fingers were still inside her, and he removed them, wet with her arousal, and spread Aurora's juices over his penis, after which he took her hand and guided her to it again. It shone from their wetness, their desire. They could wait no longer.

As if responding to a silent cue, as Harper rolled over onto her, Aurora opened her legs to receive him, her need so profound she could scarcely breathe. Harper's pressure traced the outer contours of her vagina, teasing, prodding gently at the entrance, the bulb parting her lips slightly, then retreating, pressing back and forth, side to side, never enough for Aurora. She wanted to scream but could not locate her voice; it seemed lost, deep within her, where she longed for Harper to plunge himself. If he did not, she would be driven wild!

Their bodies gleamed with a thin matte of perspiration, they breathed as one, and she wanted their bodies to be one. Panting, reaching, welcoming . . . and finally . . . finally, when Aurora thought she could endure the wait no longer, Harper penetrated her with a thrust that did bring forth a scream—a deep, low, ecstatic scream. He throbbed inside her, against the walls of her body, his urgency growing as she strained and pushed herself to meet him, crying out with each retreat and with each entry, each thrust a new sensation, different, deeper than the last. Aurora wrapped her legs around him now and they moved together, bucking wildly, in a duet of raw, intense pleasure, as wave upon wave of orgasm drove her, crashed upon her. Harper increased his speed, plunging ever deeper, and at last he cried out. Aurora tightened the throbbing muscles that held him prisoner and pulled from him the spurting, shooting fluid, abandoning herself to new heights of frenzied passion as he filled her with himself, both of them coming, coming, coming. Together. They fell back finally, exhausted, spent. And it didn't matter that they had just met. Aurora felt she had been waiting for Harper Styles all of her life.

"We're almost there," Harper informed her softly. Aurora felt the car maneuver an easy turn and opened her eyes. She looked up at him.

His sharp, strong profile was lit by the bright morning sun that was reflecting off his dark glasses. She still weakened with desire at the sight of him.

She had awakened before Harper to find herself beside him in the master stateroom, although she hadn't recalled walking there. After their lovemaking, she didn't think her legs would have carried her anywhere. Leaning on an elbow, she had spent a full ten minutes watching him sleep, marveling at the power of his sleek, nude body, even in slumber. His handsome face was in repose, and she wondered at the response it evoked in her.

Pulling on a robe she found tossed over a chair, she made her way barefoot to the salon. His tuxedo, shirt, shoes, underwear; her dress and sandals, her panties, too, were all strewn across the carpeting where they had been left the night before. The jukebox was still lit.

Crossing to it, she reviewed the record selections. She was surprised at its offerings, but Harper had said the collection was eclectic. There were old songs— standards—and big band numbers interspersed with short classical pieces and an occasional Broadway show tune. Many of the titles were abbreviated in a code of sorts. Choosing at random, Aurora pressed H-1—the letter for Harper's initial and the digit for her own at the beginning of the alphabet. The selection read: Venus/Holst.

Aurora watched the exposed innards of the old machine remove a disc, and observed the needle move over it as it began to revolve on the turntable.

She pulled the cord on the draperies, unveiling a glass wall that overlooked the horizon. The sun, still low, seemed almost to touch the glittering water. Sliding the partition aside, she stepped onto a small upper deck. The cool morning breeze washed over her as the music played, ever so softly.

From behind her, a hand came to rest on her shoulder. She raised her head to accept his kiss on her neck.

"Good morning," he whispered.

"Mmm. Good morning."

Enfolded in Harper's arms, she leaned back against him, the rough terry of his scarlet robe rubbing the soft fabric of her own—another of his or one left behind by a guest. For a while, they watched the sun climb higher in the sky.

"Harper. The music . . . what is it?"

"The second movement from *The Planets*. Like it?"

"It's . . . wonderful. It's exactly the way I feel . . . exactly."

He turned her around and kissed her. "Me too."

Jack had prepared coffee, orange juice, and croissants, on which they breakfasted, and then Harper looked at the ship's clock.

"Say! We'd better get moving! I've a meeting in an hour!"

The Porsche came to a halt in the circular driveway in front of the house—Harper's house.

"Umm . . . thank you," Aurora murmured, moving closer to him.

"Oh, Rory," he said with a smile, pulling her into a gentle embrace. His equally gentle kiss contained an echo of the previous night's pleasure. "I'll call you this evening."

"Good," she replied, a beaming smile widening her lips.

Chapter Thirteen

Harper's house, she thought as she climbed quietly up the stairs. Aurora knew that Tadzio and Maritza had wanted her to spend the night with Harper Styles—that was obvious—nonetheless, Aurora's sense of modesty made her unwilling to be seen entering the house wearing last night's wardrobe. She would feel less vulnerable after a shower and a swim.

But as her foot reached the top step, the door to Tadzio's room opened slowly and Vance appeared, carefully closing the door behind him. Aurora recognized Tadzio's silk nightshirt—the very one she'd once transformed into a dress. She doubted Vance wore anything beneath it.

He yawned and, turning toward his own room, spied Aurora. Smiling, he stretched his arms, after which he leaned back against the wall and folded them in front of him.

"Well, good morning," he said, nodding his head so that his tousled hair fell over his left eye.

She returned the nod and took a step past him.

"You dress up nice for breakfast."

She stopped and faced him, her color rising. But she was at a loss for words.

Vance was still grinning. "Your room is down there, in case you're lost," he said, pointing his finger in its direction.

"So is *yours,*" she replied, hurrying down the hallway with as much dignity as she could muster.

Since Aurora did not know the kind of role she would be reading for, she wasn't sure what she should wear. Trusting her instincts while bearing in mind Maritza's constant council—"Simple! Simple!"—she decided upon a Halston summer-wool jersey in a shade of dusty rose. Its color would balance any escaping blush while complementing the red tones of her hair.

The house had been quiet for most of the day, but it was afternoon now, so Maritza sat in the dining room. Its large windows overlooked the pool and Vance, who was exercising on the grass alongside of it.

As Aurora entered the room, the countess placed her cup of espresso in its delicate porcelain saucer and then dragged deeply on her empty ebony cigarette holder; Aurora wondered if Maritza expected to find residual smoke lurking inside.

Giving up the attempt, the older woman looked up and studied her protégé.

"Am I all right?" asked Aurora.

"Except for the brooch, perfect. Come here."

Dutifully, Aurora sat down in the chair and Maritza removed the pin. "Well? Tell me?"

"Tell you what?" But Aurora knew.

"Did you two . . . hit it off, as they say?"

Aurora's eyes remained on the brooch that Maritza had placed in her hand. "He's a wonderful man."

"Yes . . . every woman I know has said as much. For a time, at least."

"Meaning?"

"Meaning that you are young and beautiful, Rory. Enjoy him. Enjoy yourself. He is handsome and powerful. He can do much for you. You could do worse."

Aurora sighed in annoyance.

"What?" asked Maritza. "What is it?"

Aurora paused, collecting her thoughts. Then, slowly, she said, "He's wonderful. Why does there have to be a . . . a price tag on it?"

"Price tag?"

"Yes. That's what you're implying, isn't it? His being powerful had nothing to do with last night. Yes, he's handsome, but—"

"Then please accept my apology."

"Thank you."

"You are seeing him again?"

Aurora felt a sudden rush inside. "He said he'd call."

"Oh. Then I'm certain he will."

Aurora detected a note of disappointment in the countess' voice and was unable to determine why. It alarmed her. "Maritza, you know him well . . . *will* he call?" She tried to disguise the anxiety in her voice.

"Most likely, Rory." The countess sighed and then added, "Yes, he will call. But now you must be off to your audition, yes?"

Aurora looked at the Piaget wristwatch Tadzio had insisted upon buying her, despite protestations. "Will the driver take me?"

"Oh, no! How unthinking!"

"What? Maritza, what's the matter?"

"Tadzio! I do love him, but at times he is such a fool! He's taken the car!"

"Well, there must be another way to get to the studio. Is there a bus—"

A loud laugh from behind interrupted her question and Aurora turned to see Vance, dripping with perspiration as he stood in the glass doorway that led to the pool.

"A *bus!*" He laughed again. "Honey, this is L.A. You gotta *drive* out here!"

Maritza rose and placed a hand on Aurora's wrist. "He's right. We'll have to see about getting you your own car."

"But Maritza—"

"What is it?"

Aurora gulped, wondering why she felt embarrassed. "I . . . I don't know how to drive."

Vance and Maritza stared at her. Aurora sensed they regarded her as a creature with two heads. In her own defense, she said, "Well I can't be the only person you know who doesn't drive!"

They continued to stare blankly at her.

"You mean . . . I am?" Her voice rose half an octave.

Maritza laughed softly, then shook her head as Vance came nearer. "Look, I've got my heap parked around in back. It's no Rolls, but it'll get us there. I'll drive you to the studio, wait for you—out of sight if you want—and then drive you back here."

Aurora wanted to decline his offer, but she realized there was no other choice. "What about a taxi?"

"Out of the question," said the countess. "*He*"—she gestured in Vance's general direction—"is right. He will drive you there."

"And I offer my services as a driving teacher as well, whenever you want. So . . . you ready to go?"

"Yes," said Aurora. "As soon as you put on a shirt."

He bristled. "Should I take a shower first?"

"Nice of you to offer," she answered, returning his stare. "But there isn't enough time."

*   *   *

238

Everything Aurora knew about Anton Kalmar had been gleaned from Maritza and Tadzio. His history was impressive. So impressive that his office came as a shock.

She had been told that Kalmar had fled Nazi Germany and had worked in England for the ten years preceding his Hollywood career. Once in Hollywood, he had directed most of the great female stars and had twice been nominated for the Academy Award. His name commanded respect in the industry. So Aurora could not understand why she was led down a long, dark, gray corridor lined with cubicles built around metal desks. There were no doors only partitions separated one person from another. The clatter of typewriters, the voices speaking into telephones or dictaphones combined to create a cacophony that set Aurora's already unsteady nerves jangling.

"Ah! Miss O'Brien!" Anton Kalmar called upon spotting her at the entrance to his cubbyhole. His name was stenciled on the outer wall, that single mark distinguishing it from the identical cubbyholes.

He thanked the guard who had accompanied Aurora and, taking her hand in his, led her to the folding bridge chair set up in front of his metal desk.

"You seem . . . disappointed," he said, studying her as he gestured to his surroundings. "Hardly what you had expected, I imagine?"

"Well . . . I admit—"

"Nor what I had expected either. I used to have an office. A real office in the main building. They've given it to some college boy."

He sniffed, picked up a script, and handed it to her. "Here. Pages twenty-five through thirty-five. Take a moment to look it over. Ask me any questions you might have. Then we'll begin. Will you excuse me?"

He rose and left her alone. Uncomfortably alone,

despite the peripheral noises. She began to read through the scene. It was very dramatic and badly written. She scanned it once, quickly, then skipped around the script to see if she could fill in some character background. Gradually she realized that it was a "psychedelic" rehash of *Dr. Jekyll and Mr. Hyde*. The role she was reading closely resembled that of the dancehall girl enslaved by the evil Hyde. She'd seen the most recent film version of that tale, and the heartbreaking performance by Ingrid Bergman. But this? Not even Bergman could have made this work. The transition from joy to terror was too abrupt, the motivation for that terror totally lacking; and the character modeled after Hyde didn't behave badly enough to warrant the reaction called for in the script.

She read the scene again.

By the time Aurora had reread it for the third time, Anton Kalmar reentered the "office."

"Ready?" he asked, sniffing once more.

"I think so."

"Questions?"

"It is a remake of *Dr. Jekyll and Mr. Hyde,* isn't it?"

"My God, you're well read too. Yes, darling, it is. Dreadful, no?"

She smiled. "Yes."

"A true, straightforward answer. Most girls would have said it had 'possibilities.' You still want this role?"

"Of course," she answered. "I'm hardly in a position to turn it down."

"'That's right. It could be a start for you. Now"—he picked up a duplicate copy of the script from the center of his desk—"you may stand or sit . . . move around . . . whatever you like. I will read Nestor and you, of course, will read Gaby. I shall cue you in at the bottom of twenty-four."

They began. As the reading progressed, Aurora

wondered if Anton Kalmar had ever been an actor. He was marvelous, bringing to the lines a meaning that did not appear on the printed page. If the actor cast in the part were half as good, he might elevate the script to more than it was. As it was, Kalmar helped her with his subtle reading of the sadistic Hyde, enabling Aurora to reach the emotion required for the climactic moment when Gaby pleaded for her life, fearing she would be murdered.

And then the scene was finished.

"Thank you. Very nice."

It was all he said.

Aurora hesitated, not sure whether to stay or to leave.

"Is that it?" she asked, her adrenaline still high.

"Yes, Miss O'Brien. That is it. Very nice. Oh, you'll certainly get a test. You had that before you walked in here."

She felt a wave of anger well up inside her and then subside. In that case, why had she needed to read? "I had the test?"

"But you knew that, of course?"

"Well, no. Actually I didn't. But I do now. It's a . . . favor?"

"Exactly."

"Whether I'm any good or not has nothing to do with it?"

"Not with the test. But you are quite good. You'd have gotten a test even if Tadzio were not my friend."

"But I wouldn't have gotten this reading. I'm beginning to understand."

It didn't do her ego much good, but she decided to believe him. She thanked him and rose.

"We have a dinner engagement on Tuesday?" he asked, not rising from behind his desk.

"Yes. Even if I *hadn't* gotten the test. . . . We all do

favors, don't we?"

Vance leaned over from the driver's seat of his rusting VW and opened the passenger door.

"You're parked in James Garner's reserved space," Aurora remarked, pointing to the sign in front of the car as she slid in beside him.

"It was vacant," he answered, starting the motor.

"What if he'd driven up?"

"I'd have moved."

Vance shifted into reverse, then stepped on the gas pedal, causing Aurora to be thrown forward. Shifting into drive, he roared out of the parking lot toward the main gate, barely missing two costumed extras en route to the commissary.

"Well, how'd it go?" he asked, mopping his neck with a red bandana. The afternoon sun was hot and the VW had no air conditioning.

Aurora allowed a few moments to elapse before answering as she watched the traffic—wealthy traffic— go by. Bentleys, Rolls Royces, Porsches. It suddenly struck her as amusing that amidst this parade of expensive machinery, the two of them were roasting in a sticky, sweaty old jalopy while on their way to a hacienda in Beverly Hills.

"What's so funny?" asked Vance.

"They are." She nodded toward the passing cars. "They are and we are." She brushed her hair back, sweeping it off her neck. "I got the test, for whatever it's worth."

"Great."

She raised an eyebrow and faced front, avoiding his glance. Even so, she could tell he hadn't missed a thing.

"Hey . . . no, really. It's great. I'm glad for you."

"Thanks," she said, digging into her totebag for a

242

ribbon and bobby pins.

She tied her hair up and back, securing it with a tortoise-shell barrette. When she finished, the effect was more Katharine Hepburn than Audrey, as if she realized she had no one else to impress this afternoon. When she looked back at Vance, he had a surly expression on his face.

"Something wrong?" she asked. "It's sweltering in here."

He opened the window all the way as he said, "You know, I meant it when I said I'm glad you got the test. You've already gotten farther than I ever did."

"You?" Aurora asked, suddenly interested. "You act?"

"Ha! I wouldn't call it that, but it's what everybody does out here. Or tries to do."

"I guess I've been lucky. I've met some of the right people."

Vance turned from the road to meet her eyes. "And I haven't? We're both in that house, aren't we?"

"Yes. We are." She thought she understood what he was getting at, but feared she had misconstrued his remark. Still, even if that was his implication, could she really take offense? Was there that much difference between them?

"You've given up, then? Acting, I mean."

"I'm sitting it out. I'm too young to be a leading man and too old to be a kid anymore. So, I rent."

"Rent?" Aurora asked. This time she didn't understand his meaning.

But he looked at her again, the same way he and Maritza had looked at her in the dining room, and suddenly she understood. "Oh," she said.

"Hey! I didn't mean *you* do! I know you don't. After all, I see the layout at the house and you're certainly not bedding the countess!"

243

"What?" Aurora resisted the urge to slap his face only because he was driving.

"Oh, come on, Aurora—can I call you Rory, too? Aurora's too much to say. Anyway," he went on, not awaiting permission, "haven't you seen the way Maritza eyes you? You don't think that's all motherly instinct, do you? Christ, how long have you been hanging around with the two of them?"

Perhaps it was the heat—or her nerves from the audition. Perhaps she was tired. Whatever the cause, she felt a sudden nausea. She held her head in her hands, the windshield swimming before her in a dizzy blur.

When her vision cleared, Aurora realized the car had stopped and they were pulled over onto a grassy shoulder of the road. Vance reached over to the small backseat and from a white styrofoam cooler he pulled out two cans of beer. He opened them and passed one to her. "Here. I got these for the beach after I drop you off. It's all I've got but at least it's cold."

She hated beer, but it didn't matter. It was cold. She drank it with gusto, then pressed the cool, sweating can to her forehead. Sighing, she leaned back against the seat.

"God," she half whispered. "I'm so naïve! I'm feeling so stupid!"

"How old are you?"

Aurora hesitated. In the world she was coming to know this was a dangerous question, even for someone still very young. "How old are you?" she countered.

"I asked you first. I'm twenty-six."

Twenty-six and he's worried, she thought. What the hell. "I'm nineteen," she answered self-consciously.

"You're a kid. But you're wising up fast."

"Am I?"

"Sure. Besides, you're safe in this setup. Maritza

244

doesn't like me, but both she and Tadzio are crazy about you."

Resting on her left hip, Aurora positioned herself between the seat and the door. "Well, I guess you're safe too. Tadzio seems to like you a lot."

"Tadzio *loves* me. I saw to that last night."

Odd, she reflected. An hour before, she would have found that remark disturbing. Now, she asked, "People . . . men . . . fall in love with you that easily?"

"Men . . . women . . . depends on how broke I am, and I am *very* broke right now. No. Not that easily. But Anton knows what Tadzio likes. I'm it. The rest was simple."

"It's all pretty cut and dried, isn't it? A job. Right?"

Vance took a swig of the beer, wiping the can's condensation on his T-shirt. "I guess that's the bottom line. But I like him. I even like *her*—the countess."

"That was obvious to everyone, even me. Tadzio saw it too."

"Yeah, I almost blew it when I gave her the eye. I didn't know for sure what the setup was, you know?"

"No. What do you mean?"

"Well, I've been in . . . situations . . . where I've . . . uh . . . serviced . . . more than one person in a house."

"God, Vance!" She laughed suddenly. "What do you do for fun?"

He wiped his mouth with the back of his tanned arm and returned the laugh. "I go to the movies."

Her laughter built, increasing in both volume and intensity. She didn't know why, but it didn't matter. Vance's laughter became uncontrollable, too, and tears rolled down his cheeks.

When they had regained their composure, Aurora realized that Vance was grinning, calmly, at her. She also realized she no longer wanted to avert her eyes from his dazzling smile. Her reason to fear him was gone.

"I'm glad we've . . . talked," she admitted softly.

"Yeah. We understand each other, I think."

She smiled. "I think."

When they were driving again, Aurora asked how Vance had come to know Anton Kalmar.

"I was young. Like you. Well, *not* like you. Anyway . . . Anton's wife . . . I think it was his second wife . . . took a liking to me. Anton was a big name then."

"I thought he still was. Until this afternoon."

"You noticed, huh? Oh, he works, but not like in the past. I mean, two Oscar nominations, Directors' Guild award. His name even got into the *New York Times* crossword puzzle—so I read in a magazine."

Aurora's mind envisioned the bleak surroundings in which she had auditioned a short while ago. "What happened to him?"

"Oh," Vance continued, "his wife wanted me, to be blunt. Anton was already heavy into coke. He bought me to keep her happy. And his career . . ."

"What about his career?"

"It's going right up his nose. Everybody knows it."

Aurora nodded. That explained why his office consisted of a converted warehouse corner, why he was working on a seamy script unworthy of a once-considerable talent. Anton Kalmar had become a risk.

"What happened to his wife?"

"She got old. Had her face done. They split. She lives in a villa in Mexico on her settlement from the divorce. Keeps twenty-five-year-old boys around her just like always." Vance turned the VW into the driveway. "And what happened to me is that I got old too. See?"

Yes, she thought with a shudder. I'm beginning to see.

"Look in the dining room, Rory," Maritza called from beneath her canopy by the pool.

Two dozen long-stemmed red roses stood at the center of the table. A card was propped against the base of the vase.

> The second movement of *The Planets* is called "Venus—Bringer of Peace."
> A metaphor for you.
>
> Harper

He wasn't even present in the room with her, yet her legs weakened momentarily, while a small spark of desire kindled and made her want him again.

She was relieved and happy. Even peaceful. And suddenly quite tired. Constantly on the go since their arrival, Aurora decided on a nap. Tadzio was still out, and she heard Vance rev up his motor and roar from the driveway, probably headed for the beach. Maritza remained at poolside, quietly reading. The house was silent.

But her sleep was not as restful as it might have been. Strange dreams, not nightmares but disturbing nonetheless, wove in and out of her mind. Henry O'Brien, her father, appeared in shadowy form, his arms outstretched to her. Then Harper, filling her own open arms with mountains of red roses, Heathcliff filling Cathy's arms with heather.

When Aurora awoke, it was early evening. Someone was knocking at her bedroom door.

"Come in," she called groggily.

Tadzio entered, dressed to go out, except for shoes, which would probably be dark brown to match the dark slacks and the silk shirt he wore.

"Hungry?" he asked.

Aurora thought for a moment, then decided. "Yes, I am."

"Good. An old friend of mine invited us for dinner, and we're due there in an hour."

An hour. She must, of course, look wonderful, even if the dress was casual.

"Tadzio, I'm . . . tired. Could you make my apologies?"

She saw color rise in his face, his brows knit together. "We're doing this for you, Rory."

He'd never voiced that fact before, and Aurora wasn't sure what her response should be.

"I know, but . . . well, it seems only fair that you'd let me know these things at least a day in advance—"

"Sometimes, darling, I don't *know* a day in advance."

"Fine, Tadzio. It's just that I need some time to relax, to unwind a little."

"Rory, if you want success—"

"I want to rest!" she blurted out. "We've only just arrived here! I don't even know my way around this house!"

"Well, don't expect Vance to show it to you this evening if you stay here!"

She stared at him. "I can't believe you said that to me," she answered quietly.

The color drained from his face, crimson became pale white beneath his bronze tan. Tears welled in his eyes as he approached the bed and sat down on the edge of the mattress.

"I'm sorry, darling," he said at last, wiping his cheeks. "Oh, God," he cried in mock fury, "I'll get tears all over my shirt and ruin the silk!" Then he began to laugh.

Aurora moved closer to him, putting an arm around his shoulder.

"Dear Tadzio, you really have it bad, haven't you?"

He nodded. "Stupid, I know. But there's something about him—it's more than just beauty. He's like . . . like a younger version of myself. Me without the money. Misguided. He needs me."

She leaned her head against him and whispered, "Or you need him to need you."

"Same thing."

She disagreed, but chose not to voice her thoughts. "He's going with you tonight?"

Tadzio nodded again, answering, "I bought him some new clothes. That's where I was all day. Shopping."

Aurora smiled. She knew him well enough to recognize that he needed only the slightest excuse for shopping. "Then go and show him off. I'd like to write a letter."

He looked into her eyes and kissed her quickly on the lips. "Did Harper call?"

"No, but he sent roses."

"I saw them. And the card. The man does have taste."

"Mmm. Definitely. Maybe he'll call tonight. That's another reason I'd like to stay in this evening."

"All right," he said, hugging her. "Take this night to be alone. We'll say you had a prior engagement."

He left her room then, and Aurora seated herself at the dressing table.

Dear Abby,
    Happy birthday, honey.
    A lot has happened, too much to write in any

249

great detail, but I want to get this off to you right away because it's been such a long time since I've written.

You'll see from the return address on this envelope that I'm no longer in New York. I know we talked about your visiting me there, but this move to California was very sudden—and I promise I'll make it up to you.

Very soon, I'd like you to come out here for a visit. I'll show you the sights as soon as I've seen them myself and know my way around a little better. I'm going to learn to drive a car, so we'll have lots of fun together. Instead of Radio City, we'll go to Disneyland, okay?

Aurora put down the pen and reread the letter. She reminded herself to write Betsey and Joe to learn the best time for Abby to come. It should be soon, she thought; time was flying by. Before long, Abby would leave childhood behind. Aurora wondered if it was as lonely a time for her little friend as it had been for her. She hoped not, but she knew that Abby's sensitive nature was much like her own.

Promising to shop tomorrow for a pretty party dress and to have it sent to her "sister," Aurora finished the letter, adding S.W.A.K. and a series of XXXs at the bottom.

She was preparing a sandwich in the kitchen when the telephone rang.

It was Harper Styles.

Chapter Fourteen

Anton Kalmar had already excused himself twice during dinner, once to go to the men's room at the rear of the plush restaurant, once to make a telephone call. On both occasions he returned to the table with a case of sniffles. Aurora wondered if he suffered from a sinus problem or if Vance's stories were true.

The third time, she was left sitting in front of her unwanted chocolate mousse. Boredom inspired reflections on the director. He'd been animated, convivial, when he'd called for her at the house. The realization that his enthusiasm again soared after each absence from the table at first shocked Aurora. Then shock turned into a kind of pity, and finally to awe as she listened to his conversation. He spoke incessantly, but it was never prattle; whatever the effect of his stimulant—or depressant—it did not appear to dull his mind or his wit. Aurora couldn't fathom why a talent, a mind of this caliber, would permit himself to become enslaved by such an addiction, an addiction that was proving anathema to his once-dazzling career.

She realized, gazing into her mousse, that she was not bored with Anton Kalmar's company but with his addiction.

The restaurant was one of those quiet little havens of the famous and rich; it was designed to provide surcease from the public eye. The high-priced private memberships assured that anyone dining here belonged to the same "club," and beyond nodding to one another or greeting an occasional table hopper, the patrons were left to themselves. Although Aurora disliked the idea that celebrities appeared to know only other celebrities, there did seem to be another side— their side—to exclusivity: in some ways, "members" could only trust one another.

Aurora watched Anton as he reemerged from the back, smiling again. He stopped at a table to chat with a television star and his wife before rejoining Aurora.

Throughout dinner, the director had been interesting, attentive, charming, and informative. Indeed, Aurora had begun to relax when, during the fish course, it became apparent that tonight was *not* going to be about sex. She felt relief. She liked the man and hoped he might become a friend, without the complication of having to fend off passes. After their initial exchange at his house party, that possibility had presented itself, although her audition at the studio had been on a strictly professional basis.

Aurora was becoming aware of subtle rules regarding men's sexual attentions that previously she had only sensed. Some men, men like Anton Kalmar, seemed to think it their duty to make an approach. For them it was an expected kind of behavior rather than a genuine wish to bed a particular woman. In their view some unspoken pressure from both sexes demanded such attempts be made. She wondered how many times both parties followed through when neither really wanted to. A ridiculous reality.

Anton summoned a waiter and ordered his second cognac. "You haven't touched your mousse," he noted.

"I can't, Anton. Dinner was excellent, but I didn't leave room for dessert." She tossed her long hair back, brushing it behind one ear with her hand, and when her eyes met his once more, she noted a strange expression on his face. He was staring at her, studying her intently.

"Anton," she said almost in a whisper, "do I have spinach or lipstick on a tooth?"

He laughed. "No, no! I just realized something about you. It was . . . well . . . startling."

"What?"

"You look like someone familiar to me."

That surprised her. Aurora had not often been told she resembled anyone else. Not since childhood, anyway, when Aunt Frances had commented upon her likeness to Henry.

"I do?"

"Yes. The likeness is quite striking. Odd, I hadn't noticed it before. Must be the candlelight. By the way, candlelight becomes you. Remember that. And always sit as you are, to the left of the flame. It illuminates your left profile, which, you must know of course, is your better side."

She nodded. Photographers had told her that. But they had also pointed out that most people were inclined to have better left profiles than right.

Changing the subject then, Anton launched into a discussion of Aurora's screen test. It was scheduled for the following week, in the midafternoon. "You'd have to get up at five in the morning to look decent by eight. This will be easier for you, and for us all. Full crew, lights, sound." He explained that a contract player would be assigned to do the test scene with her. Then he handed her the same "sides" from the script she'd read at the audition.

"Gaby's French, isn't she?" asked Aurora.

"Yes. Although she has lived in the States for some

253

time. There are a few foreign words, but you seemed to have grasped the pronunciation at your reading in my office. Besides, should you be cast in the role, we'll have a dialogue coach to help you with the accent."

She glanced over the scene again. The lines were no problem; there weren't that many of them. But it was a highly charged, emotional scene; Aurora was grateful she'd have time to work on it before the test. She was about to ask about her costume when she noticed Anton staring again.

"I'm sorry," he offered in apology, "but it is really quite amazing." Then he asked, "Rory, my dear, have you friends out here? I mean besides Tadzio and the countess?"

She almost said no; then she thought better of it. Anton was a friend, in a way, although she knew that wasn't what he meant. Harper Styles? But who could possibly know about Aurora and him? And there was one other.

"I knew someone who came to New York to do a film. We met on the set. I don't know if we're still friends, though."

"Have you been in touch since your arrival?"

"No," she answered.

"One needs friends in this town. Perhaps I know this . . . man. It is a man, isn't it?"

She nodded. "His name is Eddie Calvert."

"Ah," said Anton, smiling, "my compliments on your discerning taste. He's one of the best A.D.s in the business."

Aurora hesitated before asking the next question but at last gave in. "How is he? What's he been doing?"

"Fine, I imagine. Always busy. I think he's working on the Streisand film. In which case he's out of town. They're due to wrap in a week or so."

Well, it wouldn't have done any good to try to look

him up after all, although she had to admit she'd like to talk with him again. Or would she, considering their last meeting . . . altercation . . . whatever?

They were midway through the drive to Harper's house when Anton pulled the car over to the side of the road. The night was clear; the smog had lifted momentarily. Aurora was just going to ask why they had stopped when Anton extracted from the glove compartment a small silver bottle and its matching silver straw.

"Anton . . ." she began.

He waved a hand, silencing her, and then snorted, inhaling the drug into his nostrils with a desperate force. Then he turned and held out the substance to her.

Aurora stared at his hands, fascinated by the delicate little shiny straw. She was curious, she confessed to herself. Still, she knew there had been a time when Anton Kalmar had been offered his first opportunity to try the powder. He had done so, and the result was exacting a toll on his career. Aurora's career was in embryo. Besides, what if she liked the stuff? Liked it a lot, as he obviously did?

"Thanks, I'll pass," she said with a nervous smile.

"Good girl," he said, unoffended. "You've never done it, have you?"

"No." She felt embarrassed, not unlike a teenager ashamed to admit her virginity. Another kind of peer pressure.

"It's part of the life, you know. Correction. Part of *my* life."

"Why, Anton?"

He shrugged. "It was fun. Chic. I accomplished so much, at first. It gave me tremendous energy and I did wonderful things. Now I do things that are not so wonderful in order to pay for my habit. It's quite expensive, you know."

Aurora's screen test went as "smoothly as could be expected," she was told by the cameraman. She hadn't been nervous, but, in her own mental replay, she didn't think it had gone well. The French accent had not presented a problem, but she had twice become tongue-tied and stumbled over pronunciation, particularly when she'd linked the guttural French *r*, produced at the back of the throat, to a word beginning with *t*, dentalized forward in the mouth. Anton had called "Cut," and the second time he'd offered to rewrite the phrase. Unsure whether this gesture was to make it easier for her or to save the time it required to get it right, Aurora asked to try it once more as written. Her training had taught her to say her lines exactly as they were written by the author, with no paraphrasing, and although she was quickly learning that in films, nothing was done exactly as written, she disliked relinquishing the discipline she'd worked so hard to attain.

They shot it once more. The third time it was perfect.

She had achieved a warm, professional rapport with the crew, especially with the lighting man. For this she was grateful; she knew he had the technical power to destroy her, regardless of her performance.

The test had taken three hours. Anton had excused himself twice, the second time for nearly half an hour. Aurora had overheard an exchange between the sound man and a production assistant. The sound man wondered aloud as to whether the director had "fallen in."

"Not yet," the production assistant had replied.

"You'll know when he's back. He sniffs his way onto the set. You'll hear him." The two men and a few others within earshot had laughed.

The studio contract player hired to act opposite Aurora in the test had seemed hostile. In the actual film, the role would be portrayed by an aging matinee idol, long past his prime and now relegated to horror movies. This picture would be a step up for him. However, the actor doing the test was obviously bored by the proceedings. The sparse offscreen conversation Aurora had with him had revealed that for the past two years other people's screen tests had comprised the bulk of his film work. He'd been feeding actors their lines, his own back to the camera most of the time. His one role had been as a surfer in an episode of a TV series. He had drowned in the first ten minutes. Beyond that, he made his living by escorting stars to parties and premières. Aurora's thoughts strayed to Vance and his situation—not all that different. It seemed that in this business a young man's life paralleled a woman's and was, at best, frustrating. Still, they were the lucky ones, and despite her sympathy for a fellow actor's dilemma, Aurora resented his I-don't-give-a-damn attitude, for it gave her nothing to work with during her highly dramatic scene. But she had acquired some technique, so she did compensate for the lack of tension.

Tired and deflated, at least she was amused when, at the end of the shoot, she emerged from the soundstage to find the Rolls waiting to meet her. She smiled as Vance, in full livery, waved at her—his eyes were crossed. It was a successful attempt to relieve her embarrassment at this ostentatious display. Quickly he got out of the car, ran around to the rear door, and, before opening it, whispered, "Get in, Garbo."

Maritza sat in the back, costumed like a dowager empress. As Aurora settled in beside her, she became

257

aware for the first time that the countess was overdressed. It concerned her only briefly. Obviously, Maritza was en route to a formal reception, and if she was not, Aurora was too exhausted to care. She'd been so eager to leave the studio that she hadn't even bothered to remove her makeup, which had been applied hours earlier and had been touched up countless times throughout the afternoon. Now she just wanted to wash her face, have a glass of wine, and sink into a bath.

She leaned back against the velvet seat and closed her eyes, sighing as the car started up and began to move slowly toward the main gate.

With her left ear she heard a soft "Tsk." She ignored it. Again she heard "Tsk." And then another.

"What is it, Maritza?" asked Aurora, her eyes still closed.

"*What* have they done to you?"

"What do you mean?"

"You allowed them to photograph you—like *that?*"

"Yes, Maritza, I did. Why?"

"I *knew* I should have gone with you and overseen things! Rory, you look like a whore!"

"Gaby is a whore, Maritza."

The short silence in the back of the car was followed by a quiet "Oh." It was the last thing Aurora heard before dropping into a weary sleep for the duration of the drive home.

The following day she had her first driving lesson with Vance.

The day after that, she was notified that she had been cast as Gaby in *Duo for One*. Her billing would immediately follow the title credit: "Introducing Aurora O'Brien."

She had three weeks before shooting began. She saw Harper often during this time, usually spending the night with him aboard the yacht, once an entire, glorious weekend.

The tranquility of these days was marred only by her nightly dreams. They were not fantasies—her life seemed more fantasy than reality—nor were they symbolic allegories. In them frightening apparitions loomed until Aurora found herself begging, within the dream, for it to be only a dream. Waking brought relief, but a certain amount of anxiety remained.

These dreams centered always around her father, the father she had never known. Why, she wondered, after all these years, was this coming to the fore? She missed him, even longed for him. Harper's kindness and consideration as a lover became more and more important. She desired him, but she needed him almost as much as she wanted him.

And still the dreams persisted. . . .

"No, no!" the costume designer fumed. "The fabric should be taut across the bustline, and it won't do that unless you wear the blouse off the shoulders."

Dutifully, Aurora slid the elastic over her shoulders, but she didn't like the effect; it was too cheap. Besides, now she would need body makeup in addition to that already applied to her face and neck.

"Good," said Jolie. "I'll go and get Marvin. You'll need a good tan."

Aurora nodded, realigning the falsie over her left breast; it seemed to be straying beneath an armpit. She hated the damned things, but she conceded Anton's point that Gaby's character should be "fuller." Nevertheless, to give credibility to the padding, her own breasts had been shoved together and pushed painfully high to create décolletage. It was not only very uncomfortable, she felt Jolie had overdone it; the artificially induced "swell of her bosom" seemed to pop out from the center of her sternum. Poor Gaby, she thought, staring at herself in the mirror. Poor Aurora, too.

At least they'd left her hair alone, allowing it to fall fully across her soon-to-be-tanned shoulders; two small combs above each temple kept the waves from cascading over her face and blocking her profile.

She had not yet met Miles Hogarth, the star of the film. Now, as Marvin opened her dressing room door, she saw him advancing toward her, past the canvas chairs, the cameras, the lights, stepping gingerly over lengths of cord and cable, his arms extended in traditional Hollywood welcome.

"Miss O'Brien," he said in a mildly affected, somewhat pseudo-British accent, "I saw your test. Truly wonderful. I am honored."

Aurora's tension melted away, and with relief, she smiled back at him. "You're very kind—and flattering. I've long admired your work."

It wasn't a lie. The work she had admired had been done in films made more than twenty years ago. Not only had Miles Hogarth once been devastatingly handsome, he'd been a brilliant actor as well. However, his brilliance had been tarnished by years of "good living," and his popularity with the public had waned as had his looks, talent, and reputation. The films in which he had recently appeared caused Aurora to regard him as a man who would do practically anything for money. Hogarth had been one of a handful of world-class actors who had been offered a chance at greatness—and he had blown it. Only his former ability made him worthy of Aurora's respect.

As they chatted, her eyes strayed over his shoulder,

beyond him, over the forest of steel trees topped with bulbs, cameras, gels, and, above them, a solid mass of lighting equipment. In the small clearing below this mass of machinery sat the tiny set that was Gaby's flat; all the surrounding technology was aimed right at it.

Strange, she thought, as Hogarth made comparisons between Fredric March's Hyde and Spencer Tracy's, it requires all this sophisticated preparation to create the illusion of a warm, homey, down-at-the-heels apartment. And this picture doesn't even have much of a budget; Aurora knew it was being made very frugally. Nonetheless, she was impressed. The set looked authentic: turn-of-the-century Boston. Only the man in the middle of the room was out of place. His back faced her as he knelt on the floor, placing a strip of gaffer's tape across a section of Oriental rug. His bright red T-shirt, faded jeans, and sneakers were anachronistic.

He rose then, calling out, "Okay, Anton, that's her first mark."

The sound of his voice sent a sting through Aurora's heart and up her backbone. He turned to face the camera, which was aimed at the spot, eyeballing the distance that would shortly be triple-checked with a tapemeasure.

He'd gained weight, although not too much; it wasn't unbecoming. His hair was shorter and he had grown a mustache. But the face was the same. He was still Eddie Calvert.

As if he had felt Aurora's eyes upon him, his own eyes darted to where she stood and met hers. She smiled a nervous, wan little grin, holding it, waiting for some kind of acknowledgment. It was not forthcoming. Eddie's face remained immobile, staring back at her with no expression. At last, he gave her a simple nod and yelled for the stand-in to take her place on the mark.

261

Hogarth was called away by Jolie, who had decided to exchange his purple satin cravat for pale blue moiré; he bowed, uttering a quick "Pardon me," and was gone.

Aurora stood alone at the edge of the metal forest. She watched as Eddie led the stand-in to the mark that would be her own first position for the master shot. The woman was perhaps a few years her senior. They had the same coloring, and were approximately the same height.

Emotion welled inside Aurora as she observed Eddie instructing the young woman to cross the set slowly and stop near the fireplace. A cameraman barked out additional demands. The lighting man followed the stand-in around the room, holding his light meter up at various intervals, yelling orders to a fourth man high on a grid, some twenty feet above them all.

And then, from somewhere amid the clutter, someone cried out, "Gimme a hand—quick!"

For a split second the moment froze in Aurora's brain as Eddie, stopping mid-gesture, shot a fleeting glance toward her.

I mustn't let this get to me, she reminded herself as those words reverberated through her head. I mustn't ruin my makeup or redden my eyes, or this job will take even longer. I can *use* this feeling for the scene. For the cameras. For Gaby.

The moment passed. The stand-in, obviously experienced in the jargon, made no offer to "give a hand." The workaday tedium of moviemaking resumed, and Aurora steeled herself for her debut.

Throughout the entire first day, her tension gradually waned as both Miles Hogarth and Anton assured her of her competence. She learned to use the master shot as a rehearsal, holding full emotion in reserve for closeups, saving it for the intimate scrutiny of the lens.

But Eddie's behavior didn't help. He avoided her during the lunch break, although this was easy to do, since crew ate before talent. As first A.D., he was forced into contact with her; however, his manner was minimally polite, professional but distant, revealing only the barest token of friendliness. His single remark on a personal level came during a pause in action; while the cameras stopped to reload, Eddie and Aurora found themselves standing next to each other. He lit a cigarette and said, "So . . . I guess you've been well."

"Yes," she answered. "I guess. And you?"

"Fine. Getting too fat, but I'm okay."

"I . . . I've thought about you," she ventured softly.

His lips parted, but his response was curtailed by Marvin, who descended upon Aurora with a powder puff, comb, mirror, and more makeup, taking advantage of the delay to eliminate shine and redress the combs at her temples. By the time he had finished, Eddie had been called back by the sound man, who was having a problem with the boom. The chance to talk, even briefly, had slipped away.

That night, Aurora sat on the deck of Harper's yacht, the script for the next day's shoot lying open in her lap. A cool breeze blew softly over the water, and the sky was still gray with the fading light near the horizon while above deep indigo seemed to drip down over it, forcing the sun into the sea.

She had again left the studio before removing her makeup, calling hasty good nights as she eagerly escaped the pressures of the first day. She also wanted to avoid a lengthy encounter with Eddie, who had, all afternoon, remained distant. The yacht, and Harper, had come to represent a safe refuge from Hollywood unreality. His lifestyle offered grace and relaxation after the hard, mechanical factory that was a movie studio. How different the stage would have been!

Aurora caught herself, realizing that she had used the subjective: would have been.

It seemed apparent to her now that a career on the stage was not to be. Movies offered the possibility of success and fame that she sensed the theater always would withhold; nonetheless, she felt in some way shortchanged. Never to know the luxury of a complete role. Never to start at the beginning and build a performance. This week, all scenes were being shot on the set of Gaby's flat. Next week, the nightclub where Gaby meets Nestor would be the set. That was now in construction. Gaby's death scene would be filmed before she was introduced to the audience!

No, she mused. She would never play Hedda Gabler or Blanche Dubois or Maggie the Cat. Might as well forget it. Well, at least accept it . . .

Aurora pulled the white terrycloth robe tighter around her against a sudden chill, and she sipped from the vodka tonic at her side. Her hair was wrapped in a white towel. Her face was clean and scrubbed shiny from a twenty-minute shower.

She and Harper had made love almost immediately upon her return from the studio. She had weakly protested. Harper hadn't allowed her time to remove her Gaby makeup but had lured her below, undressing her all the way to the master cabin.

Afterward, she'd glanced at her makeup, now a dozen hours stale and smeared from lovemaking. The mirror reflection was garish.

"God," she mused aloud, "Maritza was right—I do look like a whore!"

Harper had studied her image then. "Why don't you wash it off?" he asked. "It makes you look . . . old."

*   *   *

Over dinner she described her first day, and they laughed over the mishaps that had occurred. At one point she casually mentioned Eddie.

"Yes," said Harper, twirling his spaghetti. "Anton said you'd . . . known him in New York."

The word *known,* and his pronunciation of it, caused Aurora to wonder if he'd meant more. But Harper didn't pursue it so she saw no reason to do so. Eddie Calvert was part of her past, a past in which a young girl had been a stand-in for someone else on a film in New York. And now . . . now she had her own stand-in.

Still bleary-eyed due to the early hour, Aurora emerged from Harper's car and waited for the guard to open the heavy metal door to the soundstage.

She called good morning to the crew, who had been setting up for an hour by now. She had run over her lines in the car on the way to the studio; fortunately, today, as far as she could tell, it would be easy for Gaby. Miles Hogarth had an extended monologue filled with "spleen and vindication" as he'd called it. All Gaby had to do was cower behind a chair.

She hoped it would be as easy to work on the same set with Eddie Calvert.

Standing near the coffee urn and munching on a buttered bagel, Aurora observed Eddie as he talked with various members of the crew, sipping his own coffee from a cardboard cup. Occasionally, his eyes strayed to her, then moved quickly back to his crew.

What is going on? she wondered. Of course, they had parted in New York under less than ideal circumstances—a door left open, but a mutual understanding that their relationship had nowhere to go; their priorities differed too greatly. Still, yesterday's cold-shoulder treatment had been totally unexpected. And unwarranted, she felt. Yesterday she had suppressed the hurt, the anger. Today she would allow her feelings, whatever they were, to surface. Regardless of their personal differences, past or present, Eddie had to be aware of what this debut meant to her. She had much at stake, and although both of them were professionals, he certainly wasn't trying to make the path smoother for her.

An hour and a half later, Aurora was back in her "Gaby drag." She was growing accustomed to the falsies and was even learning how to move so the errant supplement did not slip beneath her arm. During her makeup session, Miles sat beside her and they ran lines. He was fine.

He was fine until they started shooting. The monologue gave him no end of trouble, requiring constant cuts and delays. Huge cue cards were hand printed and held just off camera for him to read as they rolled. Finally a decision was made to shoot in short, thirty-second takes. These would subsequently be spliced, edited, and intercut with reaction shots of Gaby. Thus, Miles needed to speak no more than four or five lines during the course of one take. Anything missed could be dubbed in as a voiceover while the film carried Aurora's image.

It was both disheartening and unsettling. During a break, she watched the once-great actor walk dejectedly to his dressing room, a pall of silence hanging over the set. She knew her nerves didn't need more coffee, but she headed in the direction of the coffee urn just the same.

Eddie was nibbling on a Danish. They found themselves next to each other for the first time that day. Conversation was unavoidable. Aurora didn't like the impasse anyway; at least they could still be friends, if he was willing. She needed a trusted friend on the set, if only to voice her concern for Miles Hogarth.

"Listen," she said quietly, "is there anything I can do to make this easier on Miles?"

Eddie stared at her for an instant and smiled. "Don't butt in. Mind your own business would be my professional advice."

"Eddie, I'm not butting in—I'm working with him. If it helps Miles, it helps me too."

"Always out for Aurora, huh?"

She placed her coffee cup down firmly on the table and, rising to her full height, said, "All right. Just what's going on here, anyway?"

"Going on?"

"Yes. We may as well clear the air now, because I'm not about to take two more weeks of this kind of treatment."

Eddie studied his coffee. "Did you ever stop to think that maybe you're getting a little of your own back?"

"Eddie, we haven't seen each other for months. I knew you were not exactly thrilled with the way we parted. Neither was I. But I didn't think you'd hold a grudge like this. What have I done to you?"

"Aurora, when we split, I was upset, yeah. But I realized you were right. We wanted different things. I let go of it. It's *this* that's got me pissed off."

"*This?* This what?" She was on the verge of yelling but checked herself, aware that their voices might carry.

"Look, you've moved up pretty fast since you got here," he said. "Fine. More power to you. But I'm pretty well respected in this town and I don't need you to pull strings to get me work!"

She stared blankly at him. Finally, she managed to say, "Eddie, I'm trying to understand what that means, but I haven't a clue. What are you talking about?"

"You don't know? You didn't get me assigned to this picture?"

In spite of her anger, she burst into laughter. "God,

Eddie! I'm lucky to have this job. You're giving me credit for clout I just don't have!"

"Oh c'mon, don't pretend, Aurora! Give me credit for some brains! Your new friend is rather well placed, but I resent your going to him to get me a job!"

"What? Anton? Eddie, I grant you that your name was mentioned, but—"

"Oh, Anton too? I didn't mean Anton. I meant your producer, baby. You went to him, didn't you?"

"Eddie, I don't even know who's producing this picture, so how could I have talked to him about you? I tested for this role and got the job. I've never met the producer."

"You really think I'm an idiot, don't you?" he said.

"I didn't, but I'm beginning to!"

He threw his half-eaten Danish on the table and lit a cigarette. Staring straight into her eyes he said, "You don't know who the producer is. Never met him."

"No!"

"Then he's a better actor than anyone in this town."

"Who, Eddie?" she demanded.

"Harper Styles," he answered. Then he turned and strode across the floor, disappearing into the maze of iron and steel.

Chapter Fifteen

Before Vance could get out of the car, Aurora opened the passenger door and quickly slid in next to him.

"I'll ride up front," she said.

They rode in silence for a time, Aurora keeping her reddened eyes, hidden by sunglasses, directly in front of her. She was aware that Vance occasionally cast a furtive glance toward her, obviously curious about her mood. Still, she made no attempt at conversation or explanation but merely dabbed at her eyes with a soggy tissue.

"Want to talk?" he ventured at last. The words were a key that seemed to unlock a door inside her head. Tears gave way to sobs, Aurora's shoulders shaking from the intensity of her anguish.

"It hurts—so much!" she blurted out, the pain as deep as it was new. She had been touched by sadness before, but this time it had reached a new depth; never had it been accompanied by humiliation and embarrassment. She felt as if a loved one had died; not since Miranda Vale's suicide had she been so distraught.

Her words of explanation were unintelligible as the

Rolls continued on its way; near-hysterical sobs shook her entire body.

When the worst of it had subsided and she was able to speak, Vance had stopped the car.

"Where are we?" she asked.

"The parking lot of a bar I know. I can't take you home in this shape—Tadzio and Maritza would never leave you alone. Besides, I thought you could use a drink. If not, we can talk right here in the car."

"You're so . . . smart," she said, grinning as she licked a salty tear at the corner of her mouth.

Vance shrugged, loosening his tie. "What's up?"

"Look, let's have that drink, okay? If I can get into the john and wash my face, maybe I won't scare the customers."

He laughed and, nervously, so did she.

Crossing the almost empty parking lot, Aurora explained to Vance the events of her first two days of shooting. He listened attentively, nodding.

Aurora headed directly for the ladies' room. She was right; in this state, she would have scared the customers. But warm water, followed by the stinging ice-cold splashes, revived her. Giving her face a closer look, she decided that some of the puffiness had retreated.

Vance had taken a table near the back; it was dimly lit. That wouldn't have mattered; there were few customers. The vinyl leopardskin décor irritated Aurora's eyes even in this light, but she was grateful to find a vodka martini waiting for her.

"Ah." She exhaled deeply after the first sip. "This is good. Thank you, doctor."

"You're welcome."

"Did you call the house and let them know where we are?" It sounded silly to her, but Maritza and Tadzio maintained an almost parental interest in her whereabouts. And Vance might be on call tonight as a driver . . . or escort.

"Well," he answered, "I didn't tell them where we were. Just that you'd been delayed at the studio and we'd be home as soon as you were released." He saw her concern and added, "Don't worry. The switchboard at the studio is closed. They can't call to check. Besides, they don't need the car tonight, so I'm free for the evening."

Aurora didn't like lying to Maritza or Tadzio. She would explain—but later. She wasn't up to it tonight, and besides, it was really only a white lie. Taking another sip of the martini, she felt herself beginning to relax and she realized she could trust Vance.

He seemed to understand and smiled at her. "What time is your call tomorrow?"

"No time. I have tomorrow off. They don't get around to Gaby again until the end of the week, thank God!"

"It's over soon, you know."

She nodded, but her own agreement with his comment disturbed her. Despite the personal complications involved in shooting her first film, she found it strange that she looked forward to the end of it. Acting was supposed to be fun—expression. So far, it had been nothing but drudgery, complicated by insult and injury. Her thoughts returned to Eddie and the news he'd thrust at her. She felt tears rising once more, but she managed to contain them.

"Oh, Vance," she said. "I feel so . . ."

"Cheap?"

She nodded. That was the right word. After her confrontation with Eddie, she had approached Anton regarding the legitimacy of her being cast in the film. He had dismissed her questions. "Darling," he'd said, "Harper merely asked me to take a special look at

271

you . . . a serious look. You got the role. That's what counts. 'Why' doesn't matter."

But it did matter! Aurora had fought the urge to ask to see the screen tests of the other actresses who had auditioned for the part of Gaby. Perhaps she could have convinced herself that she did deserve the job, that she was better suited for the role than the others. But she knew such a request would be ridiculous. She was too embarrassed to ask and most likely the studio would refuse her—if they'd bothered to save the footage of the screen tests. And besides, what if one of the other tests was better? That would only confirm Aurora's worst fear, that she had gotten this role because she was sleeping with the producer! Of course, she hadn't known that Harper Styles was the producer. She'd just felt strongly about Harper. He was a wonderful man . . . wasn't he?

Eddie's words had cut deeply. Now, thinking back to his curt manner—his hostility—she cringed, knowing that he'd assumed the worst. But was he so insecure he thought he'd been hired because of strings she had pulled?

In a flash, Aurora understood his anger more clearly. Their situations were not dissimilar; both she and Eddie feared they'd gotten their jobs because of someone they'd bedded. Eddie with Aurora; Aurora with Harper. That robbed their work of any joy. Dignity and pride were replaced by feelings of shame and . . . yes . . . cheapness.

All this Aurora shared with Vance over two more martinis. By the time they arrived back at the house, she was not drunk, but well on her way to being so. And she was weary, exhausted by her own emotions. It had been quite a day.

*   *   *

272

There were two messages waiting for her. "Six P.M. Harper called." "Seven-thirty. Call Harper."

She crumpled both slips of paper in her fist and dragged herself up the stairs for a bath.

After a long soak, she felt better. Instead of toweling herself dry, Aurora donned her terrycloth robe just long enough to walk from the bathroom to her bedroom. Then, disrobed and naked, she allowed the remaining dampness on her body to evaporate, cooling and relaxing her even more.

"Yes?" she replied to a knock at her door.

"Rory, it's Maritza. Harper's called again. I told him you were bathing and you'd phone him back."

"Fine. Thank you."

"It's the third time he's called, darling."

"I know. Thank you."

The countess said no more, but Aurora heard no departing footsteps so she knew Maritza was still outside the door. When Aurora made no move to speak or admit her, the countess finally said, "All right. Good night, dear," and was gone.

Aurora sat on the satin-sheeted bed, then fell back against the matching ruffled pillow sham, dark hair fanning out and framing her face in a sharp contrast to the ice blue backdrop. Sighing, she turned toward the telephone on the nightstand beside the bed.

Am I playing games? she asked herself. By this time, after three calls, Harper certainly knew something was wrong. She examined her conscience. No, she decided, this isn't a game; I'm not the one doing the manipulating. And I'm angry. Hurt. With good reason. Maybe I do want to punish him a little.

On the other hand, she knew the only way for her to proceed was to be honest with him. Harper deserved a chance to defend himself, to offer his side of the story, just as she deserved to tell him how she felt.

Nonetheless, she continued to stare at the telephone without moving to lift the receiver.

I can't, she reasoned. I'll only get weepy again. Instinctively she sensed that her own vulnerability, her own need of him, might make her back down from the rightness of her outrage.

But was it rightness or self-righteousness?

Don't back down on this, she told herself. He got me this job and never told me he was producing the film. He lied by omission, and compromised me.

It sounded old-fashioned to her; puritanical.

But she did not telephone him.

Harper's calls and messages continued. Two the following morning; one in the afternoon while she lounged at the pool. Each time, she was tempted. She wanted to, needed to, talk with him. It was precisely that need that held her back. There suddenly appeared to be something untrustworthy about him, and Aurora's guard was up, despite her own desire to pour our her feelings to him, to have him take her in his arms and assure her that it would be all right, as if he would forgive her.

Flowers arrived in the late afternoon with a card that read: "What's wrong?" It was signed with the initial *H*.

That night, Aurora wrestled with disturbing dreams. She awoke exhausted at four A.M. Lying on the bed, she tried to recall the dreams, but they were only blurs of tension and anxiety, with no specific images remaining. A fight between Harper and her father—a fight over her—was all she could remember. It had ended violently with one of them wounded. Aurora had dreamt of her father in the past, but never so vividly and never involved with anyone in her present life. It perplexed her.

By the time her next shooting call arrived, at the end of the week, Vance had answered more than a dozen calls from Harper and had run interference whenever Tadzio or Maritza had tried to learn what was troubling their protégé. Aurora had spent much of the time in her room, feigning a virus, but she did sneak out with Vance for a driving lesson. Upon returning, she found that Harper had stopped by, expressing deep concern. This upset Aurora—after all, this was Harper's house—but she didn't feel strong enough to confront him.

She was nervous, and not from camera fright, when she arrived at the studio.

Eddie seemed friendlier, but that might be due to guilt. Aurora's reaction to his disclosure that afternoon had probably convinced him of his mistaken assumption. Being friendly was probably as close as he could come to making an outright apology; Aurora knew him well enough to realize that.

However, as she stepped onto the set, she felt like a fool, felt they were all laughing at her. Her eyes darted about the labyrinth of machinery, seeking the faces of the men and women almost obscured by it. No, they weren't staring or laughing; they weren't paying any attention to her. They were merely doing their jobs. Eddie too.

Anton appeared to be particularly high when he arrived. He raced about the set, excitedly throwing out ideas and then changing them as soon as the setup had been arranged. Each new inspiration was more "brilliant"—his word—than the one before. Aurora could see his behavior's effect on the crew. Their frustrated glances were directed at Anton, not at her.

After the lunch break they did another take of a shot they'd tried to get since early morning. At least Miles was secure in his lines now—they'd run through the scene more than twenty times.

Before the cameras rolled, Anton walked up to Aurora and asked quietly, "Why haven't you called Harper?"

Fear, then fury, welled up inside her. Must *everyone* know the details of her personal life?

"Why do you ask, Anton?"

"He is very upset. He thinks you are angry with him."

"I'm not ready to speak with him. I will. I want to, you know. But I can't. Not yet."

He patted her arm in a fatherly gesture, and she was moved by the small show of concern.

Somewhere around three—there were no clocks on the set and Gaby could not wear a wristwatch—Eddie shouted, unexpectedly, "Okay, that's a wrap for today! Tomorrow, all!"

What? thought Aurora. There were two more angles and setups to shoot.

Then, in the shadowland beyond the set, she saw Harper Styles. He was talking, head to head, with Anton, but his eyes were on her, although his lips moved in response to Anton's voice.

Aurora felt her face reddening and she looked about for possible escape.

She watched as Anton moved toward Jolie for a few words. The wardrobe mistress was only a few feet away, but Anton took a circuitous route around the set rather than cutting straight across; thus, he avoided Aurora.

Gradually, the set began to clear, the heavy soundstage door opening and booming shut as the crew, one by one, made individual exits. Eddie was the last to leave; she could feel his eyes burning into her as Harper's noncommittal stare met hers.

Then Eddie said, too loudly, "Congratulations. You move fast." And he sauntered from the set, nearly brushing Harper on his way out.

Now they were alone Harper, half-lit, stood amidst the black skeletons of pipe and cable. Aurora knew he was curious about Eddie's departing comment, but she remained, motionless, in the middle of Gaby's room, only a worklight above her. Its naked bulb reduced the charming salon to a rickety, tacky set. The illusion was gone, and Aurora felt as stripped as the furnishings around her.

She sighed, tilting her head characteristically, and returned Harper's stare across the chasm of the soundstage.

Slowly he walked toward her, the heels of his shoes echoing throughout the stilled studio. His steel gray, double-breasted gabardine suit jacket was taut across his powerful chest, pulled down by the weight of his hands, which were plunged into the two front pockets.

He stepped just beyond the lens of the nearest camera and glanced briefly down at the floor. Then he brought his eyes up to meet Aurora's.

"Well?" he asked, almost in a whisper.

Adrenaline was coursing through her, causing her heart to pound at a dizzying pace. Despite Harper's everpresent authority, Aurora detected a new vulnerability in him, perhaps a sadness, she had not seen before. Her knees weakened as she looked back at the green eyes, so like her own. For the first time she realized it was Harper to whom Anton had referred that evening over dinner. She saw it now. Yes, they were very alike. She caught herself, remembering to think first, before she permitted herself to speak. This was not a reconciliation; it was—it had to be—a showdown.

"Well?" she responded, unsure of what else to safely say.

"Why haven't you answered any of my calls?"

"Why didn't you tell me you were producing this picture!"

"Don't answer a question with a question. It's neither good dialogue nor acceptable conversation."

"All right. I've avoided you because I'm hurt. You've been dishonest with me. Question answered. Your turn!"

She felt her breathing beginning to thicken but forced herself to continue on this track. This confrontation was something she would have avoided, but she knew that was not possible now. She was frightened, though, because as much as she feared losing her self-respect, she feared the loss of Harper even more.

He spoke with measured slowness. "I thought if you knew that, you'd assume I had arranged this job for you."

"Harper, did you think I wouldn't find out? And . . . and now that I have—it's even worse!"

He strode toward her, the gray streaks at his temples glowing silver under the glare of the worklight. His hand came up to her shoulders and touched her skin. Quickly she shrank away and turned to walk from the set. "Don't," she said. "You'll get makeup all over your suit."

As she moved past him, he reached out and grabbed her upper arm, whirling her around to face him.

"You've got to understand—" he began, but she yanked herself free of his grasp.

"Don't do that! Don't grab at me, Harper, because I hate it!" She tried to calm herself. "Besides, I'm wearing three-inch heels—you almost broke my ankle!"

"I'm sorry," he said softly, his hand coming up to her face, this time with tenderness. "I am . . . truly. I . . ."

It was the first time she had ever seen him at a loss for

words. His face was hidden in shadow now, obstructing her view of his eyes, but his voice betrayed emotion.

She turned and gently kissed his cheek, the scent of his cologne and the aroma of his body causing a sudden lightheadedness. Aurora allowed his left arm to wind around her neck. He did not kiss her but moved closer and quietly caressed her. They stood in silent embrace, an embrace that was . . . what? The only description she could find was *friendly,* not a word she would have used to define their relationship. It seemed as though Harper, too, was reaching out for comfort, for solace, perhaps even for love.

"Let me get my makeup off. Then we can talk," she said. They were holding hands. She led him over the tripod stands, around and past the coils of cable and wire, beyond the set to the little door upon which a nameplate read: Aurora O'Brien.

Quickly she knotted her hair at the top of her head and applied cold cream to her face. Harper took a seat on the sofa and watched.

She didn't like removing makeup in front of him. It was silly, but it seemed to destroy another illusion she wished to retain, even though he'd seen her—made love to her—without any makeup at all.

Then it was time to remove her costume. There was no other room in which to change, no screen to allow her discretion. She smiled at her first instinct—to ask him to step outside. She began to remove the tight waistband, feeling awkward and uncertain.

Suddenly, Harper was up from the sofa.

"I . . . I have to change, and . . ."

He came nearer until they stood face to face. "Go ahead."

She laughed nervously. "Harper, it's like a striptease with you here."

He took one more step, bringing his body almost

against hers. "Only if you're doing it by yourself," he murmured.

Then his lips were at her earlobes, the rush of his breath mingling with his whispered words of entreaty, of need, of love. Aurora felt the electricity of his hands as they moved with agonizing slowness over the smooth down of her shoulders, his palms never actually making contact with her skin. He brought his face to hers and bent to kiss her now-parted lips; as she leaned her head back to accept him, he pulled his head away and ran the tip of his tongue up the length of her neck, resting at the other earlobe that he teased slightly with his teeth.

"Harper," she said breathlessly, feeling the increasing flame between her thighs. "Wait . . . we're . . . someone could . . ."

Without leaving her, he kicked the dressing room door; it slammed shut. His fingers worked the drawstring at the top of her costume blouse. It fell, and as he traveled the gentle slope and swell of her breasts, he stopped, shaking his head.

"Darling, what has Jolie done to you?"

She giggled and blushed as his hands undid the back of the brassiere. "It's to make them look bigger."

"Maybe for the film. But I love them the way they are—without this damned contraption!" With that, she was free of the constriction; the relief she felt at her body's release from its prison was second only to the sensations now evoked by Harper's thumbs as they moved back and forth across her hardening nipples.

"There, now," he said. He caressed the red welts where the brassiere wire had dug into her flesh. "You are beautiful, so beautiful." His voice was deep, his breathing heavy as his lips opened to engulf her own, moving over her face, then down to her breasts with an urgency he'd not displayed since that first night aboard his yacht.

He led her to the sofa; her skirt fell to the floor as he pulled her over on top of him. He had removed his vest and jacket but was still clothed. From her straddled position, Aurora pulled loose his tie and shirt, and buried her head beneath his chin, aware of the friction of his beard and the musky scent of his skin.

His hands went to her buttocks and she felt him move into a more erect sitting position, his back against the sofa, his legs on the floor. Aurora heard the teeth of his zipper, while, with his free fingers, he teased her clitoris. His other hand was at her back, holding her up to keep her from falling. He buried his face between her breasts, roaming over them hungrily with his mouth.

Slowly, she felt the first pressure against the deeper folds of her vagina as his thick, hardened phallus opened her still wider and wider. She began moving gradually down its length until the entire shaft was buried inside her. Wave upon wave of heat, of pleasure, engulfed her. Just as slowly, she rose onto her knees, her hands on his shoulders, her neck arched backward. Then she sank down again with a suddenness that caused Harper to plunge so deeply that he gasped with pleasure.

Aurora's rhythm began to quicken as she rode. She was in control of the motion except when she straightened her knees, allowing him to push up and into her with a driving force that made her cry out his name. "Harper! Oh God, Harper!"

Again and again she plunged down over him, thrusting him inside her at ever-increasing speed until she thought she would faint. Suddenly his head fell forward and their eyes met, the world outside their own reduced, for this moment, to unimportance. No words, no sounds other than their rapid, staccato breathing as

281

they approached the summit—faster, faster, deeper, deeper—and together they came, both of them crying out, this time in unison, as the power of Harper's climax washed over Aurora, filling her with his orgasm and heightening her own. With a final tightening of her sphincter muscles, she exacted from him the last ounce of pleasure; he shuddered and groaned at their release, and they fell back against the sofa for support, drained and throbbing.

After they rested in each other's arms for a while, Harper stroked her dampened hair, and asked, "Forgive me?"

"Mmm, almost. Just as long as you know why I was so upset."

He paused momentarily and then, with a sly grin curving his mouth, he said, "I suppose, to prove that I don't cast every woman I've been to bed with, I'll have to marry you, won't I?"

Had she heard him correctly? Had he actually proposed?

Aurora lifted her head and looked at him. Now he was smiling broadly at her.

"Well," she replied, returning the grin, "I suppose to prove that I don't go to bed with a producer in order to get cast, I'll . . . have to say yes."

Chapter Sixteen

Abby picked up the contract that lay on the mattress and, flipping to the last page, read aloud from the rider:
"'Artist's name and billing amended to read: Aurora Styles.'"

Aurora smiled at the sight of the child sprawled across the enormous bed; Abby was crushing the layers of floor-length pale rose satin and lace but didn't seem to notice. A spray of pink baby's breath was nestled in her hair, which Aurora had arranged in a delicate coronet of braids.

It had been so long since they had seen each other that, despite the occasional photographs she'd received in the mail, Aurora was surprised at how the child had grown. She was still very much a little girl, yet there was unmistakable evidence, however fleeting, that before long a young woman would emerge. At one moment she attempted to behave like an adult, while in the next this young-lady-to-be demanded to be babied. She might easily have tried Aurora's patience, but she wasn't just any little girl; she was loved—and spoiled— by her foster sister who had asked her to be flower girl at her wedding. Tadzio and Vance, and even Maritza, who had never expressed a fondness for children, catered to the child, introducing her to the magic and wonder and luxury of Aurora's new world. Disneyland would have paled by comparison, even to a little girl from a small town back East.

Aurora glanced at the clock. "My God! Abby, it's twelve forty-five! The ceremony starts in fifteen minutes and I'm not even dressed!"

On cue, Maritza entered the upstairs bedroom. The arriving guests' chatter could be heard as the countess opened and quickly closed the door.

She was all over the room at once, barking orders: "Abby, that gown will look as though you've slept in it! Off the bed with you! Rory, come here. It's time to get you dressed! Every newspaper and magazine in town is here—you must hurry!"

Her manner belied the cool elegance one normally associated with the countess, and from her gown, Aurora could tell that Maritza had decided upon her role: mother-of-the-bride. Vanity prevented her from going too far, however. She wore a deep rose silk—no "sensible" lace for the countess. The gown combined grace and dignity with a hint of sensuality in its drape and cut. It clung to her still-magnificent figure enticingly, not vulgarly.

Aurora stood at the center of the room as Maritza advanced with her gown, and while the two women worked at the dozens of silk-covered buttons at her back and halfway up her arms, Aurora studied the three of them in the mirror's reflection.

She was thrilled to have Abby present. She had promised the child a visit to New York, but that had not been possible, not even during the whirlwind weekend when she and the countess had flown there to select her wedding gown. "The California designers just won't do, Rory. Bergdorf's it will be, and the gown simply must be designed especially for you—I don't

mean custom tailored, I mean custom *designed*."
Aurora had succumbed to Maritza's wishes, although she had wanted only a simple ceremony, attended by a few friends, and an afternoon frock would have been fine.

But this was, she had been reminded countless times, Hollywood. Even weddings had to be productions, especially when the groom was a prominent figure in the movie business. And certainly, Aurora thought, Abby wouldn't have been treated to quite this much splendor at a simple wedding in New York. She wanted to make up for any broken promises, for she knew only too well what a promise means to a child; she didn't want Abby to suffer as she had.

Maritza continued to fuss and cluck as she had all morning, indeed, all week, whereas Abby's eyes were fixed on Aurora and her gown.

"Can I touch it?" she asked.

"Of course," said Aurora.

"Absolutely not!" snapped Maritza.

"My hands are clean," said the child, backing away when she saw the countess' narrowed eyes.

"I don't want anyone to touch anything!" ordered Maritza. She seemed particularly nervous; perhaps she felt that something might go amiss, even after meticulous planning; or perhaps it was because she was trying to stop smoking, at Aurora's request. Her hand, when not working the buttons, appeared to be reaching for a nonexistent cigarette. Her ebony holder lay on the dressing table and now Abby was playing with it.

"Gosh, Rora," she said, waving it in the air, "it's like a magic wand and you're the fairy princess!"

Aurora smiled at the child and at Maritza's frown. "Yes, honey, except this is real life, not a fairy tale." She felt she had to remind herself.

She also had to remind herself not to sit in the Oscar

de la Renta "fairytale" gown. The flowing yards of shimmering ivory silk covered with millions of hand-sewn beads and seed pearls almost took her breath away. It was the most beautiful gown she had ever seen, and in less than fifteen minutes she would float down the stairs and—as Abby had said, it was like a fairy tale!—Harper would take her hand and she would become Mrs. Harper Styles! This went beyond her dreams, beyond anything she had ever wanted!

Now Maritza was securing the veil, a simple wisp of gossamer and a crown of tiny beaded roses. Abby reached for the bouquet, but Maritza cautioned her with a blood-red fingernail. "Those roses are very delicate, Abigail! I'll see to them! You take your flowers—they're on the desk in that blue box."

Maritza handed the spray of mauve rosebuds to Aurora and then stepped back to survey her handi-work. Aurora, framed in the full-length antique oval mirror, felt a surge of anxiety and she laughed excitedly. "I'm so nervous!" she exclaimed.

The countess stood in the doorway. She was very still, and for a split second Aurora thought she detected a strained expression. It seemed to be a blend of pride and of sadness, wistful acceptance.

"There's no reason to be nervous, Rory," said Maritza, recovering her composure. "You are absolute perfection."

"Not since the union of Rita Hayworth and Ali Khan has Hollywood seen such splendor," wrote one enthusiastic columnist.

It mattered little to the "audience" that of the one thousand or more in attendance, most were unknown to Aurora and many were only nodding acquaintances of Harper, Maritza, or Tadzio. This was Hollywood, and Harper Styles' marriage was providing the town with a grand show. Nor did it concern anyone that many actors and actresses, from the old guard and the new, had been ordered to appear, the studios exerting pressure on them to do so.

For weeks, the exclusive stores and boutiques along Rodeo Drive had found it highly profitable to help Hollywood royalty live up to its image. Dressmakers, jewelers, and, in the last two days, hairdressers had scurried from mansion to mansion, convincing each client that she alone would eclipse every woman present in grace and beauty—even the bride, whoever she was.

This situation amused, rather than impressed, Aurora. However, she had taken pride in helping to arrange the ceremony; she, too, wanted it to run smoothly. With minimal assistance, or interference, from Maritza and Tadzio, Aurora had chosen the décor. She peered out from the bedroom window at the activity below. More and more people were arriving with each passing minute.

At the front of the house, unemployed actors outfitted in red coats scurried about, parking Cadillacs, Rolls Royces, Bentleys, and other luxurious conveyances. Guests were climbing the steps to be greeted by a tuxedoed doorman who directed them toward the entry desks. Aurora wondered how well her system would work.

Each invitation was politely double-checked against an alphabetical list. A–G, to the left; H–P, to the right; and Q–Z, straight ahead. Behind each desk sat a beautiful young woman, a model or an unemployed actress who was delighted to make personal contact with the legends pouring through the door, and to be

287

earning some money.

In the event that a name was not found on the list, the matter was to be handled with extreme delicacy and discretion, lest a legitimate guest be offended. Aurora knew some mixups were bound to occur—St. Laurent under *L* instead of *S,* for example. Any crashers who were detected would be politely asked to leave. If a problem arose, Vance was to handle the situation as unobtrusively as possible.

Once they had been passed into the house, the guests' wraps would be checked. This was by far the easiest job, for the day was beautiful and the reception was scheduled to take place in Harper's sumptuous garden.

Aurora smiled as she remembered her own coat-check days; she wondered if the person hired for this occasion knew that the bride had spent awhile at this thankless task, and not so very long ago. She laughed. Today's help would make out well—far better than she had at La Grille! Aurora had stipulated that everyone "on call" was to be handsomely paid for their services; she didn't want anyone to regret today's "performance."

Entwined around and beneath the banister of the staircase which she would momentarily descend were evergreens. When Tadzio had suggested palm fronds, Maritza and Aurora had giggled aloud.

"She's not wearing a sarong," the countess had said, laughing.

They had decided on white rosebuds to surround the improvised altar at the center of the living room–salon. Tadzio had wanted lilies and on this, Maritza had been in agreement. But Aurora had complained that lilies reminded her of funerals. And she loathed yellow, despite the many times she'd been told the color was becoming to her.

The small orchestra was nestled outside the French

288

doors, on a section of the patio at the nearest end of the pool, in order to be audible in the garden and inside the house; as well. The pool itself had been strewn with water lilies—Aurora did not object to these, since they would be floating—and gardenias. Three-quarters of the pool had been covered with transparent Plexiglas, and a railing, trimmed with mauve and white roses, had been erected at its edge, thereby creating, over the water, a dance floor that would be lit from beneath when evening arrived.

Earlier that morning, Aurora had watched the workmen construct the huge white canopy over the entire garden. Under it, guests could take shelter from the California sun while partaking of appetizers and drinks. Dinner would be buffet style, served on a wall-length sideboard inside the house.

Aurora smiled at the thought of Maritza on the phone for the past month, arguing, demanding, ordering from caterers. Shipments had come from her network across the globe. The patés *had* to come from Paris. The caviar *must* be flown from Russia, the smoked salmon *directly* from Scotland. Aurora hoped that Harper's recent films had made him vast amounts of money; this simple little ceremony was about to cost him a fortune!

The wedding cake had been kept a mystery, Maritza and Tadzio having remained very secretive and coy whenever they alluded to its spectacular design. Aurora knew only that the pastry chef was flying in from Paris or New York to decorate it in person! Perhaps Abby was right and this *was* a fairy tale!

A sharp rap on the bedroom door announced the exquisite Yolanda Gentry, who peered into the room with schoolgirlish excitement. "It's time! Rory, it's time!" she cried.

It amazed Aurora that Yolanda could be so

289

genuinely enthused. The aging starlet had been selected by the studio as one of the bridesmaids, and that was fine; Aurora liked her. But Yolanda had just gone through her third divorce, so Aurora had expected a somewhat more blasé attitude from the woman toward marriage. Apparently this lavish spectacle, the importance of this union caused even the most jaded guest to quiver with anticipation.

Aurora was no exception. She didn't deceive herself for a moment; the "event of the season" had little to do with her. Any bride of Harper Styles would have elicited the same fervor; as far as Hollywood was concerned, this was his wedding. But that mattered little to Aurora; she knew it was theirs.

She stood at the top of the stairs, butterflies in her stomach, her knees shaking. Abby was beside her and they hugged; this calmed her somewhat. Then Maritza took her trembling hand and said, "Be happy, darling. You're on."

The ceremony went off without incident, the only awkward moment coming at the reception line when Eddie Calvert suddenly appeared. Aurora wondered how he had made the A-list and then remembered she had sent him the invitation. She hadn't really expected him to show up.

"May I kiss the bride?" he asked.

Aurora smiled politely, but inside a spasm of panic gripped her. What kind of kiss would he bestow upon her in front of Harper and God knew how many members of the press?

But he gave her only a polite peck on the cheek and then went immediately to the bar.

Bride and groom sat now, not unlike a king and queen surveying their domain. The elite, the crème de la crème, had gathered to pay homage to Harper Styles and his wife. For the moment, Aurora allowed herself the luxury of feeling important, of being someone.

But her real satisfaction in the afternoon's production came from the look of sheer rapture on Abby's beaming face. The older, more sophisticated guests masked their excitement, although Harper remarked in a whisper that "the circus really impressed the hell out of them all." But the effect of the proceedings on a ten-year-old child was evident in her expression of wonderment as she looked from famous face to famous face. Abby was meeting all the heroes and heroines of her favorite TV shows and movies. Aurora hoped it wasn't too much for her.

"Oh, Rory!" gushed the little girl. "You're so *lucky!*"

Harper rose before Aurora could reply. "Abby," he said, extending his arms, "may I have the honor of this dance?"

The child held out her hands as if mesmerized. Then she rediscovered her manners and turned to Aurora. "Is it okay, Rory? May I dance with Harper?"

"Of course, honey. Go ahead."

She laughed as Harper led the little girl onto the pool dance floor.

"That one's going to be stunning in a few years," Maritza observed.

"Yes, I think you're right." Aurora watched the dancing guests make room for Harper and his small partner; then she glanced past them to the cake. It was magnificent, but ridiculous too. Standing five feet and six tiers high, it was topped with a miniature Aurora, in wedding gown, posed before an old-fashioned tripod camera, behind which stood a miniature Harper, leaning over to peer through the lens at his bride. Bride and groom were surrounded by mountains of freshly peaked whipped cream.

Aurora returned her gaze to the dancers as Harper bent to accommodate Abby's small frame to his towering height. The child appeared enchanted as they moved to the strains of "You Stepped Out of a Dream." Other couples made room, then cleared the floor to stand in a circle around the two lone dancers. Harper smiled down at the little girl, occasionally glancing over her head to wink at Aurora, and Abby gazed up at Harper in hypnotic adoration.

"Just like Cinderella at the ball," Aurora commented aloud to no one in particular. A tear twinkled in her eye and trickled down her cheek. When it reached her lips, she wiped it away with her left hand, almost scratching her face with one of the faceted edges of her diamond. Then her eyes took in the dazzling prisms of the spectacular four-carat stone, Harper's wedding gift to her.

She reached for her champagne flute; the diamond glittered, then disappeared, then glittered again, darting in and out of sparkling view as the lights above and around the table captured, then released, the energy, the fire, the ice of the stone.

"It's like magic," said Aurora with a sigh. "Everything is like magic. And it all feels so right!"

Part II

Chapter Seventeen

The commercial for fabric softener ended with the gurgling coo of a baby who was apparently delirious over the velvety smoothness of his blanket, heretofore "too scratchy for baby's tender skin."

Aurora recognized the young mother in the ad as a fellow acting student from New York. Well, she thought, it's work—but I'm glad I'm not doing it!

Still, what she was doing didn't seem any more challenging, did it?

The music and fade-in to the prologue of the show began before she could continue her ruminations, and she welcomed the escape.

On the small screen, Vance held an exquisitely beautiful woman in his arms, kissing her passionately, at which point the door behind the couple opened to reveal another woman, Vance's wife, wearing an expression of stunned surprise. Aurora giggled aloud.

The teaser ended and a new one began as Aurora rose from the kitchen table to pour her third cup of coffee, cautioning herself that she really must curb her caffeine intake. Except for the dialogue coming from the small portable television set on the countertop, the house was quiet and she was glad to be alone.

Vance's image returned and Aurora's grin widened. Although he was undoubtedly an abysmal actor, he had scored, nonetheless, an enormous personal success in the two years since his first appearance on *Once More, Love,* the soap opera to which Vance referred as *Not Again, Nothing.* The ratings for the program had soared after the introduction of his character, Merritt Pomerance, who was, of course, a womanizer —and a kleptomaniac, to boot.

Aurora was happy for him. The working hours were far from Vance's dream schedule—no time for the beach, these days—but he was making good money and had acquired a self-respect and pride that he'd not had during his escort days.

Not that he was taking it all that seriously, Aurora knew. She had been to his home for lunch only last week, and he'd reduced her to tears of laughter with tales of his "work" on the show, which had been rewarded by the announcement of his nomination for a daytime Emmy.

Their hilarity had ceased, however, upon the late arrival of Eva Morley.

Although Eva seemed a bit stern at times, Aurora liked her. What the woman lacked in humor was more than compensated for by common sense and ambition.

"The nomination gives you bargaining power when you renew your contract, so don't just write it off as silly hype," she said, and the subject was closed.

Over the last few years, Aurora had mentioned several times to Harper that she had wanted to invite Vance and Eva to dinner, but he had given her an emphatic no, claiming that Vance was only a "soap-opera person" and soaps did not constitute A-list.

That Aurora found ridiculous. Harper's using it as an excuse infuriated her. She knew he looked down on Vance because of Vance's past and he harbored no love

296

for Eva. Harper had alluded to his feelings only once before, and at the time Aurora had expressed her anger. Subsequently, Harper had switched to the A-list excuse for his refusal to have Vance or Eva in his home.

Eva Morley was one of the best things that had ever happened to Vance, and fortunately he had been smart enough to recognize the fact. They had been living together since the day Vance had given notice to Tadzio, a day Aurora would not soon forget.

It had been understood and expected that Maritza and Tadzio—and Vance—would be gone from the house by the time Aurora and Harper arrived home from their honeymoon trip. After two months of travel by yacht, plane, and automobile, the newly married couple had looked forward to settling down—alone together—in their Beverly Hills home.

But upon their return, they did not find a trio but a quartet. The day after the wedding, Aurora and Harper had departed, and Eva Morley had moved in.

Aurora had suspected the presence of a woman in Maritza's life, but only by inference. Eva had not been at the wedding, nor had she visited the house. But during the honeymoon, Aurora had seen two photographs, one in a newspaper, the other in a magazine. They were reminiscent of her own early days with Tadzio and the countess. As usual, the pictures showed Maritza on Vance's arm, but there was an unknown woman with Tadzio.

Like Aurora, Eva was dark and tall. Aurora estimated her to be four or five years her senior, but this woman had a maturity beyond her years, a depth to her face that indicated wisdom. She was, in many ways, regal.

A few weeks after seeing the two photographs, Aurora happened to notice a blind item in a society column, an item that obviously alluded to her friends.

297

She knew then that Eva Morley would have to be dealt with.

Her suspicions were confirmed when she and Harper arrived home; the woman in the photographs, the woman who had appeared on Prince Tadzio Breslau's arm, reclined languidly along the length of the living-room sofa, a copy of F. Scott Fitzgerald's short stories held in her jeweled hand.

Eva looked up, directly at Aurora. Neither spoke, but as they stared at each other, Aurora was aware of a tacit understanding between them. Harper stopped briefly at the entrance to the room, then quickly stepped into it, calling Tadzio's name. Eva did not move, but she followed Harper with her eyes, after which she brought them again to rest upon Aurora.

"Which story are you reading?" Aurora asked, somehow finding herself amused without knowing why.

"'Babylon Revisited.' I've read it before."

"Well, I'm glad you didn't lock us out in the snow."

"It's a little chilly . . . but that doesn't really amount to snow, does it? Not in Beverly Hills, anyway. You've read it too, then?" Artfully, Eva arched one eyebrow.

"But only once. I'm Aurora Styles," she said, extending her hand as she walked toward the sofa.

"Eva Morley," the other woman answered as the raised voices of Harper and Tadzio reached them from the pool area. "I think perhaps I may be leaving here soon."

Aurora gave a short laugh. "I think perhaps you're right, Eva."

She was.

The chauffeur had only enough time to carry the luggage upstairs, run to the bathroom, and gulp down the beer Vance offered him before he began to carry other luggage downstairs and load it into the trunk of the Rolls.

Vance greeted Aurora and wrapped her in his arms. She kissed him on the cheek; it was good to see him again. She'd missed him—and Tadzio and Maritza. But their reunion was aborted by further shouting from outside. Maritza must have been upstairs—hiding.

Harper was obviously in a rage. They heard Tadzio tearfully explaining that time had gotten away from him; he'd planned to move into the hotel a week ago. However, there'd been a few premières and a party or two. . . .

Harper was having none of it. Then Vance came down the stairs, two bags in each hand, Eva following with another. "This is all of our stuff," he said to Aurora. "Maritza and Tadzio will take a lot longer."

But instead of carrying the bags out to the car, he placed them in the entrance hall.

Eva looked at him with a smile; then Vance ran back upstairs to help the others pack. He raced past the countess, who was making as poised an entrance as she could muster.

She embraced Aurora and then said, "Eva, may I speak with you?"

The two women went out onto the veranda, closing the glass doors behind them. Although their voices were raised, it was difficult for Aurora to hear them over the racket from upstairs.

Aurora joined Harper at the bar and touched his hand. He took a swig of Scotch and said, "Have one?"

"It's still too early for me," she said. "But you go ahead."

"Welcome home," he muttered, attempting humor despite his anger.

"It's all right, darling. I mean, I'm used to them. They didn't mean to—"

"I know, Aurora, but it's ridiculous and inconsiderate. I've not lived in this house for months, and now, with you, I just—"

"Harper, they're leaving. It'll be over and they'll be gone."

It was not, after all, as if her friends were being turned out into the streets. It would require time to heal Tadzio's wounded pride, but heal it would, as would Maritza's.

And then the front doorbell chimed. Aurora left Harper at the bar to finish his drink and calm his anger while she went into the hall and opened the door.

"Someone call for a cab?" asked the uniformed driver.

From the top of the stairs Vance called, *"I did."*

As he descended, he screamed, "Eva!" at the top of his lungs. The chauffeur struggled past him with more luggage to load into the Rolls.

Eva and Maritza had come back into the living room and now stood, waiting.

To Aurora, Vance explained, "My car died." Then he turned to Eva, ignoring the others present. "I'm not going with them. I'm taking only what I came here with . . . unless you want to come with me. But decide. Now."

"What?" Maritza roared, and she launched into a tirade of shocking expletives Aurora had rarely heard her use.

Tadzio tripped, almost tumbling down the stairs; then he tried to make sense of the countess' rampage while Harper turned his back on them all. Aurora remained in the hallway, unsure of what to do or say, sensing that it was unwise to do or say anything at all just now.

As Tadzio began to absorb the meaning of the unfolding scene, he, too, started to yell, employing Maritza's vocabulary but hurling his invective in

Vance's direction.

Vance and Eva did nothing but stare at each other, and Aurora observed that what had occurred seemed to be as great a surprise to the principals involved as it was to everyone else.

"Well?" Vance asked nervously.

Quickly, Eva turned to Maritza, who immediately became quiet. The two women faced one another and then Eva said, "Good-bye. I love you." And she fled from the living room, through the hall, the foyer, and out the front door, following the luggage-laden cabbie.

Tadzio remained halfway down the staircase, and now Vance looked up toward him.

"After all I've done for you!" Tadzio managed, tears welling in his eyes.

"It's time, Tadzio," Vance answered, picking up the remaining suitcase. "And it's my—our—last chance."

"You two? Sneaking around behind our backs!"

"No . . . not that. But we're alike, she and I. I think it took this to make us see it." Vance moved to the door, turned, and softly said, "For what it's worth . . . I've loved you, too."

Aurora continued to sip her coffee in front of the television set. As far as she knew, the heated farewell that day had been the last time Vance and Tadzio had seen each other. Eva and Vance had escaped to a nearby hotel and had later found an apartment.

Aurora remembered her own farewell to Maritza and Tadzio; it had been hastier than she would have liked. But in the long run, perhaps that was best. They were the kindest, most generous of friends. And, although Harper was right on a technicality—they had overstayed their visit—guilt continued to gnaw at her. In effect, her friends had been thrown out, and in a manner beneath the dignity of either. Aurora knew them well and she understood that this was the ultimate injury.

The bags had been loaded into the car; Tadzio, Maritza, and Aurora stood in the hallway. Tadzio embraced Aurora and said, "You'll come to New York and visit, of course. We both know this is none of your doing." He glanced quickly at the countess. "I'll wait in the car," he added, hurrying from the hall.

Maritza seemed to be staring at Aurora, as if trying to memorize her eyes, her hair, her features. So much had remained unspoken, and now, perhaps for the last time, they were alone. The countess raised her long, elegant hands and framed Aurora's face with her palms. Both had tears in their eyes when Maritza spoke. "Eva . . . she was . . . is . . . very like you."

Aurora nodded. She'd seen the similarity in the magazine photos.

"Maritza," she began, her lips trembling, "oh, I'll miss you so much!"

"And I you, dearest. But we have achieved what we wanted for you, haven't we? Remember that, Rory. You are a success." The countess pulled her close and they embraced tightly. Then she turned and with practiced steadiness strode from the house without a backward glance.

It had been awkward with Harper in the week that followed. But as time wore on and studio business occupied more of his thoughts, the entire incident seemed to fade in the glare of more immediate concerns. The subject was never mentioned again, although it continued to prey on Aurora's conscience.

That was why she had sent the telegram to the network on the day Vance's first episode aired, and it was one of the reasons for their periodic luncheons. If Aurora was not permitted to invite Vance and Eva to be guests in her own home, she would not be stopped from seeing them in theirs. Harper made no mention of these visits; he seemed to know there were certain boundaries he had no right to cross. And, as part of their unspoken bargain, Aurora did not mention Vance and Eva.

News of Tadzio and the countess was never difficult to obtain, although Aurora never visited them in New York or anywhere else. But they popped up frequently in the papers, a new woman on Tadzio's arm, a new man on Maritza's. The prince's taste ran now to dark young men, the latest was named Lance, while the countess remained true to type with a series of tallish brunettes. Postcards arrived occasionally from Paris, New York, or Rome; once, a brief but chatty letter, written by Tadzio and signed by both. Aurora was pleased that at least they were all still in touch. Her parting words to Maritza had been true: she missed them.

Once More, Love faded out and Aurora switched off the set.

On the table to her left sat the new script; she had avoided looking through it since its arrival by studio messenger that morning. She groaned as she had when she'd first glimpsed its title: *Lickety-Split*.

Not another one, she thought.

It would be her fourth film. This time it was a comedy, written and scheduled to be directed by a television sitcom veteran, probably a studio hack.

Maritza's parting words to her echoed in her ears. *You are a success.* But by whose yardstick? Yes, she had made a successful marriage. Yes, she was a movie star. But she was a grade-B movie star and certainly not one that any of the critics or her peers could deem an actress.

Over the last six months, Aurora had begun to consider her own definition of the word *success*.

Her first film, *Duo for One,* had enjoyed a minor success. Released during the summer, it was lascivious enough to intrigue the teenaged moviegoing public, and Miles Hogarth's name had helped to draw an older audience. As for herself, Aurora had been shamefully embarrassed by the angles Anton had chosen to shoot—and the use to which those angles were put by the editor in the final cut. During her one big, emotional scene, a scene to which she had brought total commitment, the camera had concentrated its lens upon her stretched, crushed, heaving breasts, making everything she did—her acting—appear ludicrous as well as laughable. In addition, the few critics who did review the film concurred. At best, they said, the actress portraying Gaby possessed potential. However, for the most part, the film and her performance had been dismissed largely as a joke.

Despite her wishes, Aurora's career was being guided and nurtured by Harper. He chose her scripts, produced her films. Fine. The second picture—he'd promised—would be different.

It was. A gothic love story in which she was terribly miscast as a shy English governess in love with her dark, brooding employer, it was a low-budget remake of *Jane Eyre,* with Aurora in the Joan Fontaine role. It flopped.

Aurora spent several months without a project, during which time Harper produced three films. One of them had a plum role, Laura in *Band of Gold,* that Aurora could easily have played.

"No," Harper had said in reply to her entreaties.

"Just let me test for the role, Harper!"

"Aurora, you're my wife. It would be beneath you to submit to a test. And if I were to cast you in the role, what would the industry say? That you'd gotten it because you're Mrs. Harper Styles. No, it's out of the question. Please don't bring it up again."

Within a week, Harper handed her the script of her third film, *Grave Matters,* in which she was murdered before the end of the first reel and spent the rest of the picture floating around in ghostly white chiffon, tormenting her killer.

So here she was, Mrs. Harper Styles, a respected member of the Hollywood community but with a career that was virtually a laughingstock to discerning audiences. Even a new television comedy hour had performed a sketch in which the leading lady's name was Luna Fashions. It hurt, even though the show was hilariously funny.

At first, the money had provided some compensation. Although she knew her salary was far below what was considered a handsome cachet, it was more than she had ever made before, and she had earned it. She was proud of that.

But as Harper's wife, she had more money than she could spend. Her own per-picture fee had increased sizably but was still the proverbial drop in the bucket when compared with Harper's income. Her money didn't seem to matter. However, Aurora kept her own bank account, and her investments had grown into an amount that Maritza might have termed a pretty penny. The separate account had been Harper's idea, a way of making Aurora secure in the money she was earning.

Nonetheless, it seemed only a consolation prize when she and Harper sat in the darkened theater for the première of *Band of Gold,* which starred a New York actress named Vivian Hamilton in the role Aurora had wanted to play—the role for which she had willingly offered to test.

Hamilton had scored a major triumph on Broadway earlier that year, winning the Tony Award for best actress over four long-established stars. Already signed to recreate her stage role in the film version of the play, Vivian Hamilton had been cast in *Band of Gold* over every up-and-coming actress in town, including Aurora Styles.

As the film unfolded before them, it quickly became apparent that this young actress was indeed a powerhouse. As Laura, she skillfully went from the age of sixteen to forty-five in what could only be termed a star performance. But, Aurora thought ruefully, what good actress couldn't, given a role that was practically actor proof? She fought off sour grapes as she sat quietly and watched. Yes, Hamilton was good. But in all honesty, Aurora knew she could have done as well. This was not conceit; it was the truth.

If envy was present in her, it was because Vivian Hamilton seemed headed for the kind of top-drawer, world-class career that any actress would covet.

Aurora and Harper put in the obligatory appearance at the lavish party following the première, and when Aurora was introduced to Hamilton, she was torn between admiration and jealousy. Yes, she admitted the jealousy—of the opportunity, the role, the adulation the actress received, beginning with the standing ovation at picture's end. Matters were not made easier when, during their brief chat at the party, Aurora discovered that Hamilton was not only a nice person but serious about her craft and eager to become better at it. Under other circumstances, they might have become friends.

The ride home was difficult. Aurora sat in the back of the Rolls, her face averted, looking out the window as the lights of Los Angeles whizzed by and faded into infinity while the sleek automobile sped along the freeway. She knew her behavior disturbed Harper, who sat silently beside her, but she hesitated to speak her mind. It seemed ungrateful to complain when she was wrapped in sable, seated in a Rolls Royce.

But the truth was unavoidable. The situation was only a mirror image of the way it had been more than two years ago, during the making of *Duo for One*. Now, instead of fearing she'd been given a role because she'd become the producer's lover, Aurora was worried that she was losing roles because she had become the producer's wife. Often, she had wanted to broach the subject to him. But the moment had never seemed right, and on those few occasions that presented an opportunity, Aurora suddenly felt childish at the prospect of bringing it up.

"Drink?" Harper asked, reaching to pull out the portable bar from its hidden recess. The car rolled over a bump that set the crystal decanters and glasses clinking.

"Yes, darling, please. I think I could use one," she answered. Perhaps now was the right time to speak. They were alone, without interruptions, and Harper was in a good mood for he knew *Band of Gold* would, in all likelihood, be a success for him and for the studio.

He flicked on the two small reading lights at either side; the interior was now illuminated as if by candlelight, casting the decanters and goblets into a glimmering, soft pink glow. The two fresh roses in the bud vases attached just above the lights stretched their lacy shadows across the velvet roof. It was a private, intimate world.

307

He poured, added ice, and handed her the vodka. Aurora didn't wait for him but sipped immediately, hoping the alcohol might give her the courage to say what she felt. She sipped again and turned to face him.

"Harper, I—"

"Wait," he commanded gently, reaching into the front pocket of his tuxedo.

He withdrew an enclosed fist, as a pleased smile crept across his handsome face. "I know tonight was difficult for you. I just wanted you to know . . . to remind you . . . of how much I love you and admire you."

"Thank you, Harper," Aurora responded, "because it *was* difficult, and I'd like to—"

"Wait," he said again. "Put down your drink for a moment."

Puzzled, she complied, placing the glass in the circular recess of the bar.

Harper extended his hand toward her, closed and turned upward. "Here," he said. "Hold out your hands."

Aurora, now more than curious, placed her palms together as he had instructed.

From his fist, a sparkling stream of diamonds trickled into her opened palms, glittering wildly in the dim amber light.

"I wish they were walnuts," he said quietly.

Aurora's memory fled back to the first night they had met and made love—and fallen in love. Tears filled her eyes and emotion welled inside her at the sweetness of his gesture.

How could she speak her mind now?

After reading the script of *Lickety-Split,* Aurora sat for a moment, confused. She was so accustomed to tired scripts and rehashed plots, so accustomed to heavy-handed suspense and dialogue, that it was difficult to believe what she had just read. Had Harper looked at this screenplay? There had to be a mistake.

It was good.

Suddenly she was elated at the prospect of beginning work on the film. Its horrid title notwithstanding, the script was well plotted, urbane, stylish, and definitely funny. Intentionally funny.

The day she reported to the studio, something else occurred that was a happy surprise. She had wondered why, when given her call two days earlier, she had not been told which scene they would be shooting first; she didn't know which lines to study. Instead of immediately going to makeup and costume, Aurora was directed to the main studio building that housed the executive offices, Harper's among them. In the large conference room, seated behind a long, oval desk of polished oak, were the creative personnel. Scripts, coffee, and bagels had been distributed. With Aurora's arrival, they were ready for their first read-through of the screenplay.

It was unheard of; at least it hadn't happened on any of the pictures she had previously filmed. But the entire cast was comprised of only five people, not counting a few day players who were as yet uncast, so a read-through was possible.

Wade Coby, the TV director, sat at the head of the table and greeted Aurora warmly. His was a familiar face, for he'd acted on television before shifting to the other side of the camera. The four other cast members were present, and Aurora was pleased to see that three of them were old pros, consummate comedy actors whose work she knew and respected. The fourth actor was unknown to her; this film, she learned, was his debut in a featured role.

As they read, Wade stopped them occasionally to offer a suggestion, mention a nuance he liked, or to explain some of the cut-aways that would be accomplished during the editing, just to punch up the comedy. It was apparent that mugging and "going for the results"—a phrase Aurora had not heard since leaving New York—would not be tolerated.

Four o'clock came and they closed their scripts. The atmosphere in the conference room was animated, exhilarated. Wade's enthusiasm had infected them all, infusing them with an eagerness to contribute their best. As much as possible, shooting would be in sequence, since much of the script dealt with only four interiors, all of which could be housed in two soundstages. No jumping back and forth from the beginning of the film to the end to accommodate the building of sets; rather, scenes would be shot in the order of their occurrence in the script. It was a first, not only for Aurora but for the other cast members as well—this procedure was seldom followed anymore—and as a result there was a special feeling in the atmosphere. It didn't matter that it was intangible; everyone could sense it.

That night over dinner, Aurora described her day to Harper. She knew she was gushing but was powerless to control herself. As she chattered on, he continued to eat and drink, staring at her with a mixture of amusement and delight.

"You're happy, hmm?" he asked.

"Oh, Harper, it's wonderful! I mean, I think this picture is really going to be *good!*"

He smiled and sipped his wine. "Let's just hope it's box-office."

He'd momentarily pricked her balloon. There it was again. Business. Didn't it matter if the product was good?

But, she reasoned, Harper was a businessman, after all, and a damned successful one. She would not allow his concern over the picture's financial success or failure to intrude on her elation. That was beyond her control anyway.

If only they would change the title, she thought. *Lickety-Split*. Really!

Chapter Eighteen

By the second week of shooting, it became apparent to Aurora that the attentions of Web Seton were more than just friendly.

In the film he was cast in the role of her ex-husband, and the plot was based on his hilarious efforts to win her back. It was Web's first featured role in a film, but his nervousness seemed to add to rather than detract from his characterization, bringing to the performance a sense of immediacy that appealed to Aurora.

He was very attractive; this she acknowledged immediately. He was also an excellent comedian, who brought out the best of Aurora's comedic abilities. Indeed, the two frequently broke each other up during filming, and an easy respect for each other's abilities gradually developed between them.

They had decided to run lines for an upcoming shot. At lunch, in Aurora's dressing room, Web took the opportunity to let his hand rest tenderly on hers.

At first, she did not pull away but let her eyes wander up to his. She smiled, sipping her coffee.

"You . . . wouldn't like to have dinner some night, would you?" he asked hesitantly.

"Sure," she replied. "Come up to the house. Harper

would love to meet you. Bring a friend."

"That's not what I had in mind, Rory."

She pushed the button of his nose with her index finger and laughed. "I know what you had in mind, Web. And I'm flattered . . . and married. Happily."

He didn't approach her again, and for that Aurora was grateful. Under other circumstances, she certainly would have been interested. He wasn't the first man to be attracted to her, but since she'd married Harper, none had tempted her.

During one of their conversations, however, something surfaced that Aurora realized she had never dealt with before.

They'd talked about their backgrounds, their life histories. Web had been married once and divorced. As he talked about his ex-wife, Aurora felt herself tensing. What was it? Most likely the fear that Web would ask her about Harper, about Harper's history before Aurora.

And she didn't know.

Of course, his vital statistics were common knowledge. Harper was born in the Midwest, in Kenosha, Wisconsin. He'd once referred to a girl with whom he had been in love, a girl who had stayed behind when he'd gone west to Hollywood. But beyond that, he'd remained elusive about specifics.

He'd been married before; that was no secret. His first wife had also been an actress. The former Mrs. Styles had been known professionally as Jennifer Beresford and had enjoyed a promising career before her marriage. Yet her films had been undistinguished, her name had faded, and apparently she had been unable to make a comeback after the divorce.

Why? Aurora wondered. Had Harper, in some way, blacklisted her? No. That wasn't like him. However, when she mentioned the name of Jennifer Beresford to anyone, Aurora was met with cautious, guarded answers. All she could glean was that Harper's first wife had left Hollywood at the age of thirty and no one seemed to know—or care—where she was now.

Harper flatly refused to discuss her. "It didn't work out," he replied in a tone that always managed to discourage further inquiry.

Aurora found his enigmatic behavior both alluring and perplexing. Harper was not a melodramatic person, but Aurora wondered if he enjoyed having his past shrouded in mystery.

On the other hand, talking with Web was easy. And he didn't inquire about Harper but confined their conversations to the present, to their work on the film, and to discussions on acting. He lent her an unauthorized biography of Helen Hayes that Aurora read with great interest.

It was in the pages of Hayes' biography that Aurora discovered the anecdote about the actress' first meeting with her future husband, Charles MacArthur.

Harper lay asleep beside Aurora as she read. Turning the page, she learned of MacArthur's first words to the young Hayes. Pouring a handful of peanuts into her palm, he said, "I wish they were emeralds." Years later, on an anniversary, he poured emeralds into Hayes' hand and said, "I wish they were peanuts."

Aurora put the book down on her lap and touched her hand to her chest. Her heart was thumping rapidly. Suddenly she was on the verge of tears as she looked over at Harper's sleeping form.

The next day she mentioned the story to Web.

"You mean you've never heard it before?" he asked, surprised. "Why, that story's a classic!"

She barely heard the rest of the conversation. She was busy masking her hurt, which was now far worse than after reading of the episode. The walnuts. The diamonds. Harper had indeed used a good line—a line he'd stolen. She couldn't help wondering how many other women had heard that same line from Harper.

But this was silly. It had happened ages ago. She had married him. And the gesture was romantic, no less so for being unoriginal. Still, Aurora felt like a fool and in an odd way, betrayed.

The diamonds had been mounted into an exquisite brooch. She never wore it again.

The months passed and *Lickety-Split* was completed. It had lived up to its promise of a happy working experience. The writers had not considered the script as sacred; changes had been made along the way and dialogue had been discussed and improved. Everyone had cooperated to the overall benefit of the film.

Life at home had remained on an even keel while shooting continued. Although occasionally Aurora missed Maritza or Tadzio, they wrote frequently and she always responded. She knew this displeased Harper, but she wasn't about to hide incoming mail.

Regular telephone calls kept her in close touch with Abby, and from the sound of the child's voice and from her appearance in the snapshots she sent, it was apparent that Aurora's foster sister was rapidly developing into a bright, levelheaded teenager. The calls to the young girl were always eagerly anticipated, and when Harper was at home, he got on an extension phone and related movie stories that never failed to thrill the youngster. It seemed that her crush—or the memory of it—still lingered, even after five years or more.

At last, *Lickety-Split* was edited, scored, and scheduled for its première. Aurora had not been so excited about an opening since her first film.

While her hairdresser arranged her coiffure, she glanced through that morning's paper. The lead story detailed an enormous drug bust, and in an accompanying article, a name that seemed familiar appeared. Olivia Butler. Why should the name ring such a bell? Unable to pinpoint it, Aurora put down the paper and centered her thoughts upon the forthcoming night's . . . triumph? She blushed at the silent voicing of the thought. But that was what she hoped it would be. The rough cut of the picture, before musical scoring, had been terrific. If the final edit and addition of music only enhanced it, *Lickety-Split* couldn't be anything but a winner. Elated by that prospect, Aurora went for an afternoon shopping tour along Rodeo Drive.

When she pulled the Mercedes into the driveway, she was puzzled. Harper's car was in the garage, and what looked like Anton Kalmar's Bentley was parked beside it.

She glanced at the delicate Piaget on her wrist. It was only four o'clock, much too early for Harper's return from the studio. And why the sudden visit from Anton? He hadn't been by for a month. As she opened the front door, she hurried into the living room. Whatever the reason for his afternoon call, Aurora looked forward to seeing him.

But she found Anton sitting on the sofa, a glass of Scotch clutched tightly in his trembling hands. He was sobbing.

Harper sat opposite him and his eyes met Aurora's as she entered the room. The atmosphere was weighted with silence.

Aurora's eyebrows rose questioningly. What could possibly have happened? She knew things had not gone well lately for the director. His last two films had fared more dismally than usual. That, together with the

317

gossip about his cocaine problem, made him an unbankable commodity, a white elephant in the industry. Yet despite Harper's unbending belief in the Hollywood structure, his unwillingness to break with what Aurora termed senseless traditions and social codes, he made an exception where Anton Kalmar was concerned. He ignored studio protocol in defense of his friend. Anton had fallen far in the eyes of the influential. Had he been anyone else, he would have been banished, permanently, from Harper Styles' life. "An outcast is an outcast," Harper would have said. And that would have ended it.

Now the director sat in a disheveled heap, a day's growth of beard on his ashen, weary face, tears streaming down his cheeks. It was an uncharacteristic display of weakness. But, Aurora wondered, *was* it uncharacteristic? His addiction was his weakness. Had it now manifested itself externally and taken complete control?

Without a word, Aurora removed her coat and poured herself a drink. Her eyes were still fixed on Harper. Finally, he held up a copy of the same newspaper Aurora had read that afternoon. The headline banner read: DRUG BUST!

Suddenly it all rushed back to her. She understood why Anton was so distressed. She also remembered why the name of Olivia Butler had seemed familiar to her.

Anton's supplier. Of course!

"Oh, my God!" Anton cried, his usually slight accent quite thick.

"Anton, stop this! There's no guarantee she'll name you—"

"No, Harper, but what if she kept a diary . . . told people . . . kept records?"

"He's right." Aurora was surprised at the emphatic

318

tone in her own voice.

"Aurora, let's not make him more hysterical!" Harper snapped.

Anger at being chastised in front of a guest almost made Aurora snap back, but this was hardly the moment for a family tiff. She sipped her drink and shrugged instead.

"Harper," said Anton, "don't you see? I'm not Olivia's only . . . patron. She supplies some very big people in this town—people who are still big. If one—just one—is exposed, we all go under. We're all linked. Oh, God, I'll be in jail for the rest of my life!"

"Not if we can get you out of the country." Harper now held Anton's attention. "Is your passport valid?"

"Yes, yes, always. But . . . my friends abroad . . . they'll be under suspicion if their own authorities see me running to them. I can't jeopardize their reputations."

"Well," said Harper, "you and Aurora have one friend who barely has any reputation to ruin. He'd take you in."

"Harper!" Aurora fairly shouted. "That's a terrible thing to say about Tadzio! I know how you feel, but he and Maritza are friends to Anton and to me."

"But I'm right, don't you think?"

She had to admit it. He was right. Tadzio certainly would not be harmed by publicity that revealed he was fraternizing with a coke head. Nonetheless Aurora resented Harper's willingness to exploit Tadzio.

"You know where he is?" Anton asked.

"Switzerland," Aurora answered.

Harper rose from his chair and crossed to Aurora. Gently he touched her face and kissed her on the lips. "Will you call him?"

*   *   *

In the old days, if they could be called that, Vance would have driven Anton to the airport. Funny that Aurora should think of that, for she was relieved that Vance was not involved in this.

They had decided it was best for Anton's car to remain in the garage. It was doubtful that anyone was looking for him yet, but it was possible, so escape would be easier in an unknown car. Of course, a Rolls would be too conspicuous, so Harper arranged for a contract player to come by that afternoon in his Chevrolet and transport Anton to the airport. The actor was totally ignorant of the situation, and Aurora was again ashamed that Harper could so coolly involve someone else in the matter. Yet what other choice was there? Their own faces were too well known, and as far as they could see, the house was not being watched. Harper did not think Anton had been followed.

It was agreed that some of the director's belongings would be forwarded to him later, after he was safely settled in Lucerne.

Lucerne. It had been so good to hear Tadzio's voice! After details about Anton's getaway were discussed, Tadzio brought Aurora up to date on his and Maritza's recent travels and adventures. As he did so, her eyes filled with tears; she suddenly missed them both very much. Briefly, she was tempted to hop on the plane with Anton and spend a week with her friends. But no—not today. Not tonight! Tonight was the première of *Lickety-Split!*

How ridiculous it all was! That morning, the première had been the most important thing in her life. Now it had paled in the light of a genuine crisis.

Quickly Aurora embraced Anton as Harper slid the patio door open. The driver-actor in the Chevrolet waited at the back of the house with the motor running, ready to speed Anton to the next plane departing

320

LAX airport.

"I'll come and visit, Anton," Aurora said, holding him closely to her. "Soon. I promise."

He nodded; emotion made words impossible. Then he rushed out to the car.

Aurora and Harper stood on the patio, watching as the Chevrolet disappeared down the road. For a moment they didn't speak. It was done and Anton was gone.

"Now," Harper finally said, indicating the time on the patio wall clock, "you'd better get dressed. We can't be late."

No, she thought. We can't be late.

It took no time for Olivia Butler to name her clients. Apparently, she had been offered leniency in exchange for doing so. The list read like a *Who's Who* of Hollywood.

In the back of the Rolls en route to the theater, Aurora and Harper sat with the late editions of the newspapers, reading about the demise of no fewer than five major Hollywood careers, Anton Kalmar's among them. He was being sought for questioning.

She glanced at her watch. It was seven-thirty. The film would begin at eight. Although she was eagerly, albeit nervously, anticipating viewing the picture, Aurora was very concerned about Anton. His flight was scheduled to depart in fifteen minutes. Would he make it or would he be detained? And would the driver of the Chevrolet be implicated in any way?

"Stop worrying." Harper grinned and placed his hand over hers. "By the time they realize he's gone, he will be."

Aurora was quiet for a moment and then asked, "Harper, what if . . . you . . . we . . . are implicated?"

321

"How?"

"I don't know the specifics of the law, but wouldn't we be what they call 'accessories after the fact'?"

Harper laughed. "Aurora, darling, this isn't a murder case. Relax. You're on the verge of a triumph this evening. Think of that. By the way, you're looking particularly beautiful."

She nodded her thanks. He'd said the word: *triumph.* She was pleased by his compliment, but her appearance had been only a secondary concern. She knew she looked marvelous. Her gown, a new Oscar de la Renta, was made of the palest pearl gray chiffon. High-throated in front and dipping to her waist in back, it was weightless and simple, to offset her diamonds and rubies. Her hair was gathered in a turn-of-the-century style that was at once demure and provocative. No, her concern over the première had nothing to do with her looking her best. She wanted the film to be a triumph.

"You're so calm, Harper. Always. I envy that."

"It's easier for me," he said. "I may lose money, but it's not my face and body up there on that giant screen. I'm not as vulnerable as the actors and actresses who take the brunt of the criticism." He laughed. "Of course, they get the lion's share of the acclaim, with a successful film."

"But aren't you at all worried about Anton?"

Harper shifted slightly in his seat and looked deeply into her eyes. "Certainly," he said quietly, "but either he'll make it to Switzerland or he won't. They'll either find out that we helped, or they won't. He is my dear friend, Aurora. I've done everything I can for him. The rest is out of my control. I can't worry about those things."

The car slowed when it ran into the traffic leading to the theater, and the Rolls joined the line of limousines waiting to move up to the entrance to discharge their famous passengers. Enormous klieg lights swept the night sky, and the butterflies in Aurora's stomach were transformed into a heavy lump of lead.

Once again, Harper was right. What control had she over any of this? Tonight's première wouldn't determine the reviews. The critics had seen the film days before at special press screenings. Their opinions were already written, ready to appear in tomorrow's edition or to be read from teleprompters on late-night newscasts. Only the audience would be seeing the film for the first time, and personnel who had worked on the film but had not been invited to the screenings.

And where is Anton now? Aurora wondered. His situation was almost a matter of life and death. Surely the première of a movie, even one of which she was so proud, shrank in importance by comparison. Who cared what people thought about the film?

She did.

". . . but the happiest surprise of the evening was the performance of Aurora Styles. Not since Carole Lombard have we seen such a deft comedic actress."

"It takes awhile to realize that Miss Styles is not going to be chased, menaced, or murdered in this very good film. One can sit back and enjoy a truly fine comedienne in a glittering performance."

"B-movie Styles moves up to the A-category in the best comedy so far this year."

On they went. Raves for Aurora and, for the most part, the picture as well. A few critics took exception to sections of the screenplay, but all were unanimous in their praise for her performance.

A week had passed since the première. The atmosphere in the theater that night had been tense for more than one reason. Everyone in the audience had read the papers, and most of those present knew the five people named by Olivia Butler. Hollywood was nervous.

Aurora's fears for Anton had subsided. He'd telephoned upon his arrival at Tadzio's chalet in Lucerne. When the FBI learned that he had left the country, the story hit the headlines for one day, but it died when an armored car robbery upstaged Anton's escape. He was safe.

And *Lickety-Split,* welcomed by the reviewers, gave everyone involved in its production cause to bask in the afterglow.

But a *triumph?*

Aurora had spoken with Web, who was already shooting another film. He'd called to ask if she was scheduled for any publicity appearances on the TV talk shows or for magazine interviews. She wasn't. Neither was he.

"Rory, you're the producer's wife. What's going on?"

She wondered too. There had been minimum advertising space taken in the newspapers or the trades, and those that appeared carried no quotes from the enthusiastic reviews. No TV commercials urged viewers to run out to their movie theaters. No billboards or posters enticed potential audiences.

"Well," Aurora stammered into the phone, "it's only been . . . a week, Web. Maybe . . . they're waiting . . . till it's in national release."

"Maybe," he answered, "but I doubt it. It's a good thing I've got a picture coming out next month and this one I'm working on now. If I had to depend on the publicity for *Lickety-Split,* I'd be forgotten."

He hadn't meant to be hurtful, she could tell. He was just being subjective. He was fairly new to the business. What had she to fear, married to Harper Styles?

324

When she hung up, Aurora leaned over and picked up the new *Variety*, which had arrived that morning. There had been little news about the film in its dailies; perhaps the voluminous weekly edition would tell her something.

It told her that the picture was not listed among the top forty box-office moneymakers. It told her that no blurbs mentioned future marketing. It told her that the studio—Harper—was not pushing the picture. Surely he wasn't using this film—*her* film—to take a tax loss!

"Why?" she asked him.

"Partly the title, darling. We've had negative response to it."

"But I said that from the beginning, Harper. I mentioned it to you before we started shooting. You could have changed the title long before the release!"

He nodded. "I make mistakes too, you know." He took her in his arms and smiled. "Aurora, you're wonderful in the film and you received great reviews. If the film loses money . . . well, what of it? The studio is doing fine. We can afford a loss, especially a critically successful one."

Aurora pulled herself from his embrace and turned her back to him, not wanting to face him while she said what she was about to say.

"Harper," she began nervously, "I'm not talking about the studio . . . I'm talking about me."

"What?"

"Me. I can't afford a loss. Not me-your-wife, but me-the-actress. I thought this film could be my chance for better roles. For public recognition. To be taken seriously." She faced him now and saw an expression of incredulity in his eyes. "Don't you understand, darling? Oh, I know it sounds peevish and selfish, but I've been doing pictures for a while and I'm going nowhere."

"Aurora, it requires time to build a career. A following."

"Not five years, Harper. Not when I'm good, in a really good film. Nobody knows *Lickety-Split* exists."

"The industry knows, Aurora. You'll see. You've gained new respect from everyone. That often takes years."

"It's not taking Vivian Hamilton years!" She'd blurted it out. In *Variety* she'd read that Hamilton had been signed for another film at twice her previous fee.

Harper launched into the whys and wherefores of movie careers: Vivian Hamilton had breezed into town on the wings of a fabulous New York stage success; she'd practically written her own ticket from the beginning. Et cetera.

Throughout it all, Aurora glared at him, seething inside. Then she said, "Hamilton also has a staff of people working for her—with her—that are legion. They slave practically twenty-four hours a day to put her in the mainstream and keep her there."

"Implying that you don't have help?" he asked defensively.

"Harper," she said quietly, "I've never had tunnel vision about success. I'm not fixated on stardom. There are far more important matters. You're one of them. I'm just tired of being a joke."

She had expected him to move closer to her and wrap her in his arms, his usual remedy whenever she was upset. But he didn't, and a puzzled, unpleasant expression marred his handsome face.

Softly he said, "I suppose that means you're growing up, doesn't it?"

Aurora didn't blink or look away when she replied, "Yes, I suppose I am."

As Christmas approached, the truth became apparent. The studio had not given the picture major publicity. There'd been hardly any campaign at all. *Lickety-Split* began to slide from public memory. Box-office receipts were, at best, grim. Without a doubt, the film was a failure. And that failure put Aurora in a mood she couldn't shake.

Despite the luxury that surrounded her, the tangible comforts and the seemingly endless supply of money, nothing satisfied her. Aurora's love and devotion to Harper remained unchanged; however, her personal success appeared to be placed permanently on hold. She realized that most of her time was spent in waiting or in disappointment: waiting for a new script, then disappointment after reading the first ten pages. It became obvious that *Lickety-Split* had been seen by too few members of the industry to alter her image; the new scripts were no better than before. All horror films, all cheap—the roles could easily have been played by two dozen other actresses under studio contract. It was only after plodding through the third such screenplay that Aurora decided to take steps she'd never dared take before.

Scripts were usually sent to her via the studio; these were potential vehicles submitted directly to the producer's wife. Little was said when she turned these down; such was the extent of her clout. However, if the script was brought home by Harper, this was a project he expected her to accept. That was a tacit agreement, one of the unspoken bonds in their marriage.

As before, the first scene of the new script told Aurora all she needed to know. Nonetheless, she plowed through page after page of being raped, chased, slapped, and terrorized by a gang of revolutionaries hellbent on keeping her, after the murder of her father, from taking over the reins of power in a banana republic.

Since she knew the budget on the picture would

prohibit actually shooting in any Latin American country—the Philippines were used by most American filmmakers for such projects—this abomination would probably be shot in the desert. Aurora had never liked the desert, and the prospect of spending weeks on location there made her even less enthusiastic about it.

Matters worsened when she read in *Daily Variety* that Vivian Hamilton had been offered *Under Eros,* the filmed version of the international best seller. Aurora had read the book, and loved it. It was a beautifully written, tightly plotted novel about a young American woman who was involved in an illicit affair with a married British officer during World War II. By any accounts, it was a plum role; more importantly, Aurora felt it was perfect for her. Talk around town had it that the producers were seeking an actress with a film background, but not someone with too much screen exposure to date. Well, she'd thought, I fit on both counts, don't I?

She had made a few telephone calls, feeling out reactions when she'd hinted at her willingess to test for the role. She'd been friendly, casual, as if she were simply keeping in touch with industry colleagues. Appearing too hungry was anathema, so she hadn't come straight out in expressing her interest. And she was not eager for Harper to learn of her attempts to find a decent script for herself.

But her efforts had proved futile. Although the paper indicated that Hamilton had not yet signed a contract, *Under Eros* was as good as hers.

Aurora turned her eyes from *Daily Variety* and glanced down at Harper's script, which lay on the sofa. *Blood Destiny.* Oh, Harper!

She found herself rehearsing *how* and *what* to say to him that night. She already knew what his arguments would be. She also knew that he had brought her the script because he was concerned about her boredom due to having no work. He probably felt this would keep her occupied—acting—and therefore, content.

But the ineptitude of this script went beyond the usual clumsy, amateurish writing and plot contrivance. The role of the female protagonist called for a girl of seventeen. Aurora knew she looked younger than her twenty-six years, but seventeen? Wasn't that pushing it?

Over dinner, she and Harper chatted pleasantly about his day at the studio, local gossip, and Web Seton, whom Harper had signed for a new film.

Over cognac in the study, Aurora searched for a way in which to broach the matter of *Blood Destiny,* but she backed off each time an opportunity presented itself until Harper asked, "Well, have you read the script yet?"

There is no backing off now, she thought. Sighing deeply, she replied, "Yes, Harper. I have."

Her tone of voice clearly told him how she felt. Pausing momentarily, Harper swirled amber liquor in a crystal snifter. Then a small but understanding smile crept onto his face. "All right," he said, "I grant you it isn't Oscar material, but you do need to get back on the screen soon."

"So people won't forget me?"

"Well . . . yes."

"Forget who, Harper?"

"You—Aurora Styles." He regarded her curiously, as if he couldn't read her meaning.

"But who is that, Harper? In movie terms, just who is Aurora Styles?"

"I don't like being spoken down to as if I were a child taking a quiz, Aurora. What are you getting at?"

"What audience will 'forget' me, Harper? Rednecks who spend their time at drive-in double features? Late-night TV freaks? God, Harper, if I never made another picture, who would really care?"

He stared at her with a look she had seen before. It put Aurora on her guard. This was the man she loved, but she knew his manipulativeness; she didn't want to be swayed from the rightness of her convictions.

"It's not as if you're without fans, darling," he said. "You see your mail. Letters come pouring in every week."

"Have you ever looked at them? Do you know the kinds of fans who write to me? Crackpots, Harper! They love me because I'm always the victim. They identify with that—if you can decipher their handwriting through the grade-school grammar and spelling!"

"You mustn't look down on your public," he said.

Anger was rising quickly, too quickly, and Aurora feared she would be unable to control it, unable to choose her words carefully. "I guess I do look down on them," she managed to grit out from between clenched teeth. "And I don't want to make these pictures anymore." She spoke quietly but firmly, hoping she conveyed her seriousness.

"There is nothing wrong with this script, Aurora."

"Oh, bullshit, Harper!" she blurted out. Her fury had reached its peak. "It's worse than ever! It's violent! It's stupid! It's senseless! The special effects department has a better part than I do!"

"You start shooting next week," he said flatly.

Aurora breathed deeply into her cognac and drained the glass before she spoke. "I won't do it," she said at last.

"Aurora, please—"

"Harper, there are better scripts lying in slush piles all over the studio. Why can't I at least—"

"Right now it would be very difficult to convince

330

anyone with a serious project that you'd be right for it."

"Oh, but you said I had gained 'new respect' from the industry after *Lickety-Split."*

"And you have. But one good film is not a track record. Especially one that . . . well, one that did less than had been expected."

"It flopped. Say it. It bombed. But how do I get a track record by going back to trash?"

His jaw tightened. "I suppose *Under Eros* is more your speed?"

It stopped her cold. Did he know she'd called around?

"Well," she said hesitatingly, "since you brought it up . . ."

"Can you be serious, Aurora? Do you really think anything that goes on in this business escapes me for long? Your interest . . . in that property was regarded with amusement."

Amusement! "And you said nothing to me?"

"How could I? I didn't want to make you feel more of a fool than you'd already made yourself."

"Fool! For wanting to do better? To be better?"

"Can we discuss this in the morning, Aurora, when you've calmed down?"

"I'll have calmed down, Harper, but I won't have changed my mind. I will not do *Blood Destiny."*

Harper rose from his leather chair and placed his empty brandy snifter on the portable bar in the corner. "We'll see," he said. Then he left the room.

Chapter Nineteen

Aurora awoke as if from a drug-induced coma. Her eyelids opened with difficulty. What had she taken last night? Nothing. Not even aspirin or a sleeping pill. Then she recalled the confrontation with Harper and knew. Exhausted, she'd wearily gone upstairs to find Harper in bed, already asleep. He was wearing pajamas, which served as a surprise and a signal. Usually, he slept naked. Pajamas meant that he was angry, off limits. Fine, she thought. She was hardly in the mood.

The morning sun streamed through the huge windows facing the bed. Too bright, she decided, wincing at sight of the bedside clock. Ten-thirty. She'd slept hours later than usual, and, of course, Harper had left hours before for the studio.

She forced herself to rise and place both feet on the floor, although the warmth, comfort, and, above all, the sanctuary of the bed called out to her. She knew herself well enough to recognize a mild depression and she was determined to fight it. Bed held no answer, only escape.

Later, dressed but without makeup, she sat and reviewed her situation over a steaming cup of coffee. In the light of late morning, without the heat of argument, she didn't question her position.

Once more, she thought longingly about *Under Eros.* Perhaps Vivian Hamilton would turn it down. Perhaps, after all, they would allow Aurora to test. She hadn't made another horror film—or horrible film—so her most recent appearance was in the worthy *Lickety-Split.* She sipped her coffee and smiled wryly. Don't kid yourself, Aurora, she cautioned. There are ten other actresses in line for the role.

Why is it so important to act? she asked. Why do I have this burning desire to express myself via the false life of a fictional woman?

She yearned now for the company of someone who could understand. As a rule, she wasn't fond of actors. She found most of them too egocentric; that and the competition and peer pressure created by the system made friendships with them difficult. Until now, the only other actor to whom she'd taken a liking was Web Seton, and that liking seemed dangerous to pursue.

As if on cue, the phone beside the breakfast table rang. Aurora answered, as taught, in the middle of the fourth ring. Any sooner and you were too eager.

"Rory?" It was Web Seton's voice.

"Oh!" she exclaimed, surprised by the coincidence and unguarded in her pleasure. "Great minds think alike!"

"Huh?"

"I was just wondering if I should call you—or leave a message."

"You shouldn't stop to wonder. Next time, just do it."

"Okay," she said, laughing. "It's almost noon. Why aren't you shooting?"

"Change in schedule. I slept late and have the rest of the day off. Thought I'd call and see how you are."

You'd be surprised, she thought. Aloud, she said, "I'm glad. You'll be working for Harper soon, I hear."

"Yeah. Good yarn. Thanks, if you had anything to do with my being hired."

"I didn't."

There was a pause, as if neither knew what else to say. Then Web asked, "Listen, instead of a chat on the phone, how about brunch?"

On impulse, she accepted. "Pick me up in an hour. Oh . . . and Web?"

"What?"

"Would you bring the script to the picture you're doing for Harper?"

"Sure . . . but haven't you read it already?"

"No. Why?"

"Just curious. There's a role in it that's perfect for you. Anyway, see you in an hour."

She chose her wardrobe carefully. Usually, Aurora dressed for herself, but today she was dressing for Web Seton.

Look out, a voice warned, cautioning against her initial choice of a clinging jersey and tight corduroy jeans. Too informal, too revealing. She switched to a beige crepe and matching man-tailored cotton slacks.

Forty-five minutes later, Aurora stood at the living-room window, waiting for Web's car to pull up. She wouldn't give him a chance to come into the house. No. She liked him too much to tempt fate.

When his car did start up the hill, she grinned. He was quickly becoming a citizen of the Hollywood establishment. The car was a Porsche.

It was a cold day for Beverly Hills, winter making itself felt more than usual. However, for the short drive to the restaurant she opened the window on her side of the car and allowed the wind to whip through her long, loose mane; the chilled air felt brisk and clean.

It did not escape her notice that Web had chosen a new restaurant, one in which they were unlikely to see people they knew. Or to be seen by them. What am I doing? she thought, feeling the pressure of Web's strong hand on her elbow as he escorted her through the room to their table.

He ordered drinks and she studied him. His wasn't a traditionally handsome face. It was perhaps too roughly hewn, the complexion too ruddy. Perfect white teeth—but everyone out here had perfect teeth. Yet that very lack of conventional good looks made him so attractive.

Between them lay the script. Aurora glanced through it, immediately disliking the title.

"The Happy Hour?" she read aloud.

"I know. I hated it too. But it's perfect, really. I play an alcoholic."

"Aha," she observed, satisfied. It was apt. "Any good?"

"Yeah, I think so. Really good. I mean, if it's well made, it could be right up there with *Lost Weekend* and *Days of Wine and Roses."*

"What's the woman's role like?"

"Good. She's my wife in the picture. But the role I thought I'd see you in comes later. It's support, but it's good. Here." He pulled out a pair of tortoise-shell-framed glasses, put them on, and took the script from her. "It's somewhere in here," he said, thumbing through to the middle.

Aurora smiled. The glasses gave Web a bookish image she hadn't seen before.

"Take a look," he suggested.

Quickly, she read through a scene. It was the role of a nurse in a glorified drunk tank; the nurse was herself a recovering alcoholic. No screaming, no histrionics, just good, solid, playable drama.

"Who got this part?" she asked, handing the script back to him.

"New girl. From New York."

No. It *couldn't* be Vivian Hamilton. The role was too small for her to even consider at this stage of her fast-moving career. Web mentioned the name of the actress, but Aurora had never heard of her. From New York. Funny, she mused. So many actresses out of work in L.A., but for the second time in a year, a "new girl from New York" had gotten a break. Maybe she never should have left New York. Nonsense, she told herself. Despite her frustration, was her lot really all that bad?

She hadn't commented on Web's last remark, and now a gentle tapping on the back of her hand returned her to the present.

"Where were you?" he asked with a grin.

"Oh, just thinking."

"About New York?"

"Sort of. Do you ever miss it?"

"Do I ever *not* miss it! But this is where it's at—money, career. You do miss it, though, don't you?"

"It's that obvious?"

"Yeah. And it's Christmas time, almost."

"Mmm. I never thought I'd long for winter weather. . . ."

". . . and snow!"

"Oh God, do I miss snow!" She joined him in laughter, their fingers lacing together across the table. Then, abruptly, the laughter ended. But their hands were still entwined. Carefully, she brought her eyes up to his.

"You're holding my hand, Web."

"On the contrary. You're holding mine."

Damn! Why was he so charming? Aurora loosened her grip and placed her hand around the Bloody Mary glass before her. "I release you," she said, attempting a smile.

"You think so?" he returned, no pretense at frivolity on his face or in his voice.

"Web . . ." she began.

"I know. Don't tell me again. You're happily married. Right?"

She hesitated for only a second, but her answer was, she knew, the truth. "Yes. I am."

"So?"

"So what?"

"So why are you here with me?"

Would it sound foolish to admit that she needed to talk? That was the truth too. But was it the only reason? She still remembered Web's embraces during their love scenes for the film, the look of his nearly nude form beneath the blankets in their movie marriage bed.

"Look . . . you know I like you. Very much. But I've never been unfaithful to Harper, and I'm not about to start. It's just that things are a little . . . strained . . . between us now. I need a friend."

"I'm not greedy," he said quietly. "If friendship is all you're prepared to offer, then I accept, with gratitude."

She sighed with relief. Although his statement did not entirely clear the air between them, at least they'd reached an understanding.

"What's the matter, Rory? Go ahead. Talk."

They ordered another round of drinks, and her worry and concern poured forth in a monologue that surprised them both. As she talked, she became more confident. Who else but another actor could understand how she felt? Another good actor who still cared about his—their—work.

When she finished, Web was silent for a time, obviously mulling over what she'd said before he spoke. "Well," he began, "it seems to me it's a matter of priorities. That is, if you want my not-too-valuable advice."

338

"Please, go on," she urged him.

"Rory, you need to act. I mean *really* need to act. That much is crystal clear. It's part of your problem."

"But you love acting too. I know you do," she protested.

"You're not listening. We both love acting. But only one of us needs it."

"Wait a minute," she said. "Run that past me again?"

"Okay. You can't live without something you need, right? You need both acting and Harper. Stop needing one of them."

"Stop needing?" she echoed. How did someone stop needing the most important factors in her life? "Well, if you're saying I should stop trying to have a career—"

"Rory, you *have* a career. But you want to *act*. And sometimes they just don't go together."

She made him stop at the bottom of the hill. "The walk will do me good."

"You're the boss," Web said, as his hand came up over the back of the seat and softly fondled her tousled hair. She let his hand stay there for a moment, briefly enjoying the sensation. When he leaned toward her, his mouth slightly open, the sun from the windshield illuminating his strong face, Aurora wanted to respond to his unspoken entreaty, but her hand came up to his chest and pushed him gently away.

"Thanks, Web. You're a friend."

"Always. And, please note, a gentleman to boot."

"Yes." She grinned. "That too."

"It's your turn to call next time, remember."

"I will." She kissed her index finger and planted it on his lips, then opened her door and got out. The Porsche sped off as she waved good-bye.

*   *   *

She had thought long and hard all day about the conversation. Web's advice was far too cut and dried to apply to the situation in any practical way, but Aurora knew that oversimplifying the problem did help to eliminate confusion. She also knew that a compromise had to be reached, one in which both parties gave a little.

Whenever Aurora was filming, a housekeeper-cook was employed. When she wasn't shooting, she enjoyed preparing the evening meal. Tonight, she took special care with it.

At the sound of Harper's car in the driveway, she was waiting at the door, dressed more formally than usual. She had piled her hair high upon her head and wore a long black velvet hostess gown, cut in a shallow V across her shoulder blades.

Kissing him on the cheek as he entered, she took his leather attaché case. "Go and shower while I mix martinis for us."

Harper looked tired and grateful for the extra attention. He returned her kiss, breathing deeply of the L'Interdit she'd dabbed on pulse spots. "What's the occasion?" he asked.

"Truce," she whispered.

"What a relief. I'll be right down."

He was quick. Having made sure their dinner was cooking on schedule, Aurora had just stirred the cocktails when Harper came downstairs and seated himself in his favorite easy chair. Refreshed from the shower and wearing a heavy wool sweater and beige Levis, he seemed younger now than when he had come home.

"About last night, Rory," he began with difficulty, "I . . . I behaved, I'm afraid, like some kind of dictator. I tried to call you to apologize, this afternoon, but—"

"I went for a drive. Brunch," she put in quickly,

saying nothing about Web.

"Fine. Let me finish." As he talked, he reached to the side of the chair where she had placed his briefcase. "I've thought about your feelings regarding *Blood Destiny,* and perhaps you're right. Besides, you're not seventeen anymore, are you?"

"No—thank God!" They both laughed.

He took two scripts from the leather case and laid them on the coffee table. "Here. Take a look at these. No horror or adventure. One is a suspense film, but not cut from the same cloth as your usual fare. Pick one."

Impulsively, she began to reach for the scripts, then stopped in mid-gesture. "And if neither of them is something I like?"

She waited for his reply. Apologizing, admitting that his judgment was off, did not come easily to Harper, she knew.

"Then we'll just keep looking," he answered.

"Oh, Harper." She rose, joining him on the arm of the chair, and kissed him tenderly.

He pulled her onto his lap and they remained there for a time, talking softly and kissing and caressing each other in the dimly lit room. Suddenly, for no apparent reason, Web Seton's image flashed through her mind. She tensed momentarily, hoping that Harper hadn't noticed.

"Something wrong?" He had noticed.

"No. I . . . I just don't want dinner to overcook. Go on into the dining room. I'll be right in."

Over the chicken Tetrazzini they talked some more, occasionally sipping the Meursault she'd chilled.

The martinis, the wine, and the after-dinner cognac had a pleasing effect upon both of them. Harper's hands strayed across the linen tablecloth to Aurora's, and he stroked her long, slim fingers, which shone like alabaster in the candle glow.

Raising his glass, he brought her hand to his lips and placed short, tender kisses at the pulse point of her wrist.

"Why don't we take our drinks upstairs?" he suggested.

He didn't wear pajamas that night.

Their lovemaking had settled into a less frequent pattern lately, although neither seemed able to go for very long without seeking the mutual gratification they both needed and enjoyed.

Tonight, however, their coming together was unusually passionate. Perhaps because they so seldom argued—*fought* was the more appropriate term—there was a special urgency both felt. As they approached each other in the darkened room, overwhelming desire surged through Aurora. His penis, fully erect, pointed toward her. He moved and came nearer, pressing his well-muscled body against hers, his lips seeking her mouth in the dark.

Aurora's knees wavered, and as she struggled to remain standing, a wave of heat burned between her legs, then rose inside her body, enveloping her breasts, her taut nipples, and her mouth, which devoured his tongue, nibbling, biting, in an aggressive display previously foreign to her.

Perspiration dotted her skin, and as her legs buckled, Harper's hands went to her elbows for support. But this time she did not want support. She gave in to the weakness, falling to her knees before him, not caressing him, not planting little kisses on the tip of his engorged member, not running her tongue along the delicious length of his shaft. Instead, she opened her mouth, her throat, and pulled him in. Giving him pleasure was more important to her tonight than anything else.

More important than her own gratification. She had to prove her need—her love—to him. As she looked up past his hard stomach, over the clearly defined pectorals to the large Adam's apple etched in sharp relief, her eyes became accustomed to the dark, and she saw his head fall back in abandon. Only the underside of his upturned jaw was visible to her now, and Aurora's love, her longing, burst inside her for the first of many times.

As she moved over him, she spread her knees wider for better balance, aware that the wetness between her legs was matting the hairs that covered her vulva. Harper moaned, calling her name, first in a whisper, then urgently. "Aurora . . . Aurora . . . Aurora!" he chanted, the litany driving her to draw on him with greater force. She felt him swell, lengthen, widen, until at last he filled her mouth with the juice of his love. Then her eyes closed and a face appeared in her mind's eye. But it wasn't the face of the man she loved . . . wanted . . . needed.

It was the face of Web Seton.

Concentrate! she commanded herself for the fourth time.

The Rolls hit a pothole and shook violently, bumping the opened script off her lap and onto the floor. She picked up the intercom phone.

"Martin?"

"Yes, ma'am," came the driver's voice.

"Would you slow down, please?"

"Sorry, Mrs. Styles," he apologized.

She thanked him and hung up.

She'd asked Harper for the use of the Rolls for the day. Her mood, her life, seemed to have improved. She decided to finish her Christmas shopping. She wanted

343

to find something special for Harper so she decided she might as well make all her holiday purchases; the car was roomy enough to hold anything she had on her shopping list. She wasn't using Harper's charge cards on this expedition; his gifts would be paid for by her earnings from the single film of which she was proud.

The script on her lap, Aurora found her place and attempted once more to use the driving time to read *Fantasy Bay,* one of the two screenplays Harper had given her.

Two days had passed since he'd brought them home. Two days since their truce and lovemaking. However, the result had been guilt, not elation. Not for the act. She had enjoyed, reveled in that. No. It was the motive behind her aggressive passion that made her feel . . . what? Words like *soiled* or *dirty* didn't apply. They were too dramatic. *Unfaithful* was the word.

But had she been unfaithful? Was imagining that her husband was another man an act of infidelity?

She read halfheartedly until the car slowed and pulled to a stop in front of the first boutique on her list. Putting down the script, she breathed a deep sigh. She'd spent yesterday reading the first one, something with the word *Stress* in the title. She hadn't liked the script or the title. Oh, it beat *Blood Destiny* by a mile, but that wasn't saying much!

The screenplay for *Fantasy Bay* was at least a change of pace. Certainly it was the best script Harper had shown her since *Lickety-Split.* She simply wasn't elated over the prospect of giving birth during a volcanic eruption. It had been done before; Lana Turner had done it during an earthquake in *Green Dolphin Street* and Rose-O-Sharon had reproduced in a raging flood in Steinbeck's *Grapes of Wrath.* Still, it had possibilities. . . .

The store was gleaming with tinsel and imitation pine. Carolers strolled and sang to the accompaniment of clinking cash registers and Swiss-imported music boxes. Aurora selected small, thoughtful gifts, elegant but not showy, for various people of the studio staff: secretaries, coaches, makeup and wardrobe people. Leather wallets or desk accessories for the men; evening purses, scarves, and perfume for the women. She disliked receiving presents that were ill suited in size or color, so she purposely avoided anything but neutral shades and conservative styles, wanting the recipients' enjoyment to extend beyond Christmas morning.

She took the longest time selecting gifts for Abby and Harper. For her foster sister she finally selected a silk dress with an empire bodice, but in a style and size that would be suitable for her for a period of several years. She also chose for her a stunning coat in coral wool, lined in softest opossum.

For Harper Aurora bought a midnight blue cashmere turtleneck sweater; a black alligator evening wallet; a miniature ship's clock for their bedroom, to match the larger one aboard the yacht; and, the most extravagant purchase she had ever made, a pair of diamond-stud cufflinks. She paid for everything in cash, which gave her an exhilarated rush of feeling. The salesclerks handled the transactions with matter-of-fact aplomb, but they were more accustomed to the sight of large amounts of cash changing hands; whereas despite the luxury surrounding her, Aurora was not. She spent freely for others, but she wouldn't be shopping with such abandon, had she been making purchases for herself.

Her arms filled with packages, she exited the last store and sank, exhausted yet happy, into the car. Martin had been following her and periodically relieving her of her burdens. Now her shopping was done and there were three weeks until Christmas.

The script of *Fantasy Bay* still lay on the back seat. The film was scheduled to start shooting in a week, with a four-day hiatus over the holiday. That would give her a good reason to keep the entertaining light, instead of being burdened with the constant business hostessing of the previous year. And she would have a project with which to keep her mind off . . . trouble. Shooting a film would allow her no time for thoughts of Web Seton.

She picked up the script again and began to read through Felicia's first scene.

She would tell Harper tonight. She would do *Fantasy Bay.*

There was much to do in the week preceding the start of filming. Miles of wrapping paper, yards of ribbon and Scotch tape, were purchased for those gifts left unwrapped by the stores. Aurora delighted in this task.

Past Christmases had been performances, with Harper's business entertaining reaching a peak during the final weeks of December. Aurora had risen to the occasion, learning names and choreographing seating so that rivals did not wind up beside one another for an entire seven-course dinner. However, she was secretly relieved that her hostess duties would be cut by more than half this year due to her shooting schedule. That was always an acceptable excuse.

The picture itself had been in production since the end of November. They had shot around the actress originally signed to play Felicia, who, Aurora learned, had withdrawn due to a real-life pregnancy. The knowledge that she had been second choice for the role wounded her pride only a little, and she made no

346

mention of it to Harper. She was happy to have the part.

Aurora's shooting schedule on *Fantasy Bay* required her to retire by ten each night and to arise by five A.M. each morning, to be in shape for her six-thirty studio call. The grind of long shooting days, studying lines on her own time, and sandwiching in appearances with Harper at various *de rigeur* parties, offered little, if any, privacy. Nonetheless, she accepted her role as working actress and producer's wife and the frenetic schedule both involved.

Shooting went smoothly enough, although she found it difficult to establish rapport with the director. Cabot Crane had personally cast the first actress to play Felicia, but Aurora knew he was doing his professional best to accept her in the role. Nonetheless, his disappointment was apparent, and she couldn't help feeling that she had been forced upon him. She didn't feel miscast though, and she was determined to bring him around, to please him with her performance. At first it was an uphill struggle, but by the end of the first week, she had followed his direction in a difficult scene, executing it with considerable ability, and Crane seemed to be warming to her. That, together with the anticipation of two more months' work on the picture, was encouraging. Certainly by the end of February, when the picture was due to wrap, Aurora would have the director in her corner.

It was Monday of the second week. She had finished a scene and made her exit from the set, lifting her hoopskirt to avoid becoming entangled in the snaking wire and metal that covered the soundstage floor. As she stood by the coffee urn awaiting the next setup, a production assistant handed her a telephone message: "Call Meyer Feld as soon as possible."

She read it once, then again, puzzled. According to

347

the message, he had phoned a half-hour before.

Why would Meyer Feld be contacting her? He was as big a name as Harper, and his films were, she admitted, of a higher caliber. Her palms moistened with anticipation as she picked up the wall phone and asked for an outside line.

She was put through to him immediately.

"Yeah? Hello?"

"Meyer, it's Aurora Styles. I just received a message—"

"Yeah, yeah. Can I see you? Today? Now?"

She hesitated, then said quickly, "Well . . . I think so. I'm on a pretty tight sched—"

"When's good?" he interrupted. "Pick a time."

"Twelve-thirty?" They'd break for lunch at noon and it would take that long to get over to his studio.

"Fine. See you." And he hung up.

She seldom left the lot for lunch. It was always easier to hop over to the commissary or send out for a salad. Now she had to remove herself from the bodice stays and the hoopskirt. She could keep her makeup intact— it was sufficiently understated—but her hair presented a problem. Arranged in a series of long, cascading corkscrew curls, it had required hours for Sergio to set. He would have a fit if she combed the curls out or crushed them beneath a hat. There was no choice. Meyer Feld would have to live with corkscrew curls.

Throwing her lynx jacket over a sweater and slacks, she darted out to her car.

Upon arriving at Three Gems Studio, Aurora was admitted to Feld's office, and she found the producer seated behind an enormous, bare desk. He was the portrait of a Hollywood mogul, down to the wire-framed glasses, bald head, and foul-smelling cigar.

"Sit, sit," he commanded. "What's wrong with your hair? You look like a bridesmaid at an Italian wedding."

Aurora laughed. "You're right. I'm shooting a picture, Meyer."

"Classy drag. You got an out?"

"An out?"

"An out clause. Can they replace you?"

"Meyer, wait a minute. Slow down. What's going on?"

"Sorry, sorry. I like to get to the point. Sometimes that gets me ahead of myself. I'm in a spot. But we can help each other out."

Aurora felt her pulse quicken. No other studio had ever wanted to borrow her from Harper for a picture. Could her appearance in *Lickety-Split* have paid off in more, and hopefully better, work?

"How can we help each other?" she asked.

"I'd like Harper to loan you to me. Twice your fee. A lead. But I wanted to feel you out on it before I speak to him."

She grinned broadly, feeling triumphant because of his faith in her and foolish for the times she'd lost faith in herself.

"Meyer . . . I don't know what to say. I'm very flattered."

"Flattered, schmattered. Can you get out of this thing you're shooting—what's it called?"

"*Fantasy Bay,* but—"

"*That* dog! Schmaltz! Belongs on TV. But I guess it's a classic compared to that slash-and-tear crap you were doing."

"It's the reason I'm doing the picture. I didn't want to go back to crap after *Lickety-Split,* so—"

"Yeah," Meyer interrupted again. "Good flick. Lousy title. You surprised this town. Didn't think you had it in you. That's why I want to borrow you."

"Thank you" was all she said, and she felt lucky to have gotten that much out.

"So . . . answer the question, for Christ's sake! Can you get out?"

"I don't know. I mean, I've been shooting for over a week already—"

"A week's nothin'. A month, we'd have problems. They'd have to reshoot half the picture."

"If you say so. But it's not up to me. When would I have to be available?"

"Right after the first of the year. Listen, Harper's your husband. He'll replace you. For this chance."

"What's the name of the picture?"

"Under Eros," he said offhandedly.

She was surprised—astounded—at her own reaction. Instead of yelling "What!" and laughing hysterically, she sat, immobile, and blinked. Could she possibly have heard him properly?

"You did say *Under Eros?"*

He nodded.

"I thought you wanted Vivian Hamilton."

"I did. Keep this under your . . . curls, because word's not out yet. I heard from her agent this morning. She won't do it."

Is she crazy? Aurora thought. "Why, Meyer?"

"Money. She wants, or her agent wants, twice our offer. It's ridiculous. She's not that big yet. Oh yeah, she will be—and she knows it. But she's not worth that price now. The deal's off. It's yours, if you want it."

"But you said at double my fee—"

"Rory, honey, you don't exactly cost a king's ransom, if you don't mind my bluntness. Twice that is still under what we tried to negotiate with Hamilton."

Vivian Hamilton had made only two films so far. God, she thought, that woman is moving fast!

"Of course I want it, Meyer." She'd be willing to do it for free. Aloud she asked, "Shall I speak to Harper or will you?"

"Go back to your set. I'll call him now and you two can discuss it at home tonight."

He rose and smiled at her, his false teeth gleaming. Impulsively, Aurora offered her right hand and said, "Thank you, Meyer."

"Uh-uh," he grunted, not taking her hand. "I don't shake on a deal till it's clinched. We'll talk."

Chapter Twenty

Damn! Aurora cursed silently as she stepped on the gas and made her turn. Of all the nights to shoot late! She'd been eager—impatient—all day to be through quickly, but everything had seemed to thwart her wishes. Her gown had torn and had needed to be sewn, a camera had jammed, and a lamp had blown. All afternoon, little annoyances had delayed shooting, forcing her to remain until six-thirty in the evening, two hours longer than she had expected. To heighten her anxiety, one of the actors consistently forgot the line that cued her entrance in the scene keeping her on set, thus necessitating several retakes.

She maneuvered the turn into the drive at the top of the hill and immediately saw Harper's Rolls in the garage. He was already home.

She let herself in through the kitchen, trying to keep her excitement from her voice as she called his name. Tossing her lynx jacket and totebag over a chair, she entered the living room and rushed to him. He sat with a stack of papers on his lap.

"Sorry I'm late—there were impossible delays. Have you eaten?"

"I waited for you. Helga left about an hour ago. She

left something in the oven. We can warm it up. Drink?"

"Oh, God, I've wanted one all day. I'll see about dinner."

Helga was a blessing. In the oven sat a small veal roast. It had dried a bit but looked promising. The housekeeper's note said it needed half an hour at 350°.

Harper had her martini ready when she rejoined him. Seated across from him on the sofa, she took the first delicious sip, then leaned back, and sighed, happy to be home. With a contented grin she asked, "Did Meyer Feld call you?"

"Yes. He did. Darling, we . . . we have to talk."

What did he mean? Aurora heard the warning tone in his voice, and tremors arose inside her. "Of course."

"First of all, congratulations," he said. "You should be very flattered." She remembered saying as much to Meyer. "Now . . . what exactly did he say to you?"

"That Vivian Hamilton wanted more money than he was willing to pay. He offered me the role in *Under Eros.*" Quickly she detailed Feld's conversation. "But didn't he tell you?"

"He did. And I don't like it."

"Why, Harper? What's wrong?" Aurora felt the fear more strongly now, but she maintained control. He hadn't said no . . . yet. It was not his permission she sought but his professional guidance. His manner told her that he wanted her to do *Under Eros* as much as she wanted it—this could be a feather in both their caps— but his hesitancy disturbed her. She was under contract to him, so if he was pleased about Meyer's offer, why did he have doubts about consenting to loan her out?

"This is what's wrong," Harper said after a long pause. "Vivian Hamilton has the potential for carving out the biggest film career since Katharine Hepburn. She knows it, so does Meyer Feld. She's sure to cop an Oscar nomination after *Too Much* opens on New

Year's. She won the Tony for the role last year."

"I guess that's why she's raised her price, Harper."

He nodded. Choosing his words slowly, he said, "Now listen carefully, Rory. I'm going to tell you something that will probably hurt, and you must remember that it is not a personal attack. It's very important that you understand that."

It was her turn to nod and then sit quietly, braced for whatever he was about to say.

Slowly, Harper asked, "Do you know what I'd do if I were Meyer Feld and I wanted an actress to lower her price?"

Oh no! she thought. The realization dulled her gaze, and she felt something heavy drop into the pit of her stomach. Without emotion, she said, "Offer it to somebody else . . . as a threat?"

"Exactly."

Tears filled her eyes. She took a gulp of the martini to steady herself and to moisten her parched lips. Harper moved closer to her on the sofa, put an arm around her, and held her close.

"You're sure, Harper?"

"I'm afraid so."

"It's not . . . not because I've already started *Fantasy Bay* and you'd have to? . . ."

"No, no. There's very little footage of you so far. Reshooting with another actress would be no major problem. And under different circumstances, do you think I'd force you to do *Fantasy Bay* and give up something important like *Eros?*"

She shook her head and lay against his chest. She could hear his heart beating quickly; she knew that having to tell her this couldn't have been easy for him.

Well, Meyer had been right about a few things, just not very honest.

"Isn't there a *chance?* . . . "

355

"Don't cling to a dream, Rory," he said. "Of course, if Hamilton doesn't lower her fee, if Feld doesn't give her what she wants, yes. Then I'd say there's a possibility. But she'd be foolish not to do the picture and he'd be crazy not to cast her in it. They're playing chess, darling, and I'm afraid you're the pawn."

Suddenly she was furious. "Pawn!" she exclaimed.

"Shh. Drink your drink and relax. I know it hurts. I told you it would. But Aurora Styles really has nothing to do with this."

"Pawn!" she repeated, unable to dismiss the word from her head. "Harper, what are you talking about?"

"Calm down and I'll explain." His tone was paternal rather than judgmental. Taking his advice, Aurora picked up her martini and sipped. In a barely audible voice she asked, "What kind of business is this that uses people as bargaining chips?"

"It's not unlike any other business, darling. You mustn't take it personally."

"Don't take it personally! Harper!"

"Aurora!"

"All right, all right." She held up a halting hand. "Go on."

"Look. There are at least three other actresses in town who would serve as a suitable threat. Meyer chose you. He could have called any of the others. Your position serves his purpose. You actually have no bearing on the situation whatsoever."

"That son of a bitch," she muttered.

Harper shrugged. "Probably. But I've not been above the same kind of tactic myself in the past. One can only be philosophical about it and move on. Besides, you can comfort yourself with one thing."

"What's that?"

"He had to offer the role to a good actress if he's going to have any credibility with Hamilton . . . and in

356

case she calls his bluff, which I doubt she will. That's something, at least."

Yes, that was something, but Aurora took little consolation from it. "But you're sure—"

"I repeat, no, I can't be absolutely sure. But I was on the phone four times yesterday with Web Seton's agent. Kahn also represents Vivian Hamilton. He knows what Meyer pulled, and he isn't worried."

"Why all the talk with him? I thought you'd settled the negotiations on Web's contract."

"I thought so too. A two-week conflict came up. We're ironing it out."

"Oh," she said, feigning disinterest. "Then his last picture is taking longer than expected?"

"No, he's finished that already. It's his next film that conflicts."

"His next film?"

"Yes," said Harper. "He's playing the husband in *Under Eros*. He signed the contract yesterday."

When Christmas week arrived, Aurora did her best to turn her mood around, to enjoy the holidays. But it was difficult.

She'd gone back to shooting *Fantasy Bay,* certainly with diminished enthusiasm. She threw out her copy of *Under Eros,* wanting to be rid of that reminder, but it continued to gnaw at her that Meyer Feld had actually offered her the role. For a while, she had toyed with the idea of legally binding him to his verbal agreement. However, Harper had cautioned her, wisely, she supposed, against such action. He doubted it could hold up in court. He knew Meyer well enough to be certain that even if Aurora had signed for the film, Feld could have found some reason to have her fired, if Hamilton suddenly acquiesced. As it was, Meyer Feld owed her one. That was something to remember, Harper noted. Finally, Aurora was convinced she would never film *Under Eros*.

On Christmas Eve morning, the *Hollywood Reporter* carried news that Meyer Feld had met Hamilton's demands halfway and the actress had accepted his offer. Shooting would begin on January second, the day after the première of her new film, *Too Much*.

Aurora had taken special pains with the house. Christmas wreaths, pines, pine cones, and sparkling lights had added a Dickensian touch to the Spanish décor. A tall, live Scottish pine stood before the windows that overlooked the side lawn. The tree was trimmed with beautiful handmade ornaments, some of which Aurora had purchased; others had come from boxes in the storage room, remnants from Christmases in Harper's past. Some of them had been chosen by Jennifer Beresford, the first Mrs. Styles. She had displayed excellent taste, a bit more flashy than Aurora would have preferred, but lovely, nonetheless. The presence of these ornaments caused Aurora to speculate on the former wife of Harper Styles.

Much of the entertaining was over, most of the parties attended. Harper had promised to return early from the studio, but until late afternoon, Helga was Aurora's only company; and the housekeeper was busy making cookies in the kitchen.

What is the matter? Aurora asked herself, for a blanket of gloom lay over the house, despite the decorations. Why am I so depressed?

But she knew. She wandered from room to room, trying to occupy her mind with last-minute holiday chores. She didn't rearrange the gifts under the tree; she'd done that four times already.

The phone rang.

"Rory!" said a familiar voice.

"Web?" Her pulse raced.

"Hi! I . . . well, it was your turn to call, but . . . anyway . . . Merry Christmas to you both."

"Thanks, Web. To you too."

There was silence on the line and then he spoke again. "I hadn't heard from you. I . . . just wondered how you've been."

"Oh fine, Web. I hear you're doing *Under Eros.*"

"Yeah," he said hesitantly. She knew immediately that he'd heard about Meyer Feld's scam. Guardedly, Web said, "It's not the lead, but it's a good part."

"I know. I've read the book."

"Look, Rory, I think it stinks—what they pulled on you."

"Web, please. I'm trying to put it out of my mind. I really feel like a fool."

"Well, don't. Listen," he said, his voice lower and more intimate, "I'd . . . I'd love to see you. For lunch? Sometime?"

It wasn't a good idea. "Web," she said, carefully choosing her words, "I think perhaps we shouldn't see each other . . . even for lunch."

He paused. "Ever?"

"Not without Harper."

"Rory, I never meant to—"

"I know, I know. It's just better this way. We'll know each other for years. As friends."

He didn't argue. They chatted inanely about the holidays. It turned out he didn't have specific plans and she felt badly for him, but she resisted the temptation to invite him over.

After several lulls in the conversation, it became apparent that there was nothing more to say. Wishing each other a Merry Christmas once more, Aurora said, "Good-bye, Web. Good luck on the film." And they hung up.

The loneliness descended more heavily. She'd missed talking to Web; they understood each other, had an easy rapport. And who else could she talk with so openly? Vance and Eva? No. They'd gone East last week. Tadzio? Maritza? Anton? Gone. Everyone gone. And there were certain subjects she could not discuss with Harper.

The word *East* brought on nostalgia for New York. For winter, snow. She'd told Web the truth—God, how she missed the snow!

Tonight, there would be a small gathering at Marvin Schwab's; he'd directed several of Harper's films. Just a few people at an informal buffet. Aurora liked him well enough; his wife was pleasant too. They'd make it an early evening, come home, have a drink beside the tree. Probably make love. Not a terrible way to spend Christmas Eve.

Still, the discontent remained. She glanced at the clock. Helga would leave soon; it was time to dress. She'd give Helga the cashmere scarf and gloves now, and they'd have a glass of sherry. That would help, wouldn't it? Diversion? Holiday cheer?

"Helga!" she called, bending to retrieve the house-keeper's gift from the multitude of packages beneath the tree.

"No," Harper whispered, nuzzling her neck as Aurora emitted a languid, contented sigh. "You stay here. Give me fifteen minutes and then come down-stairs."

He kissed her and her arms went around his neck; he smelled so good in the morning. But putting his hands on her shoulders, he said, "Release me, wench!"

Aurora giggled and opened her eyes, squinting against the morning sun coming through the still-drawn draperies.

She lay in bed for the quarter-hour he'd requested. Soon the aroma of fresh coffee sweetened the air.

The party the night before had been pleasant enough and today was Christmas; her outlook was brighter. All that remained of her previous discomfort was the lingering humiliation over the Feld-Hamilton fiasco, underscored at Schwab's party by his guests' calculated diplomacy. Not a single mention was made of *Under Eros,* which under ordinary circumstances would have been one of the main topics discussed. Word was all over town of Meyer Feld's successful ploy, signing the star he wanted at the expense of Aurora Styles.

But she would not permit that to spoil Christmas Day. Setting her thoughts on Harper's reaction to her gifts, she glanced at the clock and then donned a velour robe.

Downstairs, she stood at the threshold, watching Harper puttering around the tree. He examined packages, shook them, listening to see if they rattled. She smiled. On the table he had set a coffeepot, juice, mugs, and rolls. Aurora leaned against the wall and cleared her throat loudly.

"Ah! Just in time!"

"Caught you sneaking around the presents, didn't I?" she scolded, coming to him with a kiss.

"I stand accused," he murmured into her ear, filling his hands with the hair at her neck.

After a few sips of coffee and nibbles of the warm rolls, they moved to the rug beneath the tree and opened their gifts.

The smaller items—"stocking stuffers," Harper called them—came first. In one tiny box, an emerald pin highlighted by tiny rubies—Christmas colors, he explained—in another, matching earrings. At last, he handed her the largest box, an enormous package

361

wrapped in gleaming silver paper and tied with a wide emerald satin bow.

She tore off the paper and removed the lid, then gasped when she folded back the green tissue paper. It was a dark, soft, luscious Russian sable coat. "Harper!" She rose from the floor, clutching the sumptuous fur to her and held it up to the mirror behind the bar.

"Model it for me?" he said.

She slipped it over her burgundy robe and, parodying her high-school runway training, slouched and posed, throwing a hip to one side. Then she went to Harper and kissed him.

"Happy, darling?" he asked.

"Mmm," she murmured. "Very happy."

Despite the debris, crumpled tissue and gift wrapping, boxes and ribbon, a kind of peace had settled over the room.

"Thank you for a lovely day, Harper," she said.

"Thank you, darling . . . but there's one more present you haven't seen."

She glanced about the room but saw nothing. Every package had been opened.

He was watching her. "This one isn't under the tree."

Aurora looked at him, puzzled.

"Stand at the center of the room, darling, and face the windows."

"Harper," she protested. But he insisted, pulling her up from the floor and planting her in the spot requested. Quickly he ran to the pullcord and announced, "This is for you. Snow!"

With one fast movement, the draperies parted.

At first, sudden shock rendered her speechless. The pool was covered with snow. White flakes blanketed the entire back lawn all the way to the dip in the sloping

362

hill beyond!

"Harper!" she cried, running to the windows.

Upon closer scrutiny she saw what he had done. As at their wedding, Plexiglas covered the water in the pool. Over it, thousands of potted white poinsettias simulated a counterpane of snow. The brilliant sunlight gleamed off their large, delicate petals.

She and Harper embraced, his hand caressing her inside the soft folds of deep sable.

"I know you miss New York, darling, and I know what these last few weeks have been for you," he said.

"But when? . . ."

"While we were at the party last night."

"Let's go outside and take a closer look!" she said.

"First, I want to make a phone call."

"Business? Today? Harper—" But immediately she saw another surprise hatching.

He dialed and, after a few moments' wait, said, "Miss Abby Linn?"

Aurora laughed at Harper's formal tone.

"Yes, honey, it's Harper. Merry Christmas! Now, before I put Rory on, I just want to make sure that your birthday is next month, right?" He paused for her reply. "Good. Well, aside from what you'll get in the mail, I think you—and we—deserve a little bonus. It's impossible to swing this before April, but since that's Rory's birthday, this can be part of her gift too." He motioned for Aurora to join him at the phone. "We'd like you to come for a visit—don't worry about school, we'll work that out, okay?" He laughed at her answer and then handed Aurora the receiver.

Before taking the phone, Aurora squeezed his hand and whispered, "I love you."

As she spoke to Abby, Aurora looked out onto the lawn.

He'd given her winter. Snow. And Abby.

Abby was coming to visit.

On New Year's morning they didn't rise until after eleven. Aurora lay beside Harper, watching him sleep and occasionally stroking a lock of his silver-streaked hair. When at last he stirred and opened his eyes, he whispered a sleepy "g'morning" and rolled her into his arms. He made tender love to her and afterward held her tightly. "Happy New Year," he said in a low, grainy, sexy voice, and she laughed throatily with him.

She was glad they hadn't gone partying the night before. They'd had a choice of dozens of parties, but neither had spent a quiet New Year's Eve in a long time, so they opted for a late supper and soft music.

Around midnight they had turned on the television set, and although a twinge of melancholy had stabbed at Aurora as the ball fell in Times Square and strains of "Auld Lang Syne" filled the air, she'd kept her emotions under control and forced herself to live in the now. She was in Beverly Hills, with an adoring husband whom she loved. She could always take a trip to New York after shooting *Fantasy Bay*. And it was good to be at home, with Harper. Tomorrow night there was another party. She needed the quiet, the peace, in order to face that.

Now, with the morning light pouring into the room and Harper humming in the shower, a new year had begun. The first business day of a new year. Tonight was the première of *Too Much*. Her head throbbed at the prospect of having to face all those people who knew about the *Under Eros* game. And, of course, Vivian Hamilton would be there. So would Web Seton.

Coffee. She needed coffee.

It helped. Aurora laid out bagels, muffins, and

364

orange juice, more for Harper than for herself; she wasn't hungry.

She leafed through the morning paper. In the entertainment section she read through the list of current movies in release. Two of Harper's films were playing. No, she thought, looking closer. Three of Harper's films.

At a small revival house, a film was advertised as "Tonight Only." Its title was *New Year's Day* and it starred Jennifer Beresford!

Why, lately, was the ghost of this woman everywhere? Aurora laughed. That thought was like the plot of one of her own movies.

She heard the shower stop upstairs. Harper would soon come down to breakfast. Aurora folded the paper and put it on the table.

Around four o'clock, Harper asked, "Aren't you having your hair done for tonight?"

Aurora glanced up from the book she had been trying to read, unable to conceal her surprise. She'd completely forgotten to make an appointment for her hairdresser to come to the house.

"No," she said, inventing an excuse. "I've decided to do it myself."

"Well, you ought to start, in that case. It's getting late."

He was right. She hesitated, then rose from her chair.

"Anything the matter, Rory?"

She turned to him. Harper wore a curious expression, apparently unaware of what troubled her. But how could he not know?

"No," she lied. "Nothing's the matter." And she left the room.

* * *

At six, Harper zipped her into the Bob Mackie gown of mint green chiffon and glittering bugle beads. Aurora's hair was down and full; wearing it that way had been easier than trying anything elaborate. She fastened the emerald and ruby Christmas earrings to her pierced lobes and then glanced at Harper's profile in the mirror. He cut an elegant figure in his midnight blue tuxedo. Placing his hands on Aurora's shoulders, he leaned toward her reflection and asked, "Darling, what is it? Something's wrong."

She was disappointed in herself. Harper had done so much to cheer her spirits; yet she felt that she was letting them both down. For a while, his efforts had succeeded; she'd thought her depression was gone. But it had returned as the evening loomed before them.

"You know what's wrong, Harper," she said, her lower lip trembling as she spoke.

"You mean about . . . the première tonight?"

She nodded, afraid to speak, lest her words might open a floodgate of tears.

"But, Rory darling," he said softly, "the worst of it is over."

"It's not. I thought it was, but . . . but it isn't." The tears she had fought so hard to contain began to well in her eyes.

"Rory," Harper cautioned, "you'll ruin your make-up."

Only in Hollywood, she thought bitterly, would a husband make that remark.

He waited for her to continue. Finally she said, "Harper, would you mind awfully if . . . if I didn't go tonight?"

His face grew stern. "Yes. I would mind."

"But the whole thing is so humiliating."

"Rory, you're acting like a child. You have the sympathy of the entire industry. They're on your side."

"That's not it," she said, said, stifling a sniffle. "I guess it meant too much to me."

"Speaking of *Too Much,* I'm expected to be there. And as my wife, so are you."

"Wives get sick sometimes and stay home," she said in a small voice.

"But you're not sick."

"I am!" she blurted out, removing the earrings and tossing them onto the dressing table. "I'm depressed— and I'm sick of pretending that it doesn't matter!"

Harper straightened and, looking at the floor, said, "All right, Rory. If you insist. But I must go. You understand that, don't you?"

She rose and put her head against his chest. "I understand. Just come home early . . . and tell me about it?"

He gave her a reassuring pat on the cheek and left the room.

When he'd left, Aurora exchanged her gown for a pair of jeans and an old sweater. But now she had another problem: how to spend the evening.

She was pleased to have been given a reprieve; watching Vivian Hamilton dazzle the première audience with her brilliance onscreen would have been too difficult to endure. Still, she didn't relish staying home alone with her thoughts.

She nibbled on cold chicken while looking, once more, through that morning's paper. Again she noticed the ad for *New Year's Day.*

A glance at the clock told her she could still catch the 7:00 P.M. show.

Grabbing her lynx jacket, she darted out to the car and sped toward the movie house.

As she drove, she questioned her own wisdom,

especially in light of her present mood. But she had only seen photographs of Jennifer Beresford in vintage fan magazines and she'd become increasingly curious.

The parking lot at the revival house was nearly empty and there was no line for tickets. By the time Aurora entered the theater, the lights were down and the opening credits had been given.

Jennifer Beresford didn't appear for the first fifteen minutes of the screenplay; it was the old-fashioned setup in which pages of exposition prepared the audience for the star's entrance.

And what an entrance! Beresford floated through a pair of double Art Deco doors in a cloud of pink chiffon; it set half the audience to giggling. Aurora was reminded of Loretta Young's appearances on her television series years before.

The story wasn't much: A man was murdered on New Year's Eve; his wife, falsely accused of the crime, became enamored of her lawyer. Every moment was predictable.

But Jennifer Beresford was not.

What struck Aurora was her similarity to the actress onscreen. Not physically, but in type: They were both tall, dark-haired; and both had ivory skin. At the time the film was made, Beresford was obviously some years younger than Aurora was now, but even then, she possessed a grandness and a certain allure.

She wasn't a bad actress either, despite the over-theatricality of her gestures and her star-turn delivery. Effective, if dated. Yes, the woman was definitely talented.

On her way out of the theater, Aurora picked up a printed schedule of the Winterfest of Film. Once in the car, she turned on the overhead light and examined the blurb alongside the listing for *New Year's Day*. It read:

An obscure film, noted for its star, Jennifer Beresford. Her third picture was typical of the vehicles chosen by her studio, which her husband ran. She made only one more film after *New Year's Day*. However, she has a small cult following, some of whom hope for a comeback. Underrated as an actress and a victim of poor scripts, one can only wonder what she might have been.

Might have been. The saddest of all words—wasn't there a poem about that? No, Aurora thought, it is only sad if one never tries. Beresford had tried. But how long? How hard? It seemed obvious that Harper had not given her the best career advice. Had she, too, tried to protest?

A chill ran down Aurora's spine as she turned the ignition key. Was Harper doing the same thing to her? What had happened to Beresford and what would happen to her? She opened the window, despite the chill. She needed fresh air.

She knew that Harper loved her, felt that he respected her talent. But could he be deliberately sabotaging that talent? It seemed too farfetched unless he didn't realize what he was doing.

Why was this coming to the fore now? She had truly thought, as Harper had told her, that the worst was over. Christmas had been lovely. Reassuring. And now these devils were back; countless doubts and fears were besieging her. If only Maritza were here; she knew Harper—she'd introduced them. But the countess was in Europe. Aurora would have to think this through on her own, without any help from her friends.

She saw the Rolls and knew Harper was already home. That was her doing; she'd asked him to come home early. "Tell me about it," she'd said. As if she'd wanted to hear about goddamned Vivian Hamilton's triumph!

A small surge of fear engulfed her as she parked; would he be angry that she wasn't home? Stop it! she commanded herself. He's your husband. You love him. You can't possibly be afraid of him!

But there it was. Fear of Harper. Not of violence; he was not a violent man. No. It was fear of his disapproval. Fear of letting him down, after all he'd done for her.

Did gratitude play that large a role in their relationship? And as to all he had done for her, hadn't he made major blunders regarding her career? Hers and Jennifer Beresford's? *Why?* That question was uppermost in her mind as she strode into the living room and saw him standing at the bar.

Throwing her jacket and bag over a chair, she took a seat on one of the barstools.

"Good evening," he said. He wasn't smiling.

He'd removed his tux jacket, tie, and cummerbund. His diamond-stud cufflinks lay on the bar; his shirtsleeves were rolled up. That seemed out of character. Harper liked to change his clothes after a formal affair.

Aurora picked up the studs, rattling them in her palm as she said, "I . . . I had to get out of the house. Cognac, please?"

He poured, and Aurora, detecting a slight tremor in his hand, wondered how much he'd had to drink. This, too, was unlike him.

"Where did you go?" he asked, sliding the snifter to her.

"Believe it or not, I went to a movie."

"Why wouldn't I believe it, Rory?" he asked.

She shrugged and drank. "Just a figure of speech, Harper. I went to a movie."

"You could have gone to a movie tonight. With me."

"Harper, please . . . let's not—"

"All right," he said, not looking at her.

"How was it?" she asked finally.

"How was what? The movie *I* saw? Stage bound. Unimaginatively directed. Brilliant script, though, and a great performance. How was yours?"

"It was informative," she replied.

"Oh? How so?"

"Let's stop the cat-and-mouse, shall we?" She exhaled deeply, tossing her hair behind her shoulders. "I went to see *New Year's Day.*"

For the briefest moment she thought his face colored with anger, but he recovered quickly. "Not very good, was it?" he asked with a wry smile.

"I'm not a critic."

"Surely you have an opinion . . . of the leading lady?"

She stared at him, looking into his eyes, trying to communicate sincerely as she asked, "Harper, what happened?"

He lowered his head into his hands and ran his fingers through his hair. His eyes were red rimmed and he suddenly seemed older—and tired.

"When we married, she was young. Eighteen. Jennifer was delightful, talented. . . ." As he began to speak of his first wife, Aurora was surprised to find she was not jealous. Yet a kind of morbid curiosity took hold of her, riveting her to Harper's story.

"I knew very little about her, but what did that matter? Few people know about my past." Aurora nodded, her hand reaching for his.

"I know I must seem secretive at times. But I felt that part of my life was better left to the fertile imaginations of the people out here. I knew they'd create a past far more interesting than the truth.

371

"She was so young, too young for a past of her own. At first she was thrilled about being in movies, becoming a star. She trusted my judgment."

He glanced away and Aurora gazed into the amber well at the bottom of her glass.

"It's fitting, I suppose, that you should have chosen to see *New Year's Day*. It was the beginning of the end." He sighed. "Although I know the end started long before that."

He poured refills of cognac and swallowed hard.

"Harper, what is it?" she asked.

Bringing the bottle down upon the bar too firmly, he raised his eyes to the ceiling. "Mental illness," he said.

He walked to the windows and gazed out over the darkened pool. Aurora's glance followed him, her own reflection looking back at her in the glass.

"New Year's Day was torn apart by the critics— Jennifer along with it. Unmercifully. Cruelly. She was a laughingstock. I'd made her that. For almost a year she refused to work. Interviews became dangerous. She was chronically late, slept all day, and wandered around the house all night like . . . like a ghost.

"But, you see, the picture she'd made before *New Year's*—her second film—was a success. Good reviews. Even Oscar talk . . . and I . . ." He bent his head and Aurora saw his shoulders droop sadly. But she was rooted to the spot, unable to go to him, incapable of giving him the comfort she knew he needed.

Harper recovered and said, "I was afraid of losing her. She was growing as an actress . . . growing away from me . . . taking charge of herself. I saw it happening, and stopped it."

"How?" Aurora asked in a choked voice.

"I knew *New Year's* was an abysmal screenplay. Dated. Even corny. I hired a heavy-handed, hammy director. Rewrote scenes. I did a magnificent job, far better than even I could have guessed.

"After its release, she was finished. Oh, I lost a fortune at the box office, but I had three other successful films running. *New Year's* actually helped at tax time.

"Her last picture was my attempt at restitution. Good script, good role. But she was too far gone by then. She couldn't do the same thing twice. It was impossible to match shots, impossible to edit. She was changing lines from one shot to the next—or forgetting them entirely. Looking beautiful one day, haggard the next. The picture was pasted together. We did what we could to save it—to save her. But we failed." He paused and sipped his drink, still staring out the windows. "It was there," he said, gesturing with his glass. "By the pool. I awoke in the middle of the night, found her sitting naked at the edge of the diving board, just staring into the water. I called to her. She never answered. I walked out onto the board and she began to scream. I tried to drag her off, but she was strong. Violent. I was afraid I'd injure her. She stayed there, her toes dangling over the water, for eight hours. I called her psychiatrist—she'd been seeing one for some time. He came. Put her in a sanitarium. I told everyone she'd left me."

"But, Harper, what became of her? Where is she now?"

He turned to look at Aurora. In a hollow voice he answered, "She died. Just wasted away and died."

The words seemed to echo in Aurora's brain. But Harper's voice shattered the painful image he'd created.

"The night before I found her at the pool, she'd learned that I'd . . . I'd been with another woman. A friend of hers, very like her in many ways. It's easy to see now that I was seeking Jennifer, trying to find her again. That is no excuse—I probably sound as unbalanced as she was." His face was creased with lines accentuated by the shadows. He drained his glass and said, "That's why I believe it's pointless to look back. We can't change the past, whatever mistakes we've made. We can only change the way we perceive the past." He replaced his glass on the bar and his eyes met Aurora's.

"I haven't thought about Jennifer in a very long time, Rory. And I've never spoken about her because it's too late to make a difference." The weary resignation in his voice compelled Aurora to go to him, embrace him, comfort him. Harper was her symbol of strength and guidance, of utter control. For the first time since they'd met she felt a strength inside her, previously unknown. Harper needed her, but it wasn't that alone. It was a trust in her own stamina—Maritza's survival instinct—that gave her a newfound confidence. She was sorry for Harper, sorrier for his first wife. But, as they went upstairs to bed, she silently gave thanks that she was not Jennifer Beresford.

Chapter Twenty-One

Fantasy Bay wrapped over schedule, the first week in March. By the end of the month, Aurora and Harper had seen a rough cut. The special effects were excellent, the volcano was spectacular, and even the scene in which Aurora gave birth was credible. More editing, music, and some additional looping would have the picture ready for release by early May, in time for spring and summer.

During filming Aurora had thought frequently of the night she'd learned the truth about Jennifer Beresford. For a week or two afterward, the atmosphere had been uneasy. Harper had seemed embarrassed over letting down his guard, and Aurora thought he felt she was judging his behavior. But she wasn't. It was enough to know he realized the consequences of his deeds. She was relieved to know the same fate would not, could not, befall her. She would not allow it.

Eventually, Harper began to treat Aurora with a new respect, consulting her on decisions he had previously reserved for himself. He now valued her opinions.

April came, and with it Abby.

The child that Aurora and Harper had put on a plane

375

back to Oakdale a few years before emerged from the exit ramp a young woman, seemingly the product of a time warp.

My God, Aurora thought. Abby was wearing the coat they'd sent her for Christmas and the style was already too young for the sophisticated teenager who came toward them with outstretched arms. She kissed Aurora, then turned to Harper and blushed. Aurora smiled. Abby still had her crush on him.

Not quite as tall as Aurora, still Abby carried herself well. Her blond hair was long and straight, parted to one side and occasionally falling over her brow in an unintentionally provocative fashion.

"I'm so warm!" She laughed, removing her coat to reveal a lithe, slim body, boyish hips, and small high breasts evident beneath her Indian cotton tunic dress. A class ring hung from a gold chain around her neck.

"Aha," said Aurora, "and what's this?"

"This," answered Abby with a secretive smile, "is from Davy."

"Davy?" Harper repeated as they walked to the car. "You've never mentioned him before."

She gave him a quick peck on the cheek. "I didn't want you to be jealous, Uncle Harper."

"Let's dispense with uncle, dear. You'll make me feel older than I am."

"I like older men," she said, winking at Aurora.

"So do I. You have excellent taste." Aurora laughed. "By the way, how old is Davy?"

"My age, but he's mature. We'll talk later, okay?"

"Oh, it's for girls only?" asked Harper, teasing.

"Women, Uncle!" Abby laughed. "Wait, my suitcase!"

"No, no. The chauffeur will take care of that. We'll wait in the car."

Climbing inside, Abby exclaimed, "Oh, I'm so glad

you're rich!" She sank into the plush seat of the Rolls. Spying the bar, she asked hesitantly, "Rora . . . could I?"

"A *drink?*" It took her aback. But then she thought, well, she's old enough for one drink. "Yes, I guess so. Harper, let's all have a drink."

"Hmm. Not here ten minutes and already on the path to ruin," he said. "What would you like, Abby?"

She pursed her lips together, staring at the bottles. "Mmm. Bourbon, please."

"Bourbon!" Harper seemed genuinely surprised but picked up the bottle and poured.

Impulsively, Aurora put her arm around her sister and squeezed her tightly. Tears glistened in her eyes. "I'm so happy, Abby. So glad you're here!"

"So am I," said Abby.

The long days of loneliness, of melancholy, seemed over at last. Abby's visit was exciting, and Aurora realized that it was time for the two of them to put their relationship on different planes. She would always be Abby's big sister, but their ties had altered with Abby's use of the word *women*.

All three held their drinks high, and as Abby's suitcase was placed in the trunk, they clinked glasses.

"To us," Harper toasted.

Louis Vuitton seemed a bit lavish for a teenager, so they decided on a handsome set of Hartman tweed to replace Abby's tattered schoolgirl suitcase.

"Tomorrow," Harper promised, putting his arm around her shoulder, "we'll see about filling those bags with new clothes for you."

"You're both so good to me," Abby said, beaming.

"It's just the beginning. We're very happy to have you here. But now I'm late for the studio. You two

377

girls—women—spend the afternoon talking . . . about me, if you like." And he left.

Alone now, they changed into swimsuits and enjoyed the pool. Abby didn't towel herself but let the warm California sun dry her long, slim body.

"You have quite a figure," Aurora declared.

"Thanks. I guess I take after you." She leaned back in the chaise and closed her eyes.

"Tell me about Davy."

Abby giggled. She put on her new sunglasses and turned to Aurora. "He's this really cute guy. And sweet," she added, not unlike a mother speaking about her son. "But he's not too smart and he's too young."

"If he's your age, that's fine."

"No it's not. There's a lot he . . . doesn't know." Abby looked pointedly at Aurora.

At first the full meaning of the remark nearly escaped her. Then she realized the statement had been made as entrée to a conversation they had never had before. Suddenly, Aurora was mildly nervous.

"Abby," she began, "are you—"

"A virgin? Yes. Well, technically."

"Meaning?"

"Davy tries. And I let him touch me sometimes, but—"

"Where?"

"Oh, not *there!*" Abby blushed. "Just a little here." Her hand fluttered over her breasts. "And I . . . I want to . . . to . . ."

"Do me a favor. Don't. Not for a while. And make sure you're protected when you do."

"I know all about it. My friend Carol told me. Said she'll take me to her doctor. Mom would kill me if she knew. But the thing is, Rora, I don't *love* Davy."

Well, that's a relief, thought Aurora. At least Abby isn't confusing sex and love. "So you want to wait until you're in love?"

"I guess. I don't know. I mean, sometimes it's hard to keep saying no. Davy wants to so badly—and me too . . . sometimes. But then something tells me *don't*."

They talked long into the afternoon.

Abby's attire at dinner persuaded Aurora that drastic changes had to be made in her sister's wardrobe.

"We're doing more shopping today," she announced at breakfast. "You need some party dresses and at least one knockout formal."

"Oh, that's okay. Last year I got asked to the junior prom. I've got a long dress."

"Well, I think we'll find something new," Aurora said. "For a very special evening next Monday."

"What's next Monday?" asked Abby.

"The Academy Awards," said Harper matter-of-factly.

"Oh! Harper! Rora!" She jumped up, ran around the table, and hugged them fiercely.

Then she began to ask questions: Would Robert Redford be there? What about Paul Newman? How should she wear her hair? Would Aurora do her makeup? "And will Vivian Hamilton be there? I saw *Too Much* just before I came out here."

"She'll be there," Harper said, glancing at Aurora. "She's nominated for Best Actress."

They returned home laden with packages. Normally, Aurora wasn't fond of shopping. But with Abby, it became an adventure. She recalled her first shopping expeditions with Maritza, when apparel at Saks and

Bergdorf's and Bloomingdale's suddenly became an everyday part of her life. She was rediscovering her own enthusiasm through Abby's eyes. Even autograph seekers bothered her less when she saw that Abby was thrilled with her sister's stardom.

That night the trio celebrated, belatedly, Abby's seventeenth birthday. Harper had ordered a small cake to be presented after dinner and he'd arranged for a few celebrities to drop by. It was apparent that Abby was ecstatic.

The following morning, photos of Vivian Hamilton and Web Seton were on the front pages of two newspapers. One caption read: WEDDING BELLS ARE NOT TOO MUCH. Their marriage was set to take place the following week. There had been no rumors about this union, no grapevine gossip. Nobody even knew they'd been dating. The news shocked Aurora more than most.

Oscar night came, and with it the familiar nerves. Aurora wasn't nominated; why was she feeling this way?

Because, came the answer. Vivian Hamilton is the favorite. Smart money is on her. Las Vegas odds are high. The actress will go from a win tonight to marriage next week, and on to raves this summer in *Under Eros,* scheduled for release at the same time as *Fantasy Bay.* How could Aurora not feel a certain nervous resentment? The woman's personality had little to do with it; Aurora had liked Hamilton. But she had achieved everything Aurora had fantasized for herself at one time or another, including Web Seton.

Masking her emotions became more difficult as she dressed in a black-with-rhinestones gown and applied the last of her makeup. With a shaky hand, she knocked on Abby's door.

"You're ready so soon, Rora! Here, zip me up? Isn't it gorgeous?" Abby whirled around to show off the full-length red chiffon they had chosen together.

"Yes, gorgeous," Aurora agreed. "Now sit down and let me do your makeup."

"You look so beautiful!" exclaimed Abby, as she seated herself before the dressing table.

"Thank you."

"Something wrong, Rora?"

"I'm . . . okay. These nights are very important out here. Just nerves. I'll be all right."

But already she felt the dull thud of a headache forming behind her eyes. She tried comforting herself with the knowledge that she would be in the company of those she loved. She wouldn't be facing this alone. She had Abby. And Harper.

Harper stood at the foot of the stairs, holding a small gift-wrapped box. "For you to wear tonight, Abby."

She tore the paper away, opened the box, and gasped with awe. Inside was a silver pin fashioned into a miniature church, a tiny diamond fixed at the center of the cross above its minuscule steeple.

"It's an abbey," Harper said with a smile, obviously pleased by his own cleverness. "Here. Let me."

Aurora watched as he fastened the pin to Abby's dress. Clearly Abby had no awareness of the gift's worth. Silver and a diamond . . . are we spoiling her? Aurora wondered.

The night wore on interminably. Fortunately, they were not seated near Web Seton or Vivian Hamilton; nominees were always closer to the front, to make it easy to dart up to the podium in case of a win. They nodded to Web, who smiled sheepishly at Aurora and waved. The gem on Hamilton's finger did not go unnoticed by anyone, especially Aurora.

Meyer Feld attempted to say hello, but Aurora snubbed him.

Abby was duly impressed, but into the third hour, even she was showing signs of boredom. Aurora's headache had not subsided; rather, it had worsened. After Hamilton won for Best Actress, the pain became severe, blossoming into a full migraine.

Finally, the ceremonies drew to a close, Johnny Carson made the usual quips about the length of the show, and they were free to leave.

Once they were out in the night air, Aurora felt some relief but she was now exhausted. The three of them climbed into the back of the Rolls, and Aurora pulled the sable up around her, resting her head in the soft folds of its collar.

"Harper . . . Abby," she said with closed eyes, "I'm . . . not feeling well."

"Rora!" Abby cried, but Aurora patted her hand. "No, it's just a bad headache." Turning to Harper, she asked, "Could you drop me at home?"

"You're not coming?" His voice showed concern. These functions were important to him, she knew, and she was relieved that he didn't make an issue of her not attending the party.

"Harper, my head is killing me. It's even making my teeth ache. I just can't do it, not tonight."

"But I don't want to go without you, Rora," Abby said in a small voice.

"Don't be silly. You'll have a wonderful time."

"But—"

"Abby, please, fill in for me?" Aurora asked.

"Are you sure?"

"I'm sure."

"Well . . ."

They drove on, Aurora silent as Abby and Harper talked about the awards. Abby asked all kinds of questions; he explained the ins and outs, the politics involved in winning the Oscar.

At the house, Aurora climbed out of the car. "Don't see me in. Go on."

"All right," Harper said. "Get some rest. Don't wait up."

"Thanks. I won't. Have a good time."

She waved as the chauffeur drove off down the driveway. Then she let herself into the darkened house.

A horrid, jangling bell screamed in Aurora's ear. She groaned, turning over on her side, but it persisted. From the fog of deep sleep, she awoke with a start and grabbed the phone on its fourth ring.

"Mrs. Styles?" a male voice asked. The dull throbbing in Aurora's head continued.

"Yes? . . ."

As he spoke, she shook her head, although it caused more pain. She switched on the bedside lamp and looked at the clock. It read 4:15 A.M. Where were Harper and Abby? Downstairs? No . . . wait . . . the call was about them. *Wake up!* she urged herself.

"I'm sorry, officer . . . I'm still a little groggy. Could you repeat what you said?"

"I think you'd better come down here, Mrs. Styles. Or we can have a car come and get you."

"No . . . I can be there in half an hour."

She hung up. Had she heard him correctly or was she having a nightmare?

No. He said there had been a fire . . . on the yacht . . . serious damage . . . Harper and Abby were

383

at the hospital. . . .

Harper and Abby? On the yacht?

She hardly remembered dressing or climbing into her car, but she was driving to the hospital. What were they doing on the yacht? It was so late . . . A fire. How had it started?

A policeman was waiting for her at the admittance desk, and when the reporters and photographers huddled in the waiting room spotted her, he quickly ushered her through a door and locked it.

"Thank you," she said. "I'm . . . a little confused. Are my sister and husband all right?"

"A little smoke inhalation. A few minor burns incurred during their escape. They'll be here overnight. It's lucky they got out when they did. Damage is pretty extensive."

They were safe! Harper's yacht . . . well, better that than either of them. "May I see them?"

He nodded. "But first . . . there's something you should know."

"What?" she asked. "If they're all right—"

The policeman interrupted her. "I don't know how the press found out, Mrs. Styles, but . . . well, they're always hanging around the precinct, sniffing for leads, and—"

"You mean about the fire?"

"No, not just that. It's . . . what they were wearing when we arrived on the scene."

"Meaning?"

"Well"—the officer drew a breath—"they were naked, Mrs. Styles. We arrived just as they jumped overboard and swam for the pier. I'm afraid the press got some photos."

The room began to swim, but the alert policeman immediately handed her a cup of water from the cooler and a Valium. "Take this. The doctor thought you might be needing it."

Aurora didn't argue.

Naked. Why? Perhaps they'd decided to spend the night aboard the yacht. If Harper had drunk too much and wanted to sleep it off . . . But then, why hadn't he called? Well, he knew she wasn't feeling up to par. Perhaps their clothes had been on fire? Perhaps . . . perhaps . . . No! *No!*

She rose. "I've got to see them. Now!" she said, heading for the door.

"Okay, but let me go with you. The only way to their rooms is through the press." He unlocked the door and placed his hand on the knob. "Ready?"

She nodded, remembering her dark glasses at the last minute.

The door opened and all hell broke loose. Flashbulbs popped, microphones were thrust at her as she was led through the sea of shoving reporters, all talking at once.

"Did you know about it, Rory?"

"Is this a shock?"

"What are your plans after they recover?"

"She's a minor, isn't she?"

"If statutory rape is involved, whose side are you on?"

Aurora felt a scream building inside her. She fought it down, pushing every obstacle out of her way, eager only to see Abby, wondering if she was all right.

Abby's arms were bandaged, but beyond that, she seemed no worse for the ordeal. Although sedated, she was awake as Aurora closed the door on the pandemonium in the corridor.

Simultaneously, both sisters broke into sobs. Aurora ran to Abby with outstretched arms, then pulled back, fearful of hurting her.

"Oh . . . you hate me!" Abby cried, turning away and burying her head in the pillow.

"Hate you? Why do you say that?"

"Oh, Rora!" She wept. "I'm sorry!"

"Shh. Don't talk. It's over. You're both safe now."

"No! I *have* to tell you!"

"You don't have to tell me anything!" Aurora said. "I don't want to hear it! I don't want to *know!*"

"You have to! Please, Rora! I've done something terrible! To you . . . I—"

"All right," she replied, her responses dulled; perhaps the Valium was doing its work. Or perhaps it was a wish to see this through, played out. Over with.

Something told her that whatever she was going to hear would change everything.

"It was my fault," Abby confessed. "I wanted to . . . and Harper . . . didn't force me. . . ."

As Abby continued, her voice a drone from afar, Aurora sat transfixed, her face expressionless while her "baby sister" explained how she had seduced Harper Styles.

Aurora left a dozing Abby to go to Harper's room.

He was dressed in a hospital robe and sat in a chair facing the door.

Immediately she saw that, other than a bandage on his forehead, he was not seriously injured.

"Are you all right?" she asked.

He nodded, his face in profile, not looking at her.

"Do you have something to wear home?"

He shook his head to indicate he didn't.

"I'll have clothes sent over . . . for both of you. I understand you can leave tomorrow."

"Yes," he replied. "In the morning."

"It *is* morning, Harper. Anyway, Abby will be asleep for at least another eight hours. I'll speak to your doctor and have the car sent for you when it's time."

"How . . . is she?"

"Upset."

"And you?" At last he'd turned to face her.

How am I? She was amazed at her unexpected calm. Perhaps the Valium . . . but somehow she didn't think so. This anesthetizing stillness came from somewhere deep inside her.

"I'm . . . numb, Harper. It's too soon to say." Wearily, she walked to the edge of the bed and sat down. "I want to know. I didn't want to before. But now . . . yes. Tell me."

"Aurora, I'm tired, and—"

"I don't care how tired you are. I'm tired, too, more than you can possibly know. But I want to hear your side of this. Now."

He sighed deeply and looked down at the floor in his characteristic way. Then, slowly at first, he began to speak.

"We . . . went to the party. Abby had a few drinks. She seemed to hold her liquor well, until later anyway. Besides, it was a party—the Oscars—and we danced. Closely. Too closely. I was afraid the crowd would notice and . . .

"I took her out to the yacht. I suppose I told myself that way I could sober her up before we came home. I was worried about what you'd say if you saw her drunk. I . . . I mixed myself a drink and gave her a Pepsi or something . . . and . . ."

He stopped speaking as if trying to regain his lost composure and then explained that he had gone to the head. When he'd returned, he couldn't find her. He called and she answered from below, from the master stateroom. He found her seated on the edge of the bed.

387

"Just as you are now," he said. "She was smiling at me. She held out her hand . . . and I took it."

For the most part, his version agreed with Abby's.

"What about the fire?" asked Aurora. "Abby doesn't know how it started."

He shrugged. "She was smoking a cigarette at one point . . . earlier on. I don't know. . . ."

"What do I tell the reporters, Harper?" This was not said with sarcasm; it was a very real consideration.

"I've called our lawyers. They're on their way here. Say nothing until we speak to them. They'll call you tomorrow, or later today, I trust."

His last word made them both look directly into each other's eyes. Then Aurora rose and picked up her purse. "One question, Harper. Only one." The word stuck in her throat. *"Why?"*

He shrugged, helpless to find an answer. At last he answered, "She was . . . young."

Aurora moved toward the door. "I'm going home."

She was stopped by his voice. "We can work this out, can't we?"

Her back was to him, but even so, he knew there were tears streaming down her cheeks.

"She's my *sister,* Harper."

When Aurora opened the door, more flashbulbs popped before she could put her dark glasses on again.

Reporters had camped on the lawn of the house and were waiting when she arrived. Aurora pushed past them, actually slamming the door on the hand of one persistent photographer.

It was light now. She went about the house turning off the lights she'd left on for Harper and Abby the night before. It was seven A.M. The phone was ringing. She went to the bar and poured herself a Scotch. Then she picked up the receiver.

The publicity department at the studio. As soon as they had spoken with the lawyers, a statement would be prepared for her to give to the papers. *Fantasy Bay*'s release would be postponed. "Fine," she answered. "I really don't care."

That was true. She didn't care. Aurora hung up. The phone rang again. Instantly.

It rang continuously for the next hour. Each time a conversation ended, the phone rang once more.

Vance and Eva called. Web called. She told all of them she would return their calls later. She was exhausted. One of Harper's business partners phoned; he was concerned over what the scandal might do to the value of the company's stock.

Scandal. He'd voiced the word. It dawned on her then that scandal was exactly what this whole mess was.

The phone rang again. It was after eight now. "I can't!" she said to herself. "I just can't, anymore!" She picked up the receiver and hung up immediately. Then she took the phone off the hook and staggered into bed.

She slept for only a few hours, then got up, made coffee, and replaced the phone on the hook. It rang. "Damn!" she said. Again she took the phone off the hook. She packed a change of clothes for Harper and Abby, then called the studio to have someone pick them up and deliver them to the hospital.

Eva and Vance came by around noon, carrying the newspapers.

"It's pretty ugly," Eva said, pouring herself coffee, "but you ought to take a look, see what you're up against."

The front pages were filled with pictures of Harper and Abby, fireman's coats wrapped around their naked bodies, their hair matted from the water, as they climbed into a waiting ambulance. And there were photographs of Aurora in dark glasses, her hands pushing the cameras away. The headlines were no better: MOVIE MOGUL AND TEEN CAUGHT IN FIRE! AURORA STYLES' SIS IN LOVE TRYST WITH HUBBY! IS SHE A MINOR?

On it went. Some of it was fact; most of it was conjecture. Invariably the emphasis was on Abby and whether or not she was underage.

"What are you going to do ?" Vance asked.

"About them?"

"No," he said slowly. "About you."

Yes . . . what about her? She'd known at the hospital that something was clearly over. Finished.

The dam burst. She reached out to Vance, who grabbed her just before her legs gave way, and a loud, anguished sob escaped from deep in her throat.

"I'm going to be sick," she whispered hoarsely, cupping her hands over her mouth.

Vance carried her into the bathroom as Eva ran to the phone.

She was stretched on the sofa now. Vance was putting another damp cloth over her brow as Eva tiptoed in and said quietly, "I've called my doctor. He's on his way. He'll give you something to calm you, darling."

"Thank you," Aurora managed to say through her sobs. Then the phone began to ring again.

This time she screamed.

Aurora had asked to be left alone. "I appreciate your help," she said through the veil of oncoming sleep the doctor had induced, "but I just need . . . to rest."

"All right," Eva agreed, obviously reluctant to go.

"She'll be okay," Vance whispered. To Aurora, he said, "If there's anything we can do, Rory . . ."

"Yes . . . yes . . ."

"Rory . . . have you thought about Abby?"

"What about her?" Sleep retreated for an instant as the name registered on her brain.

"Well . . . will she . . . stay? And where?"

"No!" Aurora cried out. Much was uncertain, but she knew one thing. She couldn't bear to see Abby. "She'll have to go—back to Oakdale. I don't know . . . just put her on a plane as soon as she can travel."

They said their good-byes and at last the house was silent. The phone was off the hook. The reporters were gone.

Aurora's eyes grew heavy as she gazed glassily at the pile of newspapers on the table beside the bed.

What to do?

The doctor had said it, hadn't he?

"Take a day or so, maybe a few. Then get away for a while. You've been under tension for months."

It all began to blur. Harper . . . Abby . . . Web Seton . . . Vivian Hamilton . . . *Under Eros* . . . a golden Oscar statuette . . . *Fantasy Bay.* All of it whirling, inside and outside. Then the doctor's parting words came to her.

"Give yourself a chance to recuperate, to heal. You need a change of scene."

Part III

Chapter Twenty-Two

Aurora spent the following week with Vance and Eva; they ran interference, shielding her from reporters and photographers. Maritza was contacted in Rome, and within days, Aurora found herself at the airport. She would fly to New York and then transfer to a connecting flight that would take her to Italy, away from the limelight.

This would be the first time Aurora had ever traveled alone on a commercial jetliner and the sight of the enormous plane almost gave her second thoughts. But she had come this far undetected, and to turn back now . . . To what? she reminded herself as she handed her ticket and passport to the attendant at the check-in counter.

"Oh!" exclaimed the young woman. "You're—" But she stopped in midsentence as Aurora nodded. From behind the oversized sunglasses, she interrupted her.

"I prefer not to advertise, if you don't mind. Where do I board my flight?"

"Gate twelve," was the reply. The attendant stamped the ticket and handed it, together with passport and boarding pass, to "Mrs. H. Styles," who quickly tucked everything into her totebag. "Any luggage to check through to Rome, Mrs. Styles?"

"No," answered Aurora. "I'm not taking much with me."

"Well, then you're all set." The attendant smiled nervously, and as Aurora turned to leave the counter, a scrap of paper was thrust at her from behind the desk. "Uh . . . Mrs. Styles . . . may I have your autograph?"

The flight crew was more accustomed to celebrated passengers. The first-class section was only half-full and no one interrupted Aurora's reading, except to serve dinner, all the way to New York. She was aware of one man's attention when she rose to use the facilities. He was stretched across the center seats in the middle aisle, and he smiled lazily as she reseated herself. His lizard cowboy boots hung over the armrest. Must be a Texas millionaire, she mused. Lucky the plane isn't crowded. Still, he was tall—lanky better described him—and even first-class seats could be confining to such long legs.

As the jet soared across the country, Aurora's eyes closed and images of the past week's happenings flew through her mind, especially of the unhappy reunion with Joe and Betsey Linn, who had flown all the way from Oakdale to accompany their youngest daughter home, only to find that Abby had run away. Poor Joe and Betsey. These two good people had given refuge to a lonely, orphaned teenager, yet their own child, at a similar age, had shocked and disappointed them.

"I wish we could do something to help," Betsey had said. "Joe and I feel so . . . so responsible."

Aurora had spent most of the time assuaging their feelings, relegating hers to the background. They were so bewildered, she thought. But are they any more bewildered than I?

396

There had been a postcard, mailed from somewhere in California—the postmark was blurred. Vance had read it aloud. It had said only: "Rora, I can't expect you to forgive me. I wish I could undo everything. I just want you to know that I'm all right—and I love you." Abby had signed it in the scrawled hand Aurora knew so well, although her tears had smudged the ink.

No, she thought. I can't forgive her. Not yet. Maybe someday, but not yet. Now the merest thought of Abby or Harper brought tiny jabbing pains in her chest and constriction in her breathing. Maritza had suggested an ocean voyage—the *Raffaello* was docked in New York—but the prospect of an entire week aboard ship with nothing to do but think, especially on the water, where Harper and Abby had—

No. A fast-flying jet to New York and another to Rome. Diversion until the pain was past. If that time would ever come . . .

When the jet landed at JFK, it was almost dark. Aurora collected her belongings and deplaned. It seemed an eternity since she had last visited New York on that whirlwind trip with Maritza to shop for her wedding gown. Oh, God, she thought, is everything I see and hear going to evoke the past?

She entered the VIP cocktail lounge, accessible only to international first-class travelers. She had two hours before her connecting flight to Rome.

It was dark inside so she removed her glasses and settled into a small booth in a far corner.

"I'm glad to see you're not the type who hides her eyes indoors. On the plane you had me worried."

Aurora looked up, startled. The tall passenger in lizard boots stood before her. He was smiling, the same lazy smile he'd displayed on the flight, but his voice bore no trace of a Texas drawl.

"Mind if I join you?" he asked, sliding into the

397

opposite side of the booth.

"It doesn't seem to matter whether I do," Aurora answered. She was more irritated than flattered by this sudden attention.

"What color are they?" he said, ignoring her remark.

"What color are what?"

"Your eyes." He leaned closer, pushing the tiny candle across the table. "Ah. That's better. They're green."

"I hope I've satisfied your curiosity," said Aurora.

"Part of it. My name's Paul Blake." He extended a hand to her.

She wondered what his game was. Did he know her face? Was this one of the million ploys he knew with just a slight twist? Watching his eyes as she shook her hand, she said, "Aurora. Aurora Styles." His eyes betrayed not the smallest flicker of recognition.

The waitress arrived. He ordered Chivas and Aurora nodded. "Two."

"Well, I guess that means you don't object to my company."

"I haven't decided yet," she said, still watching his eyes, which were a deep, smoky blue. "I just like the same Scotch."

"I'd have offered you some on the plane, but you seemed engrossed in your reading . . . and I admit, with apologies, I was exhausted."

She smiled as their drinks were served. Well, at least he would fill part of the two-hour wait until her Alitalia flight.

"What were you reading?" he asked.

"When?"

"On the plane. What was so all-consuming?"

She laughed. "You won't believe this, but my mind was elsewhere the whole time. I can tell you the title, but I swear I don't remember a word of what I read."

"Then I'd rather not know its name," said Paul Blake, his smile wider than before.

"Why not? I don't think I understand—"

"Occupational hazard. I write books, and if it turned out that you were reading one of mine and didn't recall a word of it, I'd be deeply wounded. Professional pride, all that ridiculous nonsense."

"What do you write?" she asked, sipping her drink.

"Oh, different things. Mostly about injustice. Untruth. Man's inhumanity to man. Not your basic relaxing prose."

"Then never fear, your book was *not* on my lap. This novel was pure escapism. Trash. Not up to your standards, I'm sure."

Paul drained his glass and signaled the waitress for another. "You never know. I've written some garbage too. That paid the bills so I could concentrate on the stuff I wanted to write." Now his eyes smiled as they looked into hers. "Guess that makes me a hypocrite, doesn't it?"

"I don't know. Maybe it just makes you honest. That's refreshing for a change." Her cheeks warmed. "Cut that last remark. In Hollywood, that's refreshing."

"What were you doing there?" he asked.

Did he really not know who she was? "Living. Or doing what I mistook for living." She downed the rest of her drink, aware that Paul Blake was studying her. At another time she might have found him attractive. No, she decided, he is attractive. There is something so un-Hollywood about him. He's handsome in a flesh-and-blood way. Like Harper? Not at all like Harper. Perhaps that was in Paul Blake's favor, but she wasn't interested. She had undergone sufficient turmoil to want to avoid any more complications.

"You're not from the Coast," she said.

"No. Just visiting—and getting the hell out as soon as I could. And you? Are you getting the hell out too?"

She nodded. "I may never go back."

"We all say that," he said. "I said it too. But the money was too tempting. The difference is that I'm smarter than I used to be." He leaned closer. "Now I just fly in, take the money, and run!"

They both laughed until he asked, "So where are you running to—or from?"

Instantly, Aurora's guard went up. "Running? Why do you use that word?"

He shrugged his shoulders. "I don't know. Writer's instinct maybe. But you haven't answered my question." And he hadn't taken his eyes from hers.

"I'm going to visit friends. In Rome." She still wondered whether he was playing a game or whether her own ego made her assume that anyone she met knew her, anyone who hadn't been stranded on a desert island. Stop the clichés, she told herself. Just drink your drink and be grateful for the diversion.

She took another sip and sighed deeply.

"I hope that's not from boredom." Paul Blake grinned enigmatically.

She shook her head.

"May I ask a personal question?"

"Ask away. If it's too personal, I just won't answer."

His index finger touched the ring finger of her left hand. "Recently widowed? Or divorced?"

She hesitated before answering. "Separated."

"Is Rome supposed to help you decide?"

"Decide what?"

"Whether to keep that ring or give it back."

She looked up into his deep blue eyes. "Neither. The decision has already been made. The ring . . . I . . . it's too long a story." A sudden welling of emotion brought tears to her eyes.

"Sorry," she said. "The interview is over. Occupational hazard."

His eyes seemed to be smiling softly at her. "I didn't mean to pry. Well, actually, I did. I wanted to know. But I didn't intend to cause you any . . . discomfort."

She sensed that he meant it. "Why did you want to know?"

"Well, I'm on my way to Rome too, and I wondered if it was pointless to suggest we try getting . . . better acquainted."

His direct approach was, in a strange way, relaxing. Aurora felt that she didn't have to maintain the defensive, that she could be direct with him. Her shoulders and neck lost some of their tension.

But she answered his question with one of her own. "Are you running away from something or someone?"

"Did I give you that impression?"

"Well, you asked me—"

"I live in Rome most of the time. I fly to New York twice a year to see my publisher. And when one of my books gets past the option stage, sometimes I come out to L.A. just to check on how the film version turned out. It's generally disappointing, but at least it keeps me from harboring illusions. It's really a pleasant life for a confirmed hypocrite."

"You're terribly hard on yourself," said Aurora.

"Not really. I've just learned not to take myself too seriously. By the way, is Styles your maiden name or is it his name?"

She was almost convinced that he really hadn't heard of her or seen her face before. "His . . . but I'm known professionally by the name of Styles . . . so I guess I'll hang onto it." This prompted another sigh.

The waitress arrived then with the check. Aurora reached for her totebag and drew out her wallet, but Paul shook his head. "Absolutely not. I insisted on imposing my company on you." He handed the waitress several bills.

"Don't you care what happens to your books?" asked Aurora as they exited the lounge.

"I did once. The first time. Even wrote the script. They threw it out and got a studio hack to jazz it up with tons of sex and violence. I swore that was the first and last time. And it was the last time I became involved with any of it. Now if they want my books, they can pay me plenty and do whatever they like to the story. It doesn't change my work, and I sleep better at night because I'm not expecting miracles anymore."

"You paint yourself as quite a cynic. Are you?"

"Partly. About fifty-fifty. A cynical romantic or an optimistic cynic. It changes with age." His slightly crooked grin had increased, and it made Aurora smile. He wasn't more than thirty-seven or eight, but he spoke like someone much older.

They were walking toward the Alitalia check-in, and as they passed the myriad departure gates, Aurora wondered if she had ever knowingly appeared in a film version of one of Paul Blake's books. She resisted the urge to ask him.

When they were settled into their seats aboard the jet, Paul said, "Ms. Styles—"

She laughed. "Aurora. I don't know if I can handle Ms."

"Aurora. What do you do by the professional name of Styles?"

He must have been lost in the Himalayas! she thought. "I acted in films."

"Past tense?"

"Most likely. I'll know more about that after I've been in Rome for a while." She considered his

402

question. "What did you think I did?"

He reached over. "It's nighttime. Do you mind?" He removed the dark glasses, which she had put on when they'd left the lounge. "I didn't know if you wore these for a reason or for affectation. Are you well known enough to be recognized without them?"

She lowered her eyelids and said, "In some circles."

"I apologize. You certainly have the face for films, but—"

"But what?"

"But you strike me as too intelligent to put up with all the crap."

She laughed ruefully. "I thought that, too. God! was I wrong!" She detected a touch of humor in her bitterness—maybe she wasn't beyond hope.

"What's so funny?" he asked.

"It's too heavy for in-flight talk. Let's see what movie they're showing." She reached for the program listing. "Oh, God," she groaned. There was no escape.

"One of yours?"

She nodded. "My latest." Her neck tension was returning.

"Well," said Paul, "that's something we don't have in common. I've never heard of this title before."

"Don't be too sure. Never underestimate the power of a studio." That statement flooded her with recent memories. It was a sobering reminder that the film about to be shown—her most recent—might also have been her last.

As the credits rolled and Harper's name filled the screen, Aurora shut her eyes. She couldn't shut out the hurt, even trying to do so made her tired. So tired! There was escape in sleep, avoidance. Cowardly? Perhaps, but it was a way of surviving. And the pain couldn't last forever. Nothing did.

Aurora fell into a sleep so deep that she was unaware of dreaming. She was also unaware of the passage of ninety minutes until Paul Blake's hand touched her arm. Disoriented, she shook herself awake as he removed his headset and placed it in the designated pocket beneath his tray.

"You're not half bad," he commented, with a grin she was unable to interpret.

"Thanks, I think."

"What I mean is, there's no storyline, and the direction is so heavy-handed it's amazing you don't come across like a robot, the way the other actors do."

She smiled, refreshed by her nap and relaxed by his comment. "Well, I had special training for this kind of film." Her smile grew wider as she remembered her first professional encounter with Anton Kalmar.

"Other dogs?" asked Paul.

She nodded. "Oh, yes. Some barked more loudly than others, but most were members of the canine family." She looked up at him and added, "We were speaking earlier of occupational hazards. One very definite hazard is to have one's husband's name above the title."

"As in Harper Styles?"

"As in Harper Styles."

"Funny, I'd have thought that would give you freedom of choice."

"No," she said. "It gave me exactly the opposite."

"Did you love him?" Paul asked suddenly. "Or is that really none of my damn business?"

"It isn't. And yes, I did love him." Emotion began to well up again. "I'm sorry, I guess I need some time before I can talk about it without behaving stupidly." She averted her eyes from his while she rummaged through her totebag for a handkerchief. When she looked up, Paul was holding out a monogrammed white linen square.

"Here," he said. "It was my fault. Let it be my handkerchief."

"Thanks." She dabbed at a tear under her eye, trying to keep the linen clear of her mascara. Then she breathed a deep sigh and a short laugh sneaked out. It surprised her.

"Something amusing in all this, I hope?" asked Paul.

"I was just thinking that on film nobody ever sees what happens to the handkerchief—you know, whether she returns it to him or tucks it in her purse."

"The latter. That way," he said slowly with his eyes fixed on hers, "I'll have a good excuse to call. I can use it the way Victorian ladies used 'forgotten' gloves."

Aurora didn't understand why his remark made her uncomfortable, but she opted for lightness to shake an oncoming mood. "Oh, I never forget my gloves."

"No," he said. "I don't suppose you do."

Neither of them spoke until the steward came by with a cocktail caddy. Paul ordered two Scotches—Chivas—and Aurora made no attempt to refuse. However, after they clinked their glasses in a friendly toast, she purposely avoided any subjects that might require further use of Paul Blake's monogrammed white linen handkerchief.

By the time the flight was nearly over, Paul and Aurora had exchanged stories of life in Hollywood and in Rome. She related anecdotes of studio mishaps, and he offered her a tantalizing list of must-see places in the Eternal City. She didn't tell him that Maritza would, most likely, serve as tour guide and den mother and that any ruins or ancient landmarks visited would be those accessible by limousine. Odd, she reflected, it might be fun—a word she hadn't used recently—to explore the sights with Paul Blake. But, as she had learned, timing played a major role in all things. And though he had proven to be a pleasant diversion on the flight, the timing was wrong.

He interrupted her thoughts as the FASTEN SEATBELT sign flashed on. "I was thinking," he said, "that I'd like to see you in a film where you were given some real acting to do."

His hand came to rest on hers. Addressing his eyes, she said, "I would too, Paul. I would too."

He patted the diamond in its platinum setting. "Well, maybe now you'll have that chance."

It was several moments before she answered, "Maybe." She doubted she had convinced either of them.

Maritza was in full view as she approached them. Aurora spotted her as soon as she and Paul had cleared customs, but the *paparazzi* had spotted Aurora. They dashed in front of the countess and encircled *"la bellissima"* as Paul tried to wave them away. On all sides flashbulbs popped.

"Via!" shouted Paul. Shutters continued to snap. His arms went around Aurora as a shield, but the *paparazzi* didn't stop.

Paul grabbed the photographer closest to them and yanked so hard that the man dropped his camera. He then shouted angrily—in Italian so Aurora had no clue as to content—and suddenly the *paparazzo* and his cronies recoiled, leaving a trembling Aurora to be enveloped by Paul Blake's protective arm.

"Darling!" cried Maritza, finally able to join them. "Rory, darling . . . are you all right?"

Paul released his grip, and Aurora smiled tenta-

tively. "Yes . . . I'm fine. Thanks to Mr. Blake here."
To Paul, with an attempt at lightness, she said, "I hope
you're really as cynical as you pretend to be. We'll
probably be in all the next editions, and you'll be
branded as the reason I left Hollywood." That struck
her as funny and produced a wry laugh. "You see,
Mr. Blake, chivalry in these times can create problems."

He reached out and pulled her dark glasses to the tip
of her nose. "*I* can live with that, Ms. Styles." He
pushed the glasses back into position.

After Aurora and Maritza exchanged embraces,
introductions were made. The countess eyed Aurora's
tall, rugged protector and asked, "Have you come to
Rome with Rory?"

Paul smiled warmly. "I'd like to say yes to that, but
actually we've met quite recently." To Aurora he
added, "And I hope it's just the start of—" When
Aurora tensed; he paused, then said, "I hope we can see
each other again."

"May we offer you a lift into the city, Mr. Blake?"
asked the countess.

He glanced at Aurora, who answered for him. "Paul,
please forgive me if I seem rude, but I really need to be
alone. I . . . well . . ."

He saved her from floundering. "Some other time,
then. I'm meeting some people." Drawing Aurora
aside, he said, "I did mean that. Some other time?"

Aurora looked up at him through her dark glasses.
"Paul, I . . . please understand . . . but I . . ."

He squeezed her gloved hand gently. "I don't mean
to rush you. Wasn't it Sam Goldwyn who said we meet
everyone in life twice? I'll wait."

His kindness touched Aurora. He didn't seem
offended by her need to lean back and kick off her
shoes, throw off her dark glasses and the pretense that

407

accompanied them—to openly admit how deeply wounded she was. Perhaps it was the only way to cleanse her wounds. Let them surface: the anger, the hurt, the grief. Grief? she thought. Yes, she was grieving. Something in which she had believed wholly and without reservation had recently died. She needed time for mourning, had to lay her love for Harper to rest.

Chapter Twenty-Three

"Well, you must tell me all about him," said Maritza as soon as they were settled in the back seat of the Mercedes.

"There's nothing to tell. I met him on the plane. Actually between planes. In New York."

Maritza regarded Aurora from behind her tinted Dior frames. "Odd, I would have thought the two of you were closer than that. Perhaps it's wishful thinking. Even on the rebound, a new romantic interest would help get Harper out of your head, and it would restore your confidence."

"I'm not interested in a new romance right now. It's the farthest thing from my mind."

"I see. That's why you dismissed Mr. Blake so abruptly."

Aurora removed her own sunglasses to better understand the countess' remark. It didn't make sense, but neither had her behavior to Paul. She heaved a deep sigh.

"Darling, there was definitely something between you and that young man."

"Maritza, please stop looking for things that just aren't there, will you? Your imagination is working overtime. We hardly said anything to give you the impression—"

"My point exactly," said the countess, cutting her off. "It was all in what wasn't said."

Aurora didn't answer, but instead concentrated on the passing view, her introduction to the outskirts of Rome. As they drove nearer to the city, row upon row of modern apartment buildings began to appear, tall, identical, gray or yellow structures, each with small storefront display windows on the ground floor. None of the indigenous orange-colored buildings or open marketplaces Aurora had seen in photographs; none of Fellini's eccentrics. She did long to visit Via Veneto at night, although she did not confide this to the countess. The only confirmation that she was in Italy, as the Mercedes swerved in and out of schizophrenic traffic, was the language on storefront signs. The closed windows of the car did not permit the calls of the crowds to penetrate, but the wild gesticulations of people dodging zooming motorcycles and beetle-sized Fiats presented an animated pantomime. Part of Aurora wished to join them, to throw her hands into the air and shout or laugh or cry; another part of her was grateful for the safety, the isolation, of the sleek automobile. It protected her, at least for the moment, from any confrontation with . . . with what? she asked herself silently. With life? She dismissed that thought as ridiculous and turned her attention to Maritza, who had begun to play travel guide with her customary gusto.

"Of course in these *borghi*—I suppose one might liken them to American suburbs, or to those boroughs in New York—you only see the *ordinary* Italians. As we get into the center of the city, you'll see why Rome is to the heart what Athens is to the mind."

Aurora nodded. She hoped that wouldn't trouble her own heart.

They were riding beside a rushing river.

"The Tiber," Maritza pointed out. "I have friends in Trastevere—which means 'across the Tiber' and is, with the ghetto, the oldest section of the city. You'll like it, I promise."

"Is that where we're staying?" asked Aurora.

"No, darling, we'll *visit* there." She pronounced the word as though she were speaking of Aurora's all-but-forgotten walkup in Greenwich Village. "Ugo has a villa in Parioli. That's where we're staying. It's more . . . well . . . elegant. And a better neighborhood. I don't think you'll be disappointed."

They were stuck in a Roman traffic jam and Maritza muttered under her breath, "Imbecile. There *must* be another route without driving through the center!"

Aurora laughed suddenly at Maritza's fury.

"You find it amusing? Well, I suppose I ought to be happy to see you laughing. But what is it, Rory?"

Aurora grinned widely. "You've stopped smoking— and I'm really glad. But your hands—" Her giggles interrupted her speech.

"What about my hands?" the countess asked with indignant curiosity.

"Your hands are going through the motions—look!"

Maritza glanced down at her fingers, which were, in fact, poised as if clutching her invisible but once ever-present ebony cigarette holder. She too began to laugh. "Well," she finally said, "I've only exchanged one vice for another, I'm afraid." She opened her alligator handbag and withdrew a small flask.

Aurora's eyes betrayed her surprise. The countess had never been a teetotaler, but alcohol was Tadzio's problem; Maritza had always maintained control

411

because, as she had often commented to Aurora, drunks were intolerable and it was essential to remember that alcohol was aging. And, as always, certain words such as *aging* were spoken with such distaste that anyone with sensibility would immediately take warning. So it seemed to Aurora wholly out of character for Maritza to have, in her own words, "exchanged one vice for another."

Aurora studied her hostess closely. The countess looked as fabulous as she had at their first meeting. Oh, perhaps occasionally one might detect something in her eyes, but whatever one perceived there, it was *not* the evidence of age. Aurora reflected on their friendship, on Vance's revelation as to the nature of the countess' interest in her, an unknown young actress. Strange, she thought, I've never really considered her deeper feelings. If, as Vance had more than suggested, Maritza's interest in Aurora went beyond friendship, why, then, had she introduced her to and encouraged the relationship with Harper? Maritza had never expressed jealousy, nor had she ever made any sexual advances toward Aurora.

Now, as the Mercedes continued to crawl through the Roman traffic, disconnected observations crossed Aurora's mind. Why, if the countess was attracted to her, had she never voiced her feelings? Fear of frightening Aurora away? Surely fear had not stopped her with Eva Morley. And Eva couldn't have been the only woman in Maritza's life. Aurora had met other female friends of the countess—certainly some of these relationships had been more than platonic—yet, never an approach, not a single overture in Aurora's direction. She was always there, in the background, as Rory's friend, confidante, adviser. Even at the airport, the countess had seemed more interested in Paul

Blake's interest in her than Aurora herself.

A shudder passed through her, despite her luxurious sable coat. It was possible that Maritza cared for—loved—her selflessly, as a mother would love a daughter. Aurora had craved that kind of unconditional love, never having experienced it, but the idea that the countess might love her in this manner held no appeal. Even less appealing was the thought that Maritza might have harbored unexpressed desires for her. Aurora shrank farther into her side of the back seat as the chauffeur swung the car onto a steep incline in the Parioli section of Rome.

The countess' flask seemed to have no bottom; she held it out to Aurora, who declined with a nod of her head.

"Ugo will take you to Cinecittà once you're settled in. Hollywood isn't the only film capital in the world, darling, and Italy will fall in love with you."

Aurora laughed. "I hope Italy is less two-faced. I hear that Italians don't hold back their feelings—it's all up front and no ulcers. Is that true?"

"I couldn't say," answered Maritza. "I've always found people to be people, wherever they are. One survives. It's an old conversation, if you recall."

"Is that why you love Rome?" asked Aurora.

"No, darling. I love it for the city's duality. I don't suppose that's a proper answer, but it's my personal feeling. Rome is sunny and beautiful, young and vibrant—everything you are—but underneath, she's decadent, ancient, masquerading, trying to please in order to survive. Yours truly." She smiled, but it wasn't a joyous smile; Aurora detected a twinge of sadness . . . or regret.

The chauffeur turned the car onto a secluded drive and announced in slurred Italian *"Siam' arrivati."*

"Well, Rory, darling," translated Maritza, "we've arrived."

Ugo Balestrino was at home to welcome them. He was very short and wore rimless glasses. His thinning black hair, Aurora noticed immediately, was dyed that color, and his olive complexion was undistinguished except for a small mole beside his temple. He certainly didn't impress Aurora as either Tadzio or Maritza's physical ideal, but he was gracious and hospitable. He put Aurora at ease within minutes of her entrance into the splendid green marble foyer of the *palazzo,* which Maritza explained was Italian for the word *building* and not, as Aurora had assumed, a palace. Nonetheless, either definition could have served, because Villa Balestrino was opulent. It was not to Aurora's taste; however, she had to admit that it was impressive in the way that museum foyers and grand hotels are impressive. Surrounded by green marble—floors and columns—and heavy brocade tapestries on every wall, Aurora didn't know where to cast her eyes first. Two suits of armor stood guard outside a paneled door, and Ugo, whose English was impeccable, if old-fashioned, explained that he called his knights Tweedle Dee and Tweedle Dum. "After your English fable, from which I first studied grammar in school."

Aurora patted a knight's visor. "Well, I never should have believed in them. They're empty-headed, after all."

Ugo beamed, although Aurora couldn't tell if it was in appreciation of her little joke or because he took pride in understanding it. Maritza had mentioned that his passions were English literature and painting. "A genuine anglophile," she'd said.

That was an understatement. After depositing Aurora's coat and bag in the hall with Jeeves, whose real name was Gennaro, he was quick to explain, Ugo led Aurora into the library. "*Eccoci!* My favorite place—and you shall see why!"

His enthusiasm drew her to him. As did the contents of his favorite place. On two of the book-lined walls, ceiling-to-floor, were Italian titles, all bound in gold-tooled leather. The remaining two walls evoked memories of Aurora's childhood. There, in matching volumes, were all the classics she had devoured so voraciously. Her eyes scanned shelf after shelf. Could Ugo have read all of these? Or was his collection like Tadzio's, new and untouched, the bindings in perfect— too perfect—condition?

As if in reply to her question, Ugo declared, "I have committed more than one of these to memory. I especially love Dickens. And Shaw. I am not as taken with your Henry James, although I do like *The Golden Bowl*. And of course, your Hemingway is marvelous. My favorite of your playwrights is Tennessee Williams. To my mind he is as great a poet as Shakespeare."

"I couldn't agree more," said Aurora.

"Good! I like people who agree with me, when they do it with sincerity."

Maritza stood at the bar, the only part of the library, except for a sofa and chairs, that was unoccupied by books. She was drinking cognac. Ugo, leading Aurora by the hand, shook the index finger of his free hand at Maritza. "Tsktsk, my dear countess, I do wish you wouldn't," he said, indicating the brandy decanter beside Maritza's glass.

"I wish I wouldn't too, but . . ." She poured again as Ugo escorted Aurora from the room.

"Do you like paintings?" he asked.

"I only know what I like."

"*Benissimo.*" He threw open a set of carved wooden double doors. "My gallery."

They entered a vast room. As in the library, the walls were covered, but with paintings. Life-sized paintings, for the most part, stunning oil portraits in carved gilt frames.

Aurora was immediately drawn to several portraits of children whose cherubic faces were framed in halos of golden curls. "Ah!" exclaimed Ugo. "You are an admirer of Sir Joshua Reynolds!"

Aurora had not identified with the artist but with the smaller of the two children in one of his paintings, a child no more than four years, the image of Abby at an early age.

"You recognize her?" asked Ugo.

Aurora shook her head. "Not anymore. It's as though I never knew her."

Her host's face assumed an expression of uncertainty, as if his mastery of English had, on this occasion, failed him.

He went on to display the rest of his collection—more of Reynolds, several Gainsboroughs, one historical painting by Angelica Kauffmann, and countless etchings by their contemporaries. His running commentary provided the distraction necessary to clear Aurora's head, so she forced herself to listen to his stories about each canvas and his tales of the rivalries at the Royal Academy, which Reynolds had helped to establish.

"You know, my interest in this period of art arose because it parallels a great literary period in England. The writers and painters were somehow linked to one another—it is no different in life, do you not agree?" He didn't wait for her reply.

"Everyone we meet and everything we do is linked to

someone or something that came before. I sincerely believe this. It is one of life's mysteries, but also one of its certainties. There is comfort in that, I find."

"Why is that?"

"Why is it a mystery, you mean?"

"No," Aurora replied. "Why do you find it comforting?"

Ugo seemed to be searching, although Aurora couldn't tell whether it was for words in English or for the answer to her question.

"I'm not sure," he said finally. "But I suppose that knowledge is somehow reassuring. There are factors in life over which we have no control. So it is easier to shrug and just go on."

"Is it?"

"Of course. If we cannot control a thing or person, we are foolish to waste time and energy on attempting it. We can accomplish nothing by force of will."

"What do you suggest as an alternative?" she asked.

"Following the flow. Like the Tiber. Nothing one does will ever change its flow. So one must flow with it. Such is life. Ask Maritza, she can tell you."

Aurora reflected upon Maritza's history—as told to her by the countess. Was it a matter of will that she had survived or was it, as Ugo claimed, that Maritza had simply "flowed" with the tides—of war, of love, of life itself? And was the act of survival also an art, not forcing or willing but flowing with the tide? Was her flight from Hollywood and Harper and the ugliness she had discovered there a matter of will or of flow? Uncertainty filled her, but she knew she had followed her instincts, which had told her she could do nothing to change the situation once it had come to light. Perhaps she was learning, in spite of herself. That thought produced a short laugh.

"Have I mispronounced something?" Ugo asked,

breaking in on Aurora's reverie.

"Not at all," she apologized. "It was my own misinterpretation. Your usage of English is . . . formidable." She allowed Ugo to conduct the rest of his tour without interruption. Whatever Rome had to offer, in addition to asylum, Aurora sensed that it promised to educate her in far more than matters of art.

Chapter Twenty-Four

Aurora wanted time to think and time not to think, but the countess, ignoring her guest's request for peace and privacy, arranged the usual round of parties and a tour, not of the ancient city—"You'll do that on your own, darling," she'd said—but of Cinecittà, where a low-budget "spaghetti" western was filming and where Aurora secretly hoped to encounter her hero, Federico Fellini.

She learned, upon their arrival at the studio, that the director was on location and would be unavailable for several weeks. She was not eager to visit the set of a western for fear that someone might offer her a role in one. Thanks to Harper, she admitted reluctantly, she had been spared that fate in Hollywood.

Ottorino Bellini, who quickly confided that he was not a descendant of the operatic composer—"He came from Catania, *signora. I* am a Roman!"— although his first name had been selected because his parents adored the music of Respighi, was a pleasant young man in his late teens or early twenties.

From the look of rapture on his face when he was introduced to Aurora, it was clear to everyone that he was willing to be whatever "Signora Styles" wanted him to be, although preferably not a brother. But that was the role Aurora was offering, and he quickly accepted. To Maritza she whispered, "I must be getting old. He strikes me as a darling boy!"

Maritza eyed the young man as though equipped with a high-powered telescope. "Hmm. He's old enough, Rory dear. Italian men never grow up anyway, so enjoy the flattery. You could do worse."

Despite Maritza's estimation of the situation, Aurora felt only a warm, sisterly affection for Ottorino Bellini, and that was a relief to her.

At any rate by the end of her first week in Rome, Aurora had, with Ottorino, visited the Forum and the Colosseum, St. Peter's, the Sistine Chapel and the Vatican Museum, and the Fontana di Trevi.

"Toss a coin over your shoulder into the *fontana, signora,* so that you will return to Rome again after this visit is past."

She complied. "Ah, yes, I remember: *Three Coins in a Fountain.*" She found a ten-lire piece in her purse and followed tradition. As she did so, she was reminded of another film. "Ottorino, do people really *wade* in the fountain, the way Sylvia did in *La Dolce Vita?* Or was that all a fable?"

"Signora!" he exclaimed, visibly alarmed, "You are not thinking to—"

"No, no!" she assured him. "Just curious."

Ottorino shrugged his shoulders. "I do not know, *signora.* I suppose I am what you would call very . . . unsophisticated. My uncle never would have given me the opportunity of assisting you if it were not for my English, which, although poor, is passable." He looked at Aurora searchingly.

"Your English is more than passable, Ottorino. I wish I could speak Italian half as well as you speak English."

"But, *signora,* Italian is easy to learn. You pronounce *tutto*—everything that you see. We have no wasted syllables, no silent sounds. Your language is the difficult one. I could teach you Italian in no time." His eyes lowered. Aurora surmised that Franco Bellini, a studio executive, had cautioned his nephew not to be a pest.

"Ottorino, if you'll teach me Italian, just enough to make myself understood and to follow conversation, I'll be eternally grateful."

The boy turned bright pink, and his dark eyes flashed with hope.

On the social side, Ugo arranged a soirée of the crême de la crême of Roman society: studio heads mixed with financiers and industrialists; opera stars and film personalities added glamour, although none upstaged Aurora or Maritza. Aurora wore white silk, Maritza black satin. And on this occasion, it was the countess who suggested the jewels. "This is the perfect evening, darling. The ruby and diamond pendant with the matching earrings, I think."

But Aurora had already made her choice. "No, Maritza. Tonight I feel like emeralds." She wore a teardrop-shaped stone in a diamond-and-platinum setting, and matching earrings.

"Yes," said Maritza approvingly. "The emeralds go better with your eyes." She leaned over the jewel box. "In that case, *I* shall wear the rubies."

Jeeves had arranged a sumptuous buffet and the champagne flowed. Aurora was introduced to many titled people, and to a number of Italian film stars whose names were less formal: Giancarlo, Nino, Alberto, Marcello. The faces of these actors were more animated than those of their Hollywood counterparts, and their conversation, although most of it was unintelligible to Aurora, seemed more relaxed. The air of formality emanated from the surroundings, not from the guests, and Aurora was aware of an understated elegance, something lacking on Rodeo Drive. Jewels and wealth were evident, but both were worn with a more casual grace. And no one, Aurora learned quickly, called anyone else by his or her first name, despite introductions. It was *signora* or *signorina* for a woman; *signore* for a man, unless someone was addressed by a professional title: *dottore, avvocato, professore*. The nobility were addressed as *contessa* or *conte, baronessa* or *barone*. Aurora reflected that this separated the classes in a way unknown to Americans; however, it also maintained a certain distance and respect. And at least, she mused, there is no need to memorize names!

Ugo had assembled everyone in the library for a concert. He had confided his third passion, music, to Aurora, although his favorite composers were not English of the eighteenth century but Mozart and Vivaldi. He and three guests waited until everyone had been seated on the folding chairs Jeeves had arranged in two rows of semicircles. Then Ugo stepped forward and announced, "We have you as our captive audience. I shall speak in English in honor of our gracious guest." He nodded in the direction of Aurora's chair. Apparently everyone present spoke English, because he did not repeat his words in Italian. "Since we will play before we dine, we shall not, I promise, bore you for long." He laughed at his little joke and then cleared his throat. "We shall play Opus 17 in B-flat by Mozart." He glanced toward the door, as if looking for someone or something.

The three musician-guests had already taken seats

and were busily adjusting the heights of their music stands.

Jeeves tiptoed into the room, carrying a plastic shopping bag that advertised SMA, the Italian supermarket chain, in bold letters. He stepped to the improvised stage area and handed the bag to Ugo, who whispered loudly, "Where did you find it?"

"In the pantry, sir," answered Jeeves in a perfect imitation of John Gielgud. "It was somehow . . . behind the jams, sir."

The *principessa* Rosconi, a mannequin-slim woman at Aurora's left, said, "Can you imagine? A Stradivarius behind the jams! That Ugo!"

She and Aurora laughed politely and the concert began. The quartet had obviously performed together before; their timing and their playing made that evident.

Suddenly, in the dimness, Aurora became aware of a hand on her thigh. Startled, she turned toward the hand's owner. The *principessa* was smiling innocently, her eyebrows arched in query. Aurora returned her smile as she quickly crossed her legs. The movement caused the *principessa*'s hand to fall from Aurora's thigh.

"Scusi, signora," said the *principessa,* still smiling.

"Ma certo," answered Aurora. Of course, indeed!

The concert ended to polite applause, after which a late supper was served. While Aurora sampled shrimp, oysters, and squid in delicately spiced sauces, she was aware of the *principessa*'s stare. The woman was quite tall, almost six feet, and her clinging taupe gown appeared to have been poured onto her. A healthy tan and frosted hair helped to make her a living Erté sculpture. Her jewels were dramatic but modest, onyx pieces set in yellow gold. Aurora found herself at one

423

point almost returning the stare, but only from curiosity. Aurora was considered tall by Roman standards; the *principessa* could have modeled. What fascinated Aurora, however, was the woman's face; it didn't seem to have undergone cosmetic lifting, yet it was devoid of lines or wrinkles of any kind. Below it and just above the Nefertiti gold collar, her neck did betray her years. Maritza's neck was less creased. Aurora marveled that this woman could easily be ten years the countess' senior!

"You're staring," Maritza commented, a quizzical expression crossing her face.

Embarrassed, Aurora excused herself, and to escape the haze of cigarette smoke that had begun to irritate her eyes, she went out onto the balcony. A cool breeze was blowing, so she wrapped her arms around herself for warmth.

"May I?" asked a voice behind her.

As Aurora turned, a shawl of taupe-colored mohair enveloped her shoulders. The *principessa*'s hands remained at Aurora's arms as she said, "Rome can become quite cool at night." From the light of the room inside, Aurora could see the woman's eyes searching hers.

She tried to move away from the *principessa* without being too abrupt, but the older woman apparently had other ideas.

"My dear *signora,* I know you are a friend of the countess, but I see no reason why we cannot be . . . close."

Despite the night chill, Aurora was becoming uncomfortably warm. "I think you're making a mistake, *principessa."*

"Nonsense. I can tell when a woman is seeking companionship. A certain glance, a—"

Aurora cut in. "I don't want to offend you, but I'm not—"

Her words were cut off by the *principessa*'s sudden attempt at an embrace. The quintessence of poise was transformed, in an instant, into a clumsy fumbler.

Aurora fended off the advance, but the older woman was strong—and undaunted. Aurora was about to slap her when Maritza said sharply, "Leave her alone, Paola!"

The woman's swift release caused Aurora to fall back against one of the potted shrubs, and its density broke what otherwise might have been a painful fall. She brushed off her white silk gown and by the time she had recovered, the *principessa* had been dismissed by the countess.

"What were you doing out here alone with her?" asked Maritza in an irritated tone of voice.

"She followed me."

"But you *were* encouraging her earlier, darling. I saw you."

"Maritza, think what you want to, you know me better than that."

"I've always thought so, Rory."

"I don't like the way you said that."

The countess stood close to Aurora and she lifted her young friend's chin gently. "I've never interfered with any choices you've made, darling. But this is Rome, and—"

"And when in Rome?" asked Aurora, anger beginning to surface.

"Just be careful. This city can do strange things to people, Rory. Don't lose your head."

"I wasn't planning to, Maritza," Aurora answered coolly. She pulled the *principessa*'s shawl from her shoulders and, handing it to Maritza, said, "Would you

return this for me? I don't want to be misinterpreted."
She left the countess on the balcony and rejoined the
party.

The crowd had thinned out. Noting that Ugo's
Stradivarius lay atop its shopping-bag case on a chair,
Aurora removed it to a safer place, setting it on the
piano. She wandered aimlessly to the table and helped
herself to a petit four. The hour was late, but Aurora
didn't feel sleepy; restless, perhaps.

Maritza entered the room. "Rory, I'm sorry. Please
don't be upset with me."

"I'm not. But I like to stand on my own feet. I can,
you know."

"Yes, darling. I've always known that." Maritza
exhaled deeply, as if to dismiss the subject, then said,
"Ugo has suggested we go for a nightcap. Just half a
dozen of us. Will you come?"

It held appeal, even before Aurora learned that they
would be served their nightcaps at a café on Via
Veneto. "I'll just get a shawl," she said, quickly adding,
"one of my own."

The *principessa* was gone by the time Aurora,
Maritza, Ugo, and three others—the banker Petrelli,
his wife, and the neurologist, *Professore* Carlucci—
crowded into the Mercedes. On this occasion, Ugo
took the wheel and sped, not unlike a Roman cabbie,
through the deserted streets. He chose the route
through the Villa Borghese, exiting the gardens at one
of the ancient portals to the city and then swerving onto
Via Veneto. He skillfully maneuvered the car into a
parking space in front of the Excelsior Hotel and soon
the sextet had taken a table on the sidewalk outside
Donay. Aurora's heart skipped a beat. No matter what
circumstances had brought her to Rome, she was on

the street—Fellini's street. She felt a sudden exhilaration, an anticipation, a sense that she was coming home; she'd visited this place so often in her imagination.

Everyone ordered espresso and Sambuca, but Aurora chose amaretto. When the liqueur arrived, she sipped the sweet almond liquid, breathing deeply of its aromatic bouquet. She did not refuse when Ugo ordered another round.

Via Veneto was not heavily populated on this particular evening. The Café de Paris, on the opposite side of the street, was no busier. No *paparazzi* hounding stars, no glamorous or notorious Romans. Aurora wondered if all the world was not more vivid and exciting in dreams than in actuality. Was Venice no more than a baroque Disneyland? Would Florence prove as disappointing? New York and Hollywood had failed her, but were they to blame or had she placed too high an expectation upon them?

Her thoughts were interrupted by the zooming buzz of motorcycles passing at Indy 500 speeds. When she looked up, a couple had stopped by the table and were greeting Ugo and his guests.

Otto and "Buffy" Danzig, as they were introduced to Aurora, were a striking couple. Both were tall, Nordic, and blond, although the *baronessa*'s hair coloring was obviously, though subtly, salon-induced. She was American; her husband spoke English, not as Ugo did, with his charming eccentricities, but flawlessly, with only the slightest trace of an accent. Both were swathed in fur: hers, a light brown mink; his, dark beaver. A woman in her late forties, perhaps early fifties, Buffy was impeccably coiffed and made up. Otto was easily in his mid-fifties, and his aristocratic features made him a likely subject for an artist of caliber. Both husband and wife projected a friendly aloofness.

Maritza, who already knew them, leaned over and whispered *sotto voce,* "She doesn't like to use the title."

Aurora whispered back, "Well, that's refreshing. Someone who can afford to be a snob and isn't."

"No, but Otto is. I'm surprised he didn't click his heels and remind Ugo that he's a baron. Of course, the title does belong to his family. It's her money and his title. Lovely combination."

Aurora did not miss the caustic tone of the countess' remark. "Funny, he doesn't strike me as a snob."

"You've just met him."

Their confidences were cut short by the arrival of Otto at their side of the table. He bent his head, raising Maritza's hand to his lips, and kissed it. *"Contessa,"* he said without inflection. Then he turned to Aurora. *"Signora."* She didn't blush when he kissed her hand; it was a Roman custom. However, her cheeks reddened when she lifted her gaze and found Otto Danzig staring into her eyes.

"You are visiting Maritza?" he asked, pulling up a chair. Aurora noticed that Buffy had taken a seat next to the neurologist, whose name Aurora couldn't remember.

"Yes. And we are guests of Ugo," she replied.

"Ah, I see." Turning to Maritza, he said, "Your friend is lovely. I suppose she's the daughter you never had."

"Something you couldn't possibly understand, Otto," answered the countess. "Unless of course you'd like to be her father."

Again, Aurora detected the undercurrent between them. In an effort to break the building tension, Aurora said, "Do you and your wife live in Rome, Mr.

428

Danzig, or are you just visiting?"

"Otto," he answered. "Buffy and I have a small pièd a terre across the river, away from the more . . . fashionable crowd." He shot a glance at Maritza, who was stirring her Sambuca into her coffee and ignoring his remark.

Turning back to Aurora, he continued. "We make our home in New York, but we travel a great deal. We have a flat in London and we divide our year between the three capitals."

"Unless they're skiing in Gstaad or sunning at Cortina d'Ampezzo, or entertaining on their island in Greece," the countess cut in, again with almost tangible sarcasm.

It was the second time in one night that Aurora had witnessed this side of the countess. She wondered what could be the cause of such hostility. Seeking a means of escape, she asked a passing waiter for directions to the *gabinetto,* and excused herself.

While she was regarding her reflection in the mirror, the ladies' room door opened and Buffy Danzig joined her.

"Signora," she began, "I must apologize that we have had no time to become acquainted. It's just that the doctor is an old friend and we had so much to catch up on."

"There's no need to apologize, Mrs. Danzig. And please call me Aurora. *Signora* makes me feel as if I'm fifty." She immediately realized her faux pas, but before she could amend her careless words, Buffy laughed.

"I'll call you Aurora if you'll call me by my nickname—everyone does—and you must promise not to weigh your words with me, Aurora. I'm old enough to be your mother, and I'm not ashamed of the fact."

"I seem to have too many mothers tonight," Aurora

thought, unaware until she heard her voice that she had spoken the words aloud.

"Oh, then you and the countess aren't—" Now Buffy's cheeks warmed with color. "I think we're even," she said. "And I really didn't mean to—"

"It's okay. Maritza and I are old friends. We go way back." She sighed deeply. "*Way* back. To my early days in New York."

Buffy's eyes flickered. "Ah! Now I remember! I wondered where I'd seen you before and that's it. You and Tadzio Breslau—" Again she cut herself off, apparently fearful of another social blunder.

"Are also dear friends, Buffy," said Aurora with a smile. She sensed that she and this woman could dispense with formality as a result of their mutual gaffes.

"I hope Otto behaved himself. I noticed him talking with you and the countess, and I'm afraid they're not overly fond of one another."

"I gathered. Is there a reason?"

"There must be, but I certainly don't know what it could be. There are many things my husband and I don't discuss." She seemed caught in her own thoughts momentarily, but quickly recovered her presence. "I'd love to become better acquainted with you, Aurora. I have so few friends in Rome—especially women who speak English. Would you come to tea? We could talk, not just chitchat. Perhaps next week?"

"Yes. I'd like that very much."

"Good." Then, with a girlish laugh, Buffy said, "We'd better rejoin the others—we don't want them to wonder about us!"

"I wouldn't encourage either of them," Maritza said when they had returned to Ugo's villa for the night.

"I don't see why it should bother you," said Aurora. "It's obvious that you and he have no love for each other, but his wife is charming and wants me to come to tea."

"I wouldn't," Maritza repeated.

"Why? Are you going to tell me that Buffy Danzig is"—she stopped and checked her wording—"another *principessa* type?"

"Hardly," answered the countess. "But why do you need them? Haven't you been meeting enough new people?"

"I'm meeting all of *your* new people, yes. Maybe I'd like to make a few friends on my own. I can't think of anyone I've met in years that you or Tadzio or Harper"—her voice fell at the mention of his name—"didn't introduce to me. You know, Maritza, I'm not nineteen anymore."

The countess cut her off. "You meet the wrong people on your own. That Paul whatever-his-name-was on the plane—"

"You offered him a lift!"

"A momentary lapse in judgment. And then there's this *child* at the studio who follows you around like a lovesick puppydog!"

"You were suggesting to me, if you recall, that perhaps he wasn't too young. And besides, you introduced me to Ottorino in the first place."

"I did not." The countess paused, then quickly amended her statement. "Well, I may have, but I didn't expect him to become your shadow!"

Aurora breathed deeply. "Maritza, I still don't understand why any of this is causing an argument between us. No wonder Otto Danzig made that crack—"

"What crack?"

"About your mothering me." She regretted the

words as soon as they were uttered. She could see from the expression on Maritza's face that she had wounded her friend.

The countess sighed, then paced the room before she had fully recovered. "He had no right to speak that way," she said finally. "I only want you to be happy."

"Maritza," said Aurora, her voice soft and quavering, "just don't suffocate me." Without looking directly at the countess, Aurora left the room and went to bed. It had unexpectedly become a very long night.

Chapter Twenty-Five

Aurora sensed that if she decided to remain in Rome for an extended period of time, she would have to find a small apartment of her own. For now, Villa Balestrino was a welcome haven, but she knew in time she would crave the privacy she was so carefully avoiding.

As she avoided any contact with Harper Styles. First letters and then telephone calls arrived at the film studio. The calls were easier to dismiss; she instructed Ottorino to take any communications from California. He obeyed and explained to Harper on six different occasions that Signora Styles was out of town on location.

The letters, although unopened, never failed to produce a physical reaction. Aurora's pulse quickened or her stomach churned. But she had learned her lesson after the first letter. She'd made the mistake of reading it, and Harper's entreaty. His avowal of never-ending love, in spite of all that had happened, upset her to the core. His words had been intended to heal the chasm between them; instead, they widened the gap. His phrasing was eloquent, but in three pages of impassioned attempts to win her back, he never once mentioned Abby's name. Nor did he consider her feelings. The three pages were filled with Harper's love, Harper's needs, Harper's this and Harper's that. When Aurora later reread the letter in a more objective frame of mind, she came to realize that Harper wasn't intentionally trying to manipulate her; this was the way he had always handled matters—and people.

But that knowledge didn't make her ready to forgive—or forget. She was beginning work on a film, an Italian film, and she didn't need any distractions in the form of letters or calls from the man she had loved—and trusted—so deeply. She tore each subsequent letter into pieces and tossed them away. That ended the possibility of succumbing to temptation when she might be in a more vulnerable mood.

She was compelled to postpone Buffy Danzig's invitation to tea, for a solid script was offered and the female lead was a flesh-and-blood role, not a mere ornament on the hero's arm. She had always refused to appear in westerns, but filming was preferable to sitting day after day at Ugo's *palazzo,* no matter how varied the reading material. Not working permitted too much time for thinking. Shopping on the Via Condotti or sipping drinks on the Hassler roof provided only temporary distraction. Too, she felt it might be wise to be less available to Maritza for a while.

Ottorino listed for her the names of the actors in the cast. Not a Hollywood name among them. In fact, she was the only *straniera,* or foreigner—the word soon became etched in her brain—signed for the film. Her faithful young friend coached her in Italian daily, although, as he explained, this was for her own edification. "All actors are dubbed in Italian films," he said.

"You mean all *stranieri* who can't speak the

language," Aurora answered.

"No, no. All voices. This is why we shoot so quickly. We dub everything later. It has always been done this way in Rome."

"Wait a minute. I know that Sophia Loren used to be dubbed by someone else, but that was before she overcame her Neapolitan dialect."

"Yes, and now Sophia dubs herself." He beamed at having won his point.

"She dubs herself?" Aurora asked in wonder.

"Of course. And so will you when I teach you to speak with a Florentine flow in your voice—the *Fiorentini* have no accent. It is beautiful. You shall see. Carla Francese is dubbing you on this film. She speaks the Italian of Dante." He blew an imaginary kiss to the air. "Her voice could seduce any man."

Aurora laughed at his attempt at worldliness. "Then why didn't they sign her for the role?"

"Because," he replied, winking, "she is old enough to be my mother. I told you, her voice is her beauty . . . like your face." His complexion turned bright crimson.

"I see," answered Aurora. She had the feeling that starring in a spaghetti western was going to be an education.

It was that and more. Because the films were dubbed after the fact, no endless retakes were required and the working hours were quite different from those in Hollywood. They began later in the morning and broke for a full two-hour lunch. Evening overtime was a rarity. The atmosphere was casual, relaxed. While cast and crew dealt with the universal tensions involved in filming, tantrums were held to a minimum, and tempered by the midday meal and flowing wine. Aurora marveled at the work accomplished in the afternoon; wine made her drowsy. She limited her intake to a single glass if she had a scene following the break.

There were as many similarities as there were differences from Hollywood sets. The sweet, pungent aroma of hashish emanated from more than one dressing room, and her male star, a rugged Italian playboy now past his prime and relegated to westerns and gangster epics, often repaired to a corner with a familiar-looking white powder. On the first day of shooting, he offered Aurora a snort, and though he was not offended by her refusal, a second offer was never made.

The crew didn't seem to have such an affinity for alcohol as their American counterparts. Aurora thought that was because wine was a part of their culture; even children drank it with dinner. In other areas however, their behavior was much the same: Men made passes at starlets and promised them bigger roles in exchange for "favors." Extras griped and played up to assistants who might someday advance and be of help to them. How little they know! thought Aurora as she observed the scenes behind the scenes. Again she reflected that Harper had done her a good turn; she had been spared such situations. Nonetheless, that did not alter her feeling toward him. She continued to refuse his calls and tear up his letters.

She did not, however, tear up the letter she received from Abby. It was postmarked Venice, California, and read:

Dear Rora,

I don't have the courage to face you, so I am sending this to you at the studio in the hope that it will be forwarded to wherever you are. I know what has happened can never be undone, but I

436

want you to know that I have accepted the blame and I am trying to learn from my mistake.

I wrote to Mom and Dad to let them know that I am all right. I don't want them to worry. I explained that I can't go back to Oakdale, but I am going to finish school out here. I've made up my mind—also about some other things. I am staying with some kids my age. We are sharing an old house, and I am learning to cook. The place is as crowded as it was at home when I was little and you took care of me. God, Rora, I'm so sorry, so truly sorry. I think the worst part of the whole mess is knowing how much I hurt you. I love you. I wish I had some way of convincing you of that. Someday, maybe . . .

For now, I just wanted you to know that. I am okay. And I love you.

Abby's signature was at the bottom and when Aurora finished reading the letter, her index finger traced the name several times. Then Giannina, the wardrobe mistress, knocked on the dressing room door, and Aurora folded and pocketed the missive. Well, she thought as she was zipped into her costume, there must be someplace in my heart for her; I didn't destroy the letter.

As she strode onto the set, she realized it provided a sharp contrast to her preoccupations. She laughed aloud at the old-fashioned delineation of the good guys and the bad. The outlaw gang came to town dressed entirely in black, they rode black horses, and their spurs were tarnished and worn.

The sheriff and his men, and of course the leading man, were outfitted in white: white fringed pants, white hats, and white boots that looked as though they had been custom-made by Tony Lama rather than by a nineteenth-century mining-town cobbler. The spurs on their boots were polished and gleaming. "Well," mused Aurora, "at least people in those days knew where they stood. There's something to be said for that."

Ottorino, sitting nearby, said, "Aurora"—she had insisted that he, too, stop addressing her as *signora*—"there are times when I fear that my English is very poor. I did not understand a word of what you meant."

"You weren't supposed to," she said with a wicked smile.

After the film wrapped, Aurora did join Buffy Danzig for tea. The Danzigs' pièd a terre was in a very old section of the city, tucked away in a corner of Trastevere, and a creaky cage of an elevator delivered Aurora to the top floor. A thin, straggly-haired maid admitted her to the small apartment. It was cozy and casually furnished, the kind of hideaway Aurora had dreamed of before meeting Tadzio and Maritza. It invited guests to kick off their shoes and curl up on the pillowy sofa. Sunlight streamed in from a minuscule terrace, and Buffy Danzig presently came from that direction to greet Aurora.

"I hope you don't mind informality," she said. "I've done the whole flat in castoffs from other apartments."

"Actually, I'm relieved. I was afraid we might be sitting down to high tea or some such thing."

"No. Sometimes we do when my husband is at home, but this is more to my liking."

"I'm glad. Mine, too."

The two women seated themselves, Aurora on the sofa—although she did not remove her shoes—and Buffy in a deep, rose-colored chair.

They chatted amicably while Inga, the maid, served both tea and espresso. Aurora chose the latter, adding

438

steamed milk and sugar to transform it into a foamy cappuccino.

The conversation remained light, each woman basking in the luxury of speaking her native language. Aurora's Italian was improving, but she still suffered headaches by day's end from the deep concentration it required.

As she and Buffy talked of films and New York and Rome, Aurora began to sense that the *baronessa* was a very lonely woman. She found this difficult to comprehend. Buffy and her husband traveled the world together, neither having to work. Yet something was missing. Buffy seemed to crave more than the company of someone who spoke English; there were colonies of expatriate Americans and Britons in Rome—and Otto Danzig spoke English fluently.

Late afternoon was blending into early evening. The Roman skies were filled with pinks and mauve, puffy, cottony clouds unlike any Aurora had seen except in Old Masters' paintings. They had moved to the terrace, high above the banks of the Tiber, and a damp chill hovered over them.

Buffy asked suddenly, "Have you any children?"

In only a month's residence in the capital, Aurora had been asked that question by countless Romans. Buffy, however, was the first American to broach the subject.

"No," she replied. "My husband—well, I should say ex-husband—never wanted children."

"Do you feel the same as he?" asked Buffy.

"I've never really thought about it. I love children, but I don't have a burning desire to be a mother." She hadn't expected a sophisticated socialite to be curious about such a thing. "Do you have any?"

Buffy reached for her brandy, as she did so wrapping her wool shawl closer around her shoulders. "No. I wasn't able to. Medically. It's too long a story." She looked out at the horizon, at the buildings with their terra cotta tiles, at the rolling clouds. "My husband has a daughter. A bit older than you, I'd imagine."

"Oh. I hadn't realized."

"Otto and I married only ten years ago. His first wife died many years before."

"I see." Aurora shifted uncomfortably, not knowing how to respond to this information. She sensed that Buffy wanted to talk, but at the same time, she didn't know whether she was in the mood to hear about anything heavy. She wanted to feel as light and airy as the passing clouds above them.

She didn't have to concern herself. The door to the flat opened and Otto Danzig entered. Nervously, Buffy rose to greet him.

"No, no, my dear, stay where you are. I'll join you there." He peered onto the terrace and nodded. Aurora smiled and Buffy came back to her chair, moving it aside to make room for her husband. "Otto, why don't I get us all something to drink—it will warm us up."

He shook his head. "I'll do it." He put several aperitif glasses on a small tray, together with several bottles, and stepped out onto the terrace.

"Otto," said Buffy, "you remember Aurora Styles. We met at Donay. She was with Ugo and his friends."

He bowed, but on this occasion his hands held the tray, so he did not bend to kiss Aurora's hand. Instead, he set the tray atop a marble sculpture whose design offered the flat surface of a pedestal table. He reached for a bottle, poured, and handed a glass to Aurora. "It was amaretto, wasn't it?"

"Why, yes!" She was genuinely surprised that he had remembered.

He poured a second glass and offered it to his wife. "And your usual, my dear?"

She accepted without words.

Then he helped himself to a brandy and leaned back, propping his feet against the base of a broken piece of statuary.

"Buffy, dear, you didn't tell me we were having company. I would have arranged to be here earlier."

"Oh, it was really sort of a last-minute thing," she said quickly. "Aurora just finished shooting a film, and I thought—"

"Did you? Was it a role to do you justice?"

Aurora was becoming increasingly uneasy, and she was grateful for the shadows of approaching night.

"It was an experience unlike any I've known in Hollywood," she replied diplomatically. Glancing at her wristwatch, and using the hour as an excuse, she said, "I didn't realize what time it is; I really must go."

"Why so soon?" asked Otto. "I've just arrived and you're running off already?"

"Ugo and Maritza will be expecting me."

"I'll ring them and tell them you'll dine with us. Buffy and I insist, don't we?"

Buffy looked helplessly from her husband to Aurora. "It would be lovely if you'd stay, although it'll be pot luck. Inga is wretched in the kitchen and cook has the day off. You'll have to put up with whatever I can manage."

Aurora considered her hostess' words, which could have been interpreted as a hint to leave. But something, she didn't know what, told her that Buffy very much wanted her to remain.

"If I may use your telephone—"

"I'll take care of it," offered Otto. "You stay here and enjoy the sunset with Buffy." He rose and left the terrace before a protest could be made.

*   *   *

441

Pot luck consisted of omelets and glazed pearl onions, leftover croissants from that morning, and Gorgonzola with fruit for dessert. They ate around the marble-topped coffee table in the den, and aside from an undercurrent that Aurora could not identify, it was a pleasant enough evening, far more to her liking than posed, stilted occasions when twenty sat down to dine.

Around eleven o'clock, Otto announced, "Come, Aurora. It's impossible to find a taxi at this hour. I'll drive you home."

"Oh, no," she protested. "I'm sure I can manage. It's late—I refuse to put you to any trouble."

"No trouble, I assure you, and I'm sure Buffy will agree. You could easily get lost; eleven is much later in Rome than it is in the States. Very few people are out on the street. I insist upon accompanying you."

"He's right, Aurora," Buffy declared. "There's no telling what might happen. Besides," she added with a nervous laugh, "it's past my usual bedtime. Another hour and I'll turn into a pumpkin!"

Buffy walked with them to the door and kissed Aurora on the cheek. "I'm so glad you came to visit. I hope we'll be great friends."

"I hope so too, Buffy," Aurora answered. Then she and Otto stepped into the elevator cage and it descended.

They rode in silence halfway to Parioli. Suddenly, Otto turned and said, "I did not say where you were when I rang up earlier. I thought that would be best."

Aurora's eyes widened in amazement. "Why? What on earth did you tell Ugo?"

"I didn't speak with Ugo. I told the butler I was calling as a favor to you, that you would be dining with friends."

"But why? Why didn't you tell them?"

Otto was again facing front, concentrating on the road ahead of them. "I thought it was obvious. Maritza hates me. I didn't want to cause you any problems."

"Wouldn't it be better if you left that up to me?" she asked, feeling annoyed.

Otto braked the car. "Aurora, what is your relationship with the countess?"

"Why are you so interested?"

"Because I hope it's strictly platonic."

"You certainly have a lot of nerve to ask—"

"Please don't be angry. I've known Maritza too long and too well, but I would like to know you better. Not if—" He broke off.

"Not if I'm her lover? Is that what you're implying? God, I'm beginning to appreciate the working classes— they say what's on their minds instead of imposing their sexual fantasies—"

"She was my daughter's lover."

The shock of his words, the flat, emotionless tone in which he spoke them, stopped Aurora short. She looked at him, wondering what he was feeling, what he was thinking.

"I'm sorry. I had no idea."

"I don't advertise the fact."

When she found her voice, Aurora asked, "Does Buffy know?"

He shook his head, still gazing straight ahead, not at her. "There are many things my wife and I never discuss. It happened before we met."

"Where is your daughter now?"

Otto turned his eyes to her. "I have no idea. I have not seen her in twelve years. I think she prefers it that way. And it's better for the family, I suppose. When people ask, she is 'traveling.'" He paused for a moment. Then, "She's thirty this year. Her eyes are gray. Pretty

443

in her way. Not as lovely as you, however."

Aurora didn't relish his changing the subject to her.
"Does Maritza know why you dislike her so?"

"Dislike is too gentle a word. We hate each other. Of course she knows. I gave Clarice an ultimatum and she chose to comply with it. Maritza will never forgive me."

"What was the ultimatum?"

"To leave the countess or be cut off from the family."

"And the family's money?" It was out before Aurora realized she had said it aloud.

He smiled, but it was a bitter smile. "I would have expected Maritza to have explained. The money belongs to my wife." His eyes questioned hers.

She averted his gaze, pursuing instead his earlier remark. "What did you use for so-called leverage in your ultimatum, if not money?"

"Our name is a very old one. Before Tadzio Breslau's ancestors could read or write their name, we were nobility."

She was surprised to hear him mention Tadzio.

"Oh, yes, this is a very small world, Aurora. Smaller than that of your Hollywood pseudonobility. European aristocracy is a closed circle. My daughter would have been cast out of it, had she not chosen to leave, because she refused to play by the rules."

"It seems to me if you haven't seen her in twelve years, she's out of your 'circle' anyway. So where's the logic in this?"

"It hasn't anything to do with logic. Clarice would be welcomed back if she were willing to modify her behavior—in public, at least."

"And become a hypocrite like all the rest of you? Is that what you'd prefer?" Aurora's voice was rising, despite her attempts to remain calm.

"I would prefer that Clarice become a proper member of her family, worthy of its title and the respect that title commands. But my daughter was unwilling to keep her . . . persuasion . . . private." Otto's placid tone soothed Aurora's response, if not her irritation.

"But tell me, what about Maritza? She isn't an . . . an outcast. How do you explain that?"

A sardonic grin formed on Otto's lips. "I concede the countess is a woman of discretion."

"The better part of valor?" Aurora laced sarcasm with impatience. "That's the only difference?"

"It is, I assure you, not a small difference, Aurora."

She breathed deeply. "I don't know, Otto. To me it sounds too much like an elite club of two-faced people, no matter how many titles are in your little circle."

"Isn't it the same in other circles? Your own, for example?" Otto asked as he braked the car in front of Ugo's gate.

"I can't answer as you'd wish," Aurora replied. "I've never pretended to be anyone other than myself, not with Maritza or Tadzio or Ugo—"

"What about Harper Styles?"

"Despite what you may have heard, Otto, I loved Harper Styles. Maybe your closed little circle can't comprehend that because there was no deceit involved." She thought a moment. "Not on my part, anyway." For the first time no tears had welled within her at the mention of Harper's name.

"People outside your Hollywood circle are speculating as to why you left him."

"For the same reason I married him. Because I loved him. I know gossips and supermarket magazines are saying that I married him to advance my career and then left him when I didn't need him anymore." A small, wry laugh escaped from her.

"That amuses you?"

"Yes it does, thank God! You see, I wasn't brought up in a noble, titled family. I wasn't sent to finishing

445

schools in Switzerland. So I don't have to worry about appearances. I'm not concerned with other people's impressions of me—and I'm not worried about my reputation because I know who I am and what I do. The rest of the world can only speculate about that."

"I would like to speculate," said Otto.

"On what?"

"On what your answer would be if I asked you to dine with me tomorrow evening. Alone." He was staring directly at her now.

Aurora drew a long breath, returning his stare. "In case you hadn't noticed, Otto, *I'm* not the home-wrecker in the Harper Styles divorce case. I don't date married men."

"Buffy and I are married in name only. As for our . . . friendships . . . we go our separate ways."

"Oh, really? And how does that suit your closed circle?"

"I've told you. As long as we observe discretion—"

"In other words, it's okay to have affairs or indulge in orgies or do whatever you please as long as discretion rules? Anything short of murder, is that it? Or is it proper to stab someone in the back as long as nobody catches you with the knife? How marvelous for all of you—it's even better than a diplomatic passport!" She reached for the door handle, but Otto gripped her wrist, restraining her.

"I'd like to get out of the car, please. I had the mistaken impression that this evening I was having a pleasant, impromptu dinner and a friendly visit. I didn't know I had been invited to take part in some kind of weird game that you and Buffy play. It's too bad, because I like her."

"It may surprise you," said Otto, "but I like her too. And we both like you. That's why we asked you to tea."

"We?" Suddenly she understood. "We! My God,

you're telling me that I was set up, aren't you? You're telling me that your wife is pimping for you!"

Otto grabbed Aurora so violently that she thought he was going to slap her. Instead, he kissed her intensely, forcing the air from her lungs. Her breath was, literally, taken away.

Gasping and pushing him fiercely from her, she stammered, "I'm sorry for your daughter, and your wife. But I'm even sorrier for you!"

She thrust open the door and, without closing it, ran into the safety of Villa Balestrino.

Chapter Twenty-Six

Otto sent a single flower. A mauve rose in the exact shade of the dress Aurora had worn to tea. The accompanying card was encased in a slim silver envelope in the middle of which was a mauve cabochon. Aurora couldn't identify the stone, but her concentration was captured by the message on the card, which read simply: "I'm sorry, too. O."

Two things piqued Aurora's curiosity. First, Otto's attention after her less than subtle rebuff. Second, her own reaction; a mixture of flattery, distaste, and indifference. There had been no interrogation upon her return to the villa the night before; Maritza had left a message similar to Otto's, and Ugo, as it happened, had dined alone.

Maritza had not yet returned; she was absent from her customary spot in the garden when Aurora sat down for a late espresso and a brioche around noon. Her solitude did not last more than a moment, for Jeeves appeared, clearing his throat as was his habit upon arriving with a message.

"Madame, you have a caller from the studio. A young gentleman named Ottorino. Are you at home?"

"Oh, of course," said Aurora, jumping from her

chair. "I'll take it in the den."

"He isn't on the telephone, madame. He is here."

Ottorino stood as Aurora entered the drawing room. His face was flushed pink, which never failed to bring a warm smile to Aurora's face. How innocent he is, she thought. So much to learn!

"*Ciao!*" she greeted him with a kiss on each blushing cheek until his reaction would have alarmed any observant stranger. His feverish complexion, together with the excitement in his eyes whenever he was in his diva's presence, gave the impression that he was in the final throes of delirium.

"I came to invite you to a screening—also to meet your voice. Carla will be there and wishes very much to know the lovely actress for whom she has lent her speech."

"Wonderful! I could do with some distraction!" Leaving Ottorino with a blank look on his face, she fetched her purse and then left word with Jeeves as to her whereabouts.

It was refreshing to climb into the tiny Fiat, her legs propped in front of her rather than stretched out, to hear her young knight babble on about studio goings-on and harmless gossip.

"Oh, I almost forgot! You had a *telefonata.*" He guided the wheel with one hand while he fished through pockets with the other. Finally, he produced a small scrap of paper. "*Ecco!*" He handed Aurora a message scrawled in almost unintelligible English. "I took it down myself," he announced proudly.

"Good! Then perhaps you can decipher it for me. Your handwriting is abominable, Ottorino!"

"It is true," he admitted. They stopped for a traffic light at Via Bissolati, and he studied the message once more. Aurora hoped that Otto wasn't going to send notes or flowers to her at the studio.

But she was mistaken. "The caller was Signor Blake," said Ottorino. "I cannot read all of it, but he said something about his handkerchief." He glanced at her. "Can that be right? It looks like *handkerchief,* and as I recall, he said you would understand. Do you?"

Aurora broke into a wide grin. "I'm beginning to. Now tell me, what is this scribbling? It looks like the word gloves...oh." Her face now grew warm, although not as pink as her young driver's. "Never mind," she said. "I don't get all the words, but I *do* get the message." She laughed and added, "Tell me, did this Signor Blake leave a number?"

"No. That was curious, because I asked him for one. I didn't write it down, but I remember that he said, 'Tell her to find me the way I found her.' He repeated it and hung up. I did not think that was very courteous of him."

"Well, Mr. Blake is very direct."

"Then you do know how to find him?"

"No...and he didn't know where to find me."

"But then, his message—"

"He means if I want to find him, I will, just as he found me. It's not so mysterious, Ottorino."

"Then why do you look so perplexed?" he asked.

Aurora shook her head slowly. "I'm not sure." She opened her totebag and dug through its bottom till she unearthed the white linen, monogrammed handkerchief. She held it, studied it for a moment, and then tucked it back inside the bag.

If Ottorino thought it odd, he didn't say a word.

Carla Francese was a delight. She and Aurora greeted each other like long-lost friends as soon as formal introductions had been made. They seemed to share a secret, perhaps because together, they formed

451

the complete person who now strode before them onscreen, a creation of craftsmen and technicians who'd merged one woman's voice with another's face and body. The result would have convinced anyone, even people who knew her well, that Aurora had mastered Italian with amazing speed.

She glanced at Carla as they sat in the small studio projection room. Short and healthfully plump, with cropped silken blond hair and arresting blue eyes, she was very animated. She was the physical antithesis of Aurora, in figure and coloring, yet when she began to speak, a transformation occurred. Her low-pitched, richly resonant voice could have been Aurora's own! Choosing her had been inspired casting on the part of the director, for Aurora/Carla became the focal point of the film, Vittorio Calabrese notwithstanding. Aurora was fascinated, but Carla seemed unaffected. Perhaps she had experienced the same "miracle" in countless films before. For Aurora, however, this was a very special afternoon.

"Allora," said Carla when the screening was over. "What do you think, eh? You and I, we make together a good film, yes?"

"Yes," answered Aurora, impressed with the results. "Much better than I'd expected."

"Eh, so maybe you stay in Italia and become a famous film actress, yes?"

Shrugging, Aurora replied, "I admit I enjoyed the schedule—it's far less demanding than in Hollywood— but I don't know how long I'll be in Rome. This is really a kind of—"

"Of what you Americans call a working vacation? This is what you mean, yes?"

"I suppose that's as good a way of phrasing it as

452

any," she answered.

"Allora," said Carla, brightening, "we make vacation now for you, yes? Next weekend my friends and I take you to Ischia. It is too cold yet to swim, but we eat, we dance, we make a wonderful little vacation, okay?"

"Maybe," said Aurora. "Yes. Why not?"

Ottorino wasn't out of earshot. "Eh, me too? I am invited too?"

Carla frowned, but Aurora answered, "Sure!" Turning to Carla she explained, "He's been my guide and my interpreter since the first day. I'd love to share the weekend with my two new friends."

Ottorino seized the opportunity to embrace Aurora, almost knocking over the table at his elbow. Carla stiffened at first, then finally relented when the young man's arms encircled her. "Okay," she agreed, "but you will have to behave like a man, not a boy. *Capisce?"*

He blushed, looking away from her. "That will depend on what I am asked to do," he replied in a small voice.

"It won't be much," promised Carla with a wink at Aurora.

Seven days passed during which Aurora did not see or hear from Otto or Buffy Danzig, with one exception: every day, a single mauve rose arrived, although, unlike the first, it was accompanied by neither gift nor card. Aurora mused that perhaps the subsequent flowers were not from Otto but from Buffy. Games were not something she longed to play.

By week's end, she had collected seven mauve roses, and instead of having Jeeves place them in separate bud vases, she arranged them together in a tall crystal receptacle. One could detect the order in which the roses had been received by the extent of their freshness,

453

the first having wilted by Friday afternoon.

Aurora was packing a small suitcase for Ischia when Jeeves knocked at her bedroom door. "Madame," he announced in his impeccable English, "there is a florist's delivery."

She looked up from the bureau. "Another rose?" She had begun to question the Danzig imagination—or lack of it.

"No, madame, this time there are several dozen. I haven't counted, but—"

"Several dozen? Mauve?"

He nodded. "Mauve."

Aurora sighed deeply. "Is there any message with them this time?"

The butler extended a silver salver on which lay a small envelope, this one of gray paper. Taking the matching card from within it, Aurora read: *"Rome was not built in a day, but the world required only a week."* It was signed, *"O."*

She laughed, even louder when Jeeves, standing in the doorway at attention, made no attempt to smile.

"Is there anything you wish me to do, madame? That is, in addition to putting the roses in another vase?"

As she tried to regain her composure, she speculated. Otto Danzig was an intelligent man, not given to clichés. What reaction had he intended to provoke? Certainly not laughter, but what, then? Addressing her attention to Jeeves, she said, "Thank you. If there are any calls this afternoon, would you say that I've left for the weekend?"

"Certainly, madame. However, if you'll forgive my boldness, I understood that you weren't leaving until tomorrow morning. I gave cook the night off, as Signor Balestrino and the countess are dining out this evening—"

"I am leaving in the morning, Jeeves," answered

Aurora brightly. "But I'd like this evening to myself. The message stands—and thank you again. Have a nice weekend."

The butler bowed and departed.

When Jeeves had left for the evening, Aurora settled herself in Ugo's den with several magazines. Absent-mindedly she leafed through an old copy of *Oggi*, and was surprised to spot a photograph of Buffy Danzig therein. The socialite was dancing in the arms of a much younger man—definitely not Otto—and Aurora's curiosity prompted her to study the caption beneath the picture. Buffy's escort had a lengthy, hyphenated name in boldfaced type, but with the help of her Italian phrase book and her own increasing understanding of the language, she determined that he wasn't simply a casual, occasional escort of the *"elegantissima baronessa Danzig"*; he was an acknowledged companion. From the expressions on the subjects' faces and the fact that they were trying to avoid the camera lens, Aurora surmised that this snapshot fell into what Otto had described as "unbecoming behavior" for members of the upper class' inner circle. Discretion had not on this occasion been observed, and the *paparazzi* had taken full advantage of the lapse, immortalizing the couple's affair. Aurora wondered if Otto's daughter, wherever she was, had seen the photograph. So much for justice and logic. There wasn't much of it around—at least not in the inner circle.

She glanced again at the cover of the magazine. It was an old edition, from the previous summer. Perhaps it was true that Otto and Buffy did go their own way; perhaps theirs was, as Otto had said, a marriage in name only. But so what? Did that matter to Aurora? Did the photograph in the magazine make it all right for Otto to pursue her—or for her to permit him to do so? She didn't even know whether she was attracted to him. His aristocratic bearing did project a kind of authority, a commanding presence, but she wasn't sure she was interested in a commanding presence after Harper. Oh, the roses were flattering, especially since their color had been carefully chosen to match her dress. And he had remembered her choice of aperitif at their first meeting. But did she find all of this adulatory, she asked herself, because she was on the rebound from Harper? Wasn't it because her self-confidence was at a low ebb? But why, then, had she rejected advances from other men she had met since her arrival in Rome? Certainly there had been many, and only one, Vittorio Calabrese, her leading man on the western film, had resorted to crude behavior. Of course, Otto had behaved . . . inelegantly . . . in his car. But that had stemmed from their inability to see eye to eye.

It was advisable, she decided in the den, to leave Otto Danzig off limits, roses and the silver case notwithstanding. He was undoubtedly seeking no more than another conquest, a dalliance, as the scandal sheets would say. And that was not what Aurora wanted.

A small, almost imperceptible smile crept onto her lips. Well, she reflected, I may not know what I do want, but I know what I don't want, and that's something. Artie was right. She hadn't thought of Artie in years. We could be friends, good friends, she thought. That was not so with Eddie or Harper. Damn Eddie's male chauvinist pride and Harper's . . . Harper's what? Harper's obsession with youth? Was constant devotion from a child-woman going to keep him from growing old? And what would happen when Harper himself began to age? When the next child-lover or the one after her would tire of caring for a weary old man? When his bronzed tan was creased with lines, when his graying hair had whitened or thinned, when his taut, firm muscles had turned flabby and made his father-fantasy figure nothing more than that of a spent old man—What would happen then, when Harper was too old, when it was his turn to be abandoned?

That thought erased the smile from Aurora's lips; it saddened her. Retribution wasn't what she wanted; revenge only soured the avenger.

Then what did she want? "God," she mused aloud, "I wish I knew!" A tear escaped, a tear she knew was for her, not for Harper Styles. She rose, when willing her eyes to stop watering failed, and dug deep into her totebag, which was propped in a corner of the sofa. Unearthing the monogrammed white linen handkerchief, Aurora dabbed at her eyes until the tears ceased to flow. Then, focusing on the monogram, her fingers traced the embroidered *PB,* the strong gothic lettering.

On a sudden impulse, she dashed to the Roma *Elenco Telefonico* and flipped through the *B*s. Bianco, Biandoni, Bianmano, Biannelli, Blake. The Anglo-Saxon name jumped out from the multisyllabled Roman names like a clarion call. Paul Blake, Via Frattina 16. That's impossible! thought Aurora. I know that street! She glanced down at her antique leather ankle boots—the *stivaletti* she had purchased at Santelli on Via Frattina only three days before.

She reached for the telephone and dialed, her heart pounding like a smitten teenager's. It rang once. Twice. A dozen times. Unsure whether her sigh was one of relief or disappointment, she hung up and resumed her reading, tucking the handkerchief into her pocket. Well, Paul Blake, she mused silently, we just don't seem to have correct timing. That ought to tell me something.

* * *

She entered her bedroom and crossed to the adjacent bath with the marble tub and brass appointments. She drew the water and added fragrant bubbles until they were on the verge of overflowing onto the glistening green marble floor. Just as she stepped out of her robe and into the foam, the telephone rang.

Damn, she thought. However, she made no attempt to leave the tub. After six or seven rings the silence resumed, and she lay back against the cushion positioned in the tub, allowing the tension to drain from her body as she freed her mind. Her eyes closed and an hour passed with Aurora unaware of time or place; she knew only that seldom had she been able to relax so thoroughly, to allow every image, formed or not, to flow away into nothingness, not unlike the bubbles dissipating around her. She opened her eyes and laughed softly at the sight of her fingers: her skin had wrinkled after being so long submerged in the water. Maritza would never know the joy of such indulgence; she would never permit her body to partake of such pleasure. "It would be *aging,*" Aurora said aloud, giggling at her rendition of the countess' accent. How odd, she mused as she dried herself off in yards of deep-piled toweling, earlier I loathed loneliness, and now I'm basking in it! No. I'm basking in being alone, not in being lonely. Therein lies the difference.

The phone rang again. This time she answered it, balancing a terrycloth turban around her damp, piled-up hair and reaching for the receiver.

"*Pronto,*" she said slowly, hoping that the caller would speak in pedantic Italian so that she might understand.

"Aurora?" came a familiar voice, its inflection one of surprise.

She, too, was surprised. She recognized the voice. It

belonged to Otto Danzig.

"Hello."

"I'm glad you're at home," he said. "I half expected Ugo or . . . someone else to answer."

She wasn't about to tell him that no one else was at the villa. "I was just going to make a call when the phone rang," she lied, "so I picked it up."

"Good. I was afraid you had already left."

"Left?" she asked.

"For Ischia. I rang the studio and learned that you're going away for the weekend, but I thought I'd try you, just the same."

"I see." She didn't know what else to say. "Thank you for the roses. And the silver case. It's . . . it's lovely. I meant to call and thank you sooner."

"No you didn't, but I quite understand. You don't believe me."

"What is to believe or not believe?"

"That I find you fascinating. That you do not represent a passing flirtation for me. Those are too easy to obtain."

"Look, Otto, I—"

"I had hoped to convince you that I do not as a rule persist in pursuing a woman unless I find her unique. But I fear that you distrust everything about me."

"Not everything," she said. "I trust that you are persistent."

"I wanted the single rose to symbolize your uniqueness."

"But today you sent several dozen. Why the change of heart?"

"Not heart, my dear. Change of tactics. You seemed to be unaffected by one rose."

"As with many, Otto. Thank you just the same. And now—"

"Now," he interrupted, "I want to see you. Tonight."

"I don't think that's possible. . . . I can return the silver case if you like."

"The trinket was not contingent upon your seeing me."

When Aurora didn't answer, he asked, "Are you afraid?"

"Afraid?" she echoed. "Of what?"

"Of me. Perhaps of yourself?"

Her face warmed uncomfortably. "Otto, this call is really useless. You can't change my feelings."

"I do not intend to change your feelings, Aurora. Only your mind. For the moment, your mind is governing your feelings. I want some time alone with you—"

She interrupted him. "Look, I've just shampooed my hair and it's soaking wet."

"Dry it," came the seductive command.

"I'm not going out with wet hair," she said, ignoring his remark.

"Then I'll come there. You are alone, I take it?"

How did he know?

"What makes you think that?" she asked.

"Because," he replied, "if you were not alone, someone else would have answered the phone. I'll ring the doorbell in fifteen minutes."

"Otto, I just don't think—"

"Good," he said, cutting her off. *"Don't* think. That's the best way to begin. I'll be right over." And he hung up.

Chapter Twenty-Seven

Aurora reasoned later that she could have been more adamant on the telephone, forceful rather than indecisive. She could have refused him entry when he rang the bell fifteen minutes after his call. But the truth was that a part of Aurora was curious, and her curiosity led her to him as strongly as if she had pursued him instead of being pursued.

Otto Danzig found Aurora fully clothed when he arrived at Villa Balestrino. Her wet hair, no longer wrapped in a towel turban, was braided in one long plait down her back. She was unsure of the manner with which to greet him, but as Otto stepped over the threshold into Ugo's foyer, Aurora sensed that another threshold of her life had been crossed. Again, she couldn't explain why. It was simply so.

They didn't speak at first. He removed his coat and she accepted it, folding it over the high-backed antique chair in the hall.

In silence they passed the two armored knights and together they went into the den where the fire cast a golden glow, erasing the chill of the late May evening.

Aurora seated herself on the tufted leather sofa at the end closest to the fire. Otto, still standing, studied her, after which he too sat down on the same sofa, although in the opposite corner.

It was Aurora who finally spoke. "I feel as if we're two actors on a set, waiting for the director to begin. Except that I wasn't given a script."

His penetrating blue eyes were still fastened to hers, and Aurora wondered if he had practiced the art of hypnotism.

"We are," he said at last.

"Are what?"

"Two actors. But we are our own directors."

"You're forgetting the script," she said.

"It will be written as the scene progresses. Surely you are experienced in the art of improvisation?"

Now she laughed. "Only when I played an orange in acting class. I don't think I was terribly convincing."

"No doubt because you were being asked to portray something to which you couldn't possibly relate. This script requires you only to be yourself. To follow your instincts."

"I'm not sure what they are just now," she admitted.

"Well, then, let me direct the scene." Otto moved closer to Aurora while remaining on his end of the sofa. "Don't fear," he said, "I believe in Mr. Bernard Shaw's persistence and determination—tempered by a good amount of patience."

Aurora was relieved. She had literally backed her way into a corner and did not relish a rebuff such as those she had more than once received onscreen.

"May I get you a brandy?" she asked. "It's usually the next line in this sort of scene and I do remember the lines."

"Allow me," he said in a caricaturish actor-voice. "That generally follows, if I am not mistaken?" He was looking at her and she could detect humor in his eyes.

"Are you smiling at me or about me?" she asked. "In

short, are you making fun of me?"

"No," he said, crossing to Ugo's opened bar. "I am amused, though."

"Why?"

He poured from two different bottles and offered her the amber liquid. "Well, I suppose because I expected you to be . . . quite different . . . tonight."

She sipped the amaretto. "How different? In what way?"

Otto seated himself again, this time a bit closer to her but once more allowing her distance between them. "Well, let me see if I can explain it." He reached out and clinked his glass against hers. "You really are who you appear to be. It surprises me and also amuses me."

She still didn't understand. "Surprises? How? And what's so funny?"

"First of all, Aurora, funny and amusing are not necessarily the same. I am referring to the evening I drove you home and to our telephone conversation a little while ago. That night in my car, when I kissed you I felt your resistance, but I sensed your mind was ruling your response. I said that to you earlier. I believed that you did not wish to be courted with gifts or roses, and yet I also felt you enjoyed the attention, since they were not refused. I came to the conclusion that you were not playing the coquette—a word that I'm certain belongs to my generation rather than to yours—but were actually confused. I admit that I rushed you at first, because I didn't know enough about you to understand that doing so was likely to turn you away from me. Which is the very last thing I want, Aurora. The very last thing."

"What do you want from me?" she asked in a small voice.

He smiled, reaching out to touch her hand in a

gentle, kindly manner. It was not a touch intended to ignite sparks of passion. "What I want from you is not what you assume, although I do not deny that you are a lovely young woman and I would be most happy to make love to you. But not"—he snapped his fingers in the air—"like this, a quick little tussle beside the fireplace and nothing more." He removed his hand and used it to swirl the liquid in his glass. "I knew very little about you until today."

"Until today?" She found herself listening intently to his every word. Her guard was down, but she wasn't sure whether he could be trusted; yet the hour, the liqueur, and the quiet surroundings were making her relaxed.

"I have done some checking. I hope you will forgive me. But a man in my position must be cautious. I had to know if you could be trusted."

"If I could be trusted!" Aurora's eyes widened. "That's what I should be saying! Of all the—"

"Please hear me out. I am very . . . taken with you, Aurora. I had to find out whether your conduct with me was authentic or whether you had been brought on the scene to entrap me."

"What in God's name are you talking about? You and your wife were the ones playing games, Otto!"

"Not this time, I assure you. Not on my part, at least. But I admit, your words to me in the car, after their sting wore off, caused me to think how clever it would be of Buffy, if she wants to be rid of me, to 'procure' for me—I dislike the word you chose to use— how clever of her to invite to tea a beautiful, intelligent woman, one who, by the nature of her profession and some recent . . . unpleasant . . . publicity in Holly-wood is fair game for the press. How ingenious it would be if that actress, in league with my wife, enticed me to fall in love with her! There would be no recourse but divorce."

Aurora's brows were knitted together. "I thought you and Buffy liked each other. That you had a marriage in name only. Those were your words, Otto."

"And that is so," he said, "as long as I have harmless little affairs. But not if I should fall in love, which I have been in the process of doing."

His words had such a cold ring. "Otto," said Aurora, "you hardly know me, and I also have something to say in the matter. For one thing, this conversation is certainly not doing much to seduce me! Checking up on me—my God, what did you do, hire private detectives?"

"Nothing quite so obvious. But I did learn some interesting facts about you."

"Oh, really?" she asked coolly. "Do I get the *Good Housekeeping* seal?"

He smiled. "I can understand your reaction. But I had to be sure. I cannot become involved in a scandal."

"Why not? Would Buffy cut you off the way you cut off Clarice?" Her face reddened visibly in the fireglow as soon as the words were out. "I'm sorry," she added. "That wasn't called for."

"No, but it is true. If I divorce Buffy, legally she retains her fortune and I am left penniless, which is distasteful to me. I'm unaccustomed to being poor."

"Broke," she corrected. "Poor has nothing to do with money." Then she laughed as his words sank in. "So you did some checking up on me to see if it was safe to make a pass at me. Well, you must have heard that I don't have romantic flings with married barons. Is that why you're here? I'd have thought what you learned would turn you away."

Otto walked to the grate and stoked the waning embers with the brass irons. Then he stared into the depths of the flame and said, "I learned that Harper

Styles didn't deserve you. I know that I probably don't either. But I can't fight the way I feel any more than you can, Aurora." His voice had taken on a soft, pleading tone.

She turned to face him as his eyes traveled from the hearth to her, and the green irises of her eyes flashed with uncertainty. This was her last opportunity to drive him from her. But she was conflicted and thereby rendered immobile.

"I don't know how I feel, Otto. I'm very vulnerable just now. But you're a married man, and you've told me flatly—in advance—that you don't plan to divorce your wife. If I had any sense I'd say good night and show you to the door. I don't need to become involved with you—or anyone—at this moment. I don't want to be hurt again. I—"

His action was so swift that Aurora gasped. He swooped her into his arms, enveloping her in a single movement. She had to wrap her arms around his neck to keep from falling.

"I would never do anything to hurt you," he said. The words echoed in her ears. She had heard them before. But that was in the past. At least she could see what she was getting into now; her eyes were open. This was a married man, and no matter what he might feel for her, he would never leave his wife.

That was probably the deciding factor.

Chapter Twenty-Eight

Aurora had never been involved in an intellectual romance, nor had she ever been a man's mistress. The clandestine nature of her relationship with Otto, the sudden need for her own apartment in Trastevere "just to feel more independent" as she had told Maritza and Ugo, the secrecy and the always-present possibility of discovery heightened the excitement, bringing about a dizzying intoxication that otherwise might have been missing. So Aurora was convinced that Otto Danzig was an ardent lover when in truth he was not. But his attention, his constant adoration, together with Aurora's knowledge that what they shared could only last awhile, provided the foundation for their unorthodox affair.

The single disturbing factor came in finding a name for their relationship. She could not call it a love affair, although as time passed she began to wonder if she did feel a kind of love for this enigmatic man, a man always in control of his emotions, even in bed; a man whose deepest feelings, despite his protestations of love, remained guarded, withheld—even from himself, she speculated.

Yet she permitted herself to be drawn into this dual

existence; being a vivacious, magnetic film actress who dashed here and there for weekends with friends while she was the lover of a man whose entire fortune rested on the discretion observed. The role of mistress was one Aurora had never dreamed of playing.

On occasion, she forced herself to endure Otto's obsession with intrigue, agreeing to an evening in public with Buffy and a studio boss, the Danzigs forming one couple and the film pair the other. That kept gossip mongers and the press at bay, the foursome snapped at this opera or that première. And although Aurora found them highly theatrical, these evening performances were never easy.

The problem was Aurora's fondness for Buffy. The fact that Buffy had lovers, though they never appeared as Aurora's date on public outings, did not alleviate her occasional pangs of guilt. That Buffy didn't know, or didn't care, about the situation offered little compensation. And all the while, Aurora noticed, or thought she noticed, a smugness on Otto's face. The slightest turn of the corners of his mouth or the amusement in his eyes hinted at his own enjoyment of his mastery of subterfuge.

They had been to the opening of *Manon Lescaut* at the Teatro dell'Opera. Aurora, never comfortable as part of Otto's foursome, became even less so because Act II dealt with a similar situation to her own. Only Puccini's sweeping music enabled her to endure the evening. Now, alone in the back seat of the limousine as Otto's chauffeur drove her home, where Otto would join her after he bid his wife good night, she reflected over the recent changes in her life. She didn't miss Hollywood or the people there. She saw Maritza and Ugo regularly, and took special pride in furnishing her *attico* with her own earnings, unlike the heroine of Puccini's opera. But little changes, subtle changes, had occurred; a certain spontaneity was missing because each remark, each question had to be rehearsed—and each answer too. An innocent "pleasant dreams" or "sleep well tonight" from Buffy took on a new and special meaning. The only time in which she enjoyed complete freedom was inside her three-room apartment with the balcony that overlooked the terra cotta rooftops of Trastevere; the hours spent there belonged solely to her.

But tonight she would not be alone. Otto would be back within the hour. Aurora sighed as the car pulled up in front of her *palazzo*. The chauffeur, as always, came around, opened her door, and waited with the motor idling until she opened the massive double door, the building entrance. Only then did he depart.

Tonight, as she turned to close the door, Aurora noticed a dark sportscar parked across the street. A man sat behind the wheel. It struck her as unusual because of the late hour and the car's striking design; it wasn't a car she'd seen on the street before. She slammed the door hard and hurried past the *portiere*'s window, on to the stairs and into the safety of her apartment. She leaned wearily against her own door after she had locked it. Her nerves were edgy from the long day. Horseback riding in the afternoon with Ottorino, followed by the tedious performance at the opera—both onstage and off.

She flopped down onto the cotton-print sofa and leaned back. Smiling to herself, she pulled Ottorino's riding crop and gloves from behind her. They had fallen under a cushion and then been forgotten. As humid air wafted in from the open balcony door, Aurora yawned sleepily and then, glancing at the clock, realized that she had little time in which to change, to shower, and to revive her dampened spirits.

Within ten minutes, she emerged from the bedroom

wearing the gray and ecru satin peignoir that was a recent gift from Otto. Beneath it she wore its matching gown. She'd brushed her hair after removing the hated combs and pins she'd endured earlier, and had poured herself an amaretto to sip while awaiting Otto.

The doorbell rang just as she settled into a corner of the sofa. Aurora smiled indulgently; it wasn't the first time that Otto had forgotten his keys. She rose and went to let him in.

"Sometimes, I swear, you're as absentminded as—" She stopped in midsentence, for she was facing Harper Styles.

The past year had not left him untouched. He looked . . . was it older? No, thought Aurora. But tired. Older in a sense that had little to do with age. He was still gloriously handsome, thinner now, and the hollows beneath his cheeks had deepened. His hair was grayer, and new lines had been added to his face. Harper Styles had changed, but, Aurora admitted immediately, so had she. Although her heart raced from the shock of seeing him, her knees no longer weakened.

Without a word being said, she held the door wide and nodded. He entered the room, his hands thrust deep inside the pockets of his gray suede jacket. His tweed slacks were creased and he needed a shave.

"So," she said at last. "It was you parked outside."

At first he didn't face her directly. "After I saw you . . . it took me awhile to . . . to summon the courage to get out of the car." His eyes traveled the length of her body, lingering at her breasts, her hips, to which the revealing satin clung. Aurora felt suddenly vulnerable.

"The bar is in the corner," she said. "Pour yourself a drink while I get a wrap. The air is getting cool."

A moment later she returned with a burgundy

470

mohair shawl around her shoulders. Harper had poured himself a brandy. She retrieved her amaretto and sank into the single armchair in the room, away from Harper and the sofa.

"I take it you were expecting someone," he said.

"Yes. But how? . . ."

"You thought I'd forgotten my key." He paused, sipped his drink, and added, "And . . . the way you're dressed."

She didn't blush. "He'll be here any minute. You'd better say whatever it is you came here to say."

He pushed Ottorino's riding crop and gloves aside, tracing the outline of one of the cabbage roses on the cushion with his index finger. "I . . . I tried reaching you by phone. . . ."

"Harper, you must understand, I've been out of town." She paused. "That's not true. I couldn't talk to you. Not then . . ."

"And now?" he asked, looking at her.

"Now?"

"You said 'then.' What about now?"

"Yes . . . I . . . we can talk. I'm not sure what about. . . ."

He didn't answer immediately, and Aurora searched her mind, her memory, for something to say, something to fill the void. Nothing came.

At last Harper said, "You know why I've come to Rome?"

"I imagine I do." It wasn't difficult to keep a hard edge out of her voice. She didn't have the will or the energy to be rude to him. She wasn't feeling anger. In truth, she was feeling very little. But this was not the old numbness, rather a curious lack of emotion.

Aurora watched as Harper reached into his jacket pocket again. He withdrew a small, unwrapped red velvet box and placed it on the lacquered coffee table between them.

She stared at the box and then said, "You've come all this way to give me another gift." A statement, not a question.

"Aurora . . . please . . ." His voice quavered.

"I'm sorry, Harper. I didn't mean to be unkind."

"Open it."

"Harper . . ."

But he opened the box for her and slid it across the table.

Aurora's eyes fell upon the exquisite brooch. An emerald and diamond forget-me-not. Several petals were missing, by design. Harper said quietly, "Loves me . . . loves me not?"

Aurora felt something give in the pit of her stomach. "It's stunning, Harper. As always." But she closed the lid of the box.

He reached out to take her hand. Looking deeply into her eyes, he asked, "What do I have to do to get you back?"

"There's nothing to do."

"Aurora, I'm lost without you. I need you. You can't imagine the humiliation I've suffered. Don't do this to me."

"That's just it, Harper. You still see things only from your point of view."

"But time has passed. We can forget, start over. Don't you see? I need you—"

Aurora nodded. "I've begun to see, Harper. It's been that way from the start, but I didn't see. 'Don't do this to *me.*' You *need* me. What about *my* needs? All I did was love you."

"Darling, you don't know what it's been like. All these months without you. I've been miserable, Aurora. I tried to explain it in my letters."

"I only read the first one, Harper." With growing

conviction, she said, "I didn't have to read the others, did I? They were all the same."

"Aurora—"

"No, Harper, you came all the way to Rome, so hear me out. In that one letter, there was no apology, no use of the word *sorry*. That word came from Abby. *She's* sorry, Harper. She's a child, and yet she knows enough not to expect me to forgive her. And have you given any thought to her? To me? To anyone but yourself?"

He was looking at her with an expression she hadn't seen before. Perhaps, she speculated, because he'd never really known her. "I'll always love you," he said quietly.

"Oh, Harper," she whispered, "you'll always love the *memory* of love." As an afterthought, she said, without malice, "Besides, it would happen again with someone else. I'm too old for you."

His eyes met hers and she smiled, finding humor in her own words as well as truth. "I'm almost thirty, Harper. And you like younger women. Women who idolize you . . . as I did." She could see that he was suffering, and she had no desire to hurt him. Putting a hand on his shoulder, she said, "You'll find someone else."

"Not like you," he answered softly. Then, glancing again at her wardrobe, he said, "You've found someone else, haven't you?"

For a moment she hesitated. Otto . . . someone else? Aloud she said, "I suppose I have."

There was a sound at the door. Harper and Aurora turned as the lock clicked and Otto Danzig entered the room.

Aurora smiled and went to greet him, but her smile faded as Otto stared at her, his eyes going from her peignoir to the drinks on the coffee table to Harper. He jingled his keys and returned them to the pocket of the black leather motorcycle jacket he had unzipped. The casting struck Aurora as almost comical: the world-weary film producer standing opposite his contemporary, an aristocrat dressed like a rebellious teenager who has caught his parents in a compromising situation!

"What is he doing here?" Otto demanded.

Aurora ran a hand through her hair and said, "Otto, this is Harper, my—"

"I know perfectly well who he is," Otto declared, walking to the sofa and sitting on an arm. "I asked what he is doing here."

Harper began to speak, but Aurora interrupted. "He came to ask me about . . . some legalities concerning our divorce."

"Oh?" Otto leaned over the coffee table and picked up the red velvet box. Without opening it, he said, "And what might be in here?"

He tossed the box casually from one hand to the other. Aurora felt a rush of alarm. Beneath Otto's words was a current of anger she had never experienced before. As he continued to speak, his accent, while not becoming thicker, grew more clipped. "I see. Mr. Styles brings his wife a little end-of-marriage gift, is that it?"

"Danzig—" Harper began.

"And what does his wife do, darling, accept?" Otto cut in. He lifted the lid of the velvet box. "Ahh! How sweet. Aurora, my darling, are you not . . . tempted?" He snapped the lid shut.

"Otto, please." She took the box from the palm of his hand. "Harper will just finish his drink and then he'll go." She turned, tucking the box into Harper's hand. "Won't you?"

He nodded and reached for his drink. Otto grabbed it from him. "Going so soon? No, no, you must *stay*, Harper. You must drink more of *my* brandy. I regret

474

only that I arrived so soon—"

"There's no reason why we can't keep this polite, Danzig."

"Polite?" Otto cried, throwing the glass across the room.

It shattered against the wall. "Polite? Tell me you didn't come here to make love to her!"

"Otto!" Aurora yelled.

Now Harper's voice had risen. "Danzig!" he said. "I came to take her back. She said no, for what it's worth."

"Take her back! To what? What can you offer her that I cannot?" Otto demanded.

Quietly, Harper answered. "From what I've seen tonight, Danzig, quite a lot. Sanity, for one thing."

It happened before Aurora could intervene. Otto swooped down, picked up the riding crop, and, raising his arm over his shoulder, struck Harper across the face. Harper recoiled, his hand at his cheek as the whip came up again.

Without thinking, Aurora grabbed Otto by the arm and cried, "No!" She could feel the strength of his taut bicep; he was fueled by a sudden outburst of uncontrolled rage.

Suddenly, Otto's arm went limp and the riding crop dropped to the floor. His eyes were glazed, as though he had entered, or just exited from, an hypnotic trance.

Aurora was as shaken by his instant recovery as she had been by his attack. Her eyes followed Otto to the bar, where he poured himself a brandy. "Please leave," he said quietly to Harper.

Aurora helped him to his feet. A long welt had appeared across his left cheek.

"Let me get you something for that," she said.

"No." Harper looked deeply into her eyes. "Danzig's right. It's better that I leave." He moved toward the door and Aurora followed him. "You realize what you've gotten yourself into, don't you?"

Tears welled in her eyes as Aurora found her voice. "I . . . Please, Harper. Just go."

He opened the door and walked into the hall. At the top of the stairs, he turned to look back at her, his eyes still questioning.

"Good-bye, Harper," said Aurora. Then she closed the door.

Chapter Twenty-Nine

The incident with Harper was never mentioned again. Otto was more attentive, more considerate than before, showering Aurora with lavish gifts on every occasion. They traveled more frequently. However, as always, each arrived by separate train or plane, whether to Venice, Paris, London; Otto on the excuse of business meetings, Aurora suddenly invited to be the guest of acquaintances who didn't exist or a studio executive she'd never met.

It was in London, at a dull performance of a Pinter play—later she couldn't recall the title—that she heard her name spoken during intermission. She had gone to the lobby for fresh air only to find it hazy and fog-ridden with cigarette smoke. As she turned to reenter the auditorium, a deep baritone voice said, in American English, "I do wish that *Ms.* Styles would stop following me!"

She knew from both sound and words that it was Paul Blake. Her eyes lit up, for she was delighted to find a familiar face. "Paul! What on earth are you doing in London?"

His blue eyes twinkled as a grin formed on his lips. He was wearing shoes instead of cowboy boots, thereby cutting an inch from his height; nonetheless, he towered over the other theatergoers in the crowd. His dark brown hair had one stray lock—perhaps due to London dampness, Aurora mused—it added a boyishness to his rugged features.

"Well," he said. "I'm here on business, and"—here his grin broke into a full smile—"I had to order some monogrammed handkerchiefs at Harrods."

"I still have it." Aurora was smiling too. "But I don't have it with me this evening."

"Oh, I say," he teased in a mock-Oxford accent, "an excuse to try to see me again, what?"

She laughed. "Watch it, Mr. Blake, I do an excellent assortment of British accents, myself."

"Occupational hazard?" he asked.

Aurora peered around, leaned forward, and lowering her voice, said, "The play is dreadful, isn't it?"

He nodded, taking her elbow. "Why don't we sneak out? I'm sure no one will miss us."

"Well . . ." Otto was expecting her back at their borrowed flat when the play was over. Still, they had time for a drink and a friendly chat; the second act would last at least an hour. "I am thirsty," she said.

"Good. Hungry too?"

She was; she hadn't eaten dinner.

"There's a pub around the corner that serves excellent shepherd's pie—and the stout is on tap."

"Sounds perfect."

The pub was dark and half empty once the intermission—interval, Paul corrected her—was over and theatergoers had filed back to their seats. Paul and Aurora settled into a high-backed wood and leather booth.

"Well, here we are again. Isn't this where we came in?"

"Where we came in?" repeated Aurora.

"The VIP lounge at JFK. When it all began." This latter remark he spoke lightly, like a line from a fifties' comedy.

"Ah, yes," said Aurora with a sigh. "Worlds ago."

Paul ordered for both of them and then said, "Now tell me, are you shooting a film here or just visiting or what?"

How should she answer? "I'm here with . . . a friend. And you? What are you really doing in London?"

If he had noticed her hesitation, he said nothing about it. "New book. New publisher. Strictly business —and those handkerchiefs, of course."

"Of course."

"Where are you staying and for how long?" he asked.

She paused again and then said, "Brown's. And just for a few days."

"Then it's back to Rome?"

She shrugged. "I suppose. That seems to be home for the time being." Her own phrasing struck her as odd, but she sipped her stout, intent on keeping the conversation light and friendly.

"Are you 'engaged' with your friend tomorrow?" Paul asked.

"I'm afraid so. I'm only free this evening because my friend had a business appointment." It sounded so . . . false, Aurora thought. Or does it? Perhaps, she silently hoped, that is because I know it's a lie. She didn't like lying, especially to Paul Blake; she sensed he could tell immediately what she was thinking.

"Well, if your friend and you would care to join me tomorrow, I'm driving out to Aylesbury for the day. I've never enjoyed going there alone. . . ."

"I'm sorry, Paul. I don't think that's possible." To change the subject, she asked, "Where is Aylesbury, anyway? I've never heard of it."

"Well," he said, "it's a medieval town right out of a

picturebook. But my reason for visiting is personal. Dates to my childhood. I spent almost ten years there when I was a boy. It's changing so fast, I don't want to lose it. Last time I was there, they'd demolished— pulled down, as they say—the Bull's Head. In the name of progress, the town is being transformed into a place I don't know. So I like to drive there whenever I'm in London."

"Sounds like a lovely place. But I didn't realize you were English."

"Mother was very American—DAR, flag waving, all that. Dad was from the redcoat side. The only thing they ever fought about. I think she was jealous of his Englishness. She even wanted to name me William, but Dad wouldn't hear of it."

"You don't strike me as a William. I can't think of you as having any other name but Paul."

"Then you do think of me!" He said it playfully, but Aurora detected a questioning seriousness in his eyes.

"Constantly!" she said, laughing. Humor seemed safer than examining his query or her own feelings.

"Then join me tomorrow—we'll have a picnic."

"I'm sorry, Paul, I can't. Really." She glanced at her watch. "In fact, I have to be going now. I hadn't realized the time."

"Flies when you're having fun," he quipped. "I'll put you in a taxi."

She allowed him to put his arm through hers as they left the pub and walked to the curb.

A cab pulled up within minutes. "Let's get together back in Rome, then," Paul said, helping Aurora into the back seat.

"Sure," she answered softly.

"I'm in the phone book," he said. He squeezed her hand and instructed the driver. "Brown's Hotel for the lady."

As the cab drove off, Aurora leaned forward to correct the address. "Not Brown's, driver. It's two hundred Queen's Gate, in South Kensington."

Otto was waiting there when she opened the door.

"Darling," he said, embracing her. "I couldn't wait until you returned. I have something for you."

"Otto, you've given me so many things—"

"Trinkets. Trifles. This is something I've wanted to have made for you, especially for you, since the night—" He didn't finish his own sentence but instead reached into his pocket and withdrew a black velvet box. A tiny box.

Aurora lifted the lid and gasped. It was a ring, the most beautiful ring she had ever seen. The setting was of raised Florentine gold, and in it, surrounded by tiny diamonds, was a magnificent emerald, perfectly faceted from every angle of its cut.

"Otto!" she exclaimed. "It's . . . it's breathtaking!"

He slid it onto the ring finger of her right hand. "To match your eyes," he said, leading her to the sofa of their borrowed quarters. Otto was "officially" staying at the Connaught; Aurora, at Brown's, as she had told Paul. Friends of Buffy were stopping at the Danzigs' own flat in Chelsea, which gave Otto a convenient excuse to be registered at the hotel.

Aurora was still gazing at the emerald when Otto began to speak. "You mean everything to me, Aurora. I could not bear to lose you."

"Lose me? Otto, why talk as though I'm going to leave you?"

"You will someday. When you meet someone who can offer you all that I cannot. I only hope he won't come along for a while." Turning her shoulders toward him, in a strange, hollow voice, he added, "I would do anything to keep from losing you, Aurora. Anything."

She traced the side of his face. "Otto, please don't talk that way. It . . . frightens me."

"I'm only stating the truth, Aurora. Before I met you, it didn't matter to me that my . . . personal life . . . had to be conducted behind the scenes, so to speak. But with you"—he entwined his hands with hers—"I want to walk with you in the sunlight, show you off to the world, and announce to everyone that you belong to me and to no one else!"

"Otto, I am yours—as much as anyone can belong to another person. I mean, nobody can own anyone in the sense that one owns a . . . a possession."

"No," he said absently. "I suppose not. I just loathe this charade, hiding you in the wings! If Buffy—" But he stopped in midsentence.

"If Buffy what?"

"Nothing. Nothing at all."

"You were going to say if Buffy left you, weren't you?"

He nodded slowly. "Yes. If she left me, I would be entitled to half her money. It's part of our prenuptial agreement."

"Otto," Aurora ventured to ask quietly, "is her money more important to you than your happiness?"

He looked at her with an expression she was unable to decipher. "*You* are my happiness," he answered.

"Then why not divorce her? I have enough money"— she laughed at this; it was Harper's money because of California divorce laws—"we don't need Buffy's money."

"I would never accept money from you, Aurora," Otto said flatly.

"But—"

"But why do I accept it from Buffy, then?" His lips twisted into an unattractive smirk. "Business. Everything between Buffy and me has been a business arrangement. Her parents and mine were close. When my first wife died and Buffy learned she could never have children, we entered into an agreement. Her family's money, my family's title. We have always been friends, but I cannot pretend a moment's passion for her and I know that she prefers young Latin types. She always has, since before our marriage. Our arrangement was also intended to give her a respectable cover."

"Ah, yes," said Aurora sarcastically, "the famed respectability of the nobility. I'd forgotten about that."

"Darling, look. For almost a year we have been free to meet as we please, travel where we like, isn't that enough for now?"

"Yes," agreed Aurora. "It's enough."

"For now," he said half-aloud. But she heard him just the same.

"The emerald is beautiful, Otto. I'll wear it always."

"As long as we're together," he said.

"Good!" she said in a lighter tone, hoping to brighten the mood that had suddenly encompassed them both. "In that case, I won't have to give it back until I'm as old as Queen Elizabeth the first. She wore Essex's ring to the very end."

Otto didn't speak; he wrapped his arms tightly around her, so tightly that they hurt her shoulders, and his eyes were far away, far from her, far from London, far from their borrowed flat in South Kensington.

A message from the clerk at the Connaught interrupted a late breakfast the following morning. A trusted "alibi" of many years' standing, Donald Charles alone knew Otto's private number at Queen's Gate, and he forwarded any urgent calls or messages.

"It's Buffy," said Otto as he replaced the telephone

receiver into its cradle. "She's in the hospital. I must return to Rome at once."

"The hospital? What is it? What's happened?"

"I don't know. I'll try to ring her physician now." He took his address book from the travel case on the desk and went into the bedroom.

Aurora paced nervously, concerned for Buffy and reflecting on the peculiarity of her concern. She was aware that Otto's wife did not possess great physical energy, but she had never discussed Buffy's state of health with Otto.

He returned to the room, his brow furrowed and his demeanor agitated. "She's had some kind of reaction to one of her medicines. An allergy, they think. She's in critical condition."

"You must go to her," Aurora said.

"Yes," he said absently. "They're not certain she'll come out of it this time."

"This time? You mean it's happened before?"

"Once before. Buffy has a number of sensitivities. The last time it was penicillin. She went into shock."

"And this time?"

Otto was tossing things haphazardly into his suitcase. "This time they aren't sure. She likes to experiment with new medications as soon as they're on the market. The doctor hasn't been able to find out what she took this time."

"But isn't he the one who prescribes her medications?" asked Aurora.

Otto nodded. "Yes, but in Italy one doesn't need a prescription. One need simply to know the name of the drug, and one can buy it at the neighborhood *farmacia.*"

"Anything? Over the counter?" Aurora couldn't believe it.

"Anything. And when Buffy gets depressed . . . well,

she's liable to try anything she hasn't tried before."

"I hadn't realized she was so troubled." A stab of guilt assaulted Aurora at her own words. Without speaking further, she began to collect the rest of Otto's shirts and to hand them to him as, mechanically, he placed them into the suitcase. Within half an hour, he was packed and gone.

To Buffy in Rome.

The cozy little three-room flat in South Kensington was suddenly suffocatingly claustrophobic. Aurora packed her own things and took a taxi to Brown's. After all, that was her London address.

A message awaited her at the desk. It was from Paul and read: If you change your mind about that picnic, my number is 379-0246.

When she reached her room, Aurora asked the operator to ring Paul's number. Timing on this occasion was on her side; he answered on the third ring.

"My friend had to leave earlier than expected. A picnic sounds delightful."

"Terrific! I'll come by in an hour. The weather's perfect—and I visited Fortnam's yesterday. The victuals are packed and ready!"

"I'll meet you in the lobby, then." Aurora had no need to be alone this afternoon, neither in Queen's Gate nor in a hotel room. Being alone meant she'd have to think, and that was the one thing she didn't want to do.

Paul Blake was the perfect diversion and tour guide combined. Wearing what he called "country tweeds," an English-cut sports jacket with side vents over a beige cashmere turtleneck sweater and matching beige slacks, with a nod of his handsome head or a gesture, using his aromatic pipe as a pointer, he introduced Aurora to sights—both authentic and fictional, he admitted—en route to the medieval town.

They reached Aylesbury in midafternoon and Paul drove straight to the Eagle. "My favorite pub," he explained. "The Angel was pulled down when I was a wee lad."

"Your English is turning Scottish," Aurora warned him.

"Never, milady. Scotch, perhaps, as long as it's the brew we both like so well. . . ." He took her hand and led her into the pub.

After they had sipped a pint of Guinness apiece, spilling foam as they clinked their heavy glass mugs, they strolled to Market Square, where Paul pointed out the historical remnants of Aylesbury's past, Elizabethan relics that had thus far escaped the wrecker's ball. At Walton's Grange, they stopped at Walton Pond. "No relation to Wal*den,*" he said. "But it is the site of the only land mine to damage the town during the war. Dad said King George the sixth visited once while he was still the duke of York. And milady," he said, tipping a nonexistent hat, "we're very progressive, you know. Even had a lady mayor once. A Mrs. Paterson, I believe. Of course, that was in the thirties, before my time."

"I had the impression nobody was before your time," said Aurora.

"What? How ancient do you think I am?" But he laughed.

"No, no. I meant that you . . . well, you seem to see people and things so clearly. It's very rare."

He took a puff on his pipe. "It's called growing up, that's all."

Aurora couldn't interpret his sidelong glance, but she was aware that he was studying her. "I'm not sure

I understand."

"You will someday. I may have said it before. I'm a patient man."

A visceral twinge caught Aurora off guard. "I'm getting hungry. I thought you offered to feed me," she said.

They were in a grassy, tree-lined enclave, much like the private parks and meadows in Ugo's eighteenth-century paintings. They spread a blanket and Paul began to arrange an assortment of sandwiches, patés, cheeses, fruit, and paper plates. He opened a bottle of burgundy. "Let's imagine we're eating off fine china," he said.

Aurora swallowed a mouthful of paté. "This is my style."

Paul was looking at her again. "Style . . ." He grinned.

"Something funny, Mr. Blake?" she asked.

"Just thinking about your name. It does suit you. Styles."

"Ah, but what's in a name? O'Brien, Styles; you're still the same person—William or Paul."

"Last night you said Paul was the only name for me." When she didn't answer, he added softly, "And Aurora is the only name for you." He leaned closer, causing Aurora to move away.

"Aurora." He repeated her name, and his hand came to rest on hers, which was absentmindedly twisting and braiding several blades of grass.

Coloring, she withdrew her hand. "Paul, this has been a perfectly lovely afternoon."

As he was looking at her hand, the emerald gem on her finger became a prism, reflecting the late afternoon sun.

"So you've made your choice," said Paul.

"About what?"

"You tell me. Is that a symbolic gesture of Harper's love or a reconciliation gift?"

Aurora averted her eyes. "Harper didn't give me this ring."

"But it's a recent acquisition."

She nodded. "Very recent." Her heart had begun to pound for a reason she couldn't fathom.

Paul drained his wineglass. "Just one question?"

"Why not? You always seem to be asking me questions." His words and his eyes were causing her to squirm uncomfortably.

"And you never seem to answer them."

"Maybe I just don't have the answers to your questions."

"Well, try this one," he said, rising from the blanket. "Why did you change your mind and come with me today? You just don't strike me as a tease."

"I told you, my friend had to leave early and that left me free."

"I assume that friend is the giver of the ring?"

She nodded, suddenly feeling ashamed. She hadn't dreamed that Paul would consider this picnic as "teasing" or leading him on. She had assumed he could read her well. She was unprepared for his next statement, which was spoken in a harder voice than he had previously displayed.

"Let me know if you ever tire of your jewelry collection, Aurora. I'm not into buying the company I keep!"

Her hand reached out to slap him, but she restrained herself. He had every reason to feel that she had teased him. And of all people, Paul deserved better than that.

"I'm sorry," she said. At a loss for words, she began to gather up the picnic paraphernalia, depositing plates and leftovers and glasses into the hamper.

As they walked in silence to the car, a light rain

began to fall, and they slid into opposite sides of the front seat, their faces avoiding each other. The raindrops against the windshield, the hum of the engine, and the slick, rhythmic *swish, swish* of the tires against the road were the only sounds in the car for the duration of the drive back to London. Occasionally, Aurora glanced in Paul's direction, but his eyes were fixed upon the road ahead. And even if he had turned to look at her, what would she have said?

It was dark when they arrived at Brown's Hotel; the rain had increased in its intensity and Paul leaned over to the back seat, unearthing an umbrella from beneath the picnic blanket.

Handing it to Aurora, he said, "You may keep it. I have dozens."

"I'll send it to you as soon as I return to Rome," she said, still stung by his earlier words.

"Don't bother. Some people collect jewels. I collect umbrellas." His eyes were studying hers as he spoke. "I'm sorry, that was rotten. My feelings got in the way."

"In the way of what?" She had begun moving closer to her door.

"Never mind. I just—" But he broke off whatever he had started to say. "I'd be a liar if I said I'm thrilled that someone else has replaced Harper Styles, Aurora. I'd only be happy if I were the man who had replaced him. And that's damned selfish of me. If you're happy . . ."

Something in his words unsettled her. "Look, Paul," she began.

"Shh. Forget the rude things I said before. Just remember one thing—you can call me any time you need me. As a friend. For anything more, the need has to be secondary."

"Secondary to what?"

His fingers brushed a damp curl at her temple, tracing the lines of her features. Then he leaned closer, kissing her gently. It was not the kind of kiss that demanded or expected a kiss in return. Still, Aurora responded. She felt warm in Paul's car, in Paul's company, and this puzzled her.

Then his arms went around her, and their kiss took on an urgency, a questioning depth. Aurora pulled herself away.

"No, Paul. I . . . no matter what you think, I'm not . . . I can't . . . I didn't mean to . . ." But she was incapable of finishing a sentence and this perplexed her even more.

"Sweet Aurora," he said. "Sweet sunrise. And you ask what's in a name." His hand stroked her cheek and for some inexplicable reason, tears of emotion began to well within her.

"Good night," she said, pushing the door lever and opening the door.

"Bands of angels," he answered.

"What?"

"Guide thee to thy rest. By a far better poet than I. Good night, sweet Aurora."

But no angels guided her sleep that night. It was a fitful, restless, dreamless sleep, one from which she awoke countless times during the night. Perhaps, she reasoned, it was the rain, which had now turned into a raging storm.

Chapter Thirty

Aurora's return to Rome and her subsequent departure for New York didn't seem to surprise Maritza. Only her New York address prompted questions. The pair were having lunch at Ugo's villa.

"But, Rory darling, why not the penthouse? After all, Tadzio would adore your company—it would be almost like old times, and—"

"And that's why I prefer to stay at a hotel this trip. No memories, good or bad. A clean break." Aurora studied her soufflé as she spoke, purposely avoiding eye contact with the countess. She wanted Maritza to believe her excuses, but feared she'd give herself away if forced to face her friend's eyes.

"You're certain that's the only reason?"

"What other reason could there be?" asked Aurora.

Maritza had pushed her plate aside, her arms folded in front of her. "I don't know. I thought perhaps . . . a man."

How much does the countess actually know? Aurora wondered, still not looking up.

"You haven't said much about London, Rory. Did you meet someone new?"

"No, not really." It wasn't a lie. Still, a guilty twinge

made her shudder. Although that had nothing to do with the damp, late afternoon chill wafting in from the open French doors, Aurora rose from the table to close them. When she looked back after fastening the lock, Maritza was staring at her hand, at the emerald ring.

"Well, *that's* new, darling, and I've never known you to buy such things for yourself." Maritza was smiling, but her inflection had clearly indicated that she was, indeed, asking a question.

Thinking as quickly as she could, Aurora said, "Oh, all right. There is someone new. And I'm not being secretive, but I'd really rather not discuss it just now. In time, I promise, but—"

"He's married." This time it wasn't a question.

Maritza examined her fingernails. Aurora came to stand beside her and looked the countess straight in the eye; she needed to know if Maritza suspected the identity of the married man with whom she was involved.

But if Maritza had any inkling that Otto Danzig was her friend's lover, she hid her suspicions behind a warning. "Rory darling, do be careful. Don't get into a situation that might hurt you even more than the breakup with Harper."

"That's hardly possible," Aurora answered a bit more curtly than she'd intended. "Sorry, I'm not being short with you. I'm just not accustomed to this 'role.' Anyway, now you know why I'm booking a room at a hotel."

"But how shall I reach you if I need to get in touch?"

"I'll let you know where I am once I'm settled. I told you, I'm not trying to hide anything from you. I haven't booked the room yet, so I can't answer your question."

Maritza's tongue slid along her lower lip as she said, "Seems everyone is leaving the Eternal City, doesn't it?"

Aurora detected several meanings in the countess' innocent question. "Oh really? What makes you say that?"

"Well . . . your friends the Danzigs just left this weekend, and I do wonder if the *baronessa* is fit to travel so soon after her . . . ordeal."

Was Maritza studying her, or was her guilty conscience working overtime?

"I understood that Otto tried to dissuade her," said Aurora, "but Buffy wants to consult her specialist in New York."

"Oh, that's right. They're in New York, too, aren't they?"

Cat and mouse. The game was not to Aurora's liking. She took a deep breath, glanced around the room, and moved toward the door. "I should get my coat. Ottorino will be here any minute."

Aurora had transported her luggage to Ugo's in a taxi. "Tell Ugo I'm sorry I missed him."

"I will. He's very fond of you. But those business meetings in Torino, you know."

"I know." She knew only too well. She wondered if Ugo had a lady friend in that industrial city.

As they reached the entrance foyer, Aurora patted the visors of each of the knights. "*Arrivederci,* Tweedle Dee," she said to one. "*E tu,* Dum."

"I wish you'd let me accompany you to the airport," said the countess, "or at least as far as downtown. The car could drop me and continue on."

"I can't stand good-byes, and besides, I promised Ottorino. He's been such a dear."

As Jeeves opened the door, the tiny Fiat could be seen turning into the drive.

"You'll never get all your luggage into that bug!" exclaimed Maritza. "Darling Rory, really—"

"Look, it'll attract less attention at Da Vinci." She

493

glanced down at the luggage stacked in the hall. "Whatever doesn't fit, we'll just have to leave behind."

As Ottorino jumped out of the driver's side of the car, Maritza made a parting remark. "Just don't ever leave that emerald behind, darling. It might come in handy someday."

Aurora kissed her on both cheeks and ran down the steps to greet her escort—and to avoid further discussion of her jewelry collection.

Aurora was able to travel in relative anonymity; departures from Italy's capital seemed to attract less attention and fewer *paparazzi* than arrivals. Or perhaps her continued absence from the Hollywood scene had plunged her into obscurity; the films she had shot in Rome were only now being released, and none of them would shake the film world or the moviegoing public into taking particular notice of its stars. No matter how wide the films' distribution, they would not make lasting impressions. Well, Aurora mused as she settled back into her seat, perhaps Ottorino was right. "Next time you come to make a film with the Maestro, yes?" Yes, sir, she thought with a laugh. If Fellini and I are still alive the next time, and if hell hasn't frozen over, et cetera.

The flight attendant had offered magazines, and, from habit, Aurora had accepted a copy of *Vogue*. Only now did she notice that it was the Italian edition. Okay, she thought, let's see just how much you've learned. She opened the cover and began to skim the pages.

Her heart skipped a beat when she reached the *People are Talking About* section. There was a photograph of Paul Blake! He didn't appear to be posing for the camera; it was a snapshot, and the author wore a candid, slightly crooked grin as he spoke, apparently to an admirer, a matronly woman in a flowered hat who was extending her pen and a copy of his book. Aurora studied the copy, translating it in her mind: "American writer Paul Blake with a reader of his newest novel, *Places*. He has recently returned to Rome from London, where his book has received critical acclaim. This very private man refused to answer when questioned about his personal life. 'Read the book,' he advised. 'That's my personal life.' This reviewer's suggestion is: take that advice. Although Blake's fictional world is not for everyone, he searches for truths, both personal and universal. His is a highly developed vision, but Blake is not without a sense of humor. When asked if he is clairvoyant, he says, 'I don't have the answers. By writing, I'm trying to find them.' *Places* is a very personal viewpoint of a very personal man."

A slow smile crept onto Aurora's lips as she closed the copy of *Vogue*. Well, she'd understood every word. Her Italian was improving. That was something. . . .

Aurora was booked at the Mayflower; she had not told the countess, but Otto had made the arrangements for her. She had nothing to do upon her arrival in New York but unpack and wait for his call. Her suite was on a high floor overlooking Central Park, and since the day was bright and clear, she could see the tops of buildings that had been under construction during her early acting days. Then, she had seen the skyline from the windows of Tadzio's penthouse on the East Side; now her view was from Central Park West. No, she reflected, it isn't just the location; points of view have far more to do with one's perception, both inner and outer.

She had unpacked, changed from the black wool pants suit and taupe silk blouse into corduroy jeans and a cashmere turtleneck. Then she had ordered lunch from room service so she wouldn't miss Otto's call. He had made her travel arrangements and the plane had been on time, but they had agreed it was best not to meet at the airport. She had taken a taxi from JFK rather than have a limousine pick her up. Only the customs official who checked her passport had mentioned her celebrity, and as on countless occasions before, she had graciously given him her autograph. He in turn had chalk-marked her luggage without going through it or asking a question. She could have been carrying drugs or explosives; her smile and her signature on a scrap of paper had worked magic.

She laughed as she washed down the last of the turkey sandwich with the white wine. All the studying and planning, followed by a series of grade-B films in two countries—and one of which she was proud, *Lickety-Split*—and what did it get her? Easy passage through customs. Well, at least that!

She glanced at the diamond-encircled Piaget on her wrist. She'd been ensconced in the hotel for three hours and Otto hadn't called. She had no way of reaching him; she didn't have his private office number in Manhattan, and she wasn't about to telephone his secretary and start tongues wagging. Nor would she call the mansion on Long Island. What if Buffy should answer? Was Aurora in town for a shopping spree— only days after their arrival? No. Too much of a coincidence.

Another hour passed; the sun began to slip below the tall trees; the sky was changing hues, but even its varied palette could not hold Aurora's attention. Waiting for a telephone to ring has to be one of the most anxiety-producing experiences of this century, she mused, trying to find humor in her growing impatience.

At dusk, Aurora grabbed her sable coat and hailed a taxi. She had left word at the desk that if anyone should call, she would return before nine.

"Where to, lady?" asked the cabbie.

She hadn't thought about destination.

"Umm . . . downtown. The Village." An idea struck her. "Yes! West Fourth and Sixth Avenue, driver. The corner."

"Oh, ya want O. Henry's?"

"Not the restaurant, but that's the corner." She leaned back, remembering how New York cab drivers braked, and perused the passing scene. They were traveling down Fifth Avenue, and all along it were new buildings, new stores. Italian names. Gucci, Rizzoli, Ferragamo. How the city had changed! And they passed bookstores on every block. A sudden curiosity caused Aurora to examine the titles on display when the cab stopped for a red light in front of Doubleday and later at Barnes & Noble. But if she had expected to see Paul Blake's new novel in the window, she was mistaken. Well, she reflected, he had said he seldom made the best-seller list. Still, she did strain in the twilight, made darker by the taxi's tinted glass window, to see if she could spot *Places*.

The cabbie turned around and asked, "Hey, lady, ya want that corner exactly or ya want me to drop ya at Ninth Street? Otherwise, I gotta go across, down Seventh Avenue, and come around—it'll take a lot longer."

"No. On second thought, let me out at Ninth. I want to go to Balducci's. I'll walk from there."

"You got it," he said, brakes screeching as he pulled up short of the corner.

Aurora paid him and got out, wrinkling her nose at the unpleasant stench coming from the Path station

497

next to the famed store. She hurried around the corner to buy some baba au rhum, recalling that she couldn't afford to shop in this store while still a Village resident. Inside, she was surrounded by delicacies from every country imaginable! The aromas intoxicated her senses. A clerk eyed her spacious totebag suspiciously, but when he took in her fur coat and doeskin boots, he smiled as if to say, okay, lady, you're no thief. Aurora was overwhelmed by the crowd of shoppers; what had happened to the friendly neighborhood Italian specialty shop? The cheese section was now bigger than the entire store had been!

She bought an assortment of cookies, the pignola kind Maria favored. Then she walked to Cornelia Street, noting many changes on the way. Trude Heller's was gone, but Bigelow's Pharmacy was still there, old and cozily reliable. Eighth Street had assumed even more of a carnival atmosphere. Its fast food stores had garish fronts, and leather-jacketed junkies stood against them, their eyelids half-closed in response to a music only they could hear. The scent of marijuana was strong enough to induce a contact high. A couple of bag ladies waddled by. One of them had planted herself on the corner of Waverly Place and Sixth Avenue years before. Aurora recalled having tried to help her across an icy street during a cold New York winter. The woman had shoved her aside with uncommon fury. "If I wanna fall, lady, I'll fall, and fuck you!" she'd shouted from a toothless mouth. This time Aurora passed her by quickly; the woman did not appear to have changed an iota. She swore at the tourists and spat with regularity.

Aurora reached Cornelia Street, ready to sigh with relief. But upon arriving at Maria's door, disappointment assailed her. The door, which had always been open on its rusty hinges, was now bolted shut. No longer a peeling black enamel, it had been painted a bright shade of purple. The window curtains—Maria had sewn them herself of white dotted swiss—were now striped canvas drapes in muted mauves and browns, with a streak of orange running through the center of each panel. The shutters were painted an orange-yellow color. This couldn't be Maria's taste!

Aurora knocked at the door.

"Yeah?" came a gruff voice from the other side.

"Is Maria there?"

"Who?"

"Maria." She spoke louder.

"Nobody named Maria lives here, lady."

"Do you know where she went?"

"Lady, I don't even know who she *is!*" came the reply.

Aurora nodded to herself as she slowly walked away. How could she have assumed Maria would still be here, after all this time? The world didn't stay the same. Aurora smiled sadly. She'd never taken the time to contact the seamstress after moving away. Maybe Maria and that sailor boyfriend of hers had run away together. She hoped so. A rueful laugh escaped as she turned on Bleecker Street, Thomas Wolfe's phrase echoing in her ears. She'd never wanted to go home again because she'd never really had a home, not until she'd thought she had one with Harper. Her *attico* in Rome had been rented only as a matter of convenience.

So where to? she asked herself. The Mayflower Hotel, to wait for Otto Danzig? And why? Odd, but New York was having its old effect upon her, forcing her to seek answers. It was so easy *not* to think in Hollywood and Rome. Diversion. Constant distraction. But there was something about New York, or maybe what she felt about New York, where she'd had the first home she'd ever made for herself.

That struck another chord. She'd made a home. In this city, on that very block where Maria no longer lived. The other places had belonged to other people. Her one-room cubbyhole on Cornelia Street had been more of a home to her—to the real person she was— than those sumptuous villas in the glamour capitals of the world. Why haven't I recognized it before? she wondered.

Because that awareness is very unsettling, she replied. It was bringing with it a deep sadness, far deeper than nostalgia for a present that had become a past; it made her want to stay, and it made her need to flee.

She hailed a taxi on Sixth Avenue and returned to her luxurious suite at the Mayflower to await Otto's call.

Otto Danzig telephoned shortly after Aurora had drawn the draperies across the windows of the living room and curled up, bootless, on the brocade sofa.

"Darling," he said, "I couldn't ring you before now. It's been an impossible three nights."

"What's the matter?" Aurora was suddenly alarmed. "Is Buffy all right?"

Otto's sigh was audible through the receiver. "She had an attack the night we got back. At the house." His voice was detached, as though he were reporting a dull day on Wall Street, one in which his investments neither rose nor fell.

"How is she now?" Aurora's interest was kindled by her lover's lack of concern.

"She's alive," he said flatly. "I finally telephoned for an ambulance and . . . they got here in time."

"What do you mean 'finally'? How long did it take them?"

It was several moments before he spoke. When he did, his voice was even colder than before. "The ambulance arrived within minutes of my call."

Aurora still didn't understand, but Otto hadn't finished speaking. "I sat there and watched her," he said, "as I watched her in the hospital in Rome. Waiting. But she didn't die."

"Otto, I—"

"Hear me, Aurora. I must tell you this. I sat at the foot of her bed. The servants were asleep. Part of me commanded my hand to reach for the telephone, but the other part . . . kept me from touching it."

"For how long, Otto?" Aurora's voice had an urgency to it. She had a need to know his mind.

"Until . . . until I realized how easy it would be. Until she began to gag. Her eyes . . . if her eyes had been closed, I think . . . I think I might have . . ."

"Might have *what?*"

His voice became soft and more distant. "I might have let her die."

Aurora sank back against the sofa cushion for support. She had broken into a damp, cold perspiration, and the hand with which she held the telephone receiver began to tremble.

"Otto," she said. "You don't mean that. You can't—"

"I might have let her die, Aurora. It would have been so easy. And it would have simplified matters for the two of us."

Suddenly she felt a chill. That she was his mistress made her feel like an accomplice. But to what? An accomplice to wishful thinking?

"Otto, I—"

"We can't talk about it over the phone, Aurora. I don't know how soon I can get into the city, and—"

"Otto," she said slowly, not having formed her thoughts clearly in her own mind, "that . . . that may

501

be for the best. . . ."

"I don't think I—"

"Perhaps we shouldn't see each other just now. Till Buffy is better. I . . . I feel . . . well . . . I can't explain it, but—"

"Aurora, tell me why you're feeling this way," he said, his cool detachment never waning.

His emotionlessness heightened her own determination. "Otto, there are things we have to talk over . . . and you're right, not on the phone. I don't think it's right for us to see each other for a while."

"Right?" he said. "Did you say 'right'? Why use that word, darling? Simply because I voice the truth about my wishes? Do they echo yours? What's wrong in admitting the truth?"

"Nothing, if that *is* the truth."

"It was my wish."

It is not mine, she answered silently. I don't know what I want, but I do not want the demise of Buffy Danzig. Nor do I want a man who is capable of wishing his wife such a fate.

"Otto, I need some time . . . alone . . . to think."

From his voice, Aurora could tell that he really didn't understand her feelings or her reluctance to share his.

"Darling," he said, "I want New York to signify for us a new beginning."

Why, Aurora wondered, did she have the unshakable feeling that just the opposite was going to happen?

502

Chapter Thirty-One

Aurora had intended to return the emerald ring since that telephone conversation a month earlier, but Buffy Danzig's condition had worsened and Otto had been unable to leave her bedside. Every attempt on his part to induce Aurora to visit the Long Island mansion failed, adding a physical distance to the growing emotional void.

Otto was not behaving any differently, nor did she feel excluded, although, had Aurora wished to use that as an excuse, it would have served her perfectly. Otto had chosen to remain at his ailing wife's bedside; he had not insisted upon coming to Manhattan when Aurora had expressed her wish to be alone.

The simple truth was Otto had shown a side of himself that deeply frightened Aurora; not because he'd voiced his desire that Buffy Danzig die but because he was capable of permitting it to happen before his eyes. His chilling detachment mirrored too vividly the emotional climate all too evident around her, from the drug-induced numbness of the junkies in the streets to the corporate immunity of executives in glass towers. This lack of involvement repulsed Aurora and hastened her decision to end her relationship with Otto

Danzig. She agreed to meet him for lunch when he finally came into the city to confer with his attorneys on legal matters.

"Darling," he said on the phone, "it has been so long. Let me arrange a quiet lunch at a little place I know, and afterward we can be alone together."

"I . . . I have an appointment midtown. In the Seagram Building." She knew that meeting in a very public restaurant such as the Four Seasons would avert a scene, the kind of scene she feared would erupt when she returned the emerald ring and said good-bye to Otto Danzig.

"But darling, we both know too many people who lunch there, who might gossip—"

"Otto, if we're seen together in a quiet, romantic little bistro, that's likely to cause talk. But two friends having lunch at a fashionable restaurant . . . nothing to hide . . ." Before he could object further, she said, "Besides, I have another appointment nearby in the afternoon. It would really be convenient." She was surprised at her own strength.

They made a date for noon.

The restaurant was crowded, and Aurora noticed several friends and a dozen acquaintances among its patrons. That was a relief.

Over a glass of white wine, she broached the subject of their not seeing each other, but she was unprepared for Otto's intensity. He refused to hear her out.

"Aurora, do not speak of ending my reason for living! I promise you, one day I'll be free and we can be together without Buffy to interfere."

"Otto, please listen. My decision has nothing to do with Buffy. Not anymore."

"No. It has everything to do with her. I cannot—will

not—let you go."

She couldn't tell him that she no longer loved him. She feared what it might do to him—and what he might do to her. But wasn't she reacting to the melodrama he so enjoyed playing out?

"Otto. I'm telling you, it has nothing to do with Buffy. I've . . . It's just over."

"You mean everything to me, Aurora. You think I must prove that to you—all right, I will! I'll—"

"You don't need to prove anything, Otto. Things have changed. I've changed. I've thought about it a lot, and—"

"There is someone else," he said darkly, his fingers tightening around the stem of his martini glass.

"There is no one else."

"I can find out who it is," he insisted.

"Otto, whether you believe me or not, there is no one else."

Their waiter stood at attention and Otto waved him away so abruptly that the menu almost fell to the floor. Aurora's eyes darted about the elegant dining room, wondering whether her choice for this meeting had been a good idea or a disastrous one. Otto wouldn't create a scandal in public—of that she was certain. But what about later? And what could she do if he decided not to let her go?

Nerves and drinking wine on an empty stomach were inducing a headache; her temples throbbed as they hadn't since the night Harper and Abby had been found on the yacht. What was she going to do?

Otto continued to speak, but Aurora's brain told her he was saying things she had heard before. She felt her own lips moving, her voice repeating, "It has nothing to do with Buffy. It's over, that's all. There is no one else."

When nausea assailed her, Aurora put the linen napkin on her plate and rose. "Otto, I'm sorry. I'm not feeling very well. I . . . I need some air. . . ." Her feet took her through the restaurant and onto the street, Otto at her heels.

"Aurora! Stop! You cannot leave me! You—"

Snap! A camera shutter clicked.

"Get out of here!" Otto shouted at the photographer.

"C'mon, Rory! Give us a big smile!" shouted the man with the camera. To Otto, he said, "She's news, mister." Then, "How's it feel to be back in the States, Rory? Are you here for a film or is Harper Styles back in the picture?"

At the mention of Harper's name, Otto's face twisted into a menacing scowl. The photographer backed away with a shrug. "Jesus, mister. No need to get upset about it!"

Aurora turned to Otto then. "Look, this isn't the way I intended—"

But Otto cut her off. "You'll come back to me, Aurora. You can't just say good-bye!" His tight-lipped words were instantly transformed as Mary and Norton Kane, two of his and Buffy's oldest friends, passed by on their way into the Seagram Building. A warm, charming smile appeared on his face, and he kissed Mary on both cheeks, then shook Norton's hand. "Aurora, of course Buffy has introduced you to the Kanes, hasn't she? In Rome last summer?"

Recovering as though she were onstage and picking up a cue, Aurora replied mechanically, "Of course. How lovely to see you again." But her knees were shaking badly.

The four exchanged amenities, and Otto said, with the Kanes still beside them, "Aurora, let me put you in a taxi. Buffy will be so sorry to have missed you."

She asked him to give her regards to his wife, and then escaped into the back seat of a cab. Closing her eyes, she gave the driver the address of Tadzio Breslau's penthouse. There was no need to stay at the Mayflower now. Only one thing troubled her as the elevator rose to the top floor. She was still wearing Otto's emerald ring.

Tadzio, unlike Maritza, had never expressed approval or disapproval of Aurora's friendship with the Danzigs. Explanations were therefore unnecessary, and he seemed delighted to have her back. "It's like old times," he said, pouring champagne.

"I wish it were," Aurora responded.

The photograph snapped in front of the Seagram Building appeared in one of the daily tabloids the following day. "I didn't think I was that interesting," she observed aloud to Tadzio.

"Well," he reasoned, "they didn't plant you on page one, darling, did they?"

However, three days later all that changed.

Aurora and Tadzio had been watching a friend in a television miniseries. Tadzio poured more champagne as the eleven o'clock news came on. The lead story began:

Socialite-heiress Elizabeth Danzig, known as Buffy to her family and friends, was found murdered earlier this evening in the Danzig mansion on Long Island. Apparently Mrs. Danzig was the victim of a burglar and—

Aurora's champagne spilled all over the Persian rug as Tadzio cried, *"What?"*

He turned up the volume as the anchorman continued. "Otto Danzig, husband of the heiress, arrived home to find his wife in her bed. 'I stopped in to say good night to her,' he said, 'but Buffy's eyes were closed. She was sleeping peacefully. . . .'"

The anchor's voice droned on, but Aurora heard nothing; she gasped, clutching her stomach as if she had been struck.

"Rory, darling! Are you all right?" Tadzio asked, rushing to her side.

Unable to reply, she sat staring blankly at the television screen, shock and disbelief paralyzing her.

She heard Tadzio but was unable to respond.

"Rory. Rory!" Tadzio stood helplessly by as Aurora wrapped her arms around her own torso and swayed from side to side as she watched the tear-blurred images of Buffy alone, then Buffy and Otto together, flash across the screen.

"It isn't true," she said at last. "It can't be true. Oh, God, don't let it be true!"

Tadzio seated himself next to her and took one of her hands in his.

"How?" Aurora mumbled. "How did it happen?"

"Rory darling, the announcer said something about a random burglary. Buffy must have surprised the thief."

Aurora was shaking her head. Something didn't connect, in Tadzio's words or those of the TV news report, but she was at a loss to give it a name. The gnawing, nagging voice at the back of her brain refused to come forward; or Aurora refused to allow it to.

Tadzio refilled the champagne flute. "Here," he said gently. "Take a sip. It will help." He held it to her lips, and after an initial hesitation, she accepted it passively. A foreboding was settling in Aurora. She knew, yet she did not know. And her inner conflict made the merest act—the holding of a crystal glass—an impossible task.

"Rory, can you stand the rest of the news report?"

It seemed an hour passed; in actuality, it was no more than a minute. The anchorman hadn't even cut to the commercial.

Mrs. Danzig had been confined to her bed since returning from the hospital several days ago. Her husband told police he had gone to the stables while his wife was sleeping. A maid discovered Mrs. Danzig, whose room was in a shambles, clothing and jewelry tossed everywhere. Mr. Danzig had to be sedated upon hearing the news.

Aurora listened, but something still didn't register. Her mind kept darting back to the first part of the news account. *Buffy's eyes were closed. She was sleeping peacefully.* But hadn't Buffy once mentioned that she had trouble sleeping? Perhaps lately she was taking sleeping pills or tranquilizers. What was wrong? Why couldn't Aurora accept what she was hearing?

"He said he'd do anything to keep from losing me," she said in a barely audible whisper. The voice at the back of her brain moved forward, gaining energy.

"What?" asked Tadzio.

"Otto," she said slowly. "He said he'd do anything." She looked up at Tadzio, whose eyes mirrored his alarm.

"Rory . . . do you realize what you're saying?"

She shuddered. "I think I'm beginning to." She closed her eyes and sighed mournfully. "He wanted her to die. He told me so. But could Otto really have . . . have . . ."

"God, Rory, are you saying it wasn't a burglar? That it was Otto Danzig?" His voice betrayed his amazement.

"I don't know . . . I wish I did. If I were convinced that he could . . . could have . . ."

Tadzio prepared cappuccino and added a generous dose of brandy, after which Aurora curled up and quietly whimpered as she fell asleep in her friend's arms. Occasionally she shivered, as though having a bad dream, but this nightmare would not be gone when she awoke. Buffy Danzig was dead, and Otto Danzig had wanted her so. Whether or not he had had anything to do with her murder, Aurora would never go back to him. Of that she was sure.

The police were investigating every possible angle, and it didn't take them long to find Otto Danzig's former mistress. That surprised Aurora. She wasn't prepared for their visit, but the following morning, Parsons announced that two gentlemen from police headquarters were waiting in the library.

"What are you going to say?" asked Tadzio.

Aurora drew a deep breath. "I wish I knew."

She had spent most of the day pondering that very question. Not that she had ever expected to be interrogated, but she had asked herself over and over, once her nerves had calmed enough to permit more rational thinking, if it was remotely possible Otto had murdered Buffy. And, if he had, how could anyone prove it? What could she say to the police? That Otto Danzig had wanted—had wished for—the death of his wife? Did that constitute an act of murder? There had been a time when Aurora had entertained such thoughts regarding Harper Styles!

Detective Ryan asked the obligatory questions: How long had Aurora known the deceased? And how long had she and the deceased's husband been—here he cleared his throat—lovers?

Aurora answered each question truthfully. Although she flinched at the word *lovers,* she did not attempt to deny the relationship. But neither Detective Ryan nor his companion, whose name Aurora couldn't remember, said anything about Otto being a potential murder suspect. Aurora finally broached the subject herself.

"Excuse me, gentlemen, but may I ask why you came to see me? I mean, is Mr. Danzig . . . implicated in any way?"

Later, she laughed at her own naïveté. After seeing so many detective movies, she ought to have known that Ryan's answer would be "Just a routine investigation, ma'am. That's all. Seems pretty clear that Mrs. Danzig was killed by a prowler. We're just doing our job, that's all."

She ventured one step further. "You don't think Mr. Danzig is in any way involved, then, do you?"

Ryan shook his head. "Looks open and shut, ma'am. He was away from the house, anyway."

"Oh, yes. The television report said he was in the stables. I suppose a groom or someone was with him?"

"Beg your pardon, ma'am?" said Ryan.

"I just wondered . . . if he . . . if he had gone riding. He's never been fond of riding alone. . . ." She had to know if Otto had an alibi. She studied Ryan's eyes for any information he might not offer verbally.

"Apparently Mr. Danzig had gone to inspect one of the horses that was sick."

"But he *did* go to the stables," Aurora pressed.

"Is there a reason to doubt that, ma'am?" asked Ryan.

Aurora tried not to twist the handkerchief in her hand; fidgeting would make her appear as nervous as she felt.

"I . . . I was just curious, that's all."

Ryan cleared his throat again. "Ma'am, you'll forgive the question, but we have to ask."

Aurora assumed this would be a question about her relationship with Otto, but she was mistaken. Ryan wanted to know her whereabouts at the time of the crime.

He caught her completely off guard. "I was here—why do you ask that?" The implication made her tremble. Was she a suspect? "Detective Ryan, I liked Buffy Danzig."

"Yes, ma'am, but if you'll forgive me, you *were* her husband's lover." Ryan's face grew pink.

"Past is the correct tense," interjected Tadzio in an obvious attempt to rescue Aurora from an awkward moment.

Ryan nodded and jotted something in his notebook. Then he addressed Aurora again. "I take it you and the husband of the deceased are no longer . . . uh . . ."

"We are no longer lovers," Aurora finished for him. She was growing increasingly impatient with the interview. "You may use the word. It's the appropriate term."

Ryan made another note. "Mrs. Styles, just one more question, if you don't mind. How long ago did your relationship with Mr. Danzig come to an end?"

She drew a deep breath. "Several days ago." After a pause, she added, "Actually, it was over a month ago, but I . . . I only told him a few days ago."

"And how did Mr. Danzig react?"

"I . . . I can't be sure. I haven't seen or spoken with him since." What if Otto hadn't believed that it was over? What if he thought he could win her back? But how could she suggest this to the police unless she knew something more?

Ryan pocketed his notes and adjusted his coat. He seemed ready to leave.

Could this be all? Aurora wondered. Didn't he have further questions about Otto? About Buffy's money? Anything?

Aurora voiced her thoughts aloud before realizing

512

she had done so. "What about the estate? I mean . . . Mr. Danzig will inherit, won't he?"

Ryan's eyes flashed, almost imperceptibly, but Aurora hadn't failed to notice.

"I suppose he will, ma'am. You're not planning to marry him now that he's free, are you?"

"As I've said, my relationship with Otto Danzig is over." *Do you suspect Otto?* Aurora found herself unable to ask the question, to ask whether a man she had loved—or had thought she'd loved—was capable of murder.

"The police assume that it was . . . a burglary?" she ventured.

Ryan nodded. "The coroner says it was cyanosis. That's technical jargon for asphyxiation. Insufficient oxygen. Seems logical. Prowler is stealing a lady's jewels while she sleeps. She wakes up and catches him in the act. He takes the pillow and—"

"Did anyone see this . . . prowler?"

Ryan shrugged noncommittally. "Maid was downstairs. Thought she saw someone running through the garden, but she's not sure."

"Where do the gardens lead?" asked Aurora as innocently as she could, but her heart betrayed her by its incessant hammering. Would the answer implicate Otto? Should it?

But Ryan's reply implicated no one. "The gardens lead to the woods, and they lead onto the main road." He hesitated. "You've never been there?"

Aurora shook her head. "No. I was just curious."

"Well, the tennis courts are off in one direction, stables in another, and the garden veers left, as I've said, to the woods." A nervous silence followed, after which Ryan, moving toward the doorway, asked, "Mrs. Styles, do you have any reason to suspect Otto Danzig of murder?"

513

Her pulse raced. Did she dare to voice her fears, her suspicions? "Well, I . . . I just wondered . . . I mean . . ."

"If you're wondering about motive, well, we did figure there might be one, but you've cleared Mr. Danzig of that possibility."

"I have?" Aurora's voice rose half an octave.

"Sure. The money isn't a strong enough motive because even if he'd divorced his wife, he'd have gotten a fortune. The only reason he'd have to kill her would be that he'd asked for a divorce and she'd refused. That might be valid if you planned to marry him now that his wife is dead, but you've stated that your relationship with him is over. You've cleared him." He paused once more and then added, "It *is* over, isn't it?"

"Yes, but—"

"You'll sign a statement to that effect?"

"Yes, I suppose so, but—"

"Fine. Then we have no more reason to trouble you."

He and his partner left Aurora standing in the center of the room. Tadzio, leaning against the bar, poured two brandies.

"Well?" he asked. "What are you going to do?"

"I haven't the slightest idea," she replied. Perhaps Otto did go to the stables, she reflected, but did he go there after he murdered his wife?

After pacing back and forth for half an hour, Aurora was ready to explode. "Let's go out for something to eat. If I don't get some air, *I'll* die of . . . of asphyxiation!"

They decided to walk the short blocks to the Brasserie. "Everything was so simple when we used to go there," she commented as they made their way down Park Avenue.

"Darling, things were simpler, but you were wearing borrowed dresses; and I do believe if we hadn't fed you, you would surely have starved yourself into a Twiggy lookalike." Tadzio seemed pleased with his remark, and he continued in the same vein. "There are other reasons not to return to the past. If you'd stayed where things were 'simpler,' we'd never have become friends. You'd not have gone to Hollywood and become a celebrity, and—"

"And I'd never have met Harper Styles or Otto Danzig. You'd lose your case in court!"

They had thought to walk the six blocks unobserved, but suddenly, seemingly from nowhere, a flashbulb popped. "Smile, Aurora! Smile for the birdie!"

Another photographer appeared, and Aurora covered her face with one hand while she held more tightly to Tadzio's sleeve with the other.

"We're almost there," she whispered breathlessly. "Let's run!"

But the two photographers were following close behind. Aurora heard one of them say, "Bet they're going to the Brasserie—c'mon!"

The other, shorter and heavier, was panting from his effort to keep up the pace. "Oh, let her alone. We've got two shots already."

"Yeah, but she covered her face and we can't get her once they're inside the restaurant." The younger man was now within arm's distance of his prey.

"Can't you boys amuse yourselves elsewhere?" Tadzio's voice was filled with contempt.

"You kidding? Wait'll you see tomorrow's papers. Aurora Styles is front-page news again!" As he spoke, the first man captured Aurora in a full-front headshot. Her hand loomed in front of her, but the picture had been taken. The camera was not the victim of her fury; the sharp, faceted corner of her emerald ring left its

515

mark on the cheek of the photographer, who recoiled, checking the scratch for signs of blood.

Aurora and Tadzio took advantage of that moment and quickly entered the restaurant. Aggressive as American *paparazzi* might be, any further pursuit would have been discouraged by the management.

Aurora was not unaware of the stares that greeted her, nor of the whispers hidden behind menus. She tried to ease the constriction in her chest and held Tadzio's arm, as before, for support. Holding her head erect, as if balancing a book on it, she strode behind the maître d' to a table in the corner. She acted her role well, exuding casual indifference to the eyes around her, but it was a difficult performance.

After absentmindedly toying with her omelette, Aurora said softly to Tadzio, "I feel as though I'm in a fishbowl."

To which he replied, "That, dear Rory, is because you are." Squeezing her hand, he asked, "Shall we go downstairs?"

She nodded. "What's at the Sutton? Maybe we can sneak into the back row. A movie theater ought to be safe."

They agreed that whatever was playing, as long as it wasn't one of her films, they would do exactly that.

But the same two photographers were waiting outside, and they had been joined by several reporters and a small equipment truck from one of the local TV news stations.

"Come on, we'll make a run for it!" said Tadzio. "Either hide your face or smile right at them. If you give them a good shot, it just might satisfy them so they'll leave us alone."

Aurora opted for the latter suggestion and flash-bulbs popped in such rapid succession that she saw green and red dots each time she blinked. When she

516

was again able to focus, a microphone had been thrust into her face.

"Miss Styles, did Otto Danzig murder his wife?" a reporter asked.

"No comment," answered Aurora.

"But surely now, you and he—"

"I have nothing to say. You have your pictures. Would you leave us alone?" Aurora's calm façade was beginning to crumble, so she and Tadzio quickened their steps. But they had to stop at Lexington Avenue for a traffic light.

"Do you really believe it was a burglar?" asked a pursuer.

"Are you and Mr. Danzig planning to marry now that Mrs. Danzig is out of the way?" put in another.

Aurora whirled around toward the woman who had asked the question. She didn't recognize her face, but she sensed that this reporter relished her task.

"You're vultures! That's what you are! Get away from me!" Her arm lashed out as it had earlier, and the photographer whose cheek bore evidence of her anger shouted, "Hey, Annie, look out! She'll kill you with that right of hers!"

The woman backed away at the same moment the light changed to green. Tadzio grabbed Aurora's arm and they made their escape.

Once inside the Sutton—later Aurora wouldn't recall the name of the film—they settled into two aisle seats in the very last row, and Aurora, finally free of their pursuers, burst into uncontrollable sobs as Tadzio hugged her and tried to comfort her.

"I'd marry you if you didn't know me so well," he said when she had calmed somewhat. "I'd take care of you and adore you, as I always have, but you're too

517

honest for that. Not to mention, of course, that Maritza would be so goddamned jealous she'd murder me in my sleep!"

As the words were uttered, Tadzio made a terrible grimace, which, even in the darkened theater, Aurora could clearly see. But instead of setting off her sobs, it served as a release. She began to giggle, then to laugh softly; then she laughed louder and louder until she was shaking. Tadzio joined her, and the two sat in the last row, convulsed, holding their rib cages to keep from falling over.

"Shut up or I'll call the manager!" hissed a man several rows in front of them.

But they couldn't stop. Trying simply sent them into louder gales of laughter. Other patrons joined in the complaints, some rudely, some politely. A bag lady at the opposite end of their row announced, "Bunch o' fuckin' loonies, that's what they are. Prob'ly on dope. Oughta be locked up!"

When Tadzio and Aurora looked at the woman who'd made that comment, her Brillo hair, silhouetted by the screen's reflection, triggered another round of convulsive giggles. The man who had first yelled at them—a large type with an enormous belly—came up the aisle. Aurora wondered if he was about to physically quiet them, and that had an immediately sobering effect.

However, a far more sobering moment followed when the man returned with the manager. The glamorous international film actress, Aurora Styles, and her companion, Prince Tadzio Breslau, were escorted to the lobby and promptly expelled from the movie theater.

"And don't come back until you can behave!" the manager called after them.

When they reached the corner of Lexington Avenue

and Fifty-seventh Street, Tadzio, still winded from laughing, said, "God, Rory, I'm glad the TV crew didn't get their hands on *that!*"

He had intended to continue the cheering effect of Aurora's hysterical release. Instead, he made her think.

"I wonder," she mused aloud.

"What's that, darling?"

"I just wonder about Otto. Tonight isn't the end of it. That frightens me." Shaking off a sudden melancholy, she added, "I think the next time I can't stop laughing, I'll think about Buffy Danzig. I have this Godawful feeling that Otto had a lot to do with it. Maybe more than a lot. And if he did, he ought to pay for what he's done if there's any justice in this world."

"At times we have to create our own justice, Rory," Tadzio said softly.

"What do you mean?"

"Just that if you want to know—have to know—the whole story, you may find yourself more involved than you already are, or care to be."

"How?"

"Well, eventually you'll need to know the truth. It'll eat away at you until you can't avoid it any longer. And then . . . then you'll make your decision."

Aurora stopped on the curb and stared at her friend. She didn't clearly understand his remark. She had always thought of Tadzio as someone who avoided analyzing situations or people, as one who lived for diversion, enjoyment, and, as he had once said, to provide entertainment. She hadn't realized that he possessed a deeper awareness but kept it to himself. Perhaps his outrage over Vance's desertion years before had been far more than the anger of a rejected lover. He had really cared. That knowledge drew Aurora closer to him, for the flaw she had perceived and accepted as a condition of friendship was instead a

519

conscious choice and not a flaw at all.

"Funny," she finally said as they again walked west, "there are so many things I don't understand."

"About what, darling?"

"Everything. You, me. Everything."

Tadzio bowed theatrically and kissed her hand. *"Bravissima!* You're growing up! I wish you didn't have to experience certain things in order to do so, but"—here he laughed—"some people go through things and others go around them. I'm a coward, so I've always opted for the latter."

"Don't sell yourself short," Aurora said, feeling closer to him than she had for some time. At last she understood Tadzio and Maritza's relationship. Each recognized the other's strength. Aloud, Aurora said, "You're no coward, Tadzio. You're a survivor."

And silently she thought, I suppose I'm learning the art.

She hoped it would become easier with practice.

Chapter Thirty-Two

Aurora slept in Tadzio's bed that night, wrapped in Tadzio's arms. For the first time in a long time, she felt warm and secure. Comforting friendship was what she needed now, and although she knew it would never be enough to sustain her, for the moment she asked no more than that.

In the morning she signed the police affidavit. After doing so a restlessness plagued her, but she was shocked from that state upon her return to the apartment.

Tadzio, not Parsons, greeted her at the door. "Otto is here," he said in a whisper. "In the library. He's been waiting almost an hour."

Involuntarily, Aurora's knees began to quiver, but there was no avoiding this confrontation. She squeezed Tadzio's hand. "Come with me," she implored.

"He said he has to see you alone." As panic crossed Aurora's face, Tadzio quickly added, "I'll be right outside the door. I promise."

None too reassured, Aurora made her way to the library and closed the door behind her.

Otto stood with his back to her. He appeared to be gazing out the window that overlooked the long expanse of Park Avenue, but he turned as the door clicked shut.

"Aurora," he said simply.

She noticed at once that his face was slightly paler than usual, his features tense and drawn. She had never seen him like this, and that added to her uneasiness.

"Otto, I . . . I don't know what to say. I'm so sorry." She truly was, but as she spoke, a voice within her asked, Is *he* sorry? Does his face show signs of remorse, or is he just weary of the publicity surrounding the death of his wife?

"I had to see you," he said, drawing a breath. "I suppose reporters have followed me, so our meeting will be in the papers. God knows everything else about us is."

"Yes . . . I suppose we're even in those supermarket magazines." She was searching for words, feeling that the ones she spoke were meaningless. Earlier, she had been convinced that he had been involved in Buffy's death. Now, seeing his haggard, worn face, she wondered if her suspicions were unfounded.

"The police were here," she said.

"I expected they would be. I didn't have to tell them about us, about Rome, London. It seems our attempts at discretion were futile." Then his eyes met hers directly. "They know how much you mean to me, Aurora."

"Otto," she began, "I . . . I'm sorry about the other day at the restaurant. I—"

"That's all in the past. Buffy is dead. We can have a new beginning. There's no more need to hide."

"Otto, I—"

"We just have to wait a little while—until this subsides. We've waited so long already, darling. Just a little longer . . ."

Aurora averted her eyes. It was over. He knew it was

over. She had ended it. In a cowardly fashion, perhaps, but in no uncertain terms.

"Otto," she began, "I know that Buffy's death has . . . has put a great strain on you, but—" What words could she use now that she stood across from him, speaking face to face? "Otto . . . I . . . I meant what I said."

"What was that? Oh!" he gave a short laugh. "You meant that it wouldn't work between us? But darling, don't you see? We're free now—free to be together."

Her voice was unsteady and low. "It's too late for us, Otto."

For a fleeting moment, an undecipherable look flashed across his face. Was it anger? Disbelief? She couldn't be sure which.

He stepped closer to her. So far they had not touched; the small Chinese rug created an abyss, a chasm between them.

Without realizing she had done so, Aurora took a step back.

"Darling," he said, "are you trying to keep me away from you? Are you frightened of me?"

In a small voice, she admitted, "I don't know, Otto. I . . . I can't be sure."

"Sure of what? Sure of my love?"

"No," she replied, almost in a whisper. She wasn't looking at him now but was focusing beyond him, fixing her gaze upon one of Tadzio's leather-bound volumes on a shelf at Otto's shoulder height.

"Otto," she said, her voice barely audible, "did you . . . did you kill Buffy?" Her heart felt as if it were beating at the base of her throat; her breathing was high and shallow; she had feared voicing the question as much as she feared his answer to it.

At first he didn't speak. He crossed the rectangular rug to stand beside her, placing his large, slim hands

523

upon her shoulders. Then, in a voice as subdued as Aurora's, he said, "I told you I would do anything to keep from losing you."

His words, together with their intensity, registered on her brain like a physical blow. Aurora cowered, clutching the sofa arm so as not to lose her balance. As she shrank from Otto's grasp, dizziness and nausea threatened to overtake her, but she managed to avoid fainting by calling upon the denial she'd employed as a child. Denial and acting prowess. Make believe, she commanded herself. This isn't really happening. Otto did not just admit that he murdered his wife—that he murdered his wife for *you,* Aurora!

Neither denial nor theatrical ability came to her rescue when that last thought struck her. He had committed murder to keep from losing her! It didn't matter that he'd already lost her—Buffy Danzig was dead because of Aurora Styles! All the denial in the world could never negate that fact, nor could it bring Buffy back to life. This was not a film in which scenes could be reshot, a script rewritten. Buffy was dead at the hand of her husband, Aurora's lover. That he was her ex-lover did not matter, for he had refused to believe that their relationship was over.

Consumed by guilt, Aurora sank down onto the sofa. Otto stood placidly over her and reached down to stroke her hair.

"Don't touch me!" she said, recoiling. "You killed her, didn't you? You killed Buffy in cold blood. Her eyes were closed and you—"

"She was sick. And weak. The doctors said she might have gone on like that for years. Years of keeping us apart. She was a very unhappy woman, Aurora. It was for the best."

But Otto's soothing tone did not have the effect he intended. Aurora's dizziness had passed, his cool voice reviving her as surely as if she had been splashed with ice water. She wondered if she might have reacted differently had he collapsed at her feet, sobbing with guilt and remorse. It was his self-control, his absolute conviction, that frightened her most. She was staring straight at him, yet Otto Danzig, through his indifference, was becoming invisible.

Drawing herself up, she rose from the sofa and crossed to the window, the same window at which Otto had stood when she'd entered the library.

"I think you'd better leave," she said, not turning to him as she spoke.

"Not without you," he replied, joining her at the window. He whirled her around to face him. "You cannot tell me to go, not after what I've done for you!" His voice, for the very first time during their interview, had risen in pitch. There was anger in it. Taking tight hold of Aurora's sleeve, he said, "You can't leave me. You love me! As I love you!"

Aurora pulled herself free of his grasp and made for the library door. "Tadzio!" she called.

"You'll come back to me, Aurora—you must!" He dashed to her side and grabbed her in an awkward, aggressive embrace that caused one of her legs to buckle under her.

"Otto, let go of me! I'll—"

"You'll what? Scream?" His lips forced themselves upon hers.

Desperately she tried to avoid his kiss, his touch. She felt dirty, defiled. She struggled with him, amazed at his physical strength.

He held her in a vise grip against the wall. Aurora tried to free a hand to slap him, to maneuver a foot so she might kick him.

Then there was a click and Tadzio stood in the doorway. Otto quickly released Aurora, who fell against the wall, panting, gasping for air.

"Get out of here, Danzig!" Tadzio commanded. "Get out and don't ever come back! I'll call the police if I have to!"

Aurora, still winded, looked up. Otto's eyes were fixed upon her. She could neither meet his stare nor avoid it. No one spoke.

Finally, apparently realizing that Tadzio needed little provocation to make good his threat, Otto turned, looked back at Aurora a last time, and left the room.

Only when Aurora heard the outer door slam did she allow her panic to surface. Her breathing became rapid, and she was unable to speak until her anxiety had passed.

For several minutes, Tadzio waited, seemingly cognizant of her state.

When she did speak, it was in a low voice. "He killed her, Tadzio. He told me. He killed her."

Tadzio nodded. "Are you going to tell the police?"

"I . . . I . . . oh, God, Tadzio, I feel as if *I'm* the one responsible! I don't know what to do!"

"Damn!" he said. "I wish I'd been eavesdropping!"

"Why?"

"Because, darling, without another witness or tangible evidence it'll boil down to your word against his if it ever goes to trial."

"But how can I prove it? He said—"

"Those very words, Rory? *'I killed my wife'?*"

"I think—I think I'm the one who used those words. But he said he'd do anything to keep from losing me. I think he said— Oh, Tadzio, I'm so confused! Maybe later I'll remember every word he said. Right now, it's all so muddled, I—"

"Well, one thing's certain. You can't go to the police, not when you're in this state of mind. They'd have no case."

"What do you mean? He *confessed* to me!"

"Yes, darling, but they'd accuse Otto, and the defense would make mincemeat of you. They'd destroy your credibility, and Otto would be acquitted. He'd go free. Remember, a person can't be tried twice for the same crime."

"But he'll go free anyway, won't he?"

Tadzio didn't answer immediately. He poured Aurora a brandy and then said, "The only way to get Otto Danzig convicted for murder is to provide proof—beyond that famous 'reasonable doubt'—or to remember—verbatim—each and every word he said and tell it calmly to the police. You'd then have to repeat it all over again in court, for both defense and prosecution. And Otto will retain the best lawyers in the business to discredit your testimony. You'll be in all the papers again. There'll be much more publicity than your divorce from Harper warranted."

"God, Tadzio, I don't know if I can handle all that. I'm so tired. . . ." Tears welled up in her eyes as she leaned back in his arms. "Tell me what to do."

"Well, I'd say first you need a rest, need to get away from the whole scene, away from New York. To go where you can relax, a place that's not too remote. Perhaps London, or—"

"Yes," Aurora said. "London might be a good idea." She could lose herself in London without getting lost. "But then what? After London?"

"Well," he said, turning her chin toward him and smiling, "things often have a way of arranging themselves. You'll do the right thing." He leaned closer and kissed her cheek gently. "You generally do, you know."

Chapter Thirty-Three

London was damp and foggy; it suited Aurora's mood. She had registered at Brown's rather than stay with friends; she wanted to be free to come and go as she pleased without being questioned by anyone. The London papers did not ignore the Danzig murder case, but it was not until Aurora's second week in the city that her photograph began to appear in the tabloids. Out of curiosity, she read the first few accounts of her "torrid affair" with Otto Danzig. When they began to sound alike, she stopped punishing herself. At times she questioned her own judgment as to whether Otto Danzig was guilty of murder. But each time she was tempted to negate her suspicions, an image of Otto in Tadzio's library flashed through her mind. And finally, in the late edition with a two-inch-high banner was the headline: OTTO DANZIG CHARGED WITH MURDER.

The headline coincided with an occurrence that served to confirm Aurora's suspicions of Otto's guilt: the appearance of the two men who seemed to follow her everywhere. At first, before she considered the more sinister aspect of their surveillance, Aurora had assumed they were reporters, or photographers. But her recent brush with these members of the media had taught her that they never went anywhere without notepads or cameras, or, in the case of television newscasters, videotape equipment and technicians. These two men, whom she might have nicknamed Tweedle Dum and Tweedle Dee but for her fondness for Ugo Balestrino's hallway guard, carried no props. They simply followed her wherever she went.

Finally, after examining in detail what she knew, Aurora came to the conclusion that Otto Danzig was guilty of murder. Her two "shadows," she decided, were to take her back to testify—the morning papers had said her signed affidavit was insufficient evidence upon which to secure a conviction—*or* they were employed by Otto to keep her from ever returning to New York. Initially, she found the latter possibility too melodramatic even for her former lover. However, as the two men dogged her every step, she began to see the matter differently. If Otto had killed—or had arranged for someone else to kill—Buffy, what would stop him from killing again? He knew that the ugly confrontation in Tadzio's library had been witnessed only by Aurora . . . and he also knew that she was never going back to him. Perhaps in his calculating mind he'd decided if he couldn't have Aurora, nobody would. Hundreds of Hollywood films depicted just such a situation. Fear suddenly prompted Aurora to demand an answer from her two shadows.

She had shopped for cosmetics on the ground floor at Harrods. Then she had gone upstairs to The Way In and browsed. After that she had looked at evening dresses. She saw in mirrors that they followed her to each department of the store. In an effort to elude them, Aurora selected three evening gowns from the racks of designer clothing and went into a dressing room to try them on. She had no intention of buying such a gown; the past year or more of traveling in Rome, London, and New York, despite visits in friends' homes, threatened to exhaust her cash supply. She had not thought to establish credit or to open charge accounts in her own name at the time of her divorce from Harper—things had occurred too quickly—and she had left Hollywood with a single suitcase. Since, all her acquisitions, except for Otto's presents, had been paid for with cash—her own cash. She laughed as she modeled the Dior gown in the three-way, full-length mirror. It was stunning. At another time she wouldn't have hesitated. Now she replaced it on the hanger and pulled her own heather-knit sweater dress over her head. There was no point in trying on the other two gowns; she couldn't afford either.

She glanced at her emerald ring, careful not to catch the yarn of her dress on the setting. Ah, she mused ruefully, you didn't buy this for yourself, and just look where it's gotten you: in a small, overheated, fluorescent-lighted dressing room at Harrods while you try to outwit your pursuers.

She waited inside the dressing room for a quarter of an hour, and when she came back out onto the selling floor, she didn't see them. Well, she'd finally gotten rid of them.

But she was mistaken. They were waiting at the escalator and stepped onto the moving staircase just far enough ahead of Aurora to make communication impossible, for several customers were between her and them.

When they reached the ground floor, they exited the store. They weren't within sight as Aurora made her way through the doors, but as soon as she was out on the street, she saw their reflections in one of the

531

windows. They had remained behind her and had taken up pursuit once more.

She turned abruptly. They seemed surprised.

"Why are you doing this?" she demanded.

The redhead replied, "Someone wants to know where you are. All the time."

"Who? Which side are you working for?"

The two men smiled without answering and then moved to the side into teeming pedestrian traffic. Aurora saw her chance and bolted, darting in and out of gridlocked cars until, breathless, she dashed into Vidal Sassoon's salon.

"Have you an appointment?" asked the receptionist.

With a furtive glance toward the street, Aurora said, "Uh, no, actually I haven't." It would be ridiculous to say that two men were following her and she hadn't even realized where she was; she had merely pushed the door—any door—and gone inside.

"I really just need a shampoo and . . . perhaps a trim. Is there a chance that someone is free?"

The receptionist checked the appointment book. "Well, if you don't mind waiting for about ten minutes, André can take you."

Aurora nodded. "Ten minutes? That's fine." Yes, she calculated, and an hour or so after that. Maybe they'll grow tired of waiting and just give up. And disappear, she thought with increasing desperation, but without believing it would happen.

When she emerged from the salon, however, her pursuers were nowhere in sight. She felt a lightness as she walked, turning back every few blocks and finding no recognizable faces behind her.

But they were seated in the lobby of Brown's Hotel when she reentered that evening. Reasoning that even hired detectives, assassins, or whatever they were, had to sleep eventually, Aurora packed, paid her bill, and checked out of the hotel at four o'clock the next morning. She didn't know whether her telephone was being monitored, so she made no advance flight reservations but took a taxi all the way to Heathrow. There she booked a seat to Paris, on the next plane scheduled to depart.

Arriving there, she spent the first night in a small hotel, and in the morning, she telephoned Maritza, who was in New York. The transatlantic connection was less than desirable, with cellophane-crinkle sounds punctuating the conversation. However, Aurora did obtain the name and address of the countess' friend on the Avenue Georges Mandel. She had never met Giles Dufort, so neither side, prosecution or defense, could link her with him in any way. Giles was out of the country, but Maritza had arranged an invitation in advance. "Just in case you need a place to stay and haven't the money for deluxe accommodations," she had said.

The apartments were lavishly decorated. Although the gilt carvings and appointments struck Aurora as ostentatious, everything was exquisitely crafted and predated the French Revolution. But Aurora recalled the coziness of places like Aylesbury, Paul Blake's boyhood home, and felt uncomfortable in her luxurious surroundings.

Why hadn't she fled to Aylesbury instead of going all the way to Paris? she asked herself. The answer was simple. One couldn't fly to the medieval English town, and she knew nobody there. Also, in Paris she could hide; in Aylesbury, she could not.

Her thoughts drifted to Paul Blake and their last meeting. She wondered if he knew of her current predicament, not of her pursuers but of her situation.

The case was not his type of reading material, but unless he'd been traveling by camel in the middle of an African desert, there could be no way he'd not have heard or read about the Danzig trial. What must he think? She went out onto the balcony that overlooked the broad expanse below. Why should it matter what Paul Blake thought of her?

Yet it did.

Aurora wandered aimlessly about the neighborhood the first day. On the second day she spent much of the afternoon viewing the Impressionists at the Orangerie, losing herself among Monet, Pissarro, Degas, and Berthe Morisot. She made up her mind to return the following day.

But on that day, her plans changed abruptly. She received a telephone call from Tadzio; she was wanted for testimony in Otto's trial. The affidavit wasn't enough. The prosecution suspected that she knew more. They needed her on the witness stand if they were going to convict Otto.

Tadzio had already called Sabine, his housekeeper in Lucerne, to alert her. "Get on the next plane to Switzerland—they've stepped up the search. They may even know you're in Paris!"

She didn't bother to ask who or how they might know. Aurora packed her luggage and hurried downstairs to make her way to the airport.

She stood at the curb, waving at each passing taxi, trying desperately to flag an empty one.

Suddenly, a dark blue Citröen screeched to a halt. A rear door flew open, and the red-haired man jumped out. Aurora backed away from the curb.

"Not this time!" he said, grabbing her by the elbow.

Aurora screamed, but the noises of the teeming traffic obliterated the sound. "Let me go!" she cried, struggling to free herself. The redhead seemed determined to drag her into the back seat of the car.

"Who are you? What do you want with me?" She was frantic, but the man refused to release his grasp on her arm.

He yanked her and she almost fell against the car. She saw the driver—the thinner, blond half of the pair—as he opened his door, as though to assist in the kidnapping. As he reached for her leg, Aurora spied an empty taxi. Turning with an abruptness that caught both her captors off guard, she brought her knee up and kicked the redhead in the groin.

He gasped, letting go of her arm as he recoiled in pain. Aurora fled into the break between cars and flung herself into the rear of the taxi. Her minimal French was sufficient for directions: the airport, as quickly as possible. She didn't have time to request that the driver lose the Citröen; she prayed that she and the taxi would arrive intact.

Her panty hose were torn and her coat was missing a button, but she had escaped her pursuers. With her continually dwindling cash, she purchased a ticket to Lucerne, hiding in the ladies' room until it was time for her flight. She wasn't taking any chances. They seemed to have radar for tracking her. Anywhere.

Only when the plane had made its ascent and Aurora had toured the cabin to check the face of every passenger aboard did she relax. For the moment, she was free. She knew it wouldn't remain that way, but it did give her breathing space to think ahead, to plan her strategy. Sooner or later she had to be lucky or they

535

had to give up. If she could elude them only a little longer, just until she was certain she knew what to do . . . Tadzio had said she would come to the right decision when her need to know the truth became too strong. But she *did* know; she no longer had any doubt. Otto had indeed murdered Buffy. The question—the decision to be made—was simply: what to do about it.

Part IV

Chapter Thirty-Four

The rolling hills of Reggio Emilia's countryside spilled into the luscious green of Tuscany. The train made an hour-long stop in Florence—Firenze, Aurora reminded herself, refreshing her Italian—and now it was speeding on its way south to Rome.

The young nun seated opposite Aurora had fallen asleep. Not so the elderly *madre* whose eyes peered about at regular intervals as though to fend off any danger, including that of enjoying the trip. When Aurora smiled at the old woman, the wrinkled face of the nun drew itself inward, not unlike an ancient tortoise would, shielding herself from whatever contagion she feared Aurora must be carrying.

That made Aurora laugh. It was a soft, subtle laugh at which no one could have taken offense, but the old nun apparently found reason to do so, and averted her eyes from the woman she had called *putana* awhile ago. For the remainder of the trip, their eyes never met.

The rapido slowed and chug-chugged into Stazione Termini. It seemed indeed forever since Aurora had last seen the Eternal City. She didn't even wait for the young novice to awaken. She collected her things and quickly left the train.

"Tassì, signora?" asked a young man as he eyed Aurora up and down.

"No, grazie." She wasn't trusting anyone who offered her a ride. She would get in line in front of the *stazione* and await her turn; that way, she would know she was taking an authentic taxi.

"Che bella ragazza!" shouted a street vendor in the now-familiar Roman dialect. It was music to Aurora's ears.

She made her way to a telephone booth outside. She felt the pride of accomplishment as she dealt with the call; she knew where to place the *gettone* and what to say when the reception desk at the studio answered.

But even her vastly improved Italian could not locate Ottorino Bellini or Carla Francese. *"Sono fuori città,"* came the reply.

How could they dare be out of town? Aurora hung up. Announcing her name to Cinecittà would be akin to hanging a sign at Piazza Navona as to her whereabouts. She telephoned the Excelsior Hotel on Via Veneto about a room, but thought better about it and didn't wait for the desk to answer.

Why don't you call *him?* she asked herself. Because, she argued silently, he probably wants nothing to do with you after that last meeting. Why was the timing always wrong?

But he said he'd be there if you needed a friend, that little mute voice reminded her.

Yes, but . . .

But what?

Aurora closed her eyes. She wasn't calling Paul Blake because friendship wasn't really what he was offering, was it? Or, if it was, would it be enough for her?

Okay, she decided, opening her eyes, Tadzio was right. Some people go around things. I am going through them. But I'm tired of having everyone else calling the shots, telling me what to do, how to live my life.

Did Paul do that? asked that persistent voice.

"Oh, shut up," Aurora said aloud. She dialed the number of a small, residential hotel on Via Emilia, behind Via Veneto. She had walked by it on her shortcuts to the Piazza di Spagna, and it was just remote enough to provide the privacy she wanted.

They had a small room on the second floor, overlooking the garden. It sounded perfect.

Aurora exited the station area; the line of people waiting for taxis curved all the way around to the side street. She walked to Via Indipendenza and got into a taxi that was parked in front of the YMCA. Nobody could possibly recognize a blond-wigged Aurora Styles—*she* would never go near a "Y."

Her hotel accommodations were modest in comparison with her recent lodgings; however, the street was quiet and the atmosphere was cozy. The furnishings had a "lived-with" air, and the scent of orange blossoms wafted in from the terrace, which was above the garden, refreshing and awakening Aurora's senses. She was even prompted, after a nap and shower, to change her mind. She dialed the desk and asked them to ring Paul's number.

She considered hanging up, but he answered before she could do so. She told him where she was and then, tentatively, she said, "Is your offer still good?"

"Which one?" he replied.

She detected the warmth in his voice. "I need a friend," she said.

"At your service." Then his tone grew serious. "I've read some of the details in the papers, Aurora. Are you in Rome for a visit—or are you running away again?"

She sighed. "I'm trying to figure that out myself.

541

Actually, I was running when I got on the train, but not in the sense you mean. It's a long story."

"Will you tell me over dinner?"

"Yes. Maybe you can help me sort it all out."

"I thought that was part of our problem on the last two occasions," he said lightly.

"No," she replied. "It was a matter of timing."

"Speaking of which, since I'm taking a movie star to eat, shall we make it 'dinner at eight'?"

"That's a lousy pun," she said, laughing nonetheless.

"But it's one of my favorite films," he said. "Almost as good as *Lickety-Split*. See you later." He hung up before Aurora could say a word.

Lickety-Split. He'd seen it! Had he known she was in it beforehand? That thought was uppermost in her mind as she rummaged through her suitcase for something silky—and uncrushed—to wear for dinner at eight.

Paul arrived at the lobby of La Residenza at seven-thirty. "It's dark enough outside to walk without the world asking for your autograph," he said. "I even know a shortcut."

"Wonderful," said Aurora. "I feel as though I've spent the last few weeks either getting on planes or into taxis. I'd love to walk. Do you think I can dispense with these?" She was wearing sunglasses, although the sun was close to setting.

"I think you'd better. Dark glasses at night in Rome are a magnet for the *paparazzi*." He took her by the arm and led her down the steps of the hotel. "You're looking smashing. Hardly like the well-dressed fugitive one conjures up in one's imagination."

She laughed. She had steamed the mauve silk chemise dress after her shower. She wore it now with matching spaghetti-strap sandals, mohair shawl over her shoulders as protection from the damp evening chill of the Roman spring. Her sable coat and lynx jacket were locked in the armoire in her room, and her few remaining jewels, including the diamond-studded Piaget, were secure in the hotel safe.

"Where's the emerald that caused our last fight?" Paul asked, smiling. "I've seen it on magazine covers, but you're not wearing it tonight."

They had exited onto Via Emilia and she stopped at the corner. "I thought you weren't interested in ladies' jewelry collections," she chided. "But you're very observant."

"Can't help it, Mrs. Styles. You and that rock have hit every scandal sheet from Trieste to the tip of the boot." His eyes drank her in, as though measuring distance for a filming. "Ah, no wonder the lady is wearing her hair à la Veronica Lake. To avoid unwanted eyes, hm?"

She was grinning widely. "Veronica Lake? Sorry, she's before my time!" Laughing, she added, "I got tired of wearing a wig—it isn't true that blonds have more fun, I assure you."

"Ironic, isn't it? I'd imagine that you're one of the world's most envied women right now."

His remark prompted a wry, guttural laugh that erupted into a happier, somewhat relieved sound. Paul had that effect on her, when she wasn't fighting him. How good it was to see him! She opened her small, beaded evening clutch purse. Inside, lodged against lipstick, compact, and passport, was a rolled-up ball of linen. "See that?" she asked. "The infamous Danzig emerald is wrapped in the handkerchief." She gasped. "My God, Paul, it's wrapped in your handkerchief!"

"Seems a bit inappropriate," he said, but his eyes were dancing with amusement. Taking her arm, he led her to the end of the street and through a massive, forbidding but unlocked iron gate. As they descended a flight of steps, Paul continued. "Now we just have to find something in which to wrap Harper's diamond, don't we?" His eyes twinkled mischievously but he spoke lightly. Aurora sensed that his words had been carefully chosen to give her room, breathing space.

"Where are we going?" she asked as they reached Piazza Barberini, which was covered with newly erected barricades. Paul's shortcut had eliminated several blocks' walk along the curve of Via Veneto. "What happened to the fountain?"

"Ah, progress. The new subway line. They've halted construction because they came upon some previously undiscovered ruins. But we are going to a quiet, modest, marvelous trattoria that's not unlike the subway discovery. It's been hidden for ages, and only natives—and expatriates like yours truly—know about it. No cameras, no film crowd, just fabulous dining."

"Where is it?"

"My secret. Trust me. All the places you've frequented with your movie friends and those in the jet set"—here he waited for a reaction, but there was none—"are beyond my means, and frankly I find them boring. If you have a sweet tooth, I'll concede and we can have *tartuffo* at Tre Scalini after dinner. But tonight, madame is dining at La Maiella."

"I've never heard of it."

"Good. I'll play guide. It's in an alleyway just off Piazza Navona. No atmosphere—that's provided by the clientele. But the food, *signora*, is"—here he scratched his cheek with the knuckle of his index finger in typical Roman fashion—"*squisito*. I promise."

La Maiella was crowded and dark; they took a table in a far corner that was illuminated only by candles in

544

Chianti bottles. While they feasted on the house specialties of *crêpes alla ricotta* and tender *villerois,* Aurora brought Paul up-to-date on her current predicament, on Buffy's murder, and on Otto's trial, which had been covered in the newspapers. By the time they were served espresso, Aurora had provided him with the details not known by the public or press: Otto's confession in Tadzio's library and her own harrowing escape from her two pursuers.

Paul had listened attentively throughout, commenting occasionally, questioning her only on points where there was a possibility of confusion.

She told him everything, relieved to share her enormous burden. And more, to share it with someone who, she sensed, could be trusted. "Well," she said, "that's it. Every bit of it. Now don't tell me that I'm still running away. I'm aware of the fact."

"I was about to say this may be the one time running away has its merits," he answered. "To which I might add that I'm glad you ran to me. Even if that sounds presumptuous." He reached across the small table and placed his hand over Aurora's smaller, slender fingers. "We all have our weaknesses."

"I haven't been very fair to you, have I, Paul?" she asked.

"No, you haven't," he said quietly.

The restaurant had thinned out considerably and now they were the last two patrons inside. "What time is it, anyway?"

"It's past eleven. Time flies . . . remember? But what about dessert? Still hungry?"

She shook her head. "I'm stuffed."

Signaling for the waiter, Paul suggested, "Then why don't we walk?"

He paid the check, after which they strolled, arms linked, to Piazza Navona. The piazza was alive with

545

tourists seated at outdoor cafés and teenagers playing with glow-in-the-dark yo-yos. The recent crackdown on drug dealers seemed to be working; the junkies were gone. But the fountains were empty. On Ottorino's guided tour, water had flowed freely, adding an exciting background sound that set off the voices of small children and street hawkers.

"There's a legend about Bernini's fountain," both Aurora and Paul said to each other at once.

"You first," said Paul.

"No, go ahead," she insisted.

"Wait. If we both know the story—"

"You're right. This is silly!" Her face was aglow, as it had been as a child, when she and Abby had spoken in unison and then entwined their fingers to play some singsong game. Abby . . . She hadn't allowed herself to think of Abby for so long. And tonight, a new feeling had replaced the hurt. A healing, although she didn't know why. Perhaps it was time to forgive. She'd write a letter. It was her turn now.

Smiling, she said, "Paul, I have to ask you—did you *really* see *Lickety-Split?*"

"I certainly did," he replied. "I told you when we saw that film of yours—on the plane—that I wanted to see you in something better. You're wonderful in it. In fact, I saw a side of you that's usually well hidden. You can be very funny when you let yourself."

"It was a very happy experience for me at the time. But how did you find it? The film was pulled from release so quickly—"

"I saw it here. In Rome. At a little *teatro parrocchiale*—in a church auditorium. I knew you'd made it awhile back, because Harper Styles' name was scrawled in red across the screen. I noticed your name was under the title, even with star billing."

Here she laughed. "Harper's name was always

separate from the rest. I think it may have been subconscious. You know, the producer provides the money, but the actors say the lines—court jesters, subject to the king."

"You've changed. I don't detect any bitterness when you talk about him."

"Paul, recently I've come to look on those years in Hollywood as having occurred in a previous lifetime." Tossing her hair back, she sighed, but it wasn't a nostalgic sigh or a regretful one. "Sometimes I feel ancient, as if I've lived a hundred years."

"I'm still interested. . . ." He grinned. "By the way, your Italian is excellent—even though the lip sync was off."

"My what?" Then she understood. "But I didn't dub myself. God! Carla Francese spoke my lines! At last she got to do something of mine that was decent!" For some reason, she found this cause for laughter, and, without knowing why, Paul joined in. Then he stopped, abruptly, and pulled her into a shadowy doorway. "I lured you here under false pretenses, Ms. Styles."

"What? What are you talking about?"

"This. I want to be more than your friend. Far more." He bent his head to kiss her and her arms went up around his neck. His kiss was gentle, questioning at first, but when Aurora responded, his tongue parted her lips and their kiss grew more and more intense. A sudden surge of desire shot through Aurora, but tonight she didn't push him away as she had in London, when they had so misunderstood each other.

They kissed again, Paul holding her body tightly against his, and her awareness of his growing arousal sparked a fire between her legs.

"Will you give me a chance, *signorina?*" he asked when she leaned her head back for air.

547

"On one condition," she murmured, still in his arms.

"Name it," he said.

"I don't want to lose your friendship."

"Greedy, hm?" He kissed the tip of her nose.

"Um-hmm. Deal?"

"I have a condition of my own."

"What's that?" she asked.

"As long as friendship takes second place. First things, first."

"It's a deal."

"Good."

"Now what?" she asked.

"My place," he said.

As they left the privacy of the doorway, a chorus of voices echoed from the *birreria* across the street. *"Bravi ragazzi! Bravo l'amore!"*

Together, laughing and swinging their hands, they made their way to Paul's apartment on Via Frattina. Even in her spaghetti-strap sandals, Aurora kept the pace.

Paul's apartment, like the *attico* Aurora had rented in Trastevere, was on the top floor, but it overlooked the city's center. It was housed in an old building on Via Frattina; its stone was the indigenous yellow-orange of Rome that, depending upon time of day, leaned more toward sunlight or terra cotta in hue. On the ground floor a *sara cinesca,* made of heavy aluminum, hid from view the contents of the silk importer's *vetrina.*

"Be careful about the third step," Paul warned. Aurora's sandal avoided the crack as she joined Paul inside the cool marble entranceway. A cage elevator at the rear of the small lobby coughed and sputtered but delivered them to the top floor.

"The penthouse?" asked Aurora as Paul unlocked

the door.

"Not quite." He threw open the massive paneled door and bowed. "Welcome to my humble abode, milady."

Aurora glanced about her, eager to learn more about Paul Blake. If the furnishings of his living room were any indication of Paul's nature, it was immediately apparent that he was a man who enjoyed comfort, but in his context, the word had a relaxed, casual connotation rather than the luxurious one of a Tadzio Breslau or a Harper Styles. Or, she mused, an Otto Danzig.

The color scheme was a pleasing combination of browns and beiges, with rust-colored accents. The pieces themselves were contemporary, durable yet sensuous velvets and textured fabrics. The objects of diversion were few and functional: a small portable television set; an equally small stereo system and tape deck with shelf-top speakers. His workspace was an area set aside and chosen with the utmost of care. A rolltop desk with myriad drawers and cubbyholes was positioned in the corner nearest the window doors leading to a small terrace. On the desk were a sturdy electronic typewriter, a brass desk lamp, and stacks of manuscript paper, separated and clipped together according to chapter. A box lay open. In it were letters, stamps, and two bottles of paper correction fluid.

The walls held several small drawings, matted and framed. Peering closely, Aurora noticed that one was a Whistler and it was not a print. A slightly larger oil painting in a simple wooden frame was signed Chauncey Ryder. His taste was strictly personal; clearly he was a man whose acquisitions were dictated only by what he really wanted.

Nor were his bookshelves similar to Tadzio's, although many of the volumes bore the same titles as the unopened and unread books in the prince's library. Again, Paul's choice was eclectic; Swift and Defoe, yet no Sterne or Fielding; Hemingway, Capote, and Doctorow; no Faulkner or Updike. The books were not in matching, leather-bound, gold-tooled editions; they were tattered hardcovers, torn paperbacks. Only a handful had virgin jackets. Obviously their owner had not yet found time to read them.

"Where are your books?" Aurora asked as Paul returned from the kitchen with a filled ice bucket.

"You're looking at them," he replied, setting the bucket on the low marble coffee table. He reached into the bar at its carved-out center and said, "It's still Chivas, *sì?*"

"*Sì,*" she answered. "But I meant your own books. Books by Paul Blake."

"Oh, those!" He grinned as he filled two old-fashioned glasses. "Do you have eight-by-ten glossies of all your movie stills tacked to your walls?"

"I never needed reminders of my triumphs," she said, taking a sip of the soothing Scotch.

"Touché." He clinked his glass against hers. "They're under my bed. Since you asked."

"What?"

"My books. Some people invite ladies up to see their etchings. My books are . . . under my bed."

Any other man she'd known would have accompanied that line with a look or gesture that would have signaled a pass. But Paul seemed to understand her need not to be rushed. Even as he had understood, in the darkened doorway, that she was, indeed, giving them a chance. He hadn't had to ask a second time, nor did she need to explain.

He rose and crossed to the fireplace. As he knelt to light the kindling, Aurora said, "I'm sorry about London."

He didn't turn but continued his efforts until the fire caught. "So was I. But I still believed in my instincts."

"About what?"

"About you." He rose and returned to the sofa. "I said to myself the first time I saw you—on the plane, hiding behind those dark glasses—I said, 'Paul Blake, that woman, whoever she is, is going to change your life.'"

"Paul, be serious."

"I've never been more serious," he said, stroking a tendril of hair near her temple. "I know it sounds like a line, but I mean every word."

"I'd like to believe you," she heard herself say.

"Good." He took the glass from her hand and placed it beside his on the table. "I knew we had more than Chivas in common." He leaned forward and began to kiss her, first at the top of her forehead, at the point of her widow's peak. "Enough of Veronica. You're with me." He brushed back the hair covering the right side of her face and fondled it in his fingers.

The warmth of the Scotch, the intimacy of the room and the fireglow, began to reignite feelings that had begun to kindle in the shadows near Piazza Navona earlier that evening.

"Come with me," he said. "I'll show you my books. . . ."

He led her by the hand down a corridor, at the end of which was a spacious bedroom. It was sparsely furnished, containing only a large oak platform bed and a matching four-season armoire. French doors opened onto another small terrace, and the midnight scent of orange blossoms, this time mingled with café aromas—toasted espresso beans and freshly baked bread—filled the room. "It's damp this evening," he said, closing the terrace doors. "There. No one to interrupt."

Aurora had left her shawl on the living-room sofa. Now Paul stepped close to her and fingered one of the spaghetti straps on her dress. Drawing her to him, he slid the thin strips of silk from her shoulders, and his fingers began to trace the contours of her body, outlined by silk and silhouetted by the hallway light. As his hands brushed her breasts, Aurora felt her nipples harden and she shuddered. It had been a long time since she had tingled so.

His index finger slid down past her navel, to the spot between her legs where the silk now clung protectively yet invitingly. As he caressed her vulva through the dress, her knees weakened, and when he gently squeezed her mound of pubic hair, a tiny moan escaped her. Silk chemise, lace panties, and panty hose were the only barriers that still separated them.

Aurora stood in his arms, supported by the arm that stroked her shoulder blades and held her back to keep her from falling. Her hands caressed his chest, but as Paul's fingers lifted her dress and played with the edges of her panties, teasing her moist lips and then withdrawing, she found her head spinning. He seemed to know exactly when to break off, when to resume his stroking, and the cycle had begun to drive her wild. Her breathing was short, coming in excited spurts, and her insides had begun to churn, to pulsate with bursts of desire, of utter wantonness. She hadn't been so aroused by a man's touch since that very first time with Harper, on his yacht; and that had been precipitated by a bizarre attraction, an unconscious yearning for a man who resembled the father she had never known. This was new: this was Paul Blake, a man unlike any she'd ever met or hoped to meet. And she wanted him for that. Yes, she thought as she felt his hands on her zipper; yes, as the silk dress fell to the floor: she wanted Paul Blake more than she had ever wanted any man.

And acknowledging this brought her hands to his face as he looked down at her in wonder.

"Oh, Aurora," he said, "my darling, let me look at you!"

She stood in the very spot where she had been since his first touch. Her taut, erect breasts heaved with her every breath as Paul cupped each of them in his hands and then brought his lips to them. His tongue flicked back and forth over her nipples and she experienced a flamelike burning inside her vagina. Yes, she wanted him!

Paul knelt and slid her panties down to her ankles. Then he unclasped the straps on her sandals, and Aurora, not completely trusting her legs, stepped out of them. He pulled down her panty hose impatiently, muttering "damn these things" under his breath. When she was completely naked before him, he placed his hands on her pelvis and, still in a kneeling position, buried his face between her legs.

Aurora heard herself cry out as his tongue parted the lips enclosing her clitoris. As he worked up and down, then around, in always surprising motions, Aurora grabbed his hair, stroking the waves yet pulling it at the same time. Her agonizing yet wondrous anticipation had caused contractions deep within her, orgasm upon orgasm, before they had even reached the bed!

"Paul!" she cried. "Please! I can't stand it anymore! Oh, God, *I want you!*"

"Shh!" he whispered. "Not yet!" He slid his wet mouth—wet from her own juices—down her inner thighs, one side at a time, and then returned his tongue to the magical orifice that awaited him with ravenous hunger.

Again, he teased her clitoris, again she came. His tongue thrust deeper, as far as it could enter, and Aurora felt her body exploding into shooting sparks.

"Oh, my lovely Aurora!" Paul cried, almost in a gasp. In a single movement, he rose to his full height and lifted her, carrying her to the bed.

Moaning with delight, she reached out for him. "Take me," he urged, and she threw back her damp hair and slid the length of his erect shaft into her mouth. He lay back against the pillow, groaning with pleasure, which triggered deeper pleasure inside Aurora. Her tongue worked around the tip of his penis and all the way to its base. She felt his thigh muscles tense and at that same moment, his hands drew her off him and he turned her onto her back.

Without either of them speaking, he rolled on top of her; his swollen penis rubbed against her until she began to writhe from side to side. "Paul!" This time she screamed.

And he entered her. A deep gasp erupted from the very depths of her womb as he penetrated and withdrew, again and again, almost leaving her body, but never actually doing so. His hands held her arms above her head; she felt imprisoned by his body, his desire, yet she wished to fill herself with him, deeply, so their bodies could somehow merge in the simple rhythm of their lovemaking. Paul established the pace, and both of them were locked into the electrifying heat that engulfed them. At intervals, he pulled himself far back enough to enable him to take one nipple and then the other into his mouth without being drawn from inside her. The combined sensations, together with the joy she derived from his pleasure, triggered physical responses Aurora had never known before, and with them, a depth of emotional happiness that made her almost cry.

At last they were both approaching the peak; Paul's thrusts and gasps were coming harder and faster, matching Aurora's increasing tempo. Quicker and shorter, then a deep plunge. Her eyes opened; shooting stars illuminated the darkness. Paul's eyes were open too, his smile unlike any Aurora had ever seen; it bespoke trust, ecstasy, and vulnerability, as well. It caused Aurora to shudder deep inside as she tightened her sphincter muscles around Paul's penis. Then they climaxed, together; their hands entwined and their bodies melded as though they had, indeed, become one.

Afterward, they fell back, spent, against the pillows. Their bodies, bathed in perspiration, glistened in the moonlight filtering through the terrace windows. Aurora lay still, listening to her heartbeat, pondering over the expression she had seen on Paul's face. His eyes were closed now as he dozed, and the corners of his mouth were curved into the same smile she had seen during their lovemaking. That filled her with happiness; she felt she had somehow glimpsed his soul. Paul had kept nothing in reserve, had held nothing back. And, she admitted, as a similar, peaceful smile crept onto her lips, neither had she.

Chapter Thirty-Five

Aurora awoke to find herself alone in Paul's bed. The aromas of espresso and of eggs cooking wafted into the room, and moments later, Paul, wearing only a chef's apron, delivered a tray to his guest.

She stretched languidly beneath the sheet. "Good morning," she said with a lazy grin.

"Mmm," Paul answered, setting the tray on the floor and pulling the sheet away. "Just let me look at you again."

Aurora felt desire rise in her as it had the night before.

He leaned down and kissed each of her breasts, causing her to shudder. "God, you do wonders for a man's ego," he said, running his fingers down the length of her body. Then, looking into her shining eyes, he said very quietly, "I don't want to turn this into a 'heavy,' Aurora, but I've fallen in love with you. I just want you to know that."

She reached out and stroked his eyebrows. "Paul, I—"

"Shh. It happened long before last night." He lowered his head and kissed her between her thighs. She wanted him again, now, but he matter-of-factly rose, picked up the breakfast tray, and said, "I make terrific omelets. And they taste lousy once they get cold."

Aurora felt herself blush; Paul brought out a side of her that was completely uninhibited. She wasn't concerned about his impression of her, so she enjoyed a freedom, sexually and emotionally, that only made her want him more. Was this love? She wasn't sure. But it was unlike anything she had known in the past, and she wasn't about to question it.

The omelet was delicious and she devoured it. "I'm starving!" she said.

"I noticed," he answered. "You have a wonderful . . . appetite." Again, his inflection triggered involuntary responses that surprised, yet delighted, her. Looking him squarely in the eye, she asked, "Do you have this effect on all women?"

He grinned broadly. "It'd be nice to think so. Of course, I've seldom cared enough to inquire. Drink your espresso, please."

She did so, then handed him the empty demitasse cup, which he placed on the tray. When he'd removed all traces of breakfast from the bed, he joined her. Tossing his apron to the floor, he whispered, "Enough of domesticity. Now you know I can cook."

"Mmm," she murmured. "That, too. . . ." And this time, it was Aurora who initiated their lovemaking. Unlike the night before, on this occasion, it was not a slow, sensuous discovery but a ravenous hunger, a playful expedition in which they tossed and turned, making a shambles of the bed linens. They laughed and tickled each other, and almost fell, entwined, to the floor. Having explored the mysteries of one another, they now reveled with childlike abandon. She sat astride him, then he grabbed her and held her in a wrestling hold while he entered her. "I love to look at you in the daylight," he said as she came, one multiple orgasm after another. Her body trembled and throbbed with sensation, wonderful sensation, and they teased and played and made love. Then they rested and made love again. Aurora felt she might drown from pleasure; she wished the day could last forever, she was so happy and content in Paul's arms.

But with the afternoon, after they had showered together and then dressed, Paul broached the sobering subject.

"What are you going to do?" he asked.

She knew he meant about Otto Danzig and New York. She had thought about it at frequent intervals during the night. Actually her decision had been reached by allowing such thoughts to surface; a part of her had probably known all along what she would have to do.

"Tadzio was right," she said. "There's only one thing I can do." Still, her pulse raced as she spoke the words. "I'm going back to New York, Paul. I have to testify. There isn't any other choice."

He was seated beside her on the sofa, stroking a wisp of hair that insisted on falling over her eye. "I'll go with you," he said quietly.

"There's no need."

"First of all, I think there is—those two bookends who keep following you. Second, I do have to deliver the next chapters to my publisher. With the Italian postal service and all their strikes, I may as well see to it that they arrive—"

"Paul," she said, taking his hand, "I appreciate your offer, but you don't have to—"

"I know I don't *have* to. I *want* to. Call it protecting my best interests." He leaned forward to kiss her, and this time Aurora felt a great tenderess for him.

Her eyes glistening, she said, "You have a way of

breaking down my resistance in all areas, you know."

"I don't think I'm breaking it down," he said. "I think you're just letting go of your resistance. But your words are very flattering, just the same." His free hand reached over to muss her hair. "There!" he said with a laugh. "I've wanted to do that since the first time we met."

She fell back against the sofa, relaxed and happy. "You're a very enigmatic man, Mr. Blake," she said.

"Like attracts like, m'dear," he answered, rising and pulling her up with him.

She stood beside him, her arms wrapping themselves around his neck, but he freed himself of her grasp. "My God," he exclaimed to the air, "she's oversexed!" He tossed her the mauve silk dress, which had lain all night in a heap on the floor. "C'mon, lady, put this on."

"Where are we going?"

"Well, if you're still serious about New York, there are a few items to attend to. Your clothes, for example."

"All my clothes are at the hotel. I'll have to make a stop there before we leave. And the tickets. We have to book seats and get flight information—"

"Okay, I'll drop you off at your hotel to collect your luggage. Then I'll stop by Alitalia and pick up two tickets. I know there's a six o'clock flight. I have a couple of errands to run; then I'll pick you up at your hotel in a taxi and we'll go right out to Da Vinci."

"Fine. I just have to get some things out of the safe. Everything else is still packed." Then she remembered. "I have two suitcases in a locker—in Milan!"

"Nothing valuable, I hope, like passports or diamonds?"

She laughed. "No, the jewels and furs travel with me. I suppose the rest of the things don't really matter."

"Funny, I had the feeling the jewels and furs didn't

matter that much to you. Perhaps I was mistaken. . . ."

"No," she said slowly. "They're only . . . trappings."
Was it Paul Blake's effect upon her or was she
becoming aware of certain truths? Or were both things
operative?

They dressed and found a taxi. By the time Aurora
reached her hotel, it was already past three-thirty. Paul
would be back for her in half an hour. She breathed a
sigh of relief as she entered the hotel courtyard. Three
hours from now she—they—would be safely aboard an
Alitalia jet headed for New York. Whatever awaited
her there, whatever the outcome of her testimony and
of Otto's trial, it was preferable to nomadic flight and
constant panic. The lightness of her step reflected her
new conviction.

But as she pushed the revolving door to enter the
lobby, her heart sank. There, seated on the flowered
loveseat beside a potted palm, was the redhead in his
familiar black suit; the blond, still in gray, stood
against the paneled wall that led to the single elevator.

Aurora didn't hesitate. She made a 360-degree circle
inside the revolving doors and headed into the outer
courtyard with only a brief, backward glance to see if
they had spotted her.

The redhead had. He was coming toward the door.
As he reached Aurora, he said, "Mr. Danzig sends his
regards."

She bolted down the steps, almost losing one of her
delicate sandals. Quickly, she bent to adjust the strap
and then hurried onto Via Emilia, turning right at the
corner.

Another peek. Now they were together, after her.
Her adrenaline soaring, Aurora headed for Paul's
shortcut and the iron gate.

They followed.

She opened the gate and ran down the steps. Coming

561

out onto the bottom of Via Veneto, she looked for a place, any place, with crowds of people. But it was still early, the afternoon *riposo* still in force; stores were closed and cafés too sparsely populated to provide cover.

She hurried along Via Barberini, trying to think ahead as she kept a lookout for any refuge. The traffic was heavy, as always. What about a bus?

Then the shocking realization hit her.

She had no money—not a lira in her beaded clutch purse. Not a *gettone* with which to telephone Paul, no way to pay for a bus or taxi to go to Paul's apartment or the airport. What was she going to do?

She turned right, up Via Sistina, in an attempt to lose her pursuers, but her high heels prevented her from running on the cracked pavement and the cobble-stoned streets. Remembering a shortcut here, an alleyway there, she managed to gain a block or two, but always the two remained in sight. Maritza's long-ago remark about Rome's duality applied also to its streets: It was easy to elude pursuit in the circular street maze of ancient times; however, amidst those circles it was equally easy to relocate one's target if it headed in a straight direction. If Aurora could have indulged in a long flight, she might have lost them in the labyrinthian jungle of one-way streets and courtyard *palazzi;* but the plane was scheduled to leave at six, Paul would be at her hotel at four. Aurora's Piaget was with her things in the hotel safe; nonetheless she knew she had to break free of her pursuers *and* reach Paul very soon. The streets were filling as the hour approached four.

She was walking fast enough to mingle with the crowd, darting in and out of traffic as shopkeepers began to open for the evening hours. In her mind, she was formulating a plan. Get to the airport, she decided. Paul will know that something is wrong. He'll know as soon as he reaches the hotel and finds me gone but not checked out. He'll put two and two together. He'll go to the airport. He'll have the tickets.

I have my passport, she reminded herself. The furs and jewels don't matter. *You* matter. And, she realized with a sudden rush, *Paul* matters. Yes—she nodded silently as she waited for the traffic light to change—Paul Blake matters. I'm in love with Paul Blake!

And with that, an idea came to her. She glanced up and down the street, first noting that her pursuers were peering in both directions, left and right; that meant they had, for the moment, lost sight of her.

Taking advantage of this sudden stroke of luck, she spotted a jewelry shop. It must be four o'clock; the *sara cinesca* had been lifted and the shop was open for business.

She dashed inside and, in her most charming Italian, explained to the clerk that she had something to sell.

He, in turn, went into the back room. She kept an eye on the *vetrina,* trying to do so in a casual manner so that neither clerk nor proprietor would suspect her of attempting to sell stolen property.

"Signora?" asked a portly, white-haired man in his late sixties. Neither he nor his employee seemed to recognize her; perhaps it was the dark glasses, or her hair, which was again parted on the left and covering half her face. Or perhaps these were two Romans who didn't attend movies or read the gossip in the papers.

She took Harper's four-carat diamond from her third finger, left hand and held it out to the jeweler.

His eyes widened in amazement even before he examined it with his glass.

"Ma signora, è stupendo!" He was apparently so impressed that he was unable to mask his reaction.

She asked how much he was willing to pay for it.

563

The man shrugged his shoulders and rubbed his chin. Aurora didn't know if that was an effort to gain time for bargaining, but she had no time.

"Per favore," she said, nodding toward his large wall clock. She explained that she had to catch a plane.

And he explained that he needed credentials, assurance that the gem was indeed hers.

She withdrew her passport and pointed to her name. With a deep breath, she asked if he had a copy of *Oggi* or *Gente* or perhaps one of the daily tabloids; *Il Tempo* and *Il Messaggero* would be more inclined to report only the facts of the case. Neither of them would carry photographs; right now she needed corroboration. This time, she could use her notoriety!

The clerk dipped below the counter and produced a copy of a magazine unfamiliar to Aurora. But the scandal sheet had heard of her! The cover photograph was no help; it was one of the New York photographs, one in which her face was covered by her hand.

But wait! Quickly she rummaged through her clutch purse until she brought forth Paul's wrinkled handkerchief. Unwrapping it, she took the emerald ring and held it next to the photograph on the magazine cover. *"Sono io,"* she repeated twice, until finally the shopowner and his employee nodded. Yes, they concurred, she and the ring did seem to fit the picture.

The owner asked why she chose to sell the diamond and not the emerald. She used the excuse that the latter was evidence in a murder case, which was why she needed to sell the diamond at once, to enable her to reach New York. In a sentence, she explained that she was being followed. She couldn't recall the word for *detectives,* but the word *assassini* came to mind. It worked magic.

The shopkeeper opened a drawer and began counting money, instructing his assistant to keep a watch at the door for anyone who resembled an assassin.

Within minutes, the jeweler was in possession of a four-carat diamond ring, and Aurora's purse was stuffed with bills. She hadn't bothered to count them; Italian money had always seemed like Monopoly money to her and right now that money need only get her to the airport.

She had wanted to ask the jeweler to phone Paul but she'd realized he was most likely at her hotel by now. However, the owner of the shop had promised to telephone La Residenza to explain to the manager what had happened and to ask him to give her message to Paul if he hadn't already been there and gone.

The kindly jeweler was unable to provide a back-door escape from his shop. There was, he explained regretfully, only the front exit.

She thanked both men profusely, then reappeared on the crowded street. Shoppers were jammed together as were Fiats and motorcycles. Aurora's eyes darted up the street, then down, and finally she saw them. Both of them. Damn them! she thought. They had seen her enter the shop, after all! They had simply taken seats at the café across the way, and were sipping Campari, waiting patiently, knowing that if she had gone inside, eventually she had to come out again.

The blond put down some money, and the redhead lifted his finger to point in her direction.

They were separated only by the traffic.

There were no empty taxis in sight.

But a bus was stopping at the corner. Aurora raced to board it, followed by her "shadows."

She edged her way through the packed conveyance, glancing constantly over her shoulder to see if the two had managed to reach the bus in time. If they had, the bus was too crowded for her to see them.

But as the bus swerved and made its way slowly

through traffic headed for San Silvestro, Aurora spied them through the window. They had seen her board the bus and were running alongside it; with rush-hour traffic conditions, that was far easier than following in a car or taxi.

She tried to clear her mind of panic. The bus would unload its passengers at the large piazza. San Silvestro was too open a space in which to lose oneself, and it was cobblestoned; she couldn't possibly outrun them. Offering to buy a passenger's shoes would prompt anyone to think she'd gone crazy; that could play right into her pursuers' hands should they claim to be her "doctors."

She dismissed the thought. Shoes, she repeated to herself.

Of course! What was found on every Roman street in even greater number than restaurants—*calzolerie*—shoe stores!

The corner before the final turn into San Silvestro was congested, a bottleneck of honking horns and yelling drivers. On a sudden impulse, Aurora pulled the cord and the center doors of the bus opened. She alighted with a dozen other passengers and at sight of the first *calzoleria,* she rushed inside.

"Desidera?" asked a clerk.

Aurora hadn't taken time to pick out a style in the *vetrina. "Stivalli,"* she said. Yes. Boots. With low heels.

"Colore?" the girl asked. Aurora shrugged and told her it made no difference. She gave her size and when the girl made no move, Aurora, searching for the way to say "hurry," instead said, *"Nero."*

It seemed the salesgirl interpreted the word *black* to be synonymous with *hurry.* That the *stivalli* were of black suede and the suede season was almost over was of little signficance to Aurora. They fit.

She withdrew the thousands of lire, not bothering to translate their amount in her head. The salesgirl handed her several bills in change and Aurora cautiously left the store wearing her new black suede boots.

She didn't see the two men, and perhaps they would not have seen her, but in her haste, Aurora had forgotten her mauve evening sandals. The salesgirl came running from the shop, calling loudly and attracting everyone's attention, *"Signora! Signora! Le scarpe! Le sandali!"* She waved the spaghetti-strap sandals in the air; only the blind would have missed them.

So they were after her again. But this time, Aurora was able to run. And run she did. In and out of side streets, always half a block ahead. They might be clever when it came to tracking her, she mused as she ran, but they couldn't win a marathon!

Nor could Aurora. Her adrenaline had been at peak level since her escape from the hotel. She was growing weary of trying to get away yet remaining within their grasp. Long-distance running wasn't her forte, and her earlier sprint had exhausted her.

Time! What time was it? Where was Paul? Had he received her message from the jeweler?

Street after street, minute after minute, Aurora led the chase and the two followed behind, sometimes almost on her heels, at other times a full block behind.

At a busy intersection on the Via del Corso, she hailed a passing taxi, jumped inside, and instructed the driver to take her to the airport. This time she remembered the word for *hurry*. *"Subito!"* she commanded. *"Subitissimo!"*

She peered out the rear window of the Fiat as it zoomed in and out of traffic.

And then another taxi was following hers. Aurora didn't have to speculate; she knew the faces of her pursuers.

She sank back into the seat and breathed deeply, trying to quell a rising anxiety. Be calm, she said to herself. They're right behind you, but you're safe as long as you're inside this taxi and they're inside theirs. Once we arrive at the airport, it'll be a different matter. For now, relax. Paul will be there and somehow you'll manage to lose these two.

She still found it difficult to accept the fact that they were Otto's men, but the redhead had affirmed it. No guesswork was necessary. Nor was there any point in wondering whether Otto would go so far as to have her killed. A man who had murdered his wife, who knew only one woman's testimony could convict him, would stop at nothing; he had nothing to lose.

Had Paul received her message? And if so, had he alerted the *carabinieri?* Interpol? Whoever would be able to secure them safe passage aboard the jet?

She shuddered. What if the jeweler had missed Paul? What if Paul was waiting, unsuspecting, unaware of her predicament, in plain sight of Otto's men?

She'd come up with something by the time they reached Da Vinci—something that would not endanger her life or Paul's. But it would have to be soon.

They were almost at the airport.

The first thing Aurora did as the terminal came into view was to pay the taxi driver. Tipping him generously, she jumped from the taxi while the bookends' taxi was still several cars behind.

She ran into the crowded building, looking first at

the overhead clock. It read five-thirty. Half an hour to wait! She hurried to the ticket line, but on her way, she saw her pursuers entering the terminal. The redhead pointed in her direction and both men began to run.

The line was long; it would be too easy for them to rush up and drag her from it. Quickly she asked a flight attendant, *"Scusi, dove è il gabinetto?"* They *couldn't* follow her into the ladies' room!

She peered about as she walked to the door marked *Donne;* Paul wasn't anywhere in sight. How long could she wait for him? And how could she board the plane without a ticket?

Perhaps she could page him. Surely her pursuers didn't know his name. But could she be certain of that? They seemed to know everything about her; it was a chance she couldn't take. She wouldn't endanger Paul. She didn't dare to consider what Otto's men had in mind for her, but she didn't want Paul hurt or . . .

She sat on one of the boudoir chairs in front of a marble countertop with its broad expanse of mirror. If only she had other clothing with her . . . The wig had worked so well in Milan, but she had only the silk dress and mohair shawl.

Then it came to her. Rehearsing her Italian carefully, she rose from the chair and crossed the length of the ladies' room until she reached the matron.

At five fifty-five, the matron was continuing to dispense towels. But now she wore a mauve silk dress that was far too tight on her. The straps were missing, but she had somehow managed to fasten it, with safety pins, to a voluminous mohair shawl. Her fist tightly clutched a wad of lire notes as she watched the American woman exit.

The door to the *gabinetto* closed behind a tall, slim

maid—or was she a nurse or a matron?—in a baggy white uniform. Her hair was braided into two long pigtails, each tied by a thin mauve silk strap-ribbon. The single incongruity of her wardrobe, in addition to the mauve beaded evening bag she carried, lay in her choice of footwear. Instead of white "sensible" oxfords, she wore boots—black suede walking boots.

Aurora's eyes darted about as she tried to determine if and how the situation had altered.

It had! Her heart began to hammer when at last she spotted Paul. She wanted to shout his name, to run to him. But he was not alone. He was talking animatedly to a man in a dark blue uniform. But what was he? A policeman? Customs official? Pilot? Was he there to help Paul . . . or to cause more trouble?

Quickly, Aurora glanced to their only means of escape: the departure gate, where passengers for the six o'clock flight to New York were now boarding.

There, carefully scrutinizing every member of the crowd filing past them, were Otto's men; the redhead to the left, the blond to the right of the entrance.

Aurora checked the overhead clock. Five fifty-seven. What do I do? she thought, her pulse racing.

She could see Paul searching the crowd with his eyes. The passengers were thinning out; fewer and fewer people blocked Aurora from the sight of her tormentors. Terror gripped her as the blond looked right at her, then past her. For the moment, the disguise was working.

With as casual a gait as she could muster, she approached Paul. Her back was toward the gate as she slowly moved closer. Paul looked in her direction, then away. And then back. There! He had recognized her!

His mouth began to speak her name, but Aurora quickly shook her head, warning him to remain silent.

She raised her purse in front of her and gestured with her thumb, pointing over her shoulder. Paul's eyes focused past her as she drew close and whispered, "The blond and the redhead. The two at the gate."

He nodded. His uniformed companion stared at her as Paul leaned over and spoke to the man in a low voice. Aurora was unable to hear the exchange. Then the uniformed man walked away.

Aurora felt Paul's hand on her arm as he turned her toward the gate.

She couldn't move. Her feet refused to follow the command of her brain. Her heart pumped loudly in her ears and sweat broke out in beads across her forehead as she looked up into his face. She had never been more frightened in her life. Paul wanted her to turn around. To face the two men. To walk toward the gate.

"I . . . can't," she whispered in a trembling voice.

"You have to," he answered, quietly but firmly. "I'm right beside you. We're in this together." His hand strengthened its hold on her arm. "Come on. You've come so far. You're not alone. It's almost over."

I'm not alone. I'm not alone. The words released the imaginary shackles that had locked her to the spot.

She turned, and very slowly they began their approach to the gate.

Aurora watched the minute hand on the clock as it moved to five fifty-nine. Even stragglers had boarded the plane; only Otto's men remained.

Aurora's feet continued to carry her forward automatically. The redhead and the blond were now closer, larger. The blond looked directly at her and suddenly recognition dawned on him. He nodded to the redhead, whose eyes flashed with anger.

"Oh God, Paul!" Aurora whispered.

"Keep walking. Don't stop." His arm propelled her,

and now they were positioned between the two men.

The redhead lurched forward, wrenching Aurora from Paul's side. His hand went over her mouth as he dragged her backward, but she saw the blond pull a revolver from his jacket and strike Paul across the shoulders.

Then, as if in slow motion, the blond's arm came up from his side. He extended it straight in front of him, and took aim at Aurora.

At the same moment, he tumbled forward and there was an earsplitting explosion as the gun went off. The shot went wild, but the sound echoed throughout the terminal and reverberated in Aurora's head. When she opened her eyes, Paul was gripping the blond by the ankles.

The gun skidded across the waxed floor as the blond freed one foot and kicked savagely at Paul's face. Aurora felt herself being dragged backward again. She lost her balance and fell. Suddenly, she was free.

Behind her, footsteps approached from several directions. Aurora turned to see a dozen *carabinieri* materialize and descend upon the redhead.

When she looked back at Paul, he was on his feet, holding on to the blond's lapels. Two policemen handcuffed the blond from behind. Then he and the redhead were led away.

Aurora looked at Paul. His face was bruised, his jacket torn. But he was smiling, and his right arm was outstretched, beckoning to her.

"Let's go!" he cried. "We've got a plane to catch!"

She rushed to him and fell into his arms. Their lips met and they kissed until she was breathless. Then, from over her shoulder, a man's voice said, "That plane, *signore*. It will not wait forever."

"*Grazie!*" Paul said to the man in uniform.

"Sì, grazie!" exclaimed Aurora. She and Paul waved, and then, hands clasped, they hurried aboard the jet.

Moments later, the engines revved, then roared as the plane prepareed for takeoff. When they were airborne, Paul unfastened his seatbelt and reached over to undo Aurora's buckle.

"Gets in the way," he said.

Her arms went around him.

"I like that getup you're wearing," Paul said, stroking her temples.

She brushed her hand lightly over the scratch on his cheek. "Maybe I can swap outfits with one of the flight attendants when we land in New York," she answered. "It seems the thing to do today."

Today . . . Her mind flashed over the past twenty-four hours she'd spent in the Eternal City. Paul's smile reflected the new aliveness she felt inside.

"You're not wearing Harper's diamond," said Paul. "Find another handkerchief to wrap it in?" He'd spoken lightly, but Aurora knew that he was merely giving her leeway, leeway she no longer needed.

"I outgrew the ring," she said, smiling back at him.

He squeezed her hand tenderly. "I see you didn't bring any reading material on this trip."

Reading material! After their harrowing experience just past, why would he mention reading?

"I packed this before I got your jeweler friend's message at the hotel. I brought it along on the chance you might be interested." Paul reached into his flight bag and withdrew a copy of a book. His book.

"Places," she read aloud, tracing a finger over the title. "'A novel by Paul Blake.' Impressive."

"Open it," he said.

Did he really expect her to read it, now?

"Darling, don't be offended, but I—"

"Just this. So you'll know I wasn't handing you a line." He opened the book to the dedication page.

Aurora glanced down and her eyes filled with tears.

"Aurora is the sunrise," the inscription read.

"Paul . . ." she said.

She never finished the sentence, but it didn't matter. She could tell from the love in Paul's eyes that he understood, as he always had.

Zebra brings you the best in
CONTEMPORARY FICTION

PAY THE PRICE   (1234, $3.95)
by Igor Cassini

Even more than fortune and fame, Christina wanted revenge on the rich, ruthless scoundrel who destroyed her life. She'd use her flawless body to steal an empire that was hers for the taking—if she was willing to PAY THE PRICE.

SOMETIMES A HERO   (1765, $3.95)
by Les Whitten

Betrayed by passion, Strabico stood to lose all he had fought for to the global power of Big Oil. He would have to stake the woman he loved and his very life on a desperate gamble against the forces of wealth and power.

AUGUST PEOPLE   (1863, $3.95)
by Ralph Graves

For Ellen, the newest daughter-in-law in the Winderman clan, August's vacation with the family is a bitter time of feeling left out of the family circle. But soon Ellen reveals the flaws in their perfect family portrait, and secrets long hidden begin to surface.

TEXAS DREAMS   (1875, $3.95)
by Micah Leigh

For Fontayne, power is an aphrodisiac. She gambles in the playground of the world's oil empire as if it were a child's sandbox; but as she nears the pinnacle of her desires, a past scandal surfaces and threatens to destroy all her carefully planned TEXAS DREAMS.

Available wherever paperbacks are sold, or order direct from the Publisher. Send cover price plus 50¢ per copy for mailing and handling to Zebra Books, Dept. 2004, 475 Park Avenue South, New York, N.Y. 10016. Residents of New York, New Jersey and Pennsylvania must include sales tax. DO NOT SEND CASH.